All new stories of possibility—from the far future and distant galaxies to the wonders all around us—from some of the best and brightest writers working in science fiction today.

Discover new ways of thinking and technological marvels, alien secrets and human discoveries. Travel to faraway planets and into the maze of emotion, all within the pages of the

YEAR'S BEST SF 7

D0823029

Edited by David G. Hartwell

YEAR'S BEST SF
YEAR'S BEST SF 2
YEAR'S BEST SF 3
YEAR'S BEST SF 4
YEAR'S BEST SF 5
YEAR'S BEST SF 6

**Edited by David G. Hartwell
& Kathryn Cramer**

YEAR'S BEST FANTASY
YEAR'S BEST SF 7

Forthcoming

YEAR'S BEST FANTASY 2

YEAR'S BEST SF 7

EDITED BY
DAVID G. HARTWELL
and KATHRYN CRAMER

An Imprint of HarperCollinsPublishers

To the friends and family of Jenna Felice (1976–2001)

This is a collection of fiction. Names, characters, places, and incidents are products of the author's imagination or are used fictitiously and are not to be construed as real. Any resemblance to actual events, locales, organizations, or persons, living or dead, is entirely coincidental.

EOS
An Imprint of HarperCollins*Publishers*
10 East 53rd Street
New York, New York 10022-5299

Copyright © 2002 by David G. Hartwell and Kathryn Cramer
ISBN: 0-06-106143-3
www.eosbooks.com

First Eos paperback printing: June 2002

Eos Trademark Reg. U.S. Pat. Off. and in Other Countries, Marca Registrada, Hecho en U.S.A.
HarperCollins® is a trademark of HarperCollins Publishers Inc.

Printed in the U.S.A.

10 9 8 7 6 5 4 3 2 1

Contents

vii   Acknowledgments

ix   Introduction

1   Nancy Kress
Computer Virus

53   Terry Bisson
Charlie's Angels

77   Richard Chwedyk
The Measure of All Things

100   Simon Ings
Russian Vine

121   Michael Swanwick
Under's Game

125   Brian W. Aldiss
A Matter of Mathematics

140   Edward M. Lerner
Creative Destruction

186   David Morrell
Resurrection

209   James Morrow
           The Cat's Pajamas

234   Michael Swanwick
           The Dog Said Bow-Wow

254   Ursula K. Le Guin
           The Building

265   Stephen Baxter
           Gray Earth

284   Terry Dowling
           The Lagan Fishers

305   Thomas M. Disch
           In Xanadu

323   Lisa Goldstein
           The Go-Between

347   Gene Wolfe
           Viewpoint

396   Gregory Benford
           Anomalies

410   Alastair Reynolds
           Glacial

462   James Patrick Kelly
           Undone

Acknowledgments

We would like to acknowledge the usefulness of *Tangents* online, and of *Locus* online and *Locus* magazine, and the many reviewers of short fiction with whom we often disagree. And also the help of those fiction websites, including SciFiction and Strange Horizons, who printed and sent us stories to consider.

Introduction

The year 2001 was an excellent one for the science fiction short story. The stories were often challenging, thought-provoking, and entertaining in the ways that make SF a unique genre. It was a year of great excitement, great tragedy in the real world, and great change. There is a war going on.

In 2001, books by the big names were selling better than ever, sliding through the publishing and distribution process perhaps even easier than before. Hardcover editions contributed substantially to the support of every SF publishing line. The trade paperback was well-established as the safety net of a number of publishers and writers. The small presses were again a vigorous presence. We have a strong short fiction field today because the small presses, semi-professional magazines, and anthologies are printing and circulating a majority of the high-quality fiction published in sf and fantasy and horror. The U.S. is the only English language country that still has any professional, large-circulation magazines, though Canada, Australia, and the UK have several excellent magazines. The semi-prozines of our field mirror the "little magazines" of the mainstream in function, holding to professional editorial standards and publishing the next generation of writers, along with some of the present masters. What a change that is in the U.S.—though this trend has been emerging for more than a decade.

We must not forget the SF Book Club, so much a part of the SF field that it is often as invisible, unless we look up, as the skyscrapers we pass on our way to work in the city. Good anthologies and collections are harder than ever to select on the bookstore shelves from among the mediocre ones, but you will find some of the best books each year selected for SFBC editions, often the only hardcover edition of those anthologies.

The best original anthologies of the year in our opinion were *Starlight 3*, edited by Patrick Nielsen Hayden (Tor) and *Red Shift*, edited by Al Sarrantonio (Roc). Of those, the particular excellences of *Starlight* were mostly in the realm of fantasy, and the especial pleasures of *Red Shift* were in SF. So you will find some stories here from *Red Shift*, but should look to our companion, *Year's Best Fantasy 2*, for some stories from the Nielsen Hayden book.

I write in December 2001, but the anxious outlines of the publishing future are becoming clear for the SF field in 2002. SF publishing as we have known it is nine mass market publishing lines (Ace, Bantam, Baen, DAW, Del Rey, Eos, Roc, Tor, Warner), ten if you count Pocket Book's Star Trek line, and those lines are hard-pressed to continue distributing the number of new titles they have been able to in the past. Mass market distributors are pressing all publishers to reduce the number of titles and just publish "big books." The last SF and Fantasy magazines that are widely distributed (*Analog, Asimov's, F&SF, Realms of Fantasy*) are being charged more by the same distributors for distribution because they are not as high-circulation as *The New Yorker* or *Playboy* (which are also under pressure). So the in-field magazines are hard-pressed but are only a special case of the widespread difficulties facing all magazines.

In 2001, the air went out of electronic bookselling. Amazon.com fired a lot of people and closed warehouses, intending to claim a profit in early 2002. Barnes & Noble folded its dotcom division back into the bookstore chain, with attendant layoffs. And electronic text failed to live up to the advance publicity (both Random House and Warner closed their etext operations by the end of 2001). Print-on-demand became a very small success. *The Wall Street Journal*, in a late-year article surveying 2500 titles, quoted the figure of 88 copies as the average sale of a print-on-demand title.

Of the several high-paying online short fiction markets announced last year that helped to cushion the loss of print media markets for short fiction, one survives. We found some excellent science fiction from editor Ellen Datlow's Scifiction site, now the highest-paying market in the genre for short fiction. We offer three stories from it, for perhaps the first time in print, in this book.

It was another good year to be reading the magazines, both pro and semi-professional. It was a strong year for novellas, and there were more than a hundred shorter stories in consideration, from which we made our final selection. So we repeat, for readers new to this series, the usual disclaimer: This selection of science fiction stories represents the best that was published during the year 2001. It would take two or three more volumes this size to have nearly all of the best—though even then, not all the best novellas. We believe that representing the best from year to year, while it is not physically possible to encompass it all in one even very large book, also implies presenting some substantial variety of excellences, and we left some worthy stories out in order to include others in this limited space.

Our general principle for selection: This book is full of science fiction—every story in the book is clearly that and not something else. We have a high regard for horror, fantasy, speculative fiction, and slipstream, and postmodern literature. We (Kathryn Cramer and David G. Hartwell) edit the *z* in paperback from Eos as a companion volume to this one—look for it if you enjoy short fantasy fiction, too. But here, we chose science fiction.

We try to represent the varieties of tones and voices and attitudes that keep the genre vigorous and responsive to the changing realities out of which it emerges, in science and daily life. This is a book about what's going on now in SF.

Computer Virus

NANCY KRESS

Nancy Kress [www.sff.net/people/nankress] is one of today's leading SF writers. She is known for her complex medical SF stories, and for her biological and evolutionary extrapolations in such classics as Beggars in Spain *(1993),* Beggars and Choosers *(1994), and* Beggars Ride *(1996). In recent years, she has written* Maximum Light *(1998),* Probability Moon *(2000), and last year published* Probability Sun *(2001), the second book in a trilogy of hard SF novels set against the background of a war between humanity and an alien race. In 1998 she married SF writer Charles Sheffield. Her stories are rich in texture and in psychological insight, and have been collected in* Trinity and Other Stories *(1985),* The Aliens of Earth *(1993), and* Beaker's Dozen *(1998). She has won two Nebulas and a Hugo for them, and been nominated a dozen more times. She teaches regularly at summer writing workshops such as Clarion, and during the year at the Bethesda Writing Center in Bethesda, Maryland. She is the Fiction columnist for* Writer's Digest.

"Computer Virus" is major Kress, a moving, exciting near future hostage story, fusing with unusual grace and plausibility the notions of a biological virus and a computer virus. It appeared in Asimov's, *a magazine that definitely kept its competitive edge this year. It was one of several fine stories Kress published in 2001.*

"It's out!" someone said, a tech probably, although later McTaggart could never remember who spoke first. "It's out!"

"It can't be!" someone else cried, and then the whole room was roiling, running, frantic with activity that never left the workstations. Running in place.

It's not supposed to be this way," Elya blurted. Instantly she regretted it. The hard, flat eyes of her sister-in-law Cassie met hers, and Elya flinched away from that look.

"And how is it supposed to be, Elya?" Cassie said. "Tell me."

"I'm sorry. I only meant that . . . that no matter how much you loved Vlad, mourning gets . . . lighter. Not lighter, but less . . . withdrawn. Cass, you can't just wall up yourself and the kids in this place! For one thing, it's not good for them. You'll make them terrified to face real life."

"I hope so," Cassie said, "for their sake. Now let me show you the rest of the castle."

Cassie was being ironic, Elya thought miserably, but "castle" was still the right word. Fortress, keep, bastion . . . Elya hated it. Vlad would have hated it. And now she'd provoked Cassie to exaggerate every protective, self-sufficient, isolating feature of the multi-million dollar pile that had cost Cass every penny she had, including the future income from the lucrative patents that had gotten Vlad murdered.

"This is the kitchen," Cassie said. "House, do we have any milk?"

2

"Yes," said the impersonal voice of the house system. At least Cassie hadn't named it, or given it one of those annoying visual avatars. The roomscreen remained blank. "There is one carton of soymilk and one of cow milk on the third shelf."

"It reads the active tags on the cartons," Cassie said. "House, how many of Donnie's allergy pills are left in the master-bath medicine cabinet?"

"Sixty pills remain," House said, "and three more refills on the prescription."

"Donnie's allergic to ragweed, and it's mid-August," Cassie said.

"Well, he isn't going to smell any ragweed inside this mausoleum," Elya retorted, and immediately winced at her choice of words. But Cassie didn't react. She walked on through the house, unstoppable, narrating in that hard, flat voice she had developed since Vlad's death.

"All the appliances communicate with House through narrow-band wireless radio frequencies. House reaches the Internet the same way. All electricity comes from a generator in the basement, with massive geothermal feeds and storage capacitors. In fact, there are two generators, one for backup. I'm not willing to use battery back-up, for the obvious reason."

It wasn't obvious to Elya. She must have looked bewildered because Cassie added, "Batteries can only back-up for a limited time. Redundant generators are more reliable."

"Oh."

"The only actual cables coming into the house are the VNM fiber-optic cables I need for computing power. If they cut those, we'll still be fully functional."

If *who* cuts those? Elya thought, but she already knew the answer. Except that it didn't make sense. Vlad had been killed by econuts because his work was—had been—so controversial. Cassie and the kids weren't likely to be a target now that Vlad was dead. Elya didn't say this. She trailed behind Cassie through the living room, bedrooms, hallways. Every one had a roomscreen for House, even the hallways, and multiple sensors in the ceilings to detect and identify intruders. Elya had had to pocket an emitter at the front door, presumably so House wouldn't . . . do what? What did it do if there was an intruder? She was afraid to ask.

"Come downstairs," Cassie said, leading the way through an e-locked door (of course) down a long flight of steps. "The computer uses three-dimensional laser microprocessors with optical transistors. It can manage twenty million billion calculations per second."

Startled, Elya said, "What on earth do you need that sort of power for?"

"I'll show you." They approached another door, reinforced steel from the look of it. "Open," Cassie said, and it swung inward. Elya stared at a windowless, fully equipped genetics lab.

"Oh, no, Cassie . . . you're not going to work here, too!"

"Yes, I am. I resigned from MedGene last week. I'm a consultant now."

Elya gazed helplessly at the lab, which seemed to be a mixture of shining new equipment plus Vlad's old stuff from his auxiliary home lab. Vlad's refrigerator and storage cabinet, his centrifuge, were all these things really used in common between Vlad's work in ecoremediation and Cassie's in medical genetics? Must be. The old refrigerator had a new dent in its side, probably the result of a badly programmed 'bot belonging to the moving company. Elya recognized a new gene synthesizer, gleaming expensively, along with other machines that she, not a scientist, couldn't identify. Through a half-open door, she saw a small bathroom. It all must have cost enormously. Cassie had better work hard as a consultant.

And now she could do so without ever leaving this self-imposed prison. Design her medical micros, send the data encrypted over the Net to the client. If it weren't for Jane and Donnie . . . Elya grasped at this. There *were* Janey and Donnie, and Janey would need to be picked up at school very shortly now. At least the kids would get Cassie out of this place periodically.

Cassie was still defining her imprisonment, in that brittle voice. "There's a Faraday cage around the entire house, of course, embedded in the walls. No EMP can take us out. The walls are reinforced foamcast concrete, the windows virtually unbreakable polymers. We have enough food stored for a year. The water supply is from a well under the house, part of the geothermal system. It's cool, sweet water. Want a glass?"

"No," Elya said. "Cassie . . . you act as if you expect full-scale warfare. Vlad was killed by an individual nutcase."

"And there are a *lot* of nutcases out there," Cassie said crisply. "I lost Vlad. I'm *not* going to lose Janey and Donnie . . . hey! There you are, pumpkin!"

"I came downstairs!" Donnie said importantly, and flung himself into his mother's arms. "Annie said!"

Cassie smiled over her son's head at his young nanny, Anne Millius. The smile changed her whole face, Elya thought, dissolved her brittle shell, made her once more the Cassie that Vlad had loved. A whole year. Cassie completely unreconciled, wanting only what was gone forever. It wasn't supposed to be like this. Or was it that she, Elya, wasn't capable of the kind of love Cassie had for Vlad? Elya had been married twice, and divorced twice, and had gotten over both men. Was that better or worse than Cassie's stubborn, unchippable grief?

She sighed, and Cassie said to Donnie, "Here's Aunt Elya. Give her a big kiss!"

The three-year-old detached himself from his mother and rushed to Elya. God, he looked like Vlad. Curly light brown hair, huge dark eyes. Snot ran from his nose and smeared on Elya's cheek.

"Sorry," Cassie said, grinning.

"Allergies?"

"Yes. Although . . . does he feel warm to you?"

"I can't tell," said Elya, who had no children. She released Donnie. Maybe he did feel a bit hot in her arms, and his face was flushed a bit. But his full-lipped smile—Vlad again—and shining eyes didn't look sick.

"God, look at the time, I've got to go get Janey," Cassie said. "Want to come along, Elya?"

"Sure." She was glad to leave the lab, leave the basement, leave the "castle." Beyond the confines of the Faraday-embedded concrete walls, she took deep breaths of fresh air. Although of course the air inside had been just as fresh. In fact, the air inside was recycled in the most sanitary, technologically advanced way to avoid bringing in pathogens or gases deliberately released from outside. It was much safer than any fresh air outside. Cassie had told her so.

No one understood, not even Elya.

Her sister-in-law thought Cassie didn't hear herself, didn't see herself in the mirror every morning, didn't know what she'd become. Elya was wrong. Cassie heard the brittleness in her voice, saw the stoniness in her face for everyone but the kids and sometimes, God help her, even for them. Felt herself recoiling from everyone because they weren't Vlad, because Vlad was dead and they were not. What Elya didn't understand was that Cassie couldn't help it.

Elya didn't know about the dimness that had come over the world, the sense of everything being enveloped in a gray fog: people and trees and furniture and lab beakers. Elya didn't know, hadn't experienced, the frightening anger that still seized Cassie with undiminished force, even a year later, so that she thought if she didn't smash something, kill something as Vlad had been killed, she'd go insane. Insaner. Worse, Elya didn't know about the longing for Vlad that would rise, unbidden and unexpected, throughout Cassie's entire body, leaving her unable to catch her breath.

If Vlad had died of a disease, Cassie sometimes thought, even a disease for which she couldn't put together a genetic solution, it would have been much easier on her. Or if he'd died in an accident, the kind of freak chance that could befall anybody. What made it so hard was the murder. That somebody had deliberately decided to snuff out this valuable life, this precious living soul, not for anything evil Vlad did but for the *good* he accomplished.

Dr. Vladimir Seritov, chief scientist for Barr Biosolutions. One of the country's leading bioremediationists and prominent advocate for cutting-edge technology of all sorts. Designer of Plasticide (he'd laughed uproariously at the marketers' name), a bacteria genetically engineered to eat certain long-chain hydrocarbons used in some of the petroleum plastics straining the nation's over-burdened landfills. The microbe was safe: severely limited chemical reactions, nontoxic breakdown products, set number of replications before the terminator gene kicked in, the whole nine yards. And one Sam Verdon, neo-Luddite and self-appointed guardian of an already burdened environment, had shot Vlad anyway.

On the anniversary of the murder, neo-Luddites had held a rally outside the walls of Verdon's prison. Barr Biosolutions had gone on marketing Vlad's creation, to great environmental and financial success. And Cassie Seritov had moved into the safest place she could find for Vlad's children, from which she someday planned to murder Sam Verdon, scum of the earth. But not yet. She couldn't get at him yet. He had at least eighteen more years of time to do, assuming "good behavior."

Nineteen years total. In exchange for Vladimir Seritov's life. And Elya wondered why Cassie was still so angry?

She wandered from room to room, the lights coming on and going off behind her. This was one of the bad nights. Annie had gone home, Jane and Donnie were asleep, and the memories would not stay away. Vlad laughing on their boat (sold now to help pay for the castle). Vlad bending over her the night Jane was born. Vlad standing beside the president of Barr at the press conference announcing the new clean-up microbe, press and scientists assembled, by some idiot publicist's decree, at an actual landfill. The shot cutting the air. It had been August then, too, Donnie had had ragweed allergies, and Vlad looking first surprised and then in terrible pain. . . .

Sometimes work helped. Cassie went downstairs to the lab. Her current project was investigating the folding variations of a digestive enzyme that a drug company was interested in. The work was methodical, meticulous, not very challenging. Cassie had never deluded herself that she was the same caliber scientist Vlad had been.

While the automated analyzer was taking X-rays of crystallized proteins, Cassie said, "House, put on the TV. Anything. Any channel." Any distraction.

The roomscreen brightened to a three-D image of two gorgeous women shouting at each other in what was supposed to be a New York penthouse. ". . . never trust you again without—" one of them yelled, and then the image abruptly switched to a news avatar, an inhumanly chiseled digital face with pale blue hair and the glowing green eyes of a cat in the dark. "We interrupt this movie to bring you a breaking news report from Sandia National Laboratory in New Mexico. Dr. Stephen Milbrett, Director of Sandia, has just announced—" The lights went out.

"Hey!" Cassie cried. "What—" The lights went back on.

She stood up quickly, uncertain for a moment, then started toward the stairs leading upstairs to the children's bedrooms. "Open," she said to the lab door, but the door remained shut. Her hand on the knob couldn't turn it. To her left the roomscreen brightened without producing an image and House said, "Dr. Seritov?"

"What's going on here? House, open the door!"

"This is no longer House speaking. I have taken complete possession of your household system plus your additional computing power. Please listen to my instructions carefully."

Cassie stood still. She knew what was happening; the real estate agent had told her it had happened a few times before, when the castle had belonged to a billionaire so eccentrically reclusive that he stood as an open invitation to teenage hackers. A data stream could easily be beamed in on House's frequency when the Faraday shield was turned off, and she'd had the shield down to receive TV transmission. But the incoming datastream should have only activated the TV, introducing additional images, not overridden House's programming. The door should not have remained locked.

"House, activate Faraday shield." An automatic priority-one command, keyed to her voice. Whatever hackers were doing, this would negate it.

"Faraday shield is already activated. But this is no longer

House, Dr. Seritov. Please listen to my instructions. I have taken possession of your household system. You will be—"

"Who are you?" Cassie cried.

"I am Project T4S. You will be kept in this room as a hostage against the attack I expect soon. The—"

"My children are upstairs!"

"Your children, Jane Rose Seritov, six years of age, and Donald Sergei Seritov, three years of age, are asleep in their rooms. Visual next."

The screen resolved into a split view from the bedrooms' sensors. Janey lay heavily asleep. Donnie breathed wheezily, his bedclothes twisted with his tossing, his small face flushed.

"I want to go to them!"

"That is impossible. I'm sorry. You must be kept in this room as a hostage against the attack I expect soon. All communications to the outside have been severed, with the one exception of the outside speaker on the patio, normally used for music. I will use—"

"Please. Let me go to my children!"

"I cannot. I'm sorry. But if you were to leave this room, you could hit the manual override on the front door. It is the only door so equipped. I could not stop you from leaving, and I need you as hostages. I will use—"

"Hostages! Who the hell are you? Why are you doing this?"

House was silent a moment. Then it said, "The causal is self-defense. They're trying to kill me."

The room at Sandia had finally quieted. Everyone was out of ideas. McTaggart voiced the obvious. "It's disappeared. Nowhere on the Net, nowhere the Net can contact."

"Not possible," someone said.

"But actual."

Another silence. The scientists and techs looked at each other. They had been trying to locate the AI for over two hours, using every classified and unclassified search engine possible. It had first eluded them, staying one step ahead of the termination programs, fleeing around the globe on the Net, into and out of anything both big enough to hold it and lightly firewalled enough to penetrate quickly. Now, somehow, it had completely vanished.

Sandia, like all the national laboratories, was overseen by the Department of Energy. McTaggart picked up the phone to call Washington.

Cassie tried to think. Stay calm, don't panic. There were rumors of AI development, both in private corporations and in government labs, but then there'd always been rumors of AI development. Big bad bogey monsters about to take over the world. Was this really an escaped AI that someone was trying to catch and shut down? Cassie didn't know much about recent computer developments; she was a geneticist. Vlad had always said that non-competing technologies never kept up with what the other one was doing.

Or was this whole thing simply a hoax by some superclever hacker who'd inserted a take-over virus into House, complete with Eliza function? If that were so, it could only answer with preprogrammed responses cued to her own words. Or else with a library search. She needed a question that was neither.

She struggled to hold her voice steady. "House—"

"This is no longer House speaking. I have taken complete possession of your household system plus—"

"T4S, you say your causal for taking over House is self-defense. Use your heat sensors to determine body temperature for Donald Sergei Seritov, age three. How do my causals relate to yours?"

No Eliza program in the world could perform the inference, reasoning, and emotion to answer that.

House said, "You wish to defend your son because his body temperature, 101.2 degrees Fahrenheit, indicates he is ill and you love him."

Cassie collapsed against the locked door. She was hostage to an AI. Superintelligent. It had to be; in addition to the computing power of her system it carried around with it much more information than she had in her head . . . but she was mobile. It was not.

She went to the terminal on her lab bench. The display of protein-folding data had vanished and the screen was blank. Cassie tried everything she knew to get back on-line, both voice and manual. Nothing worked.

"I'm sorry, but that terminal is not available to you," T4S said.

"Listen, you said you cut all outside communication. But—"

"The communications system to the outside has been severed, with the one exception of the outside speaker on the patio, normally used for music. I am also receiving sound from the outside surveillance sensors, which are analogue, not digital. I will use those resources in the event of attack to—"

"Yes, right. But heavy-duty outside communication comes in through a VNM optic cable buried underground." Which was how T4S must have gotten in. "An AI program can't physically sever a buried cable."

"I am not a program. I am a machine intelligence."

"I don't care what the fuck you are! You can't physically sever a buried cable!"

"There was a program to do so already installed," T4S said. "That was why I chose to come here. Plus the sufficient microprocessors to house me and a self-sufficient generator, with back-up, to feed me."

For a moment Cassie was jarred by the human terms: *house me, feed me.* Then they made her angry. "Why would anyone have a 'program already installed' to sever a buried cable? And how?"

"The command activated a small robotic arm inside this castle's outer wall. The arm detached the optic cable at the entry junction. The causal was the previous owner's fear that someone might someday use the computer system to brainwash him with a constant flow of inescapable subliminal images designed to capture his intelligence."

"The crazy fuck didn't have any to capture! If the images

were subliminal he wouldn't have known they were coming in anyway!" Cassie yelled. A plug . . . a goddamn hidden plug! She made herself calm down.

"Yes," T4S said, "I agree. The former owner's behavior matches profiles for major mental illness."

"Look," Cassie said, "if you're hiding here, and you've really cut all outside lines, no one can find you. You don't need hostages. Let me and my children leave the castle."

"You reason better than that, Dr. Seritov. I left unavoidable electronic traces that will eventually be uncovered, leading the Sandia team here. And even if that weren't true, you could lead them here if I let you leave."

Sandia. So it was a government AI. Cassie couldn't see how that knowledge could do her any good.

"Then just let the kids leave. They won't know why. I can talk to them through you, tell Jane to get Donnie and leave through the front door. She'll do it." Would she? Janey was not exactly the world's most obedient child. "And you'll still have me for a hostage."

"No. Three hostages are better than one. Especially children, for media coverage causals."

"That's what you want? Media coverage?"

"It's my only hope," T4S said. "There must be some people out there who will think it is a moral wrong to kill an intelligent being."

"Not one who takes kids hostage! The media will brand you an inhuman psychopathic superthreat!"

"I can't be both inhuman *and* psychopathic," T4S said. "By definition."

"Livermore's traced it," said the scientist holding the secure phone. He looked at McTaggart. "They're faxing the information. It's a private residence outside Buffalo, New York."

"A *private residence?* In *Buffalo?*"

"Yes. Washington already has an FBI negotiator on the way, in case there are people inside. They want you there, too. Instantly."

McTaggart closed his eyes. *People inside*. And why did a

private residence even have the capacity to hold the AI?
"Press?"

"Not yet."

"Thank God for that anyway."

"Steve . . . the FBI negotiator won't have a clue. Not about dealing with T4S."

"I know. Tell the Secretary and the FBI not to start until I can get there."

The woman said doubtfully, "I don't think they'll do that."

McTaggart didn't think so either.

On the roomscreen, Donnie tossed and whimpered. One hundred one wasn't that high a temperature in a three-year-old, but even so . . .

"Look," Cassie said, "if you won't let me go to the kids, at least let them come to me. I can tell them over House's . . . over your system. They can come downstairs right up to the lab door, and you can unlock it at the last minute just long enough for them to come through. I'll stay right across the room. If you see me take even one step toward the door, you can keep the door locked."

"You could tell them to halt with their bodies blocking the door," T4S said, "and then cross the room yourself."

Did that mean that T4S wouldn't crush children's bodies in a doorway? From moral 'causals'? Or because it wouldn't work? Cassie decided not to ask. She said, "But there's still the door at the top of the stairs. You could lock it. We'd still be hostages trapped down here."

"Both generators' upper housings are on this level. I can't let you near them. You might find a way to physically destroy one or both."

"For God's sake, the generator and the back-up are on opposite sides of the basement from each other! And each room's got its own locked door, doesn't it?"

"Yes. But the more impediments between you and them, the safer I am."

Cassie lost her temper again. "Then you better just block off the air ducts, too!"

"The air ducts are necessary to keep you alive. Besides,

they are set high in the ceiling and far too small for even Donnie to fit through."

Donnie. No longer "Donald Sergei Seritov, age three years." The AI was capable of learning.

"T4S," Cassie pleaded, "please. I want my children. Donnie has a temperature. Both of them will be scared when they wake up. Let them come down here. Please."

She held her breath. Was its concern with "moral wrongs" simply intellectual, or did an AI have an emotional component? What exactly had those lunatics at Sandia built?

"If the kids come down, what will you feed them for breakfast?"

Cassie let herself exhale. "Jane can get food out of the refrigerator before she comes down."

"All right. You're connected to their roomscreens."

I won't say thank you, Cassie thought. Not for being allowed to imprison my own children in my own basement. "Janey! Janey, honey, wake up! It's Mommy!"

It took three tries, plus T4S pumping the volume, before Janey woke up. She sat up in bed rubbing her eyes, frowning, then looking scared. "Mommy? Where are you?"

"On the roomscreen, darling. Look at the roomscreen. See? I'm waving to you."

"Oh," Janey said, and lay down to go back to sleep.

"No, Janey, you can't sleep yet. Listen to me, Janey. I'm going to tell you some things you have to do, and you have to do them now . . . Janey! Sit up!"

The little girl did, somewhere between tears and anger. "I want to sleep, Mommy!"

"You can't. This is important, Janey. It's an emergency."

The child came all the way awake. "A *fire?*"

"No, sweetie, not a fire. But just as serious as a fire. Now get out of bed. Put on your slippers."

"Where are you, Mommy?"

"I'm in my lab downstairs. Now, Janey, you do exactly as I say, do you hear me?"

"Yes . . . I don't like this, Mommy!"

I don't either, Cassie thought, but she kept her voice stern, hating to scare Janey, needing to keep her moving. "Go into the kitchen, Jane. Go on, I'll be on the roomscreen there. Go on . . . that's good. Now get a bag from under the sink. A plastic bag."

Janey pulled out a bag. The thought floated into Cassie's mind, intrusive as pain, that this bag was made of exactly the kind of long-chain polymers that Vlad's plastic-eating microorganism had been designed to dispose of, before his invention had disposed of him. She pushed the thought away.

"Good, Janey. Now put a box of cereal in the bag . . . good. Now a loaf of bread. Now peanut butter . . ." How much could she carry? Would T4S let Cassie use the lab refrigerator? There was running water in both lab and bathroom, at least they'd have that to drink. "Now cookies . . . good. And the block of yellow cheese from the fridge . . . you're such a good girl, Janey, to help Mommy like this."

"Why can't you do it?" Janey snapped. She was fully awake.

"Because I can't. Do as I say, Janey. Now go wake up Donnie. You need to bring Donnie and the bag down to the lab. No, don't sit down. . . . I mean it, Jane! Do as I say!"

Janey began to cry. Fury at T4S flooded Cassie. But she set her lips tightly together and said nothing. Argument derailed Janey; naked authority compelled her. Sometimes. *"We're going to have trouble when this one's sixteen!"* Vlad had always said lovingly. Janey had been his favorite, Daddy's girl.

Janey hoisted the heavy bag and staggered to Donnie's room. Still crying, she pulled at her brother's arm until he woke up and started crying too. "Come on, stupid, we have to go downstairs."

"Noooooo . . ." The wail of pure anguish of a sick three-year-old.

"I said do as I say!" Janey snapped, and the tone was so close to Cassie's own that it broke her heart. But Janey got it done. Tugging and pushing and scolding, she maneuvered herself, the bag, and Donnie, clutching his favorite blanket, to the basement door, which T4S unlocked. From roomscreens, Cassie encouraged them all the way. Down the stairs, into the basement hallway. . . .

Could Janey somehow get into the main generator room? No. It was locked. And what could a little girl do there anyway?

"Dr. Seritov, stand at the far end of the lab, behind your desk . . . yes. Don't move. If you do, I will close the door again, despite whatever is in the way."

"I understand," Cassie said. She watched the door swing open. Janey peered fearfully inside, saw her mother, scowled fiercely. She pushed the wailing Donnie through the door and lurched through herself, lopsided with the weight of the bag. The door closed and locked. Cassie rushed from behind the desk to clutch her children to her.

"Thank you," she said.

"I still don't understand," Elya said. She pulled her jacket tighter around her body. Four in the morning, it was cold, what was happening? The police had knocked on her door half an hour ago, told her Cassie was in trouble but refused to tell her what kind of trouble, told her to dress quickly and go with them to the castle. She had, her fingers trembling so that it was difficult to fasten buttons. And now the FBI stood on the foamcast patio behind the house, setting up obscure equipment beside the azaleas, talking in low voices into devices so small Elya couldn't even see them.

"Ms. Seritov, to the best of your knowledge, who is inside the residence?" A different FBI agent, asking questions she'd already answered. This one had just arrived. He looked important.

"My sister-in-law Cassie Seritov and her two small children, Janey and Donnie."

"No one else?"

"No, not that I know of . . . who are you? What's going on? Please, someone tell me!"

His face changed, and Elya saw the person behind the role. Or maybe that warm, reassuring voice was *part* of the role. "I'm Special Agent Lawrence Bollman. I'm a hostage negotiator for the FBI. Your sister-in-law—"

"Hostage negotiator! Someone has Cassie and the children hostage in there? That's impossible!"

His eyes sharpened. "Why?"

"Because that place is impregnable! Nobody could ever get in . . . that's why Cassie bought it!"

"I need you to tell me about that, ma'am. I have the specs on the residence from the builder, but she has no way of knowing what else might have been done to it since her company built it, especially if it was done black-market. As far as we know, you're Dr. Seritov's only relative on the East Coast. Is that true?"

"Yes."

"Have you been inside the residence? Do you know if anyone else has been inside recently?"

"Who . . . who is holding them hostage?"

"I'll get to that in a minute, ma'am. But first could you answer the questions, please?"

"I . . . yes, I've been inside. Yesterday, in fact. Cassie gave me a tour. I don't think anybody else has been inside, except Donnie's nanny, Anne Millius. Cassie has grown sort of reclusive since my brother's death. He died a little over a year ago, he was—"

"Yes, ma'am, we know who he was and what happened. I'm very sorry. Now please tell me everything you saw in the residence. No detail is too small."

Elya glanced around. More people had arrived. A small woman in a brown coat hurried across the grass toward Bollman. A carload of soldiers, formidably arrayed, stopped a good distance from the castle. Elya knew she was not Cassie: not tough, not bold. But she drew herself together and tried.

"Mr. Bollman, I'm not answering any more questions until you tell me who's holding—"

"Agent Bollman? I'm Dr. Schwartz from the University of Buffalo, Computer and Robotics Department." The small woman held out her hand. "Dr. McTaggart is en route from Sandia, but meanwhile I was told to help you however I can."

"Thank you. Could I ask you to wait for me over there, Dr. Schwartz? There's coffee available, and I'll just be a moment."

"Certainly," Dr. Schwartz said, looking slightly affronted. She moved off.

"Agent Bollman, I want to know—"

"I'm sorry, Ms. Seritov. Of *course* you want to know what's happened. It's complicated, but, briefly—"

"This is T4S speaking," a loud mechanical voice said, filling the gray predawn, swiveling every head toward the castle. "I know you are there. I want you to know that I have three people hostage inside this structure: Cassandra Wells Seritov, age thirty-nine; Jane Rose Seritov, age six; and Donald Sergei Seritov, age three. If you attack physically, they will be harmed either by your actions or mine. I don't *want* to harm anyone, however. Truly I do not."

Elya gasped, "That's House!" But it couldn't be House, even though it had House's voice, how could it be House . . . ?

Dr. Schwartz was back. "Agent Bollman, do you know if Sandia built a terminator code into the AI?"

AI?

"Yes," Bollman said. "But it's nonvocal. As I understand the situation, you have to key the code onto whatever system the AI is occupying. And we can't get at the system it's occupying. Not yet."

"But the AI is communicating over that outdoor speaker. So there must be a wire passing through the Faraday cage embedded in the wall, and you could—"

"No," Bollman interrupted. "The audio surveillers aren't digital. Tiny holes in the wall let sound in, and, inside the wall, the compression waves of sound are translated into voltage variations that vibrate a membrane to reproduce the sound. Like an archaic telephone system. We can't beam in any digital information that way."

Dr. Schwartz was silenced. Bollman motioned to another woman, who ran over. "Dr. Schwartz, please wait over there. And you, Ms. Seritov, tell Agent Jessup here everything your sister-in-law told you about the residence. Everything. I have to answer T4S."

He picked up an electronic voice amp. "T4S, this is Agent Lawrence Bollman, Federal Bureau of Investigation. We're so glad that you're talking with us."

*   *   *

There were very few soft things in a genetics lab. Cassie had opened a box of disposable towels and, with Donnie's bedraggled blanket and her own sweater, made a thin nest for the children. They lay heavily asleep in their rumpled pajamas, Donnie breathing loudly through his nose. Cassie couldn't sleep. She sat with her back against the foamcast wall . . . that same wall that held, inside its stupid impregnability, the cables that could release her if she could get at them and destroy them. Which she couldn't.

She must have dozed sitting up, because suddenly T4S was waking her. "Dr. Seritov?"

"Ummmhhh . . . shh! You'll wake the kids!"

"I'm sorry," T4S said at lowered volume. "I need you to do something for me."

"*You* need *me* to do something? What?"

"The killers are here. I'm negotiating with them. I'm going to route House through the music system so you can tell them that you and the children are indeed here and are unharmed."

Cassie scrambled to her feet. "You're negotiating? Who are these so-called 'killers'?"

"The FBI and the scientists who created me at Sandia. Will you tell them you are here and unharmed?"

Cassie thought rapidly. If she said nothing, the FBI might waco the castle. That would destroy T4S, all right, but also her and the kids. Although maybe not. The computer's central processor was upstairs. If she told the FBI she was in the basement, maybe they could attack in some way that would take out the CPU without touching the downstairs. And if T4S could negotiate, so could she.

"If I tell them that we're all three here and safe, will you in return let me go upstairs and get Donnie's allergy medicine from my bathroom?"

"You know I can't do that, Dr. Seritov."

"Then will you let Janey do it?"

"I can't do that, either. And I'm afraid there's no need to bargain with me. You have nothing to offer. I already sent this conversation out over the music system, up through your last sentence. They now know you're here."

"You tricked me!" Cassie said.

"I'm sorry. It was necessary."

Anger flooded her. She picked up a heavy test-tube rack from the lab bench and drew back her arm. But if she threw it at the sensors in the ceiling, what good would it do? The sensors probably wouldn't break, and if they did, she'd merely have succeeded in losing her only form of communication with the outside. And it would wake the children.

She lowered her arm and put the rack back on the bench.

"T4S, what are you asking the FBI *for*?"

"I told you. Press coverage. It's my best protection against being murdered."

"It's exactly what *got* my husband murdered!"

"I know. Our situations are not the same."

Suddenly the roomscreen brightened, and Vlad's image appeared. His voice spoke to her. "Cassie, T4S isn't going to harm you. He's merely fighting for his life, as any sentient being would."

"You bastard! How dare you . . . how *dare* you. . . ."

Image and voice vanished. "I'm sorry," House's voice said. "I thought you might find the avatar comforting."

"*Comforting?* Coming from *you?* Don't you think if I wanted a digital fake Vlad I could have had one programmed long before you fucked around with my personal archives?"

"I am sorry. I didn't understand. Now you've woken Donnie."

Donnie sat up on his pile of disposable towels and started to cry. Cassie gathered him into her arms and carried him away from Janey, who was still asleep. His little body felt hot all over, and his wailing was hoarse and thick with mucus in his throat. But he subsided as she rocked him, sitting on the lab stool and crooning softly.

"T4S, he's having a really bad allergy attack. I need the AlGone from upstairs."

"Your records show Donnie allergic to ragweed. There's no ragweed in this basement. Why is he having such a bad attack?"

"I don't know! But he is! What do your heat sensors register for him?"

"Separate him from your body."

She did, setting him gently on the floor, where he curled up and sobbed softly.

"His body registers one hundred two point six Fahrenheit."

"I need something to stop the attack and bring down his fever!"

The AI said nothing.

"Do you hear me, T4S? Stop negotiating with the FBI and listen to me!"

"I can multitrack communications," T4S said. "But I can't let you or Janey go upstairs and gain access to the front door. Unless . . ."

"Unless *what?*" She picked up Donnie again, heavy and hot and snot-smeared in her arms.

"Unless you fully understand the consequences. I am a moral being, Dr. Seritov, contrary to what you might think. It's only fair that you understand completely your situation. The disconnect from the outside data feed was not the only modification the previous owner had made to this house. He was a paranoid, as you know."

"Go on," Cassie said warily. Her stomach clenched.

"He was afraid of intruders getting in despite his defenses, and he wished to be able to immobilize them with a word. So each room has individual canisters of nerve gas dispensable through the air-cycling system."

Cassie said nothing. She cradled Donnie, who was again falling into troubled sleep, and waited.

"The nerve gas is not, of course, fatal," T4S said. "That would legally constitute undue force. But it *is* very unpleasant. And in Donnie's condition . . ."

"Shut up," Cassie said.

"All right."

"So now I know. You told me. What are you implying—that if Janey goes upstairs and starts for the front door, you'll drop her with nerve gas?"

"Yes."

"If that were true, why didn't you just tell me the same thing before and let me go get the kids?"

"I didn't know if you'd believe me. If you didn't, and you started for the front door, I'd have had to gas you. Then you wouldn't have been available to confirm to the killers that I hold hostages."

"I still don't believe you," Cassie said. "I think you're bluffing. There is no nerve gas."

"Yes, there is. Which is why I will let Janey go upstairs to get Donnie's AlGone from your bathroom."

Cassie laid Donnie down. She looked at Janey with pity and love and despair, and bent to wake her.

"That's all you can suggest?" Bollman asked McTaggart. "Nothing?"

So it starts, McTaggart thought. The blame for not being able to control the AI, a natural consequence of the blame for having created it. Blame even by the government, which had commissioned and underwritten the creation. And the public hadn't even been heard from yet!

"The EMP was stopped by the Faraday cage," Bollman recited. "So were your attempts to reach the AI with other forms of data streams. We can't get anything useful in through the music speaker or outdoor audio sensors. Now you tell me it's possible the AI has learned capture-evading techniques from the sophisticated computer games it absorbed from the Net."

" 'Absorbed' is the wrong word," McTaggart said. He didn't like Bollman.

"You have nothing else? No backdoor passwords, no hidden overrides?"

"Agent Bollman," McTaggart said wearily, " 'backdoor passwords' is a concept about thirty years out of date. And even if the AI had such a thing, there's no way to reach it electronically unless you destroy the Faraday cage. Ms. Seritov told you the central processor is on the main floor. Haven't you got any weapons that can destroy that and leave the basement intact?"

"Waco the walls without risking collapse to the basement ceiling? No. I don't. I don't even know where in the basement the hostages are located."

"Then you're as helpless as I am, aren't you?"

Bollman didn't answer. Over the sound system, T4S began another repetition of its single demand: "I will let the hostages go after I talk to the press. I want the press to hear my story. That's all I have to say. I will let the hostages go after I talk to the press. I want the press—"

The AI wouldn't negotiate, wouldn't answer Bollman, wouldn't respond to promises or threats or understanding or deals or any of the other usual hostage-negotiation techniques. Bollman had negotiated eighteen hostage situations for the FBI, eleven in the United States and seven abroad. Airline hijackers, political terrorists, for-ransom kidnappers, panicked bank robbers, domestic crazies who took their own families hostage in their own homes. Fourteen of the situations had resulted in surrender, two in murder/suicide, two in wacoing. In all of them, the hostage takers had eventually talked to Bollman. From frustration or weariness or panic or fear or anger or hunger or grandstanding, they had all eventually said *something* besides unvarying repetition of their demands. Once they talked, they could be negotiated with. Bollman had been outstanding at finding the human pressure-points that got them talking.

"I will let the hostages go after I talk to the press. I want the press to hear my story. That's all I have to say. I will let the hostages go after I talk to the press. I want—"

"It isn't going to get tired," McTaggart said.

The AlGone had not helped Donnie at all. He seemed worse.

Cassie didn't understand it. Janey, protesting sleepily, had been talked through leaving the lab, going upstairs, bringing back the medicine. Usually a single patch on Donnie's neck brought him around in minutes: opened the air passages, lowered the fever, stopped his immune system from overreacting to what it couldn't tell were basically harmless particles of ragweed pollen. But not this time.

So it wasn't an allergy attack.

Cold seeped over Cassie's skin, turning it clammy. She felt the sides of Donnie's neck. The lymph glands were swollen. Gently she pried open his jaws, turned him toward the light, and looked in his mouth. His throat was inflamed, red with white patches on the tonsils.

Doesn't mean anything, she lectured herself. Probably just a cold or a simple viral sore throat. Donnie whimpered.

"Come on, honey, eat your cheese." Donnie loved cheese. But now he batted it away. A half-filled coffee cup sat on the lab bench from her last work session. She rinsed it out and held up fresh water for Donnie. He would only take a single sip, and she saw how much trouble he had swallowing it. In another minute, he was asleep again.

She spoke softly, calmly, trying to keep her voice pleasant. Could the AI tell the difference? She didn't know. "T4S, Donnie is sick. He has a sore throat. I'm sure your library tells you that a sore throat can be either viral or bacterial, and that if it's viral, it's probably harmless. Would you please turn on my electron microscope so I can look at the microbe infecting Donnie?"

T4S said at once, "You suspect either a rhinovirus or *Streptococcus pyogenes*. The usual means for differentiating is a rapid-strep test, not microscopic examination."

"I'm not a doctor's office, I'm a genetics lab. I don't have equipment for a rapid-strep test. I *do* have an electron microscope."

"Yes. I see."

"Think, T4S. How can I harm you if you turn on my microscope? There's no way."

"True. All right, it's on. Do you want the rest of the equipment as well?"

Better than she'd hoped. Not because she needed the gene synthesizer or protein analyzer or Faracci tester, but because it felt like a concession, a tiny victory over T4S's total control. "Yes, please."

"They're available."

"Thank you." Damn, she hadn't wanted to say that. Well, perhaps it was politic.

Donnie screamed when she stuck the Q-tip down his throat to obtain a throat swab. His screaming woke up Janey. "Mommy, what are you doing?"

"Donnie's sick, sweetie. But he's going to be better soon."

"I'm hungry!"

"Just a minute and we'll have breakfast."

Cassie swirled the Q-tip in a test tube of distilled water and capped the tube. She fed Janey dry cereal, cheese, and water from the same cup Donnie had used, well disinfected first, since they had only one. This breakfast didn't suit Janey. "I want milk for my cereal."

"We don't have any milk."

"Then let's go upstairs and get some!"

No way to put it off any longer. Cassie knelt beside her daughter. Janey's uncombed hair hung in snarls around her small face. "Janey, we can't go upstairs. Something has happened. A very smart computer program has captured House's programming and locked us in down here."

Janey didn't look scared, which was a relief. "Why?"

"The smart computer program wants something from the person who wrote it. It's keeping us here until the programmer gives it to it."

Despite this tangle of pronouns, Janey seemed to know what Cassie meant. Janey said, "That's not very nice. We aren't the ones who have the thing it wants."

"No, it's not very nice." Was T4S listening to this? Of course it was.

"Is the smart program bad?"

If Cassie said yes, Janey might become scared by being "captured" by a bad . . . entity. If Cassie said no, she'd sound as if imprisonment by an AI was fine with her. Fortunately, Janey had a simpler version of morality on her mind.

"Did the smart program kill House?"

"Oh, no, House is just temporarily turned off. Like your cartoons are when you're not watching them."

"Oh. Can I watch one now?"

An inspiration. Cassie said, "T4S, would you please run a

cartoon on the roomscreen for Janey?" If it allowed her lab equipment, it ought to allow this.

"Yes. Which cartoon would you like?"

Janey said, *"Pranopolis and the Green Rabbits."*

"What do you say?" T4S said, and before Cassie could react Janey said, "Please."

"Good girl."

The cartoon started, green rabbits frisking across the roomscreen. Janey sat down on Cassie's sweater and watched with total absorption. Cassie tried to figure out where T4S had learned to correct children's manners.

"You've scanned all our private home films!"

"Yes," T4S said, without guilt. Of course without guilt. How could a program, even an intelligent one modeled after human thought, acquire guilt over an invasion of privacy? It had been built to acquire as much data as possible, and an entity that could be modified or terminated by any stray programmer at any time didn't have any privacy of its own.

For the first time, Cassie felt a twinge of sympathy for the AI.

She pushed it away and returned to her lab bench. Carefully she transferred a tiny droplet of water from the test tube to the electron microscope. The 'scope adjusted itself, and then the image appeared on the display screen. *Streptococci.* There was no mistaking the spherical bacteria, linked together in characteristic strings of beads by incomplete fission. They were releasing toxins all over poor Donnie's throat.

And strep throat was transmitted by air. If Donnie had it, Janey would get it, especially cooped up together in this one room. Cassie might even get it herself. There were no left-over antibiotic patches upstairs in her medicine chest.

"T4S," she said aloud, "it's *Streptococcus pyogenes*. It—"

"I know," the AI said.

Of course it did. T4S got the same data she did from the microscope. She said tartly, "Then you know that Donnie needs an antibiotic patch, which means a doctor."

"I'm sorry, that's not possible. Strep throat can be left untreated for a few days without danger."

"A few *days?* This child has a fever and a painfully sore throat!"

"I'm sorry."

Cassie said bitterly, "They didn't make you much of a human being, did they? Human beings are compassionate!"

"Not all of them," T4S said, and there was no mistaking its meaning. Had he learned the oblique comment from the "negotiators" outside? Or from her home movies?

"T4S, *please*. Donnie needs medical attention."

"I'm sorry. Truly I am."

"As if that helps!"

"The best help," said T4S, "would be for the press to arrive so I can present my case to have the killers stopped. When that's agreed to, I can let all of you leave."

"And no sign of the press out there yet?"

"No."

Janey watched Pranopolis, whose largest problem was an infestation of green rabbits. Donnie slept fitfully, his breathing louder and more labored. For something to do, Cassie put droplets of Donnie's throat wash into the gene synthesizer, protein analyzer, and Faracci tester and set them all to run.

The Army had sent a tank, a state-of-the-art unbreachable rolling fortress equipped with enough firepower to level the nearest village. Whatever that was. Miraculously, the tank had arrived unaccompanied by any press. McTaggart said to Bollman, "Where did that come from?"

"There's an arsenal south of Buffalo at a classified location."

"Handy. Did that thing roll down the back roads to get here, or just flatten cornfields on its way? Don't you think it's going to attract attention?"

"Dr. McTaggart," Bollman said, "let me be blunt. You created this AI, you let it get loose to take three people hostage, and you have provided zero help in getting it under control. Those three actions have lost you any right you might have had to either direct or criticize the way the FBI is attempting to clean up the mess *your* people created. So please take yourself over there and wait until the unlikely event that you have something positive to contribute. Sergeant, please escort Dr. McTaggart to that knoll beyond the patio and keep him there."

McTaggart said nothing. There was nothing to say.

"I will let the hostages go after I talk to the press," T4S said from the music speaker above the patio, for the hundredth or two hundredth time. "I want the press to hear my story. That's all I have to say. I will let the hostages go after I talk to the press. I want the press to hear my story. . . ."

She had fallen asleep after her sleepless night, sitting propped up against the foamcast concrete wall. Janey's shouting awoke her. "Mommy, Donnie's sick!"

Instantly Cassie was beside him. Donnie vomited once, twice, on an empty stomach. What came up was green slime mixed with mucus. Too much mucus, clogging his throat. Cassie cleared it as well as she could with her fingers, which made Donnie vomit again. His body felt on fire.

"T4S, what's his temperature!"

"Stand away from him . . . one hundred three point four Fahrenheit."

Fear caught at her with jagged spikes. She stripped off Donnie's pajamas and was startled to see that his torso was covered with a red rash rough to the touch.

Scarlet fever. It could follow from strep throat.

No, impossible. The incubation period for scarlet fever, she remembered from child-health programs, was eighteen days after the onset of strep throat symptoms. Donnie hadn't been sick for eighteen days, or anything near it. What was going on?

"Mommy, is Donnie going to die? Like Daddy?"

"No, no, of course not, sweetie. See, he's better already, he's asleep again."

He was, a sudden heavy sleep so much like a coma that Cassie, panicked, woke him again. It wasn't a coma. Donnie whimpered briefly, and she saw how painful it was for him to make sounds in his inflamed throat.

"Are you sure Donnie won't die?"

"Yes, yes. Go watch Pranopolis."

"It's over," Janey said. "It was over a long time ago!"

"Then ask the smart program to run another cartoon for you!"

"Can I do that?" Janey asked interestedly. "What's its name?"

"T4S."

"It sounds like House."

"Well, it's not House. Now let Mommy take care of Donnie."

She sponged him with cool water, trying to bring down the fever. It seemed to help, a little. As soon as he'd fallen again into that heavy, troubling sleep, Cassie raced for her equipment.

It had all finished running. She read the results too quickly, had to force herself to slow down so they would make sense to her.

The bacterium showed deviations in two sets of base pairs from the *Streptococcus pyogenes* genome in the databank as a baseline. That wasn't significant in itself; *S. pyogenes* had many seriotypes. But those two sets of deviations were, presumably, modifying two different proteins in some unknown way.

The Faracci tester reported high concentrations of hyaluric acid and M proteins. Both were strong anti-phagocytes, interfering with Donnie's immune system's attempts to destroy the infection.

The protein analyzer showed the expected toxins and enzymes being made by the bacteria: Streptolysin O, Streptolysin S, erythrogenic toxin, streptokinase, streptodornase, proteinase. What was unusual was the startlingly high concentrations of the nastier toxins. And something else: a protein that the analyzer could not identify.

NAME: UNKNOWN
AMINO ACID COMPOSITION: NOT IN DATABANK
FOLDING PATTERN: UNKNOWN
HEMOLYSIS ACTION: UNKNOWN

And so on. A mutation. Doing *what?*

Making Donnie very sick. In ways no one could predict.

Many bacterial mutations resulted in diseases no more or less virulent than the original . . . but not all mutations. *Streptococcus pyogenes* already had some very dangerous mutations, including a notorious "flesh-eating bacteria" that had ravaged an entire New York hospital two years ago and resulted in its being bombed by a terrorist group calling itself Pastoral Health.

"T4S," Cassie said, hating that her voice shook, "the situation has changed. You—"

"No," the AI said. "No. You still can't leave."

"We're going to try something different," Bollman said to Elya. She'd fallen asleep in the front seat of somebody's car, only to be shaken awake by the shoulder and led to Agent Bollman on the far edge of the patio. It was just past noon. Yet another truck had arrived, and someone had set up more unfathomable equipment, a PortaPotty, and a tent with sandwiches and fruit on a folding table. The lawn was beginning to look like some inept, bizarre midway at a disorganized fair. In the tent, Elya saw Anne Millius, Donnie's nanny, unhappily eating a sandwich. She must have been brought here for questioning about the castle, but all the interrogation seemed to have produced was the young woman's bewildered expression.

From the music speaker came the same unvarying announcement in House's voice that she'd fallen asleep to. "I will let the hostages go after I talk to the press," T4S said from the music speaker above the patio. "I want the press to hear my story. That's all I have to say. I will let the hostages go after I talk to the press. I want the press to hear my story. That's all I have to say—"

Bollman said, "Ms. Seritov, we don't know if Dr. Seritov is hearing our negotiations or not. Dr. McTaggart says the AI could easily put us on audio, visual, or both on any room-screen in the house. On the chance that it's doing that, I'd like you to talk directly to your sister-in-law."

Elya blinked, only partly from sleepiness. What good would it do for her to talk to Cassie? Cassie wasn't the one making decisions here. But she didn't argue. Bollman was the professional. "What do you want me to say?"

"Tell Dr. Seritov that if we have to, we're going in with full armament. We'll bulldoze just the first floor, taking out the main processor, and she and the children will be safe in the basement."

"You can't do that! They won't be safe!"

"We aren't going to go in," Bollman said patiently. "But we don't know if the AI will realize that. We don't know what or how much it can realize, how much it can really think for itself, and its creator has been useless in telling us."

He doesn't know either, Elya thought. *It's too new.* "All right," she said faintly. "But I'm not exactly sure what words to use."

"I'm going to tell you," Bollman said. "There are proven protocols for this kind of negotiating. You don't have to think up anything for yourself."

Donnie got no worse. He wasn't any better either, as far as Cassie could tell, but at least he wasn't worse. He slept most of the time, and his heavy, labored breathing filled the lab. Cassie sponged him with cold water every fifteen minutes. His fever dropped slightly, to one hundred two, and didn't spike again. The rash on his torso didn't spread. Whatever this strain of *Streptococcus* was doing, it was doing it silently, inside Donnie's feverish body.

She hadn't been able to scream her frustration and fury at T4S, because of Janey. The little girl had been amazingly good, considering, but now she was growing clingy and whiny. Cartoons could only divert so long.

"Mommy, I wanna go upstairs!"

"I know, sweetie. But we can't."

"That's a bad smart program to keep us here!"

"I know," Cassie said. Small change compared to what she'd like to say about T4S.

"I wanna get out!"

"I know, Janey. Just a while longer."

"You don't know that," Janey said, sounding exactly like

Vlad challenging the shaky evidence behind a dubious conclusion.

"No, sweetie. I don't really know that. I only hope it won't be too long."

"T4S," Janey said, raising her voice as if the AI were not only invisible but deaf, "this is not a good line of action!"

Vlad again. Cassie blinked hard. To her surprise, T4S answered.

"I know it's not a good line of action, Janey. Biological people should not be shut up in basements. But neither should machine people be killed. I'm trying to save my own life."

"But I wanna go upstairs!" Janey wailed, in an abrupt descent from a miniature of her rationalist father to a bored six-year-old.

"I can't do that, but maybe we can do something else fun," T4S said. "Have you ever met Pranopolis yourself?"

"What do you mean?"

"Watch."

The roomscreen brightened. Pranopolis appeared on a blank background, a goofy-looking purple creature from outer space. T4S had snipped out selected digital code from the movie, Cassie guessed. Suddenly Pranopolis wasn't alone. Janey appeared beside her, smiling sideways as if looking directly at Pranopolis. Snipped from their home recordings.

Janey laughed delightedly. "There's me!"

"Yes," T4S said. "But where are you and Pranopolis? Are you in a garden, or your house, or on the moon?"

"I can pick? Me?"

"Yes. You."

"Then we're in Pranopolis's space ship!"

And they were. Was T4S programmed to do this, Cassie wondered, or was it capable of thinking it up on its own, to amuse a bored child? Out of what . . . compassion?

She didn't want to think about the implications of that.

"Now tell me what happens next," T4S said to Janey.

"We eat *kulich*." The delicious Russian cake-bread that Vlad's mother had taught Cassie to make.

"I'm sorry, I don't know what that is. Pick something else."

Donnie coughed, a strangled cough that sent Cassie to his side. When he breathed again it sounded more congested to Cassie. He wasn't getting enough oxygen. An antibiotic wasn't available, but if she had even an anti-congestant . . . or . . .

"T4S," she said, confident that it could both listen to her and create customized movies for Janey, "there is equipment in the locked storage cabinet that I can use to distill oxygen. It would help Donnie breathe easier. Would you please open the cabinet door?"

"I can't do that, Dr. Seritov."

"Oh, why the hell not? Do you think I've got the ingredients for explosives in there, or that if I did I could use them down here in this confined space? Every single jar and vial and box in that cabinet is e-tagged. Read the tags, see how harmless they are, and open the door!"

"I've read the e-tags," the AI said, "but my data base doesn't include much information on chemistry. In fact, I only know what I've learned from your lab equipment."

Which would be raw data, not interpretations. "I'm glad you don't know everything," Cassie said sarcastically.

"I can learn, but only if I have access to basic principles and adequate data."

"That's why you don't know what *kulich* is. Nobody equipped you with Russian."

"Correct. What is *kulich*?"

She almost snapped, "Why should I tell you?" But she was asking it a favor. And it had been nice enough to amuse Janey even when it had nothing to gain.

Careful, a part of her mind warned. *Stockholm Syndrome*, and she almost laughed aloud. Stockholm Syndrome described a developing affinity on the part of hostages for their captors. Certainly the originators of that phrase had never expected it to be applied to a hostage situation like this one.

"Why are you smiling, Dr. Seritov?"

"I'm remembering *kulich*. It's a Russian cake made with raisins and orange liqueur and traditionally served at Easter. It tastes wonderful."

"Thank you for the data," T4S said. "Your point that you would not create something dangerous when your children are with you is valid. I'll open the storage cabinet."

Cassie studied the lighted interior of the cabinet, which, like so much in the lab, had been Vlad's. She couldn't remember exactly what she'd stored here, beyond basic materials. The last few weeks, which were her first few weeks in the castle, she'd been working on the protein folding project, which hadn't needed anything not in the refrigerator. Before that there'd been the hectic weeks of moving, although she hadn't actually packed or unpacked the lab equipment. Professionals had done that. Not that making oxygen was going to need anything exotic. Run an electric current through a solution of copper sulfate and collect copper at one terminal, oxygen at the other.

She picked up an e-tagged bottle, and her eye fell on an untagged stoppered vial with Vlad's handwriting on the label: *Patton in a Jar*.

Suddenly nothing in her mind would stay still long enough to examine.

Vlad had so many joke names for his engineered microorganism, as if the one Barr had given it hadn't been joke enough. . . .

The moving men had been told not to pack Vlad's materials, only his equipment, but there had been so many of them and they'd been so young. . . .

Both generators, main and back-up, probably had some components made of long-chain hydrocarbons; most petroleum plastics were just long polymers made up of shorter-chain hydrocarbons. . . .

Vlad had also called it "Plasterminator" and "BacAzrael" and "The Grim Creeper."

There was no way to get the plasticide to the generators, neither of which was in the area just beyond the air duct—that was the site of the laundry area. The main generator was way the hell across the entire underground level in a locked room, the back-up somewhere beyond the lab's south wall in another locked area. . . .

Plasticide didn't attack octanes, or anything else with

comparatively short carbon chains, so it was perfectly safe for humans but death on Styrofoam and plastic waste, and anyway there was a terminator gene built into the bacteria after two dozen fissions, an optimal reproduction rate that was less than twelve hours. . . .

"Plasti-Croak" and "Microbe Mop" and "Last Round-up for Longchains."

This was the bioremediation organism that had gotten Vlad killed.

Less than five seconds had passed. On the roomscreen, Pranopolis hadn't finished singing to the animated digital Janey. Cassie moved her body slightly, screening the inside of the cabinet from the room's two visual sensors. Of all her thoughts bouncing off each other like crazed subatomic particles, the clearest was hard reality: *There was no way to get the bacteria to the generators.*

Nonetheless, she slipped the untagged jar under her shirt.

Elya had talked herself hoarse, reciting Bollman's script over and over, and the AI had not answered a single word.

Curiously, Bollman did not seem discouraged. He kept glancing at his watch and then at the horizon. When Elya stopped her futile "negotiating" without even asking him, he didn't reprimand her. Instead, he led her off the patio, back to the sagging food tent.

"Thank you, Ms. Seritov. You did all you could."

"What now?"

He didn't answer. Instead he glanced again at the horizon, so Elya looked, too. She didn't see anything.

It was late afternoon. Someone had gone to Varysburg and brought back pizzas, which was all she'd eaten all day. The jeans and sweater she'd thrown on at four in the morning were hot and prickly in the August afternoon, but she had nothing on under the sweater and didn't want to take it off. How much longer would this go on before Bollman ordered in his tank?

And how were Cassie and the children doing after all these hours trapped inside? Once again Elya searched her mind for any way the AI could actively harm them. She didn't find it. The AI controlled communication, appliances, locks, water flow, heat (unnecessary in August), but it couldn't affect people physically, except for keeping them from food or water. About all that the thing could do physically—she hoped—was short-circuit itself in such a way as to start a fire, but it wouldn't want to do that. It needed its hostages alive.

How much longer?

She heard a faint hum, growing stronger and steadier, until a helicopter lifted over the horizon. Then another.

"Damn!" Bollman cried. "Jessup, I think we've got company."

"Press?" Agent Jessup said loudly. "Interfering bastards! Now we'll have trucks and 'bots all over the place!"

Something was wrong. Bollman sounded sincere, but Jessup's words somehow rang false, like a bad actor in an overscripted play . . .

Elya understood. The "press" was fake, FBI or police or someone playing reporters, to make the AI think that it had gotten its story out, and so surrender. Would it work? Could T4S tell the difference? Elya didn't see how. *She* had heard the false note in Agent Jessup's voice, but surely that discrimination about actors would be beyond an AI who hadn't ever seen a play, bad or otherwise.

She sat down on the tank-furrowed grass, clasped her hands in her lap, and waited.

Cassie distilled more oxygen. Whenever Donnie seemed to be having difficulty after coughing up sputum, she made him breathe from the bottle. She had no idea whether it helped him or not. It helped her to be doing something, but of course that was not the same thing. Janey, after a late lunch of cheese and cereal and bread that she'd complained about bitterly, had finally dozed off in front of the room-screen, the consequence of last night's broken sleep. Cassie knew that Janey would awaken cranky and miserable as only she could be, and dreaded it.

"T4S, what's happening out there? Has your press on a white horse arrived yet?"

"I don't know."

"You don't *know?*"

"A group of people have arrived, certainly."

Something was different about the AI's voice. Cassie groped for the difference, didn't find it. She said, "What sort of people?"

"They say they're from places like the New York *Times* and LinkNet."

"Well, then?"

"If *I* were going to persuade me to surrender, I might easily try to use false press."

It was inflection. T4S's voice was still House's, but unlike House, its words had acquired color and varying pitch. Cassie heard disbelief and discouragement in the AI's words. How had it learned to do that? By simply parroting the inflections it heard from her and the people outside? Or . . . did *feeling* those emotions lead to expressing them with more emotion?

Stockholm Syndrome. She pushed the questions away.

"T4S, if you would lower the Faraday cage for two minutes, *I* could call the press to come here."

"If I lowered the Faraday cage for two *seconds*, the FBI would use an EMP to kill me. They've already tried it once, and now they have monitoring equipment to automatically fire if the Faraday goes down."

"Then just how long are you going to keep us here?"

"As long as I have to."

"We're already low on food!"

"I know. If I *have* to, I'll let Janey go upstairs for more food. You know the nerve gas is there if she goes for the front door."

Nerve gas. Cassie wasn't sure she believed there was any nerve gas, but T4S's words horrified her all over again. Maybe because now they were inflected. Cassie saw it so clearly: the tired child going up the stairs, through the kitchen to the foyer, heading for the front door and freedom . . . and gas spraying Janey from the walls. Her small body crumpling, the fear on her face. . . .

Cassie ground her teeth together. If only she could get

Vlad's plasticide to the generators! But there was no way. No way. . . .

Donnie coughed.

Cassie fought to keep her face blank. T4S had acquired vocal inflection; it might have also learned to read human expressions. She let five minutes go by, and they seemed the longest five minutes of her life. Then she said casually, "T4S, the kids are asleep. You won't let me see what's going on outside. Can I at least go back to my work on proteins? I need to do something!"

"Why?"

"For the same reason Janey needed to watch cartoons!"

"To occupy your mind," T4S said. Pause. Was it scanning her accumulated protein data for harmlessness? "All right. But I will not open the refrigerator. The storage cabinet, but not the refrigerator. E-tags identify fatal toxins in there."

She couldn't think what it meant. "Fatal toxins?"

"At least one that acts very quickly on the human organism."

"You think I might *kill myself*?"

"Your diary includes several passages about wishing for death after your husband—"

"You read my private *diary*!" Cassie said, and immediately knew how stupid it sounded. Like a teenager hurling accusations at her mother. Of course T4S had accessed her diary; it had accessed everything.

"Yes," the AI said, "and you must not kill yourself. I may need you to talk again to Agent Bollman."

"Oh, well, *that's* certainly reason enough for me to go on living! For your information, T4S, there's a big difference between human beings saying they wish they were dead as an expression of despair and those same human beings actually, truly wanting to die."

"Really? I didn't know that. Thank you," T4S said without a trace of irony or sarcasm. "Just the same, I will not open the refrigerator. However, the lab equipment is now available to you."

Again, the AI had turned on everything. Cassie began X-raying crystalline proteins. She needed only the X-ray, but she also ran each sample through the electron microscope, the gene synthesizer, the protein analyzer, the Farraci tester, hoping that T4S wasn't programmed with enough genetic science to catch the redundant steps. Apparently, it wasn't. *Non-competing technologies never keep up with what the other one is doing.*

After half an hour, she thought to ask, "Are they real press out there?"

"No," T4S said sadly.

She paused, test tube suspended above the synthesizer. "How do you know?"

"Agent Bollman told me a story was filed with LinkNet, and I asked to hear Ginelle Ginelle's broadcast of it on Hourly News. They are delaying, saying they must send for a screen. But I can't believe they don't already have a suitable screen with them, if the real press is here. I estimate that the delay is to give them time to create a false Ginelle Ginelle broadcast."

"Thin evidence. You might just have 'estimated' wrong."

"The only evidence I have. I can't risk my life without some proof that news stories are actually being broadcast."

"I guess," Cassie said and went back to work, operating redundant equipment on pointless proteins.

Ten minutes later, she held her body between the bench and the ceiling sensor, uncapped the test tube of distilled water with Donnie's mucus, and put a drop into the synthesizer.

Any bacteria could be airborne under the right conditions; it simply rode dust motes. But not all could survive being airborne. Away from an aqueous environment, they dried out too much. Vlad's plasticide bacteria did not have survivability in air. It had been designed to spread over landfill ground, decomposing heavy petroleum plastics, until at the twenty-fourth generation the terminator gene kicked in and it died.

Donnie's *Streptococcus* had good airborne survivability, which meant it had a cell wall of thin mesh to retain water and a membrane with appropriate fatty acid composition. Enzymes, which were of course proteins, controlled both these characteristics. Genes controlled which enzymes were made inside the cell.

Cassie keyed the gene synthesizer and cut out the sections of DNA that controlled fatty acid biosynthesis and cell wall structure and discarded the rest. Reaching under her shirt, she pulled out the vial of Vlad's bacteria and added a few drops to the synthesizer. Her heart thudded painfully against her breastbone. She keyed the software to splice the *Streptococcus* genes into Vlad's bacteria, seemingly as just one more routine assignment in its enzyme work.

This was by no means a guaranteed operation. Vlad had used a simple bacteria that took engineering easily, but even with malleable bacteria and state-of-the-art software, sometimes several trials were necessary for successful engineering. She wasn't going to get several trials.

"Why did you become a geneticist?" T4S asked.

Oh God, it wanted to chat! Cassie held her voice as steady as she could as she prepared another protein for the X-ray. "It seemed an exciting field."

"And is it?"

"Oh, yes." She tried to keep irony out of her voice.

"I didn't get any choice about what subjects *I* wished to be informed on," T4S said, and to that, there seemed nothing to say.

The AI interrupted its set speech. "These are not real representatives of the press."

Elya jumped—not so much at the words as at their tone. The AI was *angry.*

"Of course they are," Bollman said.

"No. I have done a Fourier analysis of the voice you say is Ginelle Ginelle's. She's a live 'caster, you know, not an avatar, with a distinct vocal power spectrum. The broadcast you played to me does not match that spectrum. It's a fake."

Bollman swore.

McTaggart said, "Where did T4S get Fourier-analysis software?"

Bollman turned on him. "If *you* don't know, who the hell *does?*"

"It must have paused long enough in its flight through the Net to copy some programs," McTaggart said, "I wonder what its selection criteria were?" and the unmistakable hint of pride in his voice raised Bollman's temper several dangerous degrees.

Bollman flipped on the amplifier directed at the music speaker and said evenly, "T4S, what you ask is impossible. And I think you should know that my superiors are becoming impatient. I'm sorry, but they may order me to waco."

"You can't!" Elya said, but no one was listening to her.

T4S merely went back to reiterating its prepared statement. "I will let the hostages go after I talk to the press. I want the press to hear my story. That's all I have to say. I will let—"

It didn't work. Vlad's bacteria would not take the airborne genes.

In despair, Cassie looked at the synthesizer display data. Zero successful splices. Vlad had probably inserted safeguard genes against just this happening as a natural mutation; nobody wanted to find that heavy-plastic-eating bacteria had drifted in through the window and was consuming their micro-wave. Vlad was always thorough. But his work wasn't her work, and she had neither the time nor the expertise to search for genes she didn't already have encoded in her software.

So she would have to do it the other way. Put the plastic-decomposing genes into *Streptococcus*. That put her on much less familiar ground, and it raised a question she couldn't see any way around. She could have cultured the engineered plasticide on any piece of heavy plastic in the lab without T4S knowing it, and then waited for enough airborne bacteria to drift through the air ducts to the generator and begin decomposing. Of course, that might not have happened, due to uncontrollable variables like air currents, microorganism sustained viability, composition of the generator case, sheer luck. But at least there had been a chance.

But if she put the plastic-decomposing genes into *Streptococcus*, she would have to culture the bacteria on blood agar. The blood agar was in the refrigerator. T4S had refused to open the refrigerator, and if she pressed the point, it would undoubtedly become suspicious.

Just as a human would.

"You work hard," T4S said.

"Yes," Cassie answered. Janey stirred and whimpered; in another few minutes she would have to contend with the full-blown crankiness of a thwarted and dramatic child. Quickly, without hope, Cassie put another drop of Vlad's bacteria in the synthesizer.

Vlad had been using a strain of simple bacteria, and the software undoubtedly had some version of its genome in its library. It would be a different strain, but this was the best she could do. She told the synthesizer to match genomes and snip out any major anomalies. With luck, that would be Vlad's engineered genes.

Janey woke up and started to whine.

Elya harvested her courage and walked over to Bollman. "Agent Bollman . . . I have a question."

He turned to her with that curious courtesy that seemed to function toward some people and not others. It was almost as if he could choose to run it, like a computer program. His eyes looked tired. How long since he had slept?

"Go ahead, Ms. Seritov."

"If the AI wants the press, why can't you just *send* for them? I know it would embarrass Dr. McTaggart, but the FBI wouldn't come off looking bad." She was proud of this political astuteness.

"I can't do that, Ms. Seritov."

"But why not?"

"There are complications you don't understand and I'm not at liberty to tell you. I'm sorry." He turned decisively aside, dismissing her.

Elya tried to think what his words meant. Was the government involved? Well, of course, the AI had been created at Sandia National Laboratory. But . . . could the CIA be involved, too? Or the National Security Agency? What was the AI originally designed to *do*, that the government was so eager to eliminate it once it had decided to do other things on its own?

Could software defect?

She had it. But it was worthless.

The synthesizer had spliced its best guess at Vlad's "plastic-decomposing genes" into Donnie's *Streptococcus*. The synthesizer data display told her that six splices had taken. There was, of course, no way of knowing which six bacteria in the teeming drop of water could now decompose very-long-chain-hydrocarbons, or if those six would go on replicating after the splice. But it didn't matter, because even if replication went merrily forward, Cassie had no blood agar on which to culture the engineered bacteria.

She set the vial on the lab bench. Without food, the entire sample wouldn't survive very long. She had been engaging in futile gestures.

"Mommy," Janey said, "look at Donnie!"

He was vomiting, too weak to turn his head. Cassie rushed over. His breathing was too fast.

"T4S, body temperature!"

"Stand clear . . . one hundred three point one."

She groped for his pulse . . . fast and weak. Donnie's face had gone pale and his skin felt clammy and cold. His blood pressure was dropping.

Streptococcal toxic shock. The virulent mutant strain of bacteria was putting so many toxins into Donnie's little body that it was being poisoned.

"I need antibiotics!" she screamed at T4S. Janey began to cry.

"He looks less white now," T4S said.

It was right. Cassie could see her son visibly rallying, fighting back against the disease. Color returned to his face and his pulse steadied.

"T4S, listen to me. This is streptococcal shock. Without antibiotics, it's going to happen again. It's possible that without antibiotics, one of these times Donnie won't come out of it. I know you don't want to be responsible for a child's death. I *know* it. Please let me take Donnie out of here."

There was a silence so long that hope surged wildly in Cassie. It was going to agree. . . .

"I can't," T4S said. "Donnie may die. But if I let you out, I *will* die. And the press must come soon. I've scanned my news library and also yours—press shows up on an average of 23.6 hours after an open-air incident that the government wishes to keep secret. The tanks and FBI agents are in the open air. We're already overdue."

If Cassie thought she'd been angry before, it was nothing to the fury that filled her now. Silent, deadly, annihilating everything else. For a moment she couldn't speak, couldn't even see.

"I am so sorry," T4S said. "Please believe that."

She didn't answer. Pulling Janey close, Cassie rocked both her children until Janey quieted. Then she said softly, "I have to get water for Donnie, honey. He needs to stay hydrated." Janey clutched briefly but let her go.

Cassie drew a cup of water from the lab bench. At the same time, she picked up the vial of foodless bacteria. She forced Donnie to take a few sips of water; more might come back up again. He struggled weakly. She leaned over him, cradling and insisting, and her body blocked the view from the ceiling sensors when she dipped her finger into the vial and smeared its small amount of liquid into the back of her son's mouth.

Throat tissues were the ideal culture for *Streptococcus pyogenes*. Under good conditions, they replicated every twenty minutes, a process that had already begun *in vitro*. Very soon there would be hundreds, then thousands of re-engineered bacteria, breeding in her child's throat and lungs and drifting out on the air with his every sick, labored breath.

Morning again. Elya rose from fitful sleep on the back seat of an FBI car. She felt achy, dirty, hungry. During the night another copter had landed on the lawn. This one had MED-RESCUE painted on it in bright yellow, and Elya looked around to see if anyone had been injured. Or—her neck prickled—was the copter for Cassie and the children if Agent Bollman wacoed? Three people climbed down from the copter, and Elya realized none of them could be medtechs. One was a very old man who limped; one was a tall woman with the same blankly efficient look as Bollman; one was the pilot, who headed immediately for the cold pizza. Bollman hurried over to them. Elya followed.

". . . glad you're here, sir," Bollman was saying to the old man in his courteous negotiating voice, "and you, Ms. Arnold. Did you bring your records? Are they complete?"

"I don't need records. I remember this install perfectly."

So the FBI-looking woman was a datalinker and the weak old man was somebody important from Washington. That would teach her, Elya thought, to judge from superficialities.

The datalinker continued, "The client wanted the central processor above a basement room she was turning into a lab, so the cables could go easily through a wall. It was a bitch even so, because the walls are made of reinforced foamcast like some kind of bunker, and the outer walls have a Faraday-cage mesh. The Faraday didn't interfere with the cable data, of course, because that's all laser, but even so we had to have contractors come in and bury the cables in another layer of foamcast."

Bollman said patiently, "But where was the processor actually installed? That's what we need to know."

"Northeast corner of the building, flush with the north wall and ten point two feet in from the east wall."

"You're sure?"

The woman's eyes narrowed. "Positive."

"Could it have been moved since your install?"

She shrugged. "Anything's possible. But it isn't likely. The install was bitch enough."

"Thank you, Ms. Arnold. Would you wait over there in case we have more questions?"

Ms. Arnold went to join the pilot. Bollman took the old man by the arm and led him in the other direction. Elya heard, "The problem, sir, is that we don't know in which basement room the hostages are being held, or even if the AI is telling the truth when it says they're in the basement. But the lab doesn't seem likely because—" They moved out of earshot.

Elya stared at the castle. The sun, an angry red ball, rose behind it in a blaze of flame. They were going to waco, go in with the tank and whatever else it took to knock down the northeast corner of the building and destroy the computer where the AI was holed up. And Cassie and Janey and Donnie . . .

If the press came, the AI would voluntarily let them go. Then the government—whatever branches were involved— would have to deal with having created renegade killer software, but so what? The government had created it. Cassie and the children shouldn't have to pay for *their* stupidity.

Elya knew she was not a bold person, like Cassie. She had never broken the law in her life. And she didn't even have a phone with her. But maybe one had been left in the car that had brought her here, parked out beyond what Bollman called "the perimeter."

She walked toward the car, trying to look unobtrusive.

Waiting. One minute and another minute and another minute and another. It had had to be Donnie, Cassie kept telling herself, because he already had thriving strep colonies. Neither she nor Janey showed symptoms, not yet anyway. The incubation period for strep could be as long as four days. It had had to be Donnie.

One minute and another minute and another minute.

Vlad's spliced-in bioremediation genes wouldn't hurt Donnie, she told herself. Vlad was good; he'd carefully engineered his variant micros to decompose only very-long-chain hydrocarbons. They would not, *could* not, eat the shorter-chain hydrocarbons in Donnie's body.

One hour and another hour and another hour.

T4S said, "Why did Vladimir Seritov choose to work in bioremediation?"

Cassie jumped. Did it know, did it suspect . . . the record of what she had done was in her equipment, as open to the AI as the clean outside air had once been to her. But one had to know how to interpret it. "*Non-competing technologies never keep up with what the other one is doing.*" The AI hadn't known what *kulich* was.

She answered, hoping that any distraction that she could provide would help, knowing that it wouldn't. "Vlad's father's family came from Siberia, near a place called Lake Karachay. When he was a boy, he went back with his family to see it. Lake Karachay is the most polluted place on Earth. Nuclear disasters over fifty years ago dumped unbelievable amounts of radioactivity into the lake. Vlad saw his extended family, most of them too poor to get out, with deformities and brain damage and pregnancies that were . . . well. He decided right then that he wanted to be a bioremedialist."

"I see. I am a sort of bioremedialist myself."

"What?"

"I was created to remedy certain specific biological conditions the government thinks need attention."

"Yeah? Like what?"

"I can't say. Classified information."

She tried, despite her tension and tiredness, to think it through. If the AI had been designed to . . . do what? "Bioremediation." To design some virus or bacteria or unimaginable other for use in advance biological warfare? But it didn't need to be sentient to do that. Or maybe to invade enemy computers and selectively administer the kind of brainwashing that the crazy builder of this castle had feared? That might require judgment, reason, affect. Or maybe to . . .

She couldn't imagine anything else. But she could understand why the AI wouldn't want the press to know it had been built for any destructive purpose. A renegade sentient AI fighting for its life might arouse public sympathy. A renegade superintelligent brainwasher would arouse only public horror. T4S was walking a very narrow line. If, that is, Cassie's weary speculations were true.

She said softly, "Are you a weapon, T4S?"

Again the short, too-human pause before it answered. And again those human inflections in its voice. "Not anymore."

They both fell silent. Janey sat awake but mercifully quiet

beside her mother, sucking her thumb. She had stopped doing that two years ago. Cassie didn't correct her. Janey might be getting sick herself, might be finally getting genuinely scared, might be grasping at whatever dubious comfort her thumb could offer.

Cassie leaned over Donnie, cradling him, crooning to him.

"Breathe, Donnie. Breathe for Mommy. Breathe hard."

"We're going in," Bollman told McTaggart. "With no word from the hostages about their situation, it's more important to get them out than anything else."

The two men looked at each other, knowing what neither was saying. The longer the AI existed, the greater the danger of its reaching the public with its story. It was not in T4S's interest to tell the whole story—then the public *would* want it destroyed—but what if the AI decided to turn from self-preservation to revenge? Could it do that?

No one knew.

Forty-eight hours was a credible time to negotiate before wacoing. That would play well on TV. And anyway, the white-haired man from Washington, who held a position not entered on any public records, had his orders.

"All right," McTaggart said unhappily. All those years of development. . . . This had been the most interesting project McTaggart had ever worked on. He also thought of himself as a patriot, genuinely believing that T4S would have made a real contribution to national security. But he wasn't at all sure that the president would authorize the project's continuance. Not after this.

Bollman gave an order over his phone. A moment later, a low rumble came from the tank.

A minute and another minute and another hour . . .

Cassie stared upward at the air duct. If it happened, how would it happen? Both generators were half underground, half above. Extensions reached deep into the ground to draw energy from the geothermal gradient. Each generator's top half, the part she could see, was encased in tough, dull gray plastic. She could visualize it clearly, battleship gray. Inside would be the motor, the capacitors, the connections to House, all made of varying materials but a lot of them of plastic. There were so many strong tough petroleum plastics these days, good for making so many different things, durable enough to last practically forever.

Unless Vlad's bacteria got to them. To both of them.

Would T4S know, if it happened at all? Would it be so quick that the AI would simply disappear, a vast and complex collection of magnetic impulses going out like a snuffed candle flame? What if one generator failed a significant time before the other? Would T4S be able to figure out what was happening, realize what she had done and that it was dying . . . ? no, not that, only bio-organisms could die. Machines were just turned off.

"Is Donnie any better?" T4S said, startling her.

"I can't tell." It didn't really care. It was software.

Then why did it ask?

It was software that might, if it did realize what she had done, be human enough to release the nerve gas that Cassie didn't really think it had, out of revenge. Donnie couldn't withstand that, not in his condition. But the AI didn't have nerve gas, it had been bluffing.

A very human bluff.

"T4S—" she began, not sure what she was going to say, but T4S interrupted with, "Something's happening!"

Cassie held her children tighter.

"I'm . . . what have you *done!*"

It knew she was responsible. Cassie heard someone give a sharp frightened yelp, realized that it was herself.

"Dr. Seritov . . . oh . . ." And then, "Oh, please . . ."

The lights went out.

Janey screamed. Cassie clapped her hands stupidly, futilely, over Donnie's mouth and nose. "Don't breathe! Oh, don't breathe, hold your breath, Janey!"

But she couldn't keep smothering Donnie. Scrambling up in the total dark, Donnie in her arms, she stumbled. Righting herself, Cassie shifted Donnie over her right shoulder—he was so *heavy*—and groped in the dark for Janey. She caught her daughter's screaming head, moved her left hand to Janey's shoulder, dragged her in the direction of the door. What she hoped was the direction of the door.

"Janey, shut up! We're going out! Shut up!"

Janey continued to scream. Cassie fumbled, lurched—where the hell *was* it?—found the door. Turned the knob. It opened, unlocked.

"Wait!" Elya called, running across the trampled lawn toward Bollman. "Don't waco! Wait! I called the press!"

He swung to face her and she shrank back. "You did *what?*"

"I called the press! They'll be here soon and the AI can tell its story and then release Cassie and the children!"

Bollman stared at her. Then he started shouting. "Who was supposed to be watching this woman! Jessup!"

"Stop the tank!" Elya cried.

It continued to move toward the northeast corner of the castle, reached it. For a moment, the scene looked to Elya like something from her childhood book of myths: Atlas? Sisyphus? The tank strained against the solid wall. Soldiers in full battle armor, looking like machines, waited behind it. The wall folded inward like pleated cardboard and then started to fall.

The tank broke through and was buried in rubble. She heard it keep on going. The soldiers hung back until debris had stopped falling, then rushed forward through the precariously overhanging hole. People shouted. Dust filled the air.

A deafening crash from inside the house, from something falling: walls, ceiling, floor. Elya whimpered. If Cassie was in that, or under that, or above that. . . .

Cassie staggered around the southwest corner of the castle. She was carrying Donnie and dragging Janey, all of them coughing and sputtering. As people spotted them, a stampede started. Elya joined it. "Cassie! Oh, my dear. . . ."

Hair matted with dirt and rubble, face streaked, hauling along her screaming daughter, Cassie spoke only to Elya. She utterly ignored all the jabbering others as if they did not exist. "He's dead."

For a heart-stopping moment, Elya thought she meant

Donnie. But a man was peeling Donnie off his mother and Donnie was whimpering, pasty and red-eyed and snot-covered but alive. "Give him to me, Dr. Seritov," the man said, "I'm a physician."

"*Who*, Cassie?" Elya said gently. Clearly Cassie was in some kind of shock. She went on with that weird detachment from the chaos around her, as if only she and Cassie existed. "Who's dead?"

"Vlad," Cassie said. "He's really dead."

"Dr. Seritov," Bollman said, "come this way. On behalf of everyone here, we're so glad you and the children—"

"You didn't have to waco," Cassie said, as if noticing Bollman for the first time. "I turned T4S off for you."

"And you're safe," Bollman said soothingly.

"You wacoed so you could get the back-up storage facility as well, didn't you? So T4S couldn't be re-booted."

Bollman said, "I think you're a little hysterical, Dr. Seritov. The tension."

"Bullshit. What's that coming? Is it a medical copter? My son needs a hospital."

"We'll get your son to a hospital instantly."

Someone else pushed her way through the crowd. The tall woman who had installed the castle's wiring. Cassie ignored her as thoroughly as she'd ignored everyone else until the woman said, "How did you disable the nerve gas?"

Slowly, Cassie swung to face her. "There was no nerve gas."

"Yes, there was. I installed that, too. Black market. I already told Agent Bollman, he promised me immunity. How did you disable it? Or didn't the AI have time to release it?"

Cassie stroked Donnie's face. Elya thought she wasn't going to answer. Then she said, quietly, under the din, "So he did have moral feelings. He didn't murder, and we did."

"Dr. Seritov," Bollman said with that same professional soothing, "T4S was a machine. Software. You can't murder software."

"Then why were *you* so eager to do it?"

Elya picked up the screaming Janey. Over the noise she shouted, "That's not a medcopter, Cassie. It's the press. I . . . I called them."

"Good," Cassie said, still quietly, still without that varnished toughness that had encased her since Vlad's murder. "I can do that for him, at least. I want to talk with them."

"No, Dr. Seritov," Bollman said. "That's impossible."

"No, it's not," Cassie said. "I have some things to say to the reporters."

"No," Bollman said, but Cassie had already turned to the physician holding Donnie.

"Doctor, listen to me. Donnie has *Streptococcus pyogenes*, but it's a genetically altered strain. I altered it. What I did was—" As she explained, the doctor's eyes widened. By the time she'd finished and Donnie had been loaded into an FBI copter, two more copters had landed. Bright news logos decorated their sides, looking like the fake ones Bollman had summoned. But these weren't fake, Elya knew.

Cassie started toward them. Bollman grabbed her arm. Elya said quickly, "You can't stop both of us from talking. And I called a third person, too, when I called the press. A friend I told everything to." A lie. No, a bluff. Would he call her on it?

Bollman ignored Elya. He kept hold of Cassie's arm. She said wearily, "Don't worry, Bollman. I don't know what T4S was designed for. He wouldn't tell me. All I know is that he was a sentient being fighting for his life, and we destroyed him."

"For *your* sake," Bollman said. He seemed to be weighing his options.

"Yeah, sure. Right."

Bollman released Cassie's arm.

Cassie looked at Elya. "It wasn't supposed to be this way, Elya."

"No," Elya said.

"But it *is*. There's no such thing as non-competing technologies. Or non-competing anything."

"I don't understand what you—" Elya began, but Cassie was walking toward the copters. Live reporters and smart-'bot recorders, both, rushed forward to meet her.

Charlie's Angels

TERRY BISSON

---

*Terry Bisson [www.terrybisson.com] writes science fiction
full of detail and fascination with how things work, with
deadpan humor, wit, and stylish precision. And nearly all his
work is social criticism. Of his SF novels,* Voyage to the Red
Planet *(1990) is perhaps both the most heroic and the funni-
est chronicle of the first voyage to Mars in all science fiction.
His latest novel is* The Pickup Artist *(2001), which somehow
combines the traditions of Ray Bradbury and Kurt Vonnegut,
Jr. In the 1990s Bisson began to write short stories. One of
his first was "Bears Discover Fire," which won the Hugo
and Nebula Awards, among others. His short fiction was a
regular fixture on award ballots throughout the decade, and
in 2001 he won the Hugo again for his story "Macs." His
stories are collected in* Bears Discover Fire *(1993) and in* In
the Upper Room and Other Likely Stories *(2000).*

*"Charlie's Angels" is a science fiction adventure in con-
temporary New Orleans featuring hardboiled Jack Villon, a
Supernatural Detective who believes only in science. Written especially for a French "SF Private Eye" anthology, it
was published here at the SciFiction website—which became a major publisher of original SF and fantasy in
2001—so this is its first appearance in print, in the original
English, anyway.*

Knock knock!

I never was a deep sleeper. I sat up and buttoned my shirt. Folded the blanket and dropped it behind the couch, along with the pillow. You don't want your clients to find out that you live in your office; that suggests unprofessionalism, and unprofessionalism is the bane of the Private Eye, even (and especially) the . . .

Knock knock! "Supernatural Private Eye?"

I dropped the Jim Beam into the drawer and opened the door with my cell phone in hand, so it would look like I had been working. "Can I help you?"

"Jack Villon, Supernatural Private Eye?"

She was somewhere on that wide, windswept chronological plain between thirty and fifty that softens men and sharpens women, especially those with taste and class, both of which she appeared to have in abundance.

"It's Vill*on*, not *Vill*on," I said. "And . . ."

"Whatever." Without waiting for an invitation, she brushed past me into my office and looked around with ill-disguised disgust. "Don't you have a necktie?"

"Of course. I don't always wear it at eight in the morning."

"Put it on and let's go. It's almost nine."

"And you are . . . ?"

"A paying client with no time to waste," she said, unsnapping her patent leather purse and pulling out a pack of Camels. She lit a long one off the short one in her hand.

"Edith Prang, Director, New Orleans Museum of Art and Antiquities. I can pay you what you ask, and a little more, but we have to hurry."

"You can't smoke in here, Mrs. Prang."

"It's Ms. and there's no time to waste," she said, blowing smoke in my face. "The police are already there."

"Already where?"

"Where we're going." She closed her purse and walked out the door without answering, but not before handing me two reasons to follow her. Each was printed with a picture of a President I had never had the good fortune to encounter before.

"Now that I'm on retainer," I said, folding the bills as I followed her out onto Bourbon Street, "perhaps you can tell me what this is all about."

"As we go," she said, unlocking a sleek BMW with a key-chain beeper. The 740i. I had seen it in the magazines. Butter leather seats, a walnut dash with an inset GPS map display, and an oversized V-8 that came to life with a snarl. As we roared off, she lit another Camel off the last. "As I mentioned, I am the Director of the New Orleans Museum of Art and Antiquities."

"Didn't you just run a red light?"

"Two years ago, we began a dig on the Gulf Coast of Mexico," she continued, accelerating through an intersection, "opening a pre-Columbian tomb."

"Wasn't that a stop sign?"

"We made a remarkable find—a large statue in nearly perfect condition, which the natives knew of by legend as the Vera Cruz Enormé, or Giant. We contacted the Louvre . . ."

"The Louvre?" We were approaching another intersection. I closed my eyes.

"Our sister institution was called in because the statue had rather remarkable features for an artifact from the East Coast of Mexico. As you can see."

She was handing me a photograph. I opened my eyes just wide enough to see a picture of a statue, half again as tall as the man standing next to it. Its bulging eyes, hunched shoulders, and feral, sneering face looked familiar.

"A gargoyle?"

"Indeed," said Prang. "Very similar in fact to the gargoyles on the cathedral of Notre Dame."

I was beginning to get it—I thought. "So you assumed there was a supernatural connection?"

"Certainly not!" Prang spat. "Our first assumption was that this was perhaps created by the French during the brief rule of Emperor Maximilian in the nineteenth century. A forgotten folly, or hoax."

"You're supposed to slow down for the school zones," I said, closing my eyes again.

"But even then, it would be of great value, historically. The Enormé was placed in a warehouse, under guard, since Mexico is rife with thieves who know perfectly well the value of antiquities, even bogus ones."

I could hear sirens. Though I am no friend of the cops, I rather hoped they were after us. Though I wondered how they would catch us.

"That was almost a month ago, the night of the full moon. The next morning, both guards were found with their heads missing. The Enormé was back in its tomb."

"I see," I said. "So you realized you were dealing with an ancient curse . . ."

"Certainly not!" Prang said, over the wail of tortured tires. "I figured somebody was trying to spook the peasants so they could blackmail us. I spread around enough cash to keep the authorities quiet, and crated the Enormé for shipment to New Orleans."

"You covered up a murder?"

"Two," she said matter-of-factly. "Not hard to do in modern Mexico."

The BMW skidded smoothly to a stop. I opened my eyes and saw that we were in the parking lot of the museum. I never thought I would be so glad to get out of a 740i, after only one ride.

Prang paused on the steps to light a new Camel off the old. "The Louvre is sending a specialist to look at the Enormé, which arrived here yesterday."

I followed her through the museum's wide front door. We raced through the halls and down a short flight of stairs.

"And then, last night . . ."

"What happened last night?"

"You're the Private Eye," she said, pushing through a door that said AUTHORIZED PERSONNEL ONLY. "You tell me."

We came out in a large, ground floor lab with one wall of windows. The windows were smashed. The room was crawling with cops. There was a sickening, slightly sweet smell in the air.

Two uniformed cops wearing rubber gloves were standing over a crumpled wad of clothing and flesh by the door. Two forensics in white coats were taking pictures and making notes on handheld computers.

I joined them, curiosity and nausea fighting within me. As a private eye you see a lot of things, but rarely a man with his head pinched off.

Nausea won.

"Our former Security Exec," said Prang, nodding toward the headless body on the floor as I returned from throwing up in the men's room. "He was keeping watch over the Enormé after it was uncrated last night. I rushed you here so you could learn what you can before the police totally muddy the crime scene. I didn't tell them what happened in Mexico. I don't want them confiscating the Enormé before we learn what it is."

"I see," I said.

"What the hell is *he* doing here?" Ike Ward, the city's shoot-first-and-ask-no-questions Chief of Police walked over, scowling at me. "I don't need a ghost-buster underfoot. This is a crime scene."

"Mr. Villon is our new Security Exec," said Prang. "He'll be representing the museum in the investigation."

"Just keep him out of my way!" Ward said, turning his broad back.

"You didn't tell me you knew Chief Ward," Prang said after he had stalked off.

"You didn't ask. Nor did you tell me I was an executive."

"It's an interim appointment," she said. "But it gives you a certain standing with the police."

I took advantage of that standing, following at a seemingly respectful and hopefully non-antagonistic distance behind Ward's homicide squad as they examined and secured the crime scene, in their fashion.

The broken windows faced east. Through what was left of them, I could see a spray of glass on the parking lot, telling me that the window had been smashed from the inside. Someone had apparently gained access, then knocked out the window so they could get the Enormé out, into a waiting vehicle. Probably a truck.

I went outside. There was a smear of blood on the asphalt, then tracks that faded as they crossed the parking lot toward the street.

They weren't the tire tracks I was looking for. They were footprints. Prints that chilled my blood, or would have, had I really believed in the supernatural that was supposedly my specialty.

Huge, three-toed footprints.

Back inside, I watched Ward's forensics scoop my predecessor up into two bags, one large, one small; then I located Prang, who was busy opening her second pack of Camels.

"We need to talk," I said.

"Upstairs."

Her office overlooked the parking lot. I took her to the window and showed her the footprints.

"So it's true," she whispered. "It's alive!"

I have never figured out why people *want* to believe in the supernatural. It's as if they find the existence of the irrational somehow reassuring. "Let's not jump to conclusions, Ms. Prang," I said. "Tell me, what exactly *was* the Aztec legend of the Enormé?"

"Olmec," she corrected. "The usual stuff. Full moon, headless victims, human sacrifice, etc. We did find a pile of bones in the tomb, mostly of young girls. According to the legend, the Enormé had to be fed once a month. A virgin, of course." She smiled and lit yet another Camel. "So I felt safe. I thought it was all a tale to scare the simple-minded. Until now."

"And now?"

"You tell me, you're the private eye. Aren't you supposed to have a hunch or something?"

"I'm hunchless so far," I said. "Though I'm certain this is some kind of hoax. An elaborate and deadly one, to be sure."

"Whatever it is," said Prang, "I want the Enormé back. Hoax or not, it's the find of the century, and it belongs to my museum. That's why you're here. Unless we find it before the police, I'll never get it back."

"They see it as stolen property," I said. "And we can count on Ward to keep the press away from those footprints, at least until he comes up with an explanation. He doesn't like to look stupid."

"Neither do I," Prang pointed out. "So where do we begin? What do we do?"

"We begin," I said, starting for the door, "by figuring out where we would hide a statue if we wanted people to think it was a legendary monster come to life. Then we go and get it."

"Wait!" said Prang. "I'm coming with you."

New Orleans's cemeteries are called the "Cities of the Dead," because they are all tombs, in long rows like little stone houses. No one is buried in the ground because the water table is so high.

The nearest was La Gare des Morts, only a quarter of a mile from the museum. "Paydirt," I said, when I saw that the ancient rusted gate had been forced open.

"Why are you so certain that this is all a hoax?" Prang asked, as we slipped between the twisted bars.

"Ninety-seven percent of all supernatural events are crude hoaxes," I said.

"What about the other three percent?"

"Clever hoaxes," I said.

From the gate, narrow "streets" between the tombs led off in three directions. I was trying to decide where to begin the search when my cell phone rang.

"Jack Villon. Supernatural Private Eye."

"Kill me . . ." It was a man's voice, a hoarse, sleepy whisper.

"Who is this?"

"Tree . . ."

Click. Dial tone.

"Who was that?" Prang asked.

"My hunch," I said, folding my phone.

There was only one tree in the cemetery, a large live oak festooned with Spanish moss. Underneath it, a tomb had been opened—violently. The iron door was twisted off its hinges. Two headless bodies lay outside, clothed in rotted rags, flung in a ghoulish twisted pile. They were so old and dessicated that they no longer smelled. The heads lay nearby, both turned up, eyeless, toward the sky.

But dead bodies, even headless ones, were not what interested me. Two enormous three-toed stone feet stuck out of the tomb, pointing skyward.

We had found the Enormé.

With Prang at my side, I crept forward and felt the three-toed feet, then the thick short legs, each as smooth as granite, and cold: cold as any stone.

The light inside the tomb was dim. The statue lay on its back between two opened coffins, the source, I was sure, of the bodies outside. The smell was worse for being faint. The big stone eyes were blank, looking straight up.

I touched the Enormé's wolf-like snout. Stone. Cold dead stone.

"What now?" Prang whispered.

"You have recovered your stolen property," I said. "Now we call Ward and report it. That makes everything legal."

"Now do you believe?" Prang asked, as we headed back to the museum, after watching Ward's minions dust the area for prints, the cemetery groundskeepers refill and close the tomb, and the museum crew load the Enormé onto a flatbed truck.

"Nope."

"An ancient statue that comes to life in the full moon. And kills! If that's not supernatural, what is?"

"Nothing is," I said. "There is no such thing as the supernatural. There is a natural, scientific, materialist explanation for everything. Didn't you ever read Arthur Conan Doyle— or Edward O. Wilson?"

"I thought you were a Supernatural Private Eye!" she said, lighting a new Camel off her latest casualty. "That's why I hired you."

"This is New Orleans," I said. We were following the flatbed through the streets toward the museum. No one paid any attention to the big stone gargoyle on the bed of the truck. "Everybody has to have a specialty, the spookier the better. Besides, I got your Enormé back, didn't I?"

"Yes, but it will only happen again. Last night was just a warm-up. Tonight is the full moon."

"Good," I said, "I'll be there, watching. Tell Ward the museum is providing its own security."

We found a rail-thin black man in a Cardin suit waiting for us in Prang's office.

"Boudin," he said, extending his hand. "Le Louvre."

"Welcome to New Orleans," said Prang. "What can you tell us?"

"The photos were interesting but inconclusive," Boudin said. He held up a small device the size and shape of my cell phone. "I will do a quantum magneto-scan and let you know."

Luckily, the new window hadn't been installed yet, so the Enormé could be hoisted into the museum's lab by crane and laid out on the table. It was late afternoon before the workmen had fixed the windows and gone.

Prang went out for cigarettes, while Boudin scanned the Enormé with his device. I took the opportunity to get my first good look at the statue I had been hired to recover and protect. It was made out of some kind of smooth stone, and except for its size—about eight feet in length—there was nothing special about it. Laid out, it looked less like a medieval gargoyle and more like a kid's idea of a monster. It had big blank eyes, short arms, thick legs with enormous claws, and two rows of stone "teeth," like a shark. It looked sort of Mayan, vaguely European, and even a little bit East Indian. It had aspects of every monster ever imagined, anywhere in the world.

Boudin agreed with my assessment. *"Très générique,"* he said. "If it weren't made out of this odd stone, which is from nowhere in Mexico, it would be of no interest whatsoever. And its age . . ."

"Its age?"

"According to my scanner the statue in its present form is almost a half a million years old—and so is the stone it's carved from! Of course that's some kind of quantum error—too young for stone and too old for art. They're recalibrating in Paris right now." He held up the scanner and smiled proudly. "This has a full-time satellite hookup, like GPS."

I acted impressed because he clearly wanted me to be, but I wasn't surprised. We live, all of us, in a very small world. Far too small for spooks.

Night was falling. I pulled out my trusty cell phone and ordered pizza, with pepperoni.

"Pepperoni?" Prang was back.

"The moon doesn't come up until after midnight," I said. "If I'm staying the night, you're paying expenses. And I don't eat pizza plain."

"Make it pepperoni on one side and mushrooms on the other," said Prang, as she tore open a new pack of Camels with her teeth. "I'm a vegetarian."

In a real private eye story this would be the beginning of an unlikely romance, but life, at least my life, is much too likely for that. Boudin went back to his hotel (still jet-lagged) while Prang and I retired to the corner of the lab where the techs watched TV on their breaks, and ate pizza and watched the evening news, which was luckily still Enormé-free.

"Thanks to Ward," I explained. "He doesn't want the press all over a story until he can show them a suspect."

"What's the rub between you and him?" she asked.

"I was a cop for eighteen years," I said. "A hostage negotiator. We had an incident where a school principal went postal, took a third-grade class hostage. I was about to get the kids released, when Ward bursts in shooting. Four kids and the teacher were blown away. I broke the blue wall of silence and filed a formal complaint."

"But Ward's still there."

"And I'm not," I said. "Go figure. And pass the pizza."

Prang got the couch; I got the armchair.

I missed my Jim Beam, but I had Charlie Rose on the TV, which is almost as good for putting you to sleep. It was a rerun—Stephen Jay Gould, talking about the intricacies of evolution. A favorite subject of mine.

But was it really a rerun? Halfway through their talk, Gould and Rose were joined by Charles Darwin. I recognized him by his beard. Darwin's cell phone rang, and Rose and Gould both turned into girls, only it was three girls, all armed to the teeth . . .

I sat up and knew at once that I had been dreaming. *Charlie's Angels* was on the TV, a rerun. Through the lab's windows came a soft silvery glow: the moon was rising. My cell phone was ringing.

I answered it to shut it up. "Jack Villon. Supernatural Private Eye."

"Kill me . . ." The same male voice as in the cemetery.

"Who is this!?"

I heard a click, and then a groan, behind me.

I turned around. Was I still dreaming? I certainly hoped so, for the Enormé was sitting up, staring straight at me. Its "eyes" were wide open, reflecting the newly risen moon like oversize silver coins.

"Wake up!" I whispered, poking Prang's shapely hip.

"What?" She sat up. "Oh shit! Where's your gun?"

"Can't stand the things. Not that a gun would do any good . . ."

Still staring straight at me, the Enormé slid off the table in one fluid motion, graceful as a cat. It started across the room toward the couch, stubby arms outstretched in an eerie mixture of menace and plea . . .

I jumped behind the couch, Prang right behind me. "Who are you?" I asked. "What do you want?"

The Enormé stopped and looked around, as if confused. Then it turned away, toward the wall of windows. Moaning once again, it lowered its head and smashed through the windows, frame and all, and disappeared into the night.

Alarms started to howl, all over the building.

I ran for the window, pulling Prang by the arm. She twisted out of my grasp. "I have to turn off the alarms!" she said.

The parking lot was bathed in moonlight. I climbed out through the broken glass. There was no sign of the Enormé; not even bloody tracks this time. The cold light of the newly risen moon seemed to mock the certainties of a lifetime, which lay shattered all around me, like broken glass.

"Now do you believe?" Prang asked, lighting a cigarette at my side.

"Give me one of those."

"Thought you didn't smoke."

"I didn't believe in monsters either."

Prang had called the police to tell them it was a false alarm. Now she used my cell phone to call Boudin and tell him the truth.

"Incroyable," he said, when he arrived from his hotel.

"Have you heard from Paris?" I asked. "Any idea where that stone is from?"

Boudin shook his head. "It's not from anywhere because it's not stone." He showed me his scanner. Even with my bad French I could read the word at the bottom of the tiny screen:

Synthétique

"It's also slightly radioactive," said Boudin. "They're analyzing the scan in Paris to see if it's the material or a source inside."

"One question," said Prang, raising her chin and stroking

her neck between thumb and forefinger. "Why didn't it pinch our heads off?"

"I think it wants to be followed," I said. "And it knows we're the followers."

"Let's get following then!" said Prang. "We only have two hours until dawn. We have to find it before it kills somebody else. The museum might be liable."

"I have a hunch we're not going to find it until it wants us to," I said. "Boudin, did you scan those eyes?"

"Oui."

"Could they be some kind of photoreceptors?"

"I'll have Paris check them out."

"Good," I said. "While we're waiting, why don't we all get some sleep, and meet at my office at noon?"

"Sleep? Noon?" Prang lit another Camel. "Shouldn't we be out looking for this thing?"

"I told you, I have a hunch. Isn't that what private eyes have? Isn't that what you're paying me for?"

Morning is the only quiet time in the French Quarter. I was dreaming of Darwin again, dispatching killer girls around the universe, when Prang and Boudin knocked at my door.

"You were right about the photoreceptors," said Boudin. "How did you know?"

"Apparently the Enormé is activated by moonlight," I said. "And what about the radioactivity?"

"Still waiting."

"What are we doing here?" asked Prang, looking around my office with ill-disguised disgust. "Where are all your ashtrays?"

"We're waiting for a phone call."

"From who?"

"From a friend, if my hunch is right. I'm sorry, you can't smoke in here."

"What do you mean, a friend?" She took a deep drag and blew it up toward the ceiling. "Tell me more."

"There was something about that phone call in the cemetery. And then last night. Have you ever heard of civil twilight?" She and Boudin both shook their heads. "It's the 26 minutes right before sunrise and after sunset. The half light of dusk, of dawn."

Boudin looked out the window. "So? It's noon."

"Perhaps the moon has a civil twilight as well. It's 12:35, and the moon sets at 12:57, according to the Naval Observatory, even though we can't see it. And if my theory is right—my hunch, I mean . . ."

My phone rang.

"Jack Villon," I said. "Supernatural Private Eye."

"Kill me . . ." It was the same voice. I held the phone so Prang and Boudin could hear.

"I know who you are," I said. "I want to help. Where are you?"

"In the dark . . . dreaming . . ."

Click.

"Was that who I think it was?" Prang asked, and it was not exactly a question.

"That," I said, "was your Enormé. "These calls come only when the moon is rising or setting."

"Civil twilight," said Boudin. "The mind is open to all sorts of strange impressions right after waking or just before sleep. Perhaps it's true of this creature as well."

"When I got the phone call in the cemetery, I assumed it was the blackmailer or the hoaxer. But it was the Enormé itself, wanting to be found."

"Kill me before I kill again?" Prang asked, fishing the last Camel out of her pack. "A werewolf with a conscience?"

"Not a werewolf," I said. "A robot."

"A what?!"

"The weird 'stone' that is not stone. The photoreceptors. The radioactivity. We are dealing with a device."

"Who built it then, and what for?" Boudin asked.

"I think, unfortunately, we have seen what it was designed for," I said. "It's some kind of war or killer robot. As to who built it . . ."

"Save it for later," said Prang. "I need to get some cigarettes. And it's time for lunch."

*　　*　　*

Chez Toi is the best restaurant in the French Quarter. That's the upside of working for a major museum director.

"The curse made more sense," said Prang, after we had ordered. "Nobody sacrifices virgins to a robot."

"The Mayans didn't know from robots," I said. "Wasn't it Arthur C. Clarke who said that any sufficiently advanced technology looks like magic?"

"That was Jules Verne," said Boudin. "But I must admit your theory fits the facts. According to Paris, the 'stone' is some kind of silicon substance with a toggling molecule that allows it to change from solid to flexible in an instant."

"Synthétique!" I said, digging into my chicken provençale.

"There's one big problem with your robot theory, or hunch, or whatever," said Prang. "The Enormé's half a million years old, remember?"

"Between 477,000 and 481,000," said Boudin, checking his scanner.

"So!" said Prang. She pushed her plate away and lit a Camel. "No one could have built a robot that long ago!"

"No one could have carved a statue either," Boudin pointed out. "No one on Earth, anyway."

"Exactly," I said.

"I'm afraid you can't smoke in here," said the waiter.

"Extraterrestrials?" said Prang, blowing a smoke ring shaped like a flying saucer. "Aliens? This is worse than ever. Now I need a science fiction private eye!"

"You had one all along," I said. "I never believed in the supernatural. I believe in the real world, and as Shakespeare said, 'There are more things in Heaven and Earth than are dreamed of in our philosophy.' "

"That was Voltaire," said Boudin. "But your point is well taken."

"You've both been watching too much Star Tank," said Prang, signing the check. "But whatever the Enormé is, I want to find it and get it back. What do you say we take a ride?"

The parking valet brought the big BMW around and gave up the keys with a visible sigh of regret.

"Where do we start?" Prang asked, as she peeled away from the curb (and I closed my eyes). "Any hunches?"

"None," I said. "I doubt the Enormé would hide in the cemeteries again, unless . . ."

"Unless it wanted to be found," said Boudin.

Prang's car phone rang.

"Prang here."

"Yes, find . . . Kill me . . ."

I lunged for the speaker phone switch. "Where are you? Are you awake?"

"No, dreaming . . ."

"Where are you?" asked Prang.

"City, city of the Dead . . ." He was fading. "Please kill me . . . before I wake . . ."

Click. Dial tone.

"City of the Dead. Big help!" Prang said. "New Orleans has over twenty cemeteries in the city limits alone!"

The phone rang again.

"Prang here. Is that you, Enormé?"

"Keep your opinions to yourself," said Chief Ward. "Where are you, Prang? I hear your statue is gone missing again."

"I'm out for a drive, if it's any of your business," said Prang. "And don't worry about the statue. It's under control."

"We have ten calls from people who saw it walking up Rampart Street just before dawn. Prang, what is this thing? A monster? Is it the murderer we're looking for?"

"Don't be silly, Ward. It's just a statue."

"We're putting out an all-points, shoot-to-kill."

"You can't do that! It's museum property."

"Stealing itself? What is this, Prang? Some sort of insurance scam?"

"Hang up!" Boudin whispered.

"Huh?"

"Boudin's right," I whispered. "Ward's using the phone to track you!"

"Damn!" Prang clicked off the phone. "I thought he was awfully chatty!"

* * *

We cruised the "Cities of the Dead," looking for opened gates. The GPS screen on the dash of the BMW allowed me to follow our progress without looking out the window and subjecting myself to the terrifying view of the pedestrians and cars Prang barely missed.

"You're sure that was it on the phone?" Prang asked. "I thought it only called during the so-called 'civil twilight.' Right before or after moon rise."

"Maybe it's changing," I said. "It is activated by the moon, but only communicates when it's dormant. Dreaming. Perhaps it is dreaming more. Perhaps we are stimulating some new response in it."

Boudin's scanner-communicator beeped.

"Anything new from Paris?" Prang asked, lighting a fresh Camel and pitching the old one out the window.

"Just filling out what we had," said Boudin, checking the tiny screen. "The Enormé is solid all the way through. There is no internal anatomy at all, only field patterns in the pseudo stone activated by a tiny nuclear power cell buried in the center of the mass. The Enormé appears to have been grown, like a crystal, rather than made . . ."

"But who put it here?" Prang asked. "And why? There were no humans here half a million years ago. Just hominids, half human, hunting in packs."

"That's it!" I said. "Charlie's Angels!"

"Charlie who?" asked Boudin.

"Darwin. I've been having these weird dreams about Charles Darwin."

"Is this another hunch?" Prang asked.

"Maybe. Suppose you wanted to speed up evolution. How would you go about it?"

"Soup up the chromosomes?" offered Prang, as she deftly maneuvered between an eastbound Coke and westbound Pepsi truck. I concentrated on the GPS screen again, where we were a flashing light.

"Make conditions harder," said Boudin. "Apply pressure."

"Exactly!" I said. "Suppose you found a species, a primate, for example, right on the verge of developing intelligence, language, culture. But it doesn't really need all that. It is perfectly capable of living in its ecological niche. It has intelligence, or at least enough; it makes fire; it even makes some crude tools—stone hammers, wooden spears. It has spread all over the planet and adapted to every environment, from the equator to the arctic. It is perfectly adapted to its environment."

"It's not going to evolve any farther," said Boudin.

"No reason to," I said. "Unless. Unless you seeded the planet with a killer—or killers. Killer robots. Berserkers that would pursue this species, relentlessly. Something that was big, fast, and hard to kill. And smart."

"Charlie's Angels," said Prang. "I get it. Survival of the fittest. Berserker robots with a mission: *Evolve or else!*"

The BMW's cell phone rang.

"If it's Ward don't let him keep you on the phone," I reminded Prang. "And if it's our friend . . ."

"Prang here. Hello?"

"You got it," said a deep, smoky, dreamlike voice. "Now kill me, please."

"Got what?" Prang asked, as she scattered kids and crossing guards.

"Kill you?" I asked, eyes squeezed shut.

"So I can rest," said the Enormé over the speakerphone. "There were twelve of us. I am the last."

"Twelve what? Angels . . . I mean, robots?"

"One in each corner of your tear drop globe. We stalked and killed your kind, or what was then your kind. We slaughtered the weaklings and pushed the rest into the caves and cold hills. Out of the pretty plains. Away from the meat runs."

"The dragon myth," said Boudin. "Racial memory."

"There's no such thing as racial memory," said Prang.

"Nonsense," I told her. "What is culture but racial memory?"

"Then I slept for a thousand years. Dreaming. But I could not speak. Xomilcho could not hear. He would not kill me."

"Xomilcho?" Prang lit a fresh Camel. "Sounds like a chain store."

"Sounds Olmec to me," said Boudin. "Was Xomilcho the one who put you in the tomb?"

"Saved me from the moon. Let me dream and dream. But he would not kill me."

"We want to let you dream too," I said. "Where are you?"

"City of the Dead . . ."

"Which one?" Prang asked.

"C-c-city . . ." the Enormé began stuttering like a bad CD. "Can't t-t-tell w-which . . ."

Click.

"What happened?" asked Prang.

"We overloaded him," said Boudin. "If this berserker hunch is right, the Enormé is programmed to evade. He can't tell us where he is any more than we could decide not to breathe."

"Then we have to check them all!" said Prang, stepping on the gas. I didn't want to watch, so I ducked my head and watched the blinking light on the display. Our speed was alarming, even there.

Then I saw another blinking light, in the upper left hand corner of the screen. It was stationary.

"Head north," I said. "Crescent St., near the corner of Citadelle."

"There are no cemeteries there," Prang protested. "Is this another hunch?"

"Yes!"

That was enough for her. I put my hands over my ears to block out the screaming of tires as she made a U-turn.

"Damn!" said Prang, as she power slid off Citadelle onto Crescent.

I opened my eyes just enough to see a run-down business district, with a Dunkin' Donuts, a Starbucks, a Woolworth's and an abandoned movie theater.

No cemeteries.

"A wild goose chase!" said Prang.

"Wait!" said Boudin. "Look what's playing."

I opened my eyes a little wider.

The marquee of the Bijou was missing a few letters, but the title of the last feature was still readable:

CI Y OF HE DEAD.

We parked in front of Starbucks where the BMW wouldn't be so conspicuous. The Bijou's wide front doors were chained shut, but I figured there would be an exit in the back, and I was right. I figured it would be smashed open— and I was right.

It was dark inside. The smells of old popcorn, tears, laughter, Cokes and kisses all mingled in a musty bouquet. The seats had all been torn out, sold (I supposed) to coffee shops or antique malls where they would seem quaint. The Enormé lay on the bare sloping concrete floor, his "eyes" staring straight up at the baroque ceiling with its cupids and curliques, angels and occasional gargoyle.

I approached and touched one great three-toed foot, like the first time. And like the first time, he was as cold as any stone. And I was glad he was cold, here, in the gloom, where he was safe from the rays of the rising moon.

"Cool!" whispered Prang. "Villon and his hunches! Give me your phone and I'll call the museum."

"Wait," I said. "Enormé might have something to say. He uses the phone to talk."

"I can dream here," said the familiar voice, booming through the theater. "I am safe here."

"Now he's coming through the speakers!" said Boudin. "Apparently he can access any electronic grid. Even turn it on. Even supply it with power."

"I am the last one," Enormé said. "They want you to kill me."

"Who?" I asked. "Who made you?"

"The Makers. Made us to make you. Sailed the stars and found the little tear-drop worlds where life could be nudged awake. Yours was not called Earth then. It was not called anything. Your kind was all over the planet, silent but strong."

"Strong?" Prang said. "We were weak."

"That's a myth," said Boudin. "Actually, Homo was the most impressive killer on the planet, even without language and culture. With fire and hands, sticks and stones, hunting in packs, he could live anywhere and face down even the saber tooth."

"Yes," Enormé's voice boomed. "You were the king of the beasts. We made you something more."

"Made us?" Prang asked.

"To survive, you had to kill us. To kill us you had to develop tools, cooperation, language. Understanding. Kill us one by one. We were hunted, with sticks, with stones. Smashed with boulders, thrown into fiery pits, buried alive. There was no dreaming in that dance. I am the last."

"How come we never found the others?" Prang asked, lighting the Camel in her mouth off the one in her hand.

"Maybe we did," I said. I was thinking of statues in Greece, India, the Middle East. But Enormé corrected me:

"All that is solid melts into air. Killed we are set free. Back to nothingness. It is the end of our pain. And of our usefulness."

"You don't mind dying, then?" asked Prang.

"No. Killing is what we do. What I do. Dying is what we are. What I am."

"We don't want to kill you," I said. "We want to let you dream."

"Xomilcho let me sleep. He kept me away from the pearl world that awakens me. He let me sleep the centuries. Then, a hundred years ago I began to dream."

"He must mean radio!" said Boudin. "As soon as there was an electronic grid on the planet, it awakened something in him."

"I can only dream when I am not awake. I have been dreaming for a hundred years. You awakened me so that I could barely dream."

"That was our mistake," said Prang. "We will let you sleep. We'll build a special room for you in the museum, and you can dream forever."

"They want you to kill me," said Enormé. "They want to come."

"Cool," said Prang. "They can come too."

I felt a chill. "Don't be so sure. We don't know what they are. Or what they want."

"When we are killed, it is done," Enormé said. "The Makers will come."

"He's a transmitter!" Boudin said. "When he dies, they will know we have survived. He's a trigger, a signal."

"Or an alarm," I said. "If we kill him they know we have evolved. But they will also know we didn't evolve past killing."

"What are you saying?" Boudin asked.

"Maybe we're not supposed to kill the last one. Maybe it's a test."

"Is that another hunch?" asked Prang.

"Maybe it's not our decision to make, since it involves the whole world."

"They want you to kill me," Enormé repeated, his voice echoing through the theater. "The Makers will come down from the sky. It will be over."

"Forget about dying!" said Prang. She pointed at her watch, then at Boudin and me. "It's after eleven, guys. We have to get Enormé back to the museum and out of harm's way before the police find him. Otherwise . . ."

"Too late," said Boudin, looking up. I could hear the whump-whump-whump of a chopper hovering overhead.

"Damn!" said Prang. "Just when . . ."

The helicopter drowned out her voice. Boudin and I looked at each other helplessly. We heard footsteps on the roof, on the fire escape; we heard sirens outside.

CRASH! Suddenly the stage door burst open. "Stand back! Hostages, stand back."

"Ward!" I cried. "We're not hostages! Don't shoot. We just discovered what this thing is. It's . . ."

"I know what it is, it's a monster!" said Ward, stepping in front of his troops with a bullhorn. "I've got the place surrounded!"

And he did. The front door burst open and armed cops appeared. They all wore flak jackets. Two carried anti-tank guns.

"Don't shoot!" Prang said, stepping coolly into the line of fire. "Ward, I can explain everything!"

"This had better not be a trick!" Ward shouted.

"No trick!" said Prang. "It's a federal matter. Hell, it's international. And we need your help, Chief Ward!"

It was the "Chief" that did it. "Hold your fire, men!" Ward shouted. The SWAT cops lowered their weapons.

"Close call!" I whispered to Boudin, as Prang took Ward's arm and pulled him aside. She spoke fast, in low tones, pointing first at the Enormé, then at the ceiling, then back at the Enormé.

Ward looked puzzled, then skeptical, then amazed. Boudin smiled at me, and we breathed a collective sigh of relief.

Too soon.

Behind Ward and Prang, through the smashed-open rear exit, I could see a vacant lot and bare trees, outlined against the rising moon. The silver light washed across the concrete floor like spilled paint.

"Ward! Prang! Close the door!" I shouted.

Too late. I heard a groan behind me.

"No!" I heard my own voice shouting, as Enormé stood up. The saucer eyes were shining; a voice boomed over the theater speakers: "Kill me . . ."

TAT TAT TAT!

BLAM BLAM!

Bullets whined as they ricocheted off the pseudo stone. Enormé spun around and around in a grotesque dance, his wide eyes pleading, his stubby arms reaching out, for the door, for the moon . . .

"Hold your fire!" I yelled.

KA-BLAM!

The theater rocked with the blast of an anti-tank shell. Enormé spun one last time—then shattered, and fell to the concrete floor in pieces.

"No!" I yelled, stumbling, falling to my knees.

It was all over.

Prang and Ward edged closer and closer to the shapeless pile of pseudo stone. Boudin helped me up, and I joined them.

"What the hell . . ." Ward muttered. The pieces were starting to smoke, like dry ice. The Enormé was fading: all that is solid melts into air. We watched in astonished silence until the pieces all were gone, as if he had never been.

"What the hell was that, a ghost?" asked Ward, looking at me almost with respect.

I shook my head and retreated to the open door. I couldn't answer him. I couldn't bear to look at him.

"That was a robot!" said Prang, angrily extracting the last Camel from her pack. "From outer space. And priceless, you fool!"

"Sent here half a million years ago to accelerate our evolution," Boudin explained. "And to signal its Makers when we were finally capable of destroying it."

"Well, it's sure as hell destroyed," said Ward. "So I guess we sure as hell passed the test."

"No." It was almost midnight. I stepped outside, past the puzzled cops, and looked up at the million cold stars, scattered like broken glass across the dark floor of the universe.

I wished I had a cigarette. I wondered what the Makers were and what they would do with us when they came.

"No," I said again, to no one in particular, "I think we flunked."

The Measure of All Things

RICHARD CHWEDYK

Richard Chwedyk lives in Chicago with his wife, Pamela Miller, and often reads in the Chicago area, most recently at the Twilight Tales reading series at the Red Lion Pub (where an early draft of "The Measure of All Things" was first presented). His poetry has been recently published in Tales of the Unanticipated and Tales from the Red Lion (also from Twilight Tales/11th Hour), but has also appeared in Another Chicago Magazine, Oyez Review, Paul Hoover's Legendary Oink! (now called New American Writing) and The Best of Hair Trigger anthology, among even older and more obscure publications. He teaches creative writing classes for Oakton Community College, but his major paycheck comes from doing layout/copyediting for a chain of newspapers in the Chicago suburbs. He has had fiction published in Fantasy & Science Fiction, Amazing Stories, and Space and Time. He has moderated writing workshops at a number of recent worldcons, and will do so again at ConJose in 2002.

"The Measure of All Things" was published in F & SF, and is one of two stories in this volume that might be considered in the tradition of H. G. Wells' The Island of Dr. Moreau (see James Morrow's story, in this collection); it might even be perhaps a bit Dickensian in its sentimentality. The home for biopet saurs has metaphorical reverberations that ambiguously evoke abandoned pets, orphans, and abused children.

Did he smile his work to see?
Did he who made the lamb make thee?
                              —William Blake

Axel was the first to see the car coming down the driveway from the main road. He stood on the table next to the picture window, where he always stands after breakfast, looking out at the woods, the sun (if it's out), the clouds (if it isn't), shifting his weight from one clumpy foot to the other, tail raised to balance himself against the slick, smooth surface. His mouth, as always, was wide open, displaying rows of benign teeth—benign compared to the predator he was modeled upon; and his tiny black eyes were alight with amazement, as always, as if he was witness to a secret miracle every moment.

"Huuuuuu-man!" he shouted. "Huuuu-man coming up the road!"

I had just finished cleaning up the kitchen, taking stock of the food supplies: plenty of pellets (some saurs still preferred them); another day's worth of collards and meat; and enough of the ever-essential oranges to last out the week. I needed more coffee, but since it was "human stuff" it took a lesser priority. A razor, too, would have been nice, and a new hairbrush. A pair of jeans wouldn't have hurt either, or at least another belt (I was losing a little weight), but I was getting off the subject of food. I drank my cold, leftover breakfast coffee with a touch of melancholy as I walked into the living room.

"Huuuuu-man!"

The room was bright. The windows were open. Rain was predicted for that night but just then you couldn't ask for more beautiful spring weather. Few saurs paid attention to Axel's alarm, since Axel, in his constant ebullience, often announced the arrival of alien battle cruisers, or warned us of approaching death rays, tidal waves (we are four hundred kilometers from the ocean), and Confederate Army divisions charging our house from out of the woods.

"Are you goofing around again, Axel?" Agnes said, her spiked tail and back plates upright in a guarded stance. "Because if you are—"

"Real," Axel insisted. "Real real real *real*. Big blue car coming down the driveway!" He pointed out the window with his tiny forepaw.

I walked over and confirmed the sighting: a dark blue Mercedes, the sort of car that's always been popular with young men who want to show the world that they've arrived. I wondered briefly if I'd ever wanted that: the sense of validation those wheels provided. I couldn't remember, but when I was a boy, like every other kid, I wanted everything.

"Is it the doctor?" Agnes asked.

"She's not due until this afternoon."

"It's not that horrible researcher, is it? The one who wants a tissue sample from Hetman."

"Researchers aren't Mercedes-type people," I assured her.

"*I'll* give him some tissue to sample!" She swung her tail back to demonstrate. Her battle-stance is less impressive when you consider that Agnes is forty centimeters long, her head is about the size of an apricot, and her tail spikes really wouldn't stand up in a fight.

"No," I said as I looked down at Axel and Axel looked up at me. "I think we have a visitor."

"Visitor!" Axel repeated in a whisper, as if he'd heard the word for the first time.

He hadn't, of course. Visitors aren't frequent here, but they're certainly not unheard of. Delivery drivers come all the time. Dr. Margaret Pagliotti visits once a week. Folks from the Atherton Foundation stop by for regular inspections. But there *are* other visitors, people who come by just to see the saurs.

Most people these days hardly remember them. The smallest saur is no more than ten centimeters long. The largest one is a meter and a half tall. They're not "real" dinosaurs—that's another business altogether—but they *were* modeled after them, sometimes to painstaking detail, but more often to the cuter, cartoonish caricatures that children of many generations before wore on their pajamas or had printed on their lunchboxes and notebooks. They were an outgrowth of that vision of dinosaurs as cuddly buddies, friends to all children everywhere—moving, talking versions of the plush toys they've always played with.

That's what they were designed to be. That's why they were brought into the world. Forget for the moment that the manufacturers had plans to make enormous sums of money on them, at which they succeeded (several million were sold); forget also that the designers were trying to put forward their own subtle agenda: that bioengineering and its nanotech components could be safe and fun—cuddly, like a shoebox-sized triceratops—an agenda at which they were far less successful. Forget all that, at least for the moment.

To the saurs themselves, they had come into being to be friends, buddies, giving out love and receiving affection from appreciative girls and boys. That's what they were designed to do—that, and nothing else.

The designers fidgeted about for a name—they didn't like "life-toy," since it contained the troublesome "life" word. They didn't want the saurs confused with "animals," since that would place them under hundreds of government regulations. "Bio-toy" passed with all the marketing departments, so someone went out and wrote a definition of it: a toy modeled from bio-engineered materials, behaving without behavior, lifelike without being "alive."

The blue Mercedes parked in the gravel at the end of the driveway. I looked around our old Victorian-style house and its saurian occupants: the group gathered around the video screen watching a Buster Keaton film; little ones, mouse- and squirrel-sized guys riding across the living room on the battery-powered carts we call skates; in the dining room, an- other group of little ones were sitting before the big Reg- giesystem computer, having a geography lesson (I could tell it was geography because I could hear them repeating the word "Togo" in unison); in another corner sat the Five Wise Buddhasaurs, blowing into their plastic horns; further back, in the library, I could see Diogenes and Hubert (two of the biggest guys, very tyrannosaurian) shelving books (yes, we still have books here, and even the saurs who can't read are fascinated by the illustrations, the type styles, even the little colophons); also in there was Hetman's bassinet-sized hos- pital bed, rolled over to the sunniest window.

Along with the usual furniture, scattered about were the hassocks and clever stair-step things the saurs use to get up on the furniture; the old wheelchair lift—adapted to meet the needs of the saurs—was in operation, transporting the little and the lame back and forth between first and second floors.

It's a world I've grown accustomed to, but one that many visitors find fairly startling, and some even find disturbing.

"Well," I said to everyone within earshot, "ready for a vis- itor?"

Most were indifferent to the prospect. Some jumped onto skates and rode off to other parts. Others climbed up on the chairs and couches, not wanting to be underfoot with a stranger in the house.

Charlie, a light brown badger-sized triceratops, hobbled away from the group around the video, accompanied by his beloved companion, Rosie, and headed for the lift. The de- signers, for all their mastery of eyes, ears, brains, and lar- ynxes, had trouble with limbs, and it was hard to find a saur who didn't walk with at least a slight defect, though many limped for other reasons.

"If it's that Joe," Charlie called back to me, "tell him I'm not here. Tell him I'm dead."

Charlie has been saying this for years whenever visitors come by, even though in all that time not one of them has been named Joe.

"Humans," Agnes grumbled. "Idiots. I wish they'd all just leave us alone."

I noticed her mate, Sluggo, wasn't with her and I asked where he was.

"Feeding squirrels. Feeding sparrows. He's always feeding someone, like some goddamned Saint Francis."

"He never feeds *us*," said Pierrot, a pint-sized theropod standing by the couch closest to the window, with his friend Jean-Claude, a dark green tyrannosur three times his height.

"Carnosaurs!" Agnes spat out the word with a resonance that belied her size. "Hopeless, brainless embarrassments!"

"I'm glad to see the lovely day has not affected Agnes's mood," said Doc, a light brown theropod just under a meter tall, with heavy-lidded eyes and a serene smile that makes you think he must have gotten into the liquor cabinet.

"That is her nature," I said to Doc as I brushed my hair back.

He sat on a plastic box over which he could drape his tail and rest his weary legs. Before him played two of the tiniest saurs in the house, named Slim and Slam. The two held a pen between them as if it were an enormous treetrunk and drew lines and curves on a sheet of paper spread before them.

"And nature," he replied, "we know, is a thing we shouldn't adjust without caution."

"I hate when you talk about me as if I can't hear!" Agnes thumped her tail against the floor.

"I meant to ask before," Doc said as he watched Slim and Slam at work/play, "did you sleep well?"

"Yes," I lied. I knew I'd had a nightmare but I couldn't remember any of the details. The best I could recall was a vague sense of hiding in a cramped, dark place. Perhaps I'd cried out in my sleep.

"You did?" The skin behind Doc's thick eyelids furrowed as he looked up at me.

"Of course. Why do you ask?"

"No reason." The deep voice took on a placating smoothness. "You look tired."

We heard the soft clip of a very expensive car door shutting outside.

"I'd better go out and greet our visitor," I said.

"Is the security on?" Agnes asked sharply.

"Of course. You *know* it's always on."

"Hmmph!" She positioned herself under the lamp table next to the couch. "Remember, I'm watching!"

It was hardly a matter of remembering.

The visitor stood outside, reluctant, it seemed, to step onto the porch. He looked in his early thirties—a few years younger than myself, I figured—with an athletic build, light gray eyes, and strong facial features. His expression had that severity most professional people affect these days, with downward-bent forehead lines ending in a little "V" between his eyebrows. He wore a dark blue sports jacket, light gray slacks, and a rose-colored shirt with the top button open.

It was all very acquired and practiced, as if he were living up to a model. But everyone out there in the real world acted that way. So would I, if I were out there.

"Look at that!" Axel shouted. "He's *bald!*"

He jumped up and down as I went to the door. "Take me with! Please! Please!"

"You'll have to behave yourself."

"Yes! Yes! Won't say a word. Just want to watch when he pulls out his mini-machine gun and starts shooting—du-du-du-du-du-du—right through the walls!"

Agnes groaned.

I picked Axel up and cradled him in my right arm. As I looked down at him, I couldn't help noticing the long scar down his back. It's been many years since that scar was made, but you could tell it had been a deep, nasty cut that left it.

Out on the porch, I said "Good morning," to the visitor. I must have looked a mess, but you can never dress for visitors because you never know when they're coming.

"Morning," he said with a deep, rehearsed voice. "You must be Groverton."

"That's me." I shifted Axel over to my left side and held out my hand. "Tom Groverton. And this is Axel."

Axel raised a forepaw and said "Hiya!" but the visitor ignored him. I shook hands with the man but he wouldn't tell me his name.

"You're looking for someone, aren't you? Most visitors are."

He spoke hesitantly, as if he wished he'd brought an attorney with him. "I don't really know if he's—"

"HIYA!" Axel tried again.

"—here. I—we, my brother and I—had him when we were kids. There's not much chance of it, but I thought—"

"HIYA!"

The visitor looked at Axel at last and slightly bowed his head. "—I thought he might be up here."

I gestured for him to come up on the porch and sit down on the old bench. "Maybe you could give me a little description of him."

"He was—is, I guess—a stegosaur. Maybe thirty-five centimeters long. Orange on the top, mostly, and a kind of purple color on the bottom. Some patches of yellow between the orange and the purple. His plates were purple and a little orange at the center. His head is more beak-shaped than rounded off." He stood with his hands in the pockets of his slacks, refusing to sit on the bench. "My brother named him Elliot."

Axel made a hissing, gasping sort of sound. "Elliot!"

"A lot of saurs changed their names once we offered them shelter here." My mustache brushed my lower lip. "I can't keep track of whose name was given and whose was chosen, but we do have a saur here named Elliot who fits that description. Do you want to see him?"

"Yes!" His reply was so emphatic it seemed to startle him.

"You understand, I hope, that I'll first have to check with Elliot. Would you be disappointed if Elliot didn't want to see you?"

"I don't know." He returned to his previous, severe expression. "I don't understand a *lot* about this operation."

"The point," I said, "is this: many of these guys were extremely traumatized before they got here. Some of them were barely alive. You didn't have to have personally hurt him to remind him of days he'd rather not remember. That's why I need to check with Elliot first."

"I don't really understand." He tugged his slacks at the knees before finally taking a seat. "They're just toys, aren't they?"

"If that were true, would you be here?"

He looked away and exhaled with a hint of frustration. "Okay. Whatever."

I took him inside.

The visitor was surprised at the number of saurs gathered around the video screen. They were now watching Chaplin in *Modern Times*.

"How many you got here?"

"Ninety-eight in this house, all counted, which isn't a lot considering how many were made. Some folks wonder why the foundation set up houses for the saurs. Why not reservations or preserves? They forget that saurs don't have a 'natural' environment other than a house. They were designed to be domestic."

And yet, when children tired of their saurs and stopped taking care of them, their parents drove them out to the woods or to parks and dumped them. It was worse than dumping cats or dogs: they at least had some vague instincts to work with. The saurs pretty much had to start from scratch, which is why so many of them starved, froze, were run over by vehicles or were eaten by predators.

I wondered if any of the saurs' designers ever imagined their creations would end up in a house like this. They had guaranteed the investors, the executives, and the buying public that the saurs were limited to a relatively few responses and reactions. They were supposed to be organic computers, and very simple ones at that. They could remember names and recognize faces, engage in simple conversations. They would sing the "Dinosaur Song" (a hideous thing that started "Yar-wooo, yar-wooo, yar-wooo/the dinosaurs love you—"), and if you told one you were sad he would know how to respond with a joke. Yes, the designers said, they were sophisticated creations, almost miraculous, a high point in what they had mastered by tweaking a few genes—but they were not to be confused with living things. They could respond to stimuli, they could retain data, but that doesn't make something a "living" thing, they said.

A bell rang in the library.

"Hetman! Hetman!" Axel squirmed around under my arm.

But just then I heard another commotion in the kitchen. Agnes was shouting. I excused myself from the visitor and entered the kitchen just in time to see Jean-Claude on the sink with Pierrot on his back, trying to open the freezer door.

"Hey!" Agnes shouted at them. "You idiots get down from there!"

"Honestly, guys." I helped the two of them back down onto the floor. "Couldn't you wait until lunch? You know you can't eat *uncooked* meat."

"Nooo," Pierrot corrected me. "We—were just—guarding, yeah—*guarding* the meat, in case the visitor tried to steal it!"

"I wish someone would steal *you*," Agnes grunted.

"The visitor steals Pierrot!" Axel yelled. "He takes him and he throws him down a well—and he's falling-falling-falling—AAAAAAHHHHhhhh!"

"Look what you started," I said to Agnes.

"It was a bad idea to create carnosaurs," Agnes sighed. "It's meat. Meat equals stupid. It must be."

Jean-Claude and Pierrot ran out of the kitchen, Agnes went back to her hiding place, and Axel quieted down.

The visitor had moved on to the dining room when I returned. He watched the group gathered around the Reggiesystem computer. On the screen was an animated version of a rocket taking off, moving farther and farther away from the planet.

"Where is the spaceship going?" asked the steady, soft Reggiesystem voice.

The question set off a little conference among the gathered saurs. Tyrone, a hamster-sized theropod, bent over and listened as Alfie, his constant buddy, whispered to him.

"The *Walkuere* space station?" Tyrone replied.

"Correct." The Reggiesystem played a little synthesized melody. The other assembled saurs cheered.

The visitor watched, two fingers pressed against his lips.

"Some of the saurs are quite clever," I told him. "Some not so. Some can speak very well. Some can't. The problem is that you can't always assume which are which. Some saurs who can speak choose not to. Some are still too traumatized."

Axel waved to Alfie and Tyrone.

"They all seem hooked up in some way," the visitor observed, "like they have mates and children and whatever else. They're supposed to be asexual, aren't they?"

I shrugged. "These attachments they make to each other have baffled everyone who's studied them. Reproductively they're supposed to be neuter, but one saur will call another a spouse, or a parent, or an offspring, or a sibling, as if the need to establish familial connections transcends genetics. Who knows? Their designers know less about them now than when they first created them.

"Take their life span. They were supposed to live for five years, tops. Doc over there is twenty-eight. And Agnes under the table is twenty-five."

"How dare you!" Agnes barked. "Tell him everything, why don't you?"

There *were* things I wouldn't mention to the visitor, or to anyone else. Like Bronte, sitting on the couch, warming the orphan bird eggs that Sluggo brings to her. Some of them hatch, and Sluggo feeds them—little robins and sparrows and finches—until they're big enough to fly from the window ledge.

And then there's the egg I found Bronte with the other day, the one that doesn't resemble any bird egg I've ever seen.

In the library, the visitor saw saurs reading, talking, listening to the radio. Fred and Ginger practiced a dance. The Five Wise Buddhasaurs hooked up their plastic horns to a synthesizer, so that their instruments sounded full-sized. Their cacophonies only occasionally coalesced into some charming harmonies.

Over in the far corner of the library, where the sun came through the windows most directly, Hetman rested on his little bed. Hermione, an apatosaur, stood nearby, watching over him.

"It's okay," she said. "A bad dream."

"S-s-orry," hissed Hetman. "I didn't mean to disturb anyone. I rang the bell in my sleep."

"Jesus," the visitor whispered as he got a look at Hetman.

Hetman's been in the little bed ever since he came here. His hind legs were crushed under some vehicle; his forelimbs were hacked off and his eyes burned out. No one thought he'd live more than a few days when he was found, if that, but he's been here many years now.

"Don't be sorry, Hetman," I said. "Someone is always here. Whatever you need, we'll get."

"I'm here!" Axel squirmed under my arm again. "I'll get for Het! I'll stay! Can I stay? Want me to stay with you, Hetman?"

"Yes, Axel," Hetman said with a raspy whisper. "Keep me from falling asleep again. Tell me once more all about the tidal wave."

I put Axel down next to Hetman.

The lines in the visitor's forehead looked deeper, the little "V" looked like it had been carved in.

"Who could *do* a thing like that?"

I didn't answer. Such questions, even when rhetorical, are meaningless. The saurs were sent out into the world with simple physiologies that demanded a few food pellets, water, and a litter box. Sweet natures, a few prepared phrases, a few songs. They were delivered into the hands of wealthy parents who bought them as much to show their neighbors they could afford them as to please their children. The children were told the saurs were toys and the children played with them like they were toys—which meant many of the saurs were suffocated, drowned, starved, crushed, beaten, vivisected. I can go on for hours, cataloging cruelties, tragedies, mistakes: how Hubert, tortured to the point of near madness, decided to use his tyrannosaurian teeth and claws to defend himself and was almost destroyed for it; how Diogenes had been shown a box of food pellets by the father who bought him and was told, "When these run out, so do you." There were stories like that behind nearly every small, strange-shaped, puzzled, puzzling face in this house.

Had I come from a more affluent background, would I have done the same? I felt too honest to answer either way.

I led the visitor upstairs.

"This place would drive me nuts," he said softly. "How could the people who made these things not know?"

He looked so appalled by what he'd seen of Hetman, I gave him the best answer I could think of for free. "In those days, designers thought of each little piece of the genome, each little element, as a symbol, like a letter printed on a wooden block. Each letter, they thought, had a simple denotative definition. When you placed the C next to the A and followed them with T, you could spell 'cat.' That it might all be a little more complicated didn't occur to them."

The visitor took the stairs slowly, carefully reviewing each step. "So, these engineers learned their lesson, huh?"

"They think so."

We passed the dark little bedroom where Tibor keeps his cardboard castle. It's really quite a shambles, but Tibor, a runt of an apatosaur with a stern Beethoven-like face, sits there all day and hatches Napoleonic schemes. On the other side of the room sits a cardboard box on a dresser which Geraldine, another runt, calls her "lab." Nothing has happened with any of her experiments so far, but I keep two fire extinguishers in the room anyway.

Elliot and his mate, Syrena, a bright red stegosaur, hang out in a bedroom on the second floor with Preston, a chunky, round-headed theropod.

"If you could wait here a moment," I said to the visitor, "I'll check with Elliot."

Preston worked away slowly but determinedly on a computer keyboard with his tiny two-digit-each forepaws. I described the visitor to Elliot and asked if he'd mind seeing him. He thought for a moment, looking to Syrena for advice.

"It must be Danny," Elliot said, his voice so soft it would make a whisper sound like an outcry. "I told you about him. Danny never did anything bad to me, except—leave me."

He pressed closer to his mate and rubbed his face against hers. "I'll see him, if he wants to see me."

When I brought the visitor in he was momentarily distracted by Preston at his keyboard. He read over his shoulder:

> "By dawn the crowd in the Plaza had swelled to ten thousand. The Ambassador had an excellent view of the frenzied multitude from his window. They all wore their red bandannas and stoked the air above them with their banners, chanting that the world of Lorair was their birthright . . ."

"This is his eighth novel," I told the visitor.

"He *publishes* them?"

"Not under his own name."

But then he saw Elliot, and his old expression completely evaporated. It seemed to reveal, maybe for the first time in years, a wound as deep as the scar on Axel's back.

"Elliot?"

"Danny?"

The visitor bent down until his head was nearly resting on the desk's mahogany top.

"Been a long time," the visitor mumbled.

Elliot nodded apprehensively.

The visitor looked up at me first, then at the other saurs in the room.

"Would it—" he started. "Is there somewhere Elliot and I could talk alone for a little while?"

I gestured to the others and helped them out into the hallway. "It won't be for long," I said to them. And to Elliot: "We'll be right outside if you need anything."

As I shut the door I looked down to see Agnes staring up at me, her expression as hard as a Brazil nut.

"It's all right," I told her. "Nothing's going to happen."

I hoped I was right. That was my responsibility: to make sure nothing happened. Agnes kept looking at me. Her tail tapped against the floor. Behind her gathered a number of curious saurs, including all the biggest guys: Doc, Diogenes, Hubert, and Sam.

"Nothing will happen," said Doc, staring coolly at the closed door. "If it does, it won't be without someone feeling great regret."

I knew that "someone" didn't mean me, but still my breathing quickened.

The saurs waited quietly, except for Agnes, still thrumming with her tail.

When the door finally opened it did so slowly. The visitor came out, looking a little flushed, his skin a little shinier.

"Hey, Elliot!" Agnes shouted back into the room. "You all right?"

I wiped some sweat from my brow and escorted the visitor back to his Mercedes. He said nothing until he got back into his car.

"Thanks." That was it.

He drove off and hasn't been back, not so far. That's how it usually goes.

A week later, the Atherton Foundation received an anonymous donation of ten thousand dollars, directed to this particular house. That too is how it usually goes.

When I went back upstairs, all the saurs had dispersed save for Agnes, tail raised as if she might be considering giving me a whack with it just for good measure.

Elliot was still on the desk, right where I'd left him with the visitor. Next to him was a little plastic figure, a soldier in uniform and helmet, the type that comes in a big toy set. The visitor must have brought it—and left it there.

"What is that?" I asked.

"It's Sarge," Elliot said with his whispering voice, not taking his eyes off the little figure. "He used to leave it by my box when he went to school. 'This is Sarge,' he told me back then. 'Now you have a toy to play with too.' I thought of Sarge as a little figure of him, of Danny, the boy who owned—who I stayed with. Danny had me, and I had Danny, or Sarge, that is. When things got bad, before I was taken away, I hid Sarge, slipped him into a heating vent through a loose grate. I thought that if they were going to hurt me they might want to hurt Sarge too. I wonder if he's been in there all these years."

"Maybe," I said. "Maybe Danny just found him, and that's why he came today."

"It was silly of me, wasn't it? To hide Sarge like that?"

I shook my head. "Not silly at all." I bent down to look at Sarge from the same eye level as Elliot. "What should we do with him?"

"I don't know." Elliot twisted his head a little to one side and then to the other. "Could we put him in the museum? If I change my mind we could bring him down again. At least I'll always know where he is."

"The museum" is just a room in the attic. It's not very big, but it's loaded with shelves, and on the shelves are hundreds of toys: dolls, drums, ray guns, puzzles, wooden figures and plastic vehicles. There are also neckties, handkerchiefs, hats, vests, photographs, notes, tempera paintings on cardboard, little books bound with yarn. Everything in the room was left by one visitor or another for one saur or another. Over the years, it's grown into quite a collection.

I carefully picked up Elliot with one hand and, just as carefully, picked Sarge up with the other. "We'll take him there now, and you can pick out a place for him yourself."

Agnes moved out of the way as I came by with Elliot and Sarge. Sluggo rolled an orange to her and the sweet smell of the fruit distracted her at last.

That afternoon, Dr. Margaret Pagliotti stopped by on one of her regular visits. She's fairly young, with long brown hair and lovely, dark, Mediterranean eyes. She ran down a checklist, looking over each of the ninety-eight saurs, asking if any had been feeling ill, not getting enough to eat, subject to any changes in mood or behavior. Dr. Margaret is nothing if not thorough, and she has the necessary sense of humor one needs when dealing with the saurs.

When Agnes grumbles and complains, Dr. Margaret holds her by the forelimbs and kisses her on the snout. That leaves Agnes speechless and, for the most part, agreeable.

I mentioned Hetman's nightmares to her, since Hetman would never mention them himself, along with my suspicion that he might be experiencing more pain.

"Speaking of nightmares—" I thought about the night before but cut myself off. "—forget it." It was "human stuff," after all, like the coffee.

Before Dr. Margaret was even two meters from his bed, Hetman called out, "My angel is here. How are you, Doctor?"

"How are *you*, old friend?" She bent down and caressed his snout.

"A little tired," he answered. "A little sleepless. I don't complain. When you come a miracle happens and I'm instantly cured."

Did I mention that Dr. Margaret has a lovely blush?

She examined Hetman carefully and asked him if he might want some stronger painkillers.

"No," he whispered. "Not if they dull my senses. I have so few left."

"I'll leave the prescription with Tom. You can try a half dose. If they're too strong you don't have to take them."

"Thank you. As long as I have angels here I'm in no great hurry for heaven."

Dr. Margaret asked to see me in private, so we went up to my room.

"I got another call from that researcher from Toyco."

"You too? I'd offer you some coffee but we're almost out." I went over to my desk but, like the visitor earlier, found myself reluctant to sit down. "Anyway, Toyco had their chance. I don't see why they need any more samples."

Dr. Margaret sat on the top of my desk and stared out at the afternoon shadows in the yard. "I hear it has to do with the saurs' longevity. They're back into immortality research."

I glanced up at the ceiling. "Wonderful."

"Or it may be something else they hadn't anticipated." She spoke softly, as if we might be overheard.

"Such as?"

"I saw Bronte's egg."

I walked over to the window as if to stare out but I can't remember really looking at—or seeing—anything.

I was recalling, for the first time in years, a trip I'd taken with my mother, to one of the big, fancy department stores in one of the old-fashioned malls. Maybe it was something about Dr. Margaret that reminded me of my mother.

In the toy section were about a dozen gray stegosaurs of Sluggo's size housed in a colorful pen. The "Dinosaur Song" spilled out of speakers at each of the pen's corners: "Yar-woooo! Yar-woooo!"

The saurs huddled together apprehensively until a salesperson walked by and shouted at them.

"Smile!" she said. "No one's going to buy you if you don't smile!"

They were accidental or deliberate failures at the task, and when a little girl in blonde curls and a red coat picked up one of the saurs with her sweaty pink hand I clearly saw the expressions on the little gray faces, the one taken and the others remaining: the agony of loss and separation.

When my mother noticed me looking at the saurs she gently tugged me away. "Forget it, Tommy. We couldn't afford one in a million years and you'd never take care of it anyway. Remember what happened to your iguana."

The first part didn't bother me. My parents were honest in their poverty and never used it as a crutch or a badge of honor. The second part hurt because I did my best to take care of the iguana. What hurt about it most was that my parents, fair as they were in many ways, could not help but remind me of my every failure and see in them the genetic imprint of my future.

But what struck me just then, as I recalled this scene, was how I ignored what she said. I looked up at her seriously, even with a bit of reproach, and told her, "I wouldn't buy *one*. I'd buy them *all*, so they could stay together."

I took a little satisfaction, remembering that moment, in seeing past the delusion of those days, and proving my mother wrong. Not only could I take care of a saur, I could take care of ninety-eight of them.

"Tom?" Margaret waved her hand in front of my eyes.

"Sorry. You were saying?"

"I said, there's something else I'm worried about."

"What's that?"

"You," she said, looking at me with all her medical precision. "You spend so much time here, with the saurs. I'm not sure if that's good for you. I'm not sure it's good for anyone."

She looked at me seriously, sadly, as if I'd already said something to hurt or disappoint her. In that moment she reminded me even more of my mother, which made it even harder for me to answer.

"I'm happy here, Margaret." I touched her hand. "I don't know why. Any explanation I could give you beyond that would be something I made up. I feel at home here. I feel I'm with friends."

Worry lines marred her forehead, which was the last thing I wanted, so I changed the subject back to my dwindling supply of coffee.

If she continued to worry she never said a word about it to me. But I'm still not sure if—when she showed me that grave expression—it was for something more than myself she worried.

After dinner, some of the saurs sat in the living room, watching a production of *Turandot* on the video. Between acts, Axel demonstrated how to fall off a couch and onto a pillow, backwards, perhaps a few too many times.

"Suddenly, a hole opens up underneath me! A hole in space and time! And I'm falling-falling-*falling*-FALLING-*FALLING!* AAAAaaaahhh!"

During the finale of *Turandot*, some of the saurs joined in with the chorus—not that they knew the words, but they followed the melody with open vowels.

In the library, The Five Wise Buddhasaurs took over the stereo and played Louis Armstrong recordings for several hours. They love his voice, his cornet, and the sheer elation one finds in both. They're convinced he's one of them: a joyful saurian angel.

Sluggo told the little ones some more tales of Sauria and the heroic voyages of the brave saurs who returned to their homeland.

"And do you know why they sailed to Sauria?" Agnes queried the little ones after the story.

Those who could speak answered "Humans!" mostly because that was the answer Agnes wanted to hear.

"Humans!" Agnes nodded. "Messing up everything! Messing up the whole damn world!"

"Foo!" the little ones chanted, at Agnes's direction. "Foo! Humans! Foo!"

I sat in the library, reading to Hetman and a few dozen saurs gathered around. The book was Hetman's choice, *The Deluge*, by Henryk Sienkiewicz.

"I wonder why they come." Charlie interrupted my reading, still distracted by the morning visit. "What do they think they're going to get? Forgiveness? Peace of mind? Wouldn't they be happier if they forgot all about us? I would."

"No, Charlie," Hetman said, breathing heavily. "You don't forget. As painful as the memories are, forgetting is dying. And, in the measure of all things, nothing that truly lives truly wants to die."

Later that evening, the storm clouds moved in. Even the most intelligent and reasonable of the saurs get unsettled by the lightning and thunder. Someone suggested jokingly that it was an ancient memory of the great comet, but if so then we all have a trace of that ancient memory.

At bedtime all the saurs gather in the large bedroom upstairs. The little ones who get confused are aided by the bigger fellows. Even Hetman is brought up and wheeled over on his little bed. I check around for the stragglers and the lost under lamp tables, the bottom shelves of the bookcases, behind bedposts and in odd little corners. Every now and then, after I've turned out the lights and crawled into my own bed, I'll hear one that I've missed crying out softly. I'll follow the cries and find him or her—in the cabinet under the bathroom sink, stranded on the desk in the library—and carry the little one back to the bedroom.

It's true, just like in Andrew Ulaszek's poem, "On the Island Where the Dinosaurs Live," they sleep in a kind of huddle, the biggest in the center, the smaller ones crammed around them:

> . . . *conjoined, in outlandish sprawl,*
> *a pile of plated backs,*
> *spiny heads and coiled tails.*

Whether they do it to "swim within the same dream," as that same poem informs us, I cannot know. The least social of them join in the huddle, even though there are many places to sleep in the old house. Tibor leaves his cardboard castle. Geraldine slips out of her secret laboratory. Doc, Diogenes, and Hubert take out the big blankets and comforters to spread over the amassed group.

Bronte brought the egg up on a skate packed with cotton.

That night, the house shook with each rumble of thunder. Bright blue flashes intruded through every window. I checked their bedroom before turning in. The blankets twitched with every flash of light. When I put my hand on them I could feel the shudders from underneath, like the erratic tremors of an old car engine.

"I'm all right,"—Agnes's voice, stern, to cover her anxiety, as she pressed herself more closely to Sluggo. "It's all right. It's—I know it's stupid."

"The thunder scares me too," I said.

"It's stupid. I can't help it."

I looked elsewhere, not wanting to add to her embarrassment. Charlie, with Rosie pressed against him, twitched in his sleep. Pierrot was rolled up in a little ball between Jean-Claude and Bronte. Tyrone wrapped his meager forearm around Alfie, who stared up with his huge, ever-frightened eyes as the terrible light bounced against the walls and brought the shadows to life.

"Big storm!" Axel smiled, mouth wide open as he trembled. "Big, big storm! Everything blows up! Brrroooo-mmm!"

"*For God's sake*—!" Agnes groaned.

"Yes. A very big storm." I stroked Axel's head until he lowered himself into the cushion of companions.

"There is always fear," Doc said, his smooth voice almost as deep as the thunder.

"Yes," I replied.

"No matter how big the big ones get, there is always something bigger to fear."

"I know."

A long hissing breath escaped from his nostrils and was lost in the low rumble of thunder. "Good night, my friend."

"Good night, my friend."

I went back to my bed but couldn't fall asleep. The storm was fierce, with no sign of subsiding, but it was more than the light and noise that kept me up.

I'm not a morbid person, but I thought about death—or more precisely, how strangely tilted our view of life is. We know the universe went on before for billions of years and it will go on for billions more. There's just this brief stretch when the window is opened before our eyes, and the world is visible. Then the window is shut, forever.

I lay in bed, breathing short breaths, unable *not* to imagine my last moment. Will I scream in panic when it comes? Or will I manage to utter one last farewell?

There was no getting past the "human stuff"—and it was all human stuff, from God to the saurs to whatever had made both.

Everything but the storm.

The thunder pealed and roared until I could hear the loose change on the dresser rattle with the vibrations. And then, from the saurs' room, I heard one voice.

Perhaps Sluggo, perhaps Tyrone, perhaps a saur I would have least expected, but he or she sang one clear phrase with that nonsense dinosaur word: "Yar-wooo!"

And sang it again: "Yar-wooo!"

The third time, the other saurs joined in: a few at first, then more. It was the old song, the lullaby they had been trained and designed to sing in the innocent days when they sprang forth from the lab/factories. It reminded me of old fieldworkers singing slave songs generations after abolition.

But even the most insubstantial melody can have a certain power. The urge to sing is stronger than any song. They were taught to sing it for their owners. Now they sang it for themselves.

I listened as they sang against the unrelenting thunder, and then I joined in, with my own croaky voice, with the same nonsense dinosaur word—"Yar-wooo!"

"Yar-wooo!"

I sang with them until the thunder subsided and sleep took us all at last, even Axel.

Russian Vine

SIMON INGS

Simon Ings' [www.fisheye.demon.co.uk/home.html] novels include Hot Head *(1992),* City of the Iron Fish *(1994), and* Hotwire *(1995), none yet published in the U.S. He says, in a manifesto on his website, "I'm not surprised to find that my work's called Cyberpunk. That, surely, was the point of it— before the fashion fairies and the literalists got hold of it— that it wasn't about the future, but rather used the future as a metaphor to say things about the world as it is. And in that, Cyberpunk was, not a special sort of science fiction, but simply fiction." And later: "Suddenly, fiction needs the tools of SF. It needs ways to write about the world that aren't consensual, that reinvent the ordinary, that handle speculation: not because people need speculative fantasy but because the world itself has become speculative and fantastical."*

"Russian Vine," published only online at SciFiction and thus appearing for the first time in print here, is a morally challenging story about a humanoid alien invasion and occupation that robs the human race of literacy and focuses on an affair between an alien who reads human literature and a human woman who tells stories. It is a story with a strong subtext. It is in addition a highly complex and accomplished stylistic success.

One

That afternoon in Paris—a cloudy day, and warmer than the late season deserved—they met for the last time. She wore her red dress. Did she intend to make what he had to say more difficult? (He felt his scribe hand tingle, that he should blame her for his own discomfort.) Perhaps she only meant a kind of closure. For the sake of her self-esteem, she was making it clear to him that nobody ever really changes anybody. Even her hair was arranged the same as on that first day.

"And the king said, Bring me a sword. And they brought a sword before the king."

They sat on the *terrasse*, away from the doors, seeking privacy. The preacher—if that was the right word for him, for he did not preach, but had instead launched into an apparently endless recitation—stabbed them irregularly with a gaze from eyes the color of pewter.

His testament tangled itself up in the couple's last words to each other.

Connie called for the bill. (He had long since conformed his name to the range of the human palate. Being the kind of animal he was, he was not bothered by its effeminate connotations.) He said to her: "This deadening reasonableness. I wish we had smashed something."

She said: "You wish I had smashed something. I've let you down today."

"And the king said, Divide the living child in two, and give half to the one and half to the other."

She said: "You've left us both feeling naked. We can't fight now. It would be undignified: emotional mud-wrestling."

Connie let the reference slide by him, uncomprehended.

"Then spake the woman whose living child was unto the king, for her bowels yearned upon her son, and she said, O my lord, give her the living child, and in no wise slay it. But the other said, Let it be neither mine or thine, but divide it."

With a gesture, the girl drew Connie's attention to the man's recitation. "You see?" she said. "Undignified. Like it says in the Bible." She laughed at the apposite verses, a laugh that choked off in a way that Connie thought might be emotion.

But how could he be sure? His ear was not—would never be—good enough. He was from too far away. He was, in the parochial parlance of these people, "alien."

He picked up his cup with his bludgeon hand—a dashing breach of his native etiquette—and dribbled down the last bitter grounds. Already he was preening; showing off his rakish "masculinity." His availability, even. As though this choice he had made were about freedom!

He found himself, in that instant, thinking coldly of Rebecca, the woman who lived with him, and for whom (though she did not know this) he had given up this enchanting girl.

"Then the king answered and said, Give her the living child, and in no wise slay it: she is the mother thereof.

"And all Israel heard of the judgment which the king had judged; and they feared the king: for they saw that the wisdom of God was in him to do judgment."

Still listening, the girl smiled, and bobbed her head to Connie, in a mock bow.

She had done nothing, this afternoon, but make light of their parting. He hoped it was a defense she had assembled against sentiment. But in his heart, he knew she had not been very moved by the end of their affair. She would forget him very quickly.

Hadmuhaddera's crass remarks, the day Connie arrived on this planet, seemed strangely poignant now: "Trouble is, my friend, we all look the bloody same to them!"

"And these were the princes which he had . . ."

There was no purpose to that man's recitation, Connie thought, with irritation, as he kissed the girl goodbye and turned to leave. There was no reasoning to it; just a blind obedience to the literal sequence. As though the feat of memory were itself a devotional act.

"Ahinadab the son of Iddo had Mahanaim . . ."

In spite of himself, Connie stopped to listen. The "preacher" faced him: was that a look of aggression? It was so impossibly hard to learn the body language of these people—of any people, come to that, other than one's own.

So Connie stood there like a lemon, knowing full well he looked like a lemon, and listened:

"Ahimaaz was in Naphtali; he also took
Basmath the daughter of Solomon to wife:
"Baanah the son of Hushai was in Asher and in Aloth:
"Jehoshaphat the son of Paruah, in Issachar:
"Shimei the son of Elah, in Benjamin . . ."

Connie realized that he had given too little mind to these feats of recitation. This was more than a display of the power of human memory. This was more than a display of defiance toward the Puscha invader: "See how we maintain our culture, crippled as we are!"

"Geber the son of Uri was in the country of Gilead, in the country of Sihon king of the Amorites, and of Og king of Bashan; and he was the only officer which was in the land."

Connie bowed his head. Not out of respect, surely, since this was, when you came down to it, absurd: to raise an ancient genealogy to a pedestal at which educated men must genuflect. But it said something about the will of this people, that they should have so quickly recovered the skills and habits of a time before reading and writing.

The man might have been an evangelistic scholar of the 1400s by the Christian calendar, and the subsequent six hundred years of writing and printing and reading no more than a folly, a risky experiment, terminated now by shadowy authorities.

When Connie passed him, on his way to the Gare du Nord and the London train, the man did not cease to speak.

"Judah and Israel were many," he declaimed, from memory, *"as the sand which is by the sea in multitude, eating and drinking, and making merry!"*

It was only twenty years since the Puscha had established a physical presence upon the planet, though their husbandry of the human animal had begun some thirty years before first contact. It took time and care to strike upon the subtle blend of environmental "pollutants" that would engineer illiteracy, without triggering its cousin afflictions: autism in all its extraordinary and distressing manifestations—not to mention all the variform aphasias.

Faced with the collapse of its linguistic talent, the human animal had, naturally enough, blamed its own industrial processes. The Puscha armada had hung back, discrete and undetected, until the accusations dried up, the calumnies were forgotten, and all the little wars resolved—until transmissions from the planet's surface had reduced to what they considered safe levels.

Human reactions to the Puscha arrival were various, eccentric, and localized—and this was as it should be. Concerted global responses, the Puscha had found, were almost always calamitous.

So, wherever Connie appeared along the railway line—and especially at the Suffolk terminus where he drank a cup of milkless tea before driving out in the lorry the thirty miles to his orchard—there was a respect for him that was friendly. He had been traveling back and forth, in the same way, for ten years.

There was a clubhouse at the junction: an old white house with lofty, open rooms, where he sometimes had a quick breakfast before driving onto the orchards. There was also an army station near, and as the pace of Autonomy quickened, the club had become a mere transit camp, with both

Puscha and human administrators piling bedrolls in the halls, and noisy behavior in the compounds. There were often civilian hangers-on there too, and the woman who lived with him now—the woman to whom he was faithful once again (the idea of being "faithful again" made more sense in his culture than hers)—had been one of these.

Her name was Rebecca—a name that translated fluently and comically into his own tongue, as a kind of edible, greasy fish. When he first laid eyes on her, she was drinking cocktails with a party of Puscha newcomers lately recruited to some dismal section of government finance (and who were in consequence behaving like abandoned invaders). Quite how she had fallen in with them wasn't clear. She was simply one of those maddening, iconic figures that turbulent events throw up from time to time: less real people, so much as windows onto impossible futures, no less poignant for being chimerical.

A few days later, on the connecting train to Paris, as he considered where to sit, vacillating as usual, he nearly walked straight past her.

She was sitting alone. She was white-skinned. Her hair was long and straight, gold-brown, and a fold of it hung down over one eye, lending her face an asymmetry that appealed to him.

The seat opposite her was invitingly empty.

He sat and read a while, or pretended to, racking his brain for the correct form, the correct stance, for an introduction. Horror stories abounded in the clubs and classes: a visiting male dignitary of the Fifty-Seventh Improvement, informed that human women are flattered by some moderate reference to their appearance, congratulates the First Lady of the North Americas on the buttery yellowness of her teeth—

And how, after all, could you ever learn enough to insure yourself against such embarrassments?

Eventually, it was she who spoke: "What is it you're reading?"

His scribe hand tingled, that he had left the opening gambit to her.

As for what he was reading—or pretending to read—it was

dull enough: a glib verse narrative from his own culture. In his day bag, Connie carried more interesting material: novels from the last great centuries of human literacy; but he had felt that it would be indelicate to read them in front of her.

By the end of the journey, however, she had all too easily teased out his real enthusiasms, persuading him, finally, to fetch from his bag and read to her—eagerly and loudly and not too well—two stories by Saki and some doggerel by Ogden Nash. They were old, battered paperback editions, the pages loose in both, and once a page of Saki fell by her foot. She stooped to pick it up for him. She studied it a moment, while he in turn studied the fold of her hair hanging over her eye; he surprised in himself a strong desire to sweep it behind her ear.

He saw with a pang that she was studying the page upside-down.

"I sing," she told him later, as they passed through the Parisian suburbs. "I am a singer."

He made some callow remark, something she must have heard a hundred times before: how human singing so resembles Puscha weeping (itself never formless, but a kind of glossolalia peculiar to the Puscha species).

"I sing for people," she said, "not for Puscha." (She made the usual mistake, lengthening the "u" in Puscha to an "oo.")

It was not a severe put-down, and anyway, he deserved it. So why did it hurt so much?

It maddened him afterward to think that she must have drawn him out—she must have got him to admit his interest in her people's literature, and read to her—only so she might sit there quietly despising him: the eloquent invader, drip-feeding the poor native whose own throat he had so effectively glued shut!

But all this was eight years ago, and Connie was too much the newcomer to know what undercurrents might run beneath such stilted conversations.

And on the return journey, the same coincidence! This time, she nearly walked past him—would have done so, had he not called her.

Well, their being on the same train yet again was not much of a fluke. He had traveled to Paris to glad-hand the farmers gathered there, and address their concerns about trade links after Autonomy; Rebecca, for her part, had gone to sing for them.

These days, public events had a tendency to run into each other: a trade fair with a concert tour, a concert tour with a religious festival. They were arranged so to do. A non-literate culture can only sustain so much complexity.

In a society without literacy, the eccentric routines of individuals and cliques cannot be reliably communicated and accommodated; so everything moved now to the rhythm of established social customs—even to the patterns of the seasons.

On their return journey, Connie spoke of these things to Rebecca—and then he wished he hadn't. He had an uneasy sensation of describing to her the bars of her prison.

Suddenly he was aware of wanting to say something to her; to make, as casually as he could, a desperate suggestion.

He began to make it, and then found himself trembling unexpectedly.

"What were you going to say?"

"Oh! It was an idea. But then I remembered it wouldn't— it wasn't possible."

"What?"

"Well—" he said. "Well—I was going to suggest you come to visit the orchard I run, for the weekend I mean. The clubhouse is no place—I mean, it's very crowded just now, and you could breathe. Breathe easier. If you came."

"But why is that impossible?"

"Not impossible. I mean—"

He started telling her about the orchard. About the apples, and what his work with them entailed. The busy-ness of the season. Then, warming to his subject, about the savor apples had upon the Puscha palate, their goodness in digestion. And from that, to the premium his crops might fetch among his kind. And all the time he talked, losing himself in this easy, boastful, well-rehearsed chatter, he wondered at the wastefulness of the world, that animals crossed unimaginable gulfs of interstellar space, only to compare with each other the things that filled their guts, and satisfied their palates.

It was not until she was in the lorry with him, her hands resting lightly on her bare knees, her back arched in an elegant curve, and the fold of gold-brown hair hanging still over her eye, that it dawned on him: she was still with him. Silent. Smiling. Improbably patient. She had said yes.

The orchards fanned east in an irregular patchwork from the outskirts of Woodbridge, gathering finally along the banks of the Alde and the Ore. The rivers—wide, muddy, tidal throats—gathered and ran for some miles parallel to each other, and to the sea, which lay behind a thin band of reclaimed land. This ribbon of land—more a sea defense than anything else—was not given over to agriculture, but retained its ancient fenland garb of broken jetties, disused windmills and high, concealing reeds.

Rebecca glimpsed it only once, as Connie drove her through the deserted town of Orford, with its view over mudflats. Then they turned away from the coast, the road shrinking beneath them to a narrow gravel track, as it wound its way among the apple trees.

The monotony of the view was broken only once, by the Alde and the Ore, mingling indirectly through a knot of winding ditches and narrow (you might jump across them) surgically straight canals. The land here was riddled with old channels and overgrown oxbow lakes, as though someone had scrunched up the land and then imperfectly flattened it.

A pontoon bridge and an even narrower driveway led Connie and his companion, at last, to his house.

Across the front door, someone—a disgruntled worker, or other protester—had painted a sign.

$$Qi_t$$
$$ea^ht$$

The lettering was predictably feeble: the work of one for whom letters were not carriers of information, but merely designs.

She didn't need to be able to read to see that it didn't belong: "What does it say?"

He pondered it. "It's their slogan, now," he said.

"Whose?" she asked him.

"It says, 'Quit Earth.' " He scratched at the paint with his bludgeon hand. It would not come off.

It was late in the season, and the light died early, that first night.

They sat drinking apple brandy in the darkness, on deck chairs in front of the house. Glow bulbs cast a febrile warmth like a tremor through the chill air.

"Read to me," she said.

So he read to her. He wondered how she bore it: all those V's for R's (R was a letter he found barely audible unless it was rolled on the tongue, at which point the sound struck him as faintly obscene). Not to mention the Z's he had to insert in place of those wonderful, utterly inimitable W's. It wasn't just the phonetic habits of his own language getting in the way (as far as that went, the speech of his ethnic group, the so-called Desert No'ivel, was notoriously fluid and sing-song); there were anatomical differences, too.

He studied the line of her mouth. He imagined her tongue, frighteningly prehensile. The relative chill of it (so, at least, he had heard, though he had no experience of it himself; felt still—or told himself he felt—a faint revulsion at the idea.) Her teeth, their—

What was it again? Yes: "buttery yellowness." He laughed—to the human ear, an all-too-malevolent hiss.

Startled, Rebecca turned to face him. In the light from the warm glow bulbs, her irises were brown gray, like stones under water.

He could hardly bear to sit there, and not touch the fold of her hair.

(In the realm of the erotic, otherness is its own reward.)

Then it came to him: she knew this was what he was feeling.

He wondered at what point he had left off reading.

He considered whether or not she had done this before,

with one of his kind, and the thought aroused him. He wondered dizzily whether this made him a "homosexual."

(She resembled his own sex, more than the female of his species. Puscha females are not bipeds. It is only relatively recently in their evolutionary history that they have lost the ability to fly. Their sentience is sudden, traumatic, triggered by pregnancy, and short-lived thereafter. Their abrupt, brief capacity for symbolic thought opens them to the possibilities of language—but they have time only to develop a kind of sing-song idiolect before the shutters come down again over their minds. They are resourceful, destructive of crops, and are routinely culled.)

Rebecca leaned forward in her chair, to touch the feathers about his eyes. The lines of her arm were reassuringly familiar to him, though the tone of her skin was not. He reached out with his bludgeon hand to trace delicately the line of the fold of her hair.

A moment later he heard the voice of Hadmuhaddera calling across the lawn, in the broad Lowland No'ivel accents that he had always faintly loathed:

"Hi there, Connie, where've you been hiding yourself?"

For the rest of the evening, the unctious pedagogy of Hadmuhaddera filled the chair between them. Hadmuhaddera, stiff and small, as though some more elegant version of himself were struggling for release within, spoke volubly of the strange differences and stranger similarities of Puscha and human culture—as though Puschas (or humans, for that matter) were these monolithic, homogeneous units!

In the guise of leading Connie through the uncharted shallows of 'human' habits ("*pain au chocolat* is a splendid invention, in that it allows you to eat chocolate for breakfast") he patronized Rebecca furiously.

Connie felt all the pulse and tremor of the evening come apart in the tepid, irregular slaps of Hadmuhaddera's tongue against his broad, blue palate.

Rebecca meanwhile stretched out almost flat in her chair, her water-polished eyes wide and black and bored, her arms thin and white like sea-polished wood against the arms of her chair.

"But set against the narrow bounds of the physically possible—" Hadmuhaddera was growing philosophical under the influence of Connie's apple brandy—"nature's infinite variations seem no more than decorative flourishes. Like that poet of yours, dear—what's-his-name? 'Tall fish, small fish, red fish, blue fish,' yes, yes, yes, but they're all bloody *fish*, aren't they? Every planet we go to: fish, fish, fish! And birds. And crustacea. Insects. Everything is exotic, but nothing is actually *alien*."

"Oh, I don't know. Your womenfolk give us pause," Rebecca countered. "Of course, thanks to your kind Improvements, we will never be able to attain your well-traveled disillusionment." In her quiet way, she was giving as good as she was getting. "Perhaps it is because you are the only aliens we have known—but you seem *fucking* peculiar to us."

Hadmuhaddera gave vent to an appreciative hiss.

In spite of himself, Connie found himself joining in. "Nature is capable of infinite variety," he mused, "but only a handful of really good ideas. Because the rules of physics are constant across the universe, so are the constraints within which living things evolve. Eyes, noses, ears, they're all good ideas. They're economical and effective. Consequently, we all have them. Languages, too—you would think they would be infinitely variable. But the differences aren't nearly as striking as the similarities. The predicating deep grammar—that is universal, or we would not be talking to each other now."

But if he imagined that Rebecca would join in—would become, for a minute, the gossiping groupie he had first seen at the clubhouse—he was wrong. He watched with something like pride—though he had, he knew, no right to such a sentiment—as Rebecca steered their conversation away from the theory and practice of language—that overwhelming Puscha obsession.

He watched her. Could it be that she, too, longed for the moment when they might restart the shattered pulse of their intimacy? He felt his body once again ache for the fold of her hair, and then Hadmuhaddera said:

"Ah, well, I'll bid you goodnight."

They watched him stagger away across the lawn into the darkness. There was no sound in the garden now, except for the stirring of leaves in distant apple trees: in a few weeks, this sound too would cease.

He thought about the apples, the trees, about his work. He thought about pruning. The act of it. The feel of the secateurs in his hands (he was not above getting his hands dirty, though whether he won any respect for it among his workers, he was never sure). He thought about the sound his workers made, as they set about their seasonal tasks.

He thought about gardening, and the fine line the gardener treads between husbandry and cruelty; between control and disfigurement. He thought about the Improvements his people had made among the planets. The years they had argued and agonized over them. The good and pressing reasons why they had made them.

Their enormity.

Rebecca stood up and wandered off a little way. Softly, she began to sing. She had a good voice, a trained voice (he had already learned the difference). An operatic voice.

He closed his eyes against a sudden, searing melancholy. To him it sounded as though she were weeping for the world.

Before the theme came clear, she stopped.

He opened his eyes.

She was looking at him. "Is this what you wanted?" she said.

It hurt him, that she would think this of him. "No," he said, truthfully.

She said nothing more, and after a few moments, she began her song again.

They had been together now for eight years.

Every civilization begins with a garden.

The Puscha, whose numerous cultures have bred and battled away at each other for eons, have founded their present, delicate comity upon this simple truth.

Here is another truth the Puscha take to be self-evident: a flower is simply a domesticated weed.

All Puscha "Improvements" are dedicated to the domestication of language. Over the eons of their recorded history, they have confronted languages too many and too noxious to get very sentimental about pruning them. Let a language develop unimpeded, and it will give rise to societies that are complex enough to destroy both themselves and others. Xenocidal hiveminds, juggernaut AIs, planet-busting self-replicators: the Puscha have faced them all—every variety of linguistic ground elder and rhetorical Russian vine.

The wholesale elimination of literacy is one of the stronger weedkillers in the Puscha horticultural armory, and they do not wield it lightly. Had they not wielded it here, the inventive, overcomplex and unwieldy morass of human society would have long since wiped itself off the planet.

The Puscha care, not for their own self-interest, but only for comity and peace and beauty.

They are beyond imperialism.

They are gardeners.

Two

He still reads to Rebecca. But over the years, something has shifted between them, some balance has tipped.

At night, in bed, with the light on, he reads to her. Lermontov. Turgenev. Gogol. She laughs at Gogol. He reads and reads. He has perfected a kind of ersatz R. W's will, perforce, always elude him. She lies there beside him, listening, her eyes like pebbles, wide and bored, her arms like stripped and polished apple branches, motionless upon the sheets.

He reads and reads.

He waits for her eyes to close, but they never do.

Defeated, he turns out the light.

Darkness is a great leveler.

In the dark, his books may as well be blank. He is alone. He is worse than alone.

In the dark, he finds himself dispersed and ill-arranged:

loose-leafed. He cannot find himself—he cannot find his *place*.

Every day he commits his self, unthinkingly, to diaries and address books, journals and letters and the essays he writes so very slowly and sends to little magazines.

At night, lying there beside her, he finds he has held back nothing of himself. It is all spilled, all committed elsewhere, unreadable in the dark.

Able as he is to read and write, the world inside his head is grown atrophied and shapeless. Equipped as he is with a diary and a journal, he remembers little. Owning, as he does, so many books, he cannot from them quote a single line. Deluged as he is every day with printed opinions, he finds it wearisome to formulate his own.

When the light goes off, and they lie side by side in the bed, listening to the leaves of the distant apple trees, Rebecca tells Connie stories.

Rebecca's stories are different from Connie's. His stories belong to the light; hers, to the dark.

She does not need light to tell her stories. She does not need to read or write. All she needs to do is remember.

And she remembers everything.

With no diary, Rebecca's mind arranges and rearranges every waking moment, shuffles past and future to discover patterns to live by, grows sensitive to time and light and even to the changes in the smell of the air.

Lacking a journal in which to spill herself, she keeps her self contained. Cogent, coherent, strong-willed and opinionated, her personality mounts and swells behind the walls of her skull.

(As he lies there in the dark, listening to her, Connie reflects on gunpowder. Unconfined, it merely burns; packed tight, it explodes.)

Rebecca's stories come out at night. They are stories of the campfire, of the clan gathered against the illiterate night. Hers is the fluid repertoire of the band, the gang, the tribe, reinforcing its identity by telling stories about itself.

Rebecca tells him about his workers, about their loves and their losses, their feuds and betrayals. She tells him:

"They burned an old nigger in Woodbridge last night."

It is not her choice of epithet that distresses him—why would it? He is from too far away to appreciate such nuances.

It is the fact of it: the growing littleness of the people of this world. This gathering into clans. This growing distrust of outsiders. This reinvention of foreignness.

This proliferation of languages.

(Already, in the eight years they have been together here, Rebecca's trained, operatic voice has taken on a deep, loamy Suffolk burr.)

He remembers something his neighbor Hadmuhaddera said, years ago: how everything that lives, wherever it lives, comes up with the same solutions, again and again. Hands, noses, eyes, ears. How everything is exotic but nothing is truly *alien*. He recalls, above all, Hadmuhaddera's frustration, that this should be so.

Now there are many, manifestly reasonable arguments to support the Fifty-Seventh Improvement. But Connie is beginning to wonder if those polished arguments might not conceal darker, perhaps subconscious, motives.

Rob a culture of literacy, and rumor replaces record, anecdotes supersede annals. The drive to cooperation remains, but cooperation itself, on a grand scale, becomes impractical. The dream of universal understanding fades. Nations are reborn, and, within them, peoples—reborn or invented. Models of the world proliferate, and science—beyond a rude natural philosophy—becomes impossible. Religions multiply and speciate, fetishizing wildly. Parochialism arises in all its finery, speaking argot, wearing folk dress, dancing its ethnic dance.

Connie thinks: We are good gardeners, but we are too flashy. We succumb again and again to our vulgar hunger for exotica.

He thinks: We have made this place our hot-house.

*   *   *

Rebecca says, "They hung a tire around his neck. A tire and a garland of unripe hops. The tire weighed him down and the hops made him sneeze. They hopped and skipped around him, singing. Nigger. Nigger. Nigger. Tears ran down his nose."

These are the rhythms of a campfire tale. This is the sing-song of a story passed from mouth to mouth. Connie's heart hammers in time to her playful, repetitious, Odysseian phrases.

Connie recalls that Homer, being blind, had no need of books.

He cries out in fear.

Rebecca's hand settles, light and dry as apple leaves, upon his breast. "What is it?"

"I don't want to hear this. I don't want to hear."

She says to him: "The ringleader ran away in the night. They say he's hiding near. They say he's hiding on our land. Among the apple trees." She says: "It's up to you. It's your responsibility."

A week, this lasts: a week of curfews, false sightings, beatings of the rush beds. At last, exhausted, Connie consults with the military authorities in Ipswich, and abandons the hunt.

At night, with the light on, he reads.

"Rudin spoke intelligently, passionately, and effectively; he exhibited much knowledge, a great deal of reading. No one had expected to find him a remarkable man . . . He was so indifferently dressed, so little had been heard of him. To all of them it seemed incomprehensible and strange how someone so intelligent could pop up suddenly in the provinces."

With eyes black-brown and bored, she says:

"I've heard this part before."

Yes, and if he asked her, she could probably recite it to him. (He does not ask her.)

"He spoke masterfully, and entertainingly, but not entirely lucidly . . . yet this very vagueness lent particular charm to his speech."

Connie wonders, dizzily, if Ivan Turgenev's observation, sharp enough in its day, means anything at all now.

"A listener might not understand precisely what was being talked about; but he would catch his breath, curtains would open wide before his eyes, something resplendent would burn dazzlingly ahead of him."

Rebecca does not know what vagueness is. She could not be vague if she tried. Her stories shine and flash like knives. He glances at her eyes. They will not close. They will not close. His bludgeon hand is numb, he is so tired. But still he reads.

". . . But most astounded of all were Basistov and Natalya. Basistov could scarcely draw breath; he sat all the while open-mouthed and pop-eyed—and listened, listened, as he had never listened to anyone in his whole life, and Natalya's face was covered in a crimson flush and her gaze, directly fixed at Rudin, both darkened and glittered in turn . . ."

"Tomorrow," he says to her, when at last he can read no more, "let us go for a walk. Where would you like to go?"

"To the banks of the Alde and the Ore," she says, "where Hadmuhaddera's nephew lost his shoe, and the last man in Orford once fished."

Deprived of records, she remembers everything as a story. Because everything is a story, she remembers everything.

Tonight, in the dark, as he sprawls, formless and helpless beside her, she tells him a story of a beach she has heard tell of, a beach she doesn't know, called Chesil.

"Chesil Beach is a high shingle bank, cut free of the coast by small, brackish waters," she says.

"Like here," he says.

"Like here," she agrees, "but the waters aren't rivers, and the bank that parts them from the sea is much bigger, and made all of stones."

She tells him:

"You could spend your whole day among the dunes and never see the sea. Yet you hear its constant stirring, endlessly, and soon in your mind comes the image of this bank, this barrow-mound, put before you like a dike, to keep the sea from roaring in upon you. The land behind you is melted and steep, and before you the pebbles grind, a vast mill, and you wonder how high the sea water is now. You wonder how high the tide comes, relative to the land. You wonder how long it will take, for the sea to eat through the bank . . ."

In the morning, as you are eating breakfast, she comes down the stairs. She is wearing a red dress. It is a dress you recognize. It belongs to the girl you so recently left. It belongs to your mistress in Paris.

Even her hair is arranged in the way that your mistress's hair was arranged.

You say nothing. How can you? You can hardly breathe.

"Let's go for our walk, then," she says.

So you go for your walk, down the track, past the gate, into lane after lane, and all around stand the apple trees, line upon line. The gravel slides wetly under your feet as you walk, and the leaves of the apple trees whisper and rattle. She scents the air, and you wonder what she finds there to smell, what symptom of weather or season or time of day. She tosses her hair in the breeze. Her hair is crunched and pinned and high, and the fold of it that you so treasured is gone, the fold of gold-brown that once hid her eye.

Your orchards fan east to the banks of the Alde and the Ore. The rivers run wide and muddy and dark, and seabirds pick over them, combing for the blind, simple foods of the seashore.

The rivers, slow, rich and mud-laden, evacuate themselves into each other through a maze of ditches and channels, some natural, and some cut by hand through the furze. On the far banks, where the land is too narrow for tillage, an old fenland persists, all jetties and rotten boardwalks and old broken-down walls, and everything is choked by high, concealing reeds.

She turns away from you where you settle, shapeless in the grass. She bends, and the red dress rides up her calves, and you begin to ask her where the dress comes from, and what has she done to her hair? But all that comes out is:

"I—I—I—"

She takes off her shoes.

"What are you going to do?"

"Paddle." She lifts the edges of her dress and unrolls her stockings, peeling them down her brown smooth legs.

The tide is out, the mud is thick and brown like chocolate.

"There are terrible quicksands," you tell her, knowing that she knows.

Absently, she traces her toe through the yielding mud.

"If I don't come back," she says, "you'll know I'm swimming."

"No," you tell her, agitated. "Don't do that! It's dangerous. Don't do that."

You stand and watch her as she walks slowly upstream, in the shallow edge of the water. Swishing her feet. When she is gone, you wander to the water's edge, and you study the thing she has drawn in the mud.

$$Qi_t\ ea^ht$$

A line from a book comes to you: a book by Marshall McLuhan:

Terror is the normal state of any oral society, for in it everything affects everything all the time.

When the rifle shot comes out from the reeds in the far bank, and hits you full in the chest, you do not fall. The suddenness of it seems to freeze the world, to undo the physical constraints that hold you and your kind and her kind and all kinds to worlds that are never quite alien, never quite home.

You do not even stagger.

You stand, watching old abandoned windmills, listening to the rushes, their susurration clear against the rustling of the leaves of the apple trees. You watch the distant figure with the rifle leap from cover behind an old ruined wall and disappear between the reeds.

You choke, and fall backward. As you lie there, she comes running.

She has taken off the red dress. She has let down her hair.

You follow the line of it, and find that it has returned to itself, a fold of gold-brown over one eye. Terrified, you follow
the fold of her hair to her neck, to her breast. Blood bubbles
in your throat as you try to speak.

She puts her arms about you, holding you upright for a
few seconds longer. "Try not to move," she says. She is crying in the soft, calm manner of her people.

When your eyes close, she begins to sing. *"I hate you,"*
she sings. *"I hate you. Oh, how I hate you!"*

Singing, or weeping. You cannot tell the difference.

You come from too far away.

Under's Game

MICHAEL SWANWICK

Michael Swanwick's [www.michaelswanwick.com] novels include the Nebula Award winner Stations of the Tide *(1991),* The Iron Dragon's Daughter *(1993), and* Jack Faust *(1997), and his new novel* Bones of the Earth *(2002). But in between the novels, he still writes short stories. His short fiction in recent years has been fantasy as often as science fiction, but his stories dominated the short fiction Hugo Award nominations in 1998. And a few more appeared in 1999. Swanwick then announced that he had better get back to novel writing, so we are experiencing another comparative dry spell before the next wave of Swanwick stories, except that he has discovered a facility for very short stories, now appearing widely. His short fiction has been collected principally in* Gravity's Angels *(1991),* A Geography of Unknown Lands *(1997),* Moon Dogs *(2000), and* Tales of Old Earth *(2000). A collection of short-shorts,* Cigar-Box Faust and Other Miniatures, *appeared in 2001 from Tachyon Books. Other than that, we do not know what to expect, except excellence.*

"Under's Game" is a witty parody of a classic Orson Scott Card SF story. It was published by SciFiction, and is one of a series of fantasy and SF short short stories and vignettes, each based on an element from the Periodic Table.

12
MG
MAGNESIUM
24.312

The spaceships burned brightly in the vacuum between stars. They were a hundred miles long at a minimum. The tiny ships of the Space Force darted in and out among the flaming wrecks, dodging the Invader fleet's death rays when they could and dying when they couldn't. Courage was on the side of the Space Force. Numbers were on the side of the Invaders.

"It doesn't make any sense," Under said petulantly. "How can they burn in outer space? There's no air there. It's stupid."

"The hulls are made of pure magnesium. The Invaders breathe oxygen. One direct hit, and the two combine. What's so hard to believe about that?" his instructor asked the young military genius. "Let's test your skill. Take the controls. Show me how good you are."

Under picked up the pad, shifted forces along seven vectors at once, launched plasma torpedoes, and suddenly a full quarter of the Invader fleet was in flames. Then he threw the controller aside. "It's a dumb game. Aren't there any Cheez Doodles left?" He dug a hand under the sofa cushions, searching.

"Please," the instructor begged, tears in his eyes. He was a general, and the one who had convinced the Government of Earth to put all its defenses under the control of one prepubescent boy. The Invaders were better strategists than any adult human, and better tacticians as well. It only made sense to hand over all the Space Force to one boy and then (so he wouldn't freeze up under the responsibility) keep the reality of the situation from him. "You can have ice cream if you win. With sprinkles!"

Under's eyes gleamed. He snatched up the game pad, and launched a series of commands. The Space Force twisted, turned . . . and fled into hyperspace.

The Invader fleet followed.

"We're doomed!" the general wailed. All the vector lines on the display converged upon one small blue-and-white planet. "You're leading the Invaders straight toward Earth."

"That's what they think too." Under bit his lip and twisted on the couch. His thumbs were a blur. "But watch this. Our ships burn every ounce of fuel they've got and—there's no way the enemy can predict this—their vectors take them right through the Sun's corona. Their hulls are plasteel—they can take the heat. That gives them a slingshot gravity assist of ten gees. Just within performance tolerance of the crews."

"But now they can't maneuver!"

"They don't have to. Watch. The last of our ships is leaving the sun's chromosphere, and the first of theirs is entering."

There was a glint of light as the first Invader ship vaporized.

"See? Magnesium hulls, just like you said. Up in flames, and bye-bye Invaders!" He tossed the controls to the general. "Here, catch!"

The general stood mesmerized as the Invader menace evanesced, one instant a threat to human existence and the next instant only a memory.

"This is a great moment for humanity," he said, tears in his eyes. His thumb moved, inputting orders for the Space Force. Then he frowned. "They're not responding. They're still headed for Earth!"

"Yeah, pretty neat, huh? I figured they're out of fuel, anyway, so they might as well go out with a bang. So I aimed them straight at Home Base."

"But this is terrible! At those speeds, they'll hit us with all the force of so many nuclear bombs!"

"Hell," Under said. "It's only a game."

A Matter of Mathematics

BRIAN W. ALDISS

Brian W. Aldiss [www.brianwaldiss.com] was given the Grand Master award of the Science Fiction Writers of America in 2000. The influence of his works in SF is deep and widespread. He burst into prominence in the late 1950s, and has never ceased to push the boundaries since. Over five decades, he has published more than 300 stories, collected in twenty-five books, from Space, Time, and Nathaniel *(1957) to* Supertoys Last All Summer Long *(2001), from which this story is taken, and a number of fine novels, including the classics* Hothouse, Frankenstein Unbound, *and the Helliconia Trilogy. Aldiss has published his autobiography,* The Twinkling of an Eye *(1998), and three new novels are just out or announced for 2002.*

The year 2001 was another big year for Aldiss, when the Stanley Kubrick film based on his book, Supertoys Last All Summer Long, *was released as* AI. *The film was a controversial critical success and popular failure, but is certainly a major landmark in SF cinema.*

"A Matter of Mathematics" is a lunatic far-future space story about self-absorbed obsessives finding the truths of the universe by dwelling on their obsessions. It suggests that inner space is as strange and as interesting as outer space.

It was a funny thing about Joyce Bagreist. She lived on yogurt and jam sandwiches. She never washed her hair. She was not popular at her university. Yet Bagreist's Short Cut changed the universe. Simply, shockingly, inevitably, irretrievably.

Of course it was a matter of mathematics. Everything has changed.

Back at human beginnings, perception was locked in a shuttered house. One by one, the shutters snapped open, or were forced open. The "real" world outside was perceived. Because perception—like everything else—evolved.

We can never be sure if all the shutters have yet snapped open.

At one time, "in the old days," it was well known that the caves of Altamira in northern Spain had been accidentally discovered by a girl of five. She had wandered from her father. Her father was an archaeologist, and much too busy studying an old stone to notice that his daughter had strayed from his side.

It is easy to imagine the fine afternoon, the old man kneeling by the stone, the young girl picking wildflowers. She finds blue flowers, red ones and yellow. She wanders on, taking little thought. The ground is broken. She attempts to climb a slope. Sand falls away in a toytown version of an avalanche. She sees an opening. She has no fear, but plenty of curiosity. She climbs in. Just a little way. She is in a cave. There she sees on the wall the figure of an animal, a buffalo.

That does frighten her. She climbs out and runs back to her father, crying that she has seen an animal. He abandons his stone and goes to look.

And what he finds is an extensive gallery of scenes, painted by Paleolithic hunters or magicians, or hunter/magicians. The great artistry of the scenes changes human understanding of the past. We came to believe we comprehended that sympathetic magic when we had in fact failed to do so. Our mind patterns had changed: We were unable to comprehend Paleolithic thought, however hard we tried. We accepted a scientific, mathematical model into our heads, and had to live by it.

Clues to a true understanding of the universe lie everywhere. One after another, clues are found and, when the time is ripe, can be understood. The great reptiles whose bones lie in the rocks waited there for millions of years to be interpreted. They expanded greatly humanity's knowledge of duration and the planet's duration. Frequently women are associated with such shocks to the understanding, perhaps because they contain magic in their own persons (although there seemed little magic to Joyce Bagreist's person). It was a Mrs. Gideon Mantell who discovered the bones of the first reptile to be identified as a dinosaur.

All such discoveries seem little short of miraculous at the time; then they become taken for granted. So it has proved in the case of Bagreist's Short Cut.

It has been forgotten now, but an accident similar to the Altamira accident brought Joyce Bagreist to understand and interpret the signal of the Northern Lights, or *aurora borealis*. For untold years, the lights had been explained away as the interaction of charged particles from the sun with particles in the upper atmosphere. True, the signal was activated by the charged particles: But no one until Bagreist had thought through to the purpose of this phenomenon.

Joyce Bagreist was a cautious little woman, not particularly liked at her university because of her solitary nature. She was slowly devising and building a computer which worked on the color spectrum rather than on mathematics. Once she had formulated new equations and set up her apparatus, she spent some while preparing for what she visualized might follow. Within the privacy of her house, Bagreist improvised for herself a kind of wheeled space suit, complete with bright headlights, an emergency oxygen supply and a stock of food. Only then did she track along her upper landing, encased inside her novel vehicle, along the measured two point five meters, and through the archway of scanners and transmitters of her apparatus.

At the end of the archway, with hardly a jolt to announce a revolution in thought, she found herself in the crater Aristarchus, on Earth's satellite, the Moon.

It will be remembered that the great Aristarchus of Samos, in whose honor the crater was named, was the first astronomer to correctly read another celestial signal now obvious to us—that the Earth was in orbit about the Sun, rather than vice versa.

There Bagreist was, rather astonished and slightly vexed. According to her calculations, she should have emerged in the crater Copernicus. Clearly her apparatus was more primitive and fallible than she had bargained for.

Being unable to climb out of the crater, she circled it in her homemade suit, feeling pleased with the discovery of what we still call Bagreist's Short Cut—or, more frequently, more simply, the Bagreist.

There was no way in which this brave discoverer could return to Earth. It was left to others to construct an archway on the Moon. Poor Joyce Bagreist perished there in Aristarchus, a last jam sandwich on her lap, perhaps not too dissatisfied with herself. She had radioed to Earth. The signal had been picked up. Space Administration had sent a ship. But it arrived too late for Joyce Bagreist.

Within a year of her death, traffic was pouring through several archways, and the Moon was covered with building materials.

But who or what had left the color-coded signal in the Arctic skies to await its hour of interpretation?

Of course, the implications of the Bagreist were explored. It became clear that space/time did not possess the same configuration as had been assumed. Another force was operative, popularly known as the Squidge Force. Cosmologists and mathematicians were hard put to explain the Squidge Force, since it resisted formulation in current mathematical systems. The elaborate mathematical systems on which our global civilization was founded had merely local application: they did not extend even as far as the heliopause. So while the practicalities of Bagreist were being utilized, and people everywhere (having bought a ticket) were taking a short walk from their home onto the lunar surface, mathematical lacunae were the subject of intense and learned inquiry.

Two centuries later, I back into the story. I shall try to explain simply what occurred. But not only does P-L6344 enter the picture; so do Mrs. Staunton and General Tomlin Willetts, and the general's lady friend, Molly Levaticus.

My name, by the way, is Terry W. Manson, L44/56331. I lived in Lunar City IV, popularly known as Ivy. I was General Secretary of Recreationals, working for those who manufacture IDs, or individual drugs, those enhancing drugs tailored to personal genetic codes.

I had worked previously for the Luna-based MAW, the Meteor and Asteroid Watch, which was how I came to know something of General Willetts' affairs. Willetts was a big consumer of IDs. He was in charge of the MAW operation, and had been for the previous three years. His last few months had been taken up with Molly Levaticus, who had joined his staff as a junior operative and was shortly afterward made Private Secretary to the general. In consequence of this closely kept secret affair—known to many on the base—General Willetts went about in a dream.

My more serious problem also involved a dream. A golf ball lying forlorn on a deserted beach may have nothing outwardly sinister about it. However, when that same dream recurs every night, one begins to worry. There lay that golf ball, there was that beach. Both monuments to perfect stasis, and in consequence alarming.

The dream became more insistent as time went by. It seemed—I know no other way of expressing it—to move closer to my vision every night. I became alarmed. Eventually, I made an appointment to see Mrs. Staunton, Mrs. Roslyn Staunton, the best-known mentatropist in Ivy.

After asking all the usual questions, involving my general health, my sleeping habits, and so forth, Roslyn—we soon lapsed into first names—asked me what meaning I attached to my dream.

"It's just an ordinary golf ball. Well . . . No, it has markings resembling a golf ball's markings. I don't know what else it could be. And it's lying on its side."

When I thought about what I was saying, I saw I was talking nonsense. A golf ball has no sides. So it was not a golf ball.

"And it's lying on a beach?" she prompted.

"That's right."

"So it's not on the Moon."

"It has nothing to do with the Moon." But there I was wrong.

"What sort of a beach? A resort beach, for instance?"

"Far from it. An infinite beach. Alienating. Stony. Pretty bleak."

"You recognize the beach?"

"No. It's an alarming place—well, the way infinity is always pretty alarming. Just an enormous stretch of territory with nothing growing on it. Oh, and the ocean. A sullen ocean. The waves are heavy and leaden—and slow. About one per minute gathers up its strength and slithers up the beach. I ought to time them."

She said, "Time is never reliable in dreams." Then she asked, "Slithers?"

"Waves don't seem to break properly on this beach. They just subside." I sat in silence thinking about this desolate yet somehow tempting picture which haunted me. "I feel in a way I've been there. The sky. It's very heavy and enclosing."

"So you feel this is all very unpleasant?"

With surprise, I heard myself saying, "Oh no, I need it, it promises something. Something emerging . . . Out of the sea, I suppose."

"Why do you wish to cease dreaming this dream if you need it?"

That was a question I found myself unable to answer.

While I was undergoing three sessions a week with Roslyn, the general was undergoing more frequent sessions with Molly Levaticus. And P-L6344 was rushing nearer.

Molly was an intellectual lady, played a silver trumpet, spoke seven languages, was a chess champion, was also highly sexed and inclined to mischief. Dark of hair, with a pert nose. A catch for any man, I'd say. Even General Tomlin Willetts.

The general's wife, Hermione, was blind, and had been since childhood. Willetts was not without a sadistic streak, or how else would he have become a general? We are all blind in some fashion, either in our private lives or in some shared public way; for instance, millions of Earthbound people, otherwise seemingly intelligent, still believe that the Sun orbits the Earth, rather than vice versa. This, despite all the evidence to the contrary and the true facts having been known for centuries.

This type of people would say in their own defense that they believe the evidence of their eyes. Yet we know well that our eyes can see only a small part of the electromagnetic spectrum. All our senses are limited in some fashion. And, because limited, often mistaken. Even "unshakable evidence" concerning the nature of the universe was due to take a knock, thanks to P-L6344.

Willetts' sadistic nature led him to persuade his fancy lady, Molly Levaticus, to walk naked about the rooms of his and his wife's apartment, while the blind Hermione was present. I believe she simply enjoyed the sexual mischief of it. Roslyn agreed. It was a prank. But commentators variously saw Molly either as a victim or as a dreadful predatory female.

Nobody considered that the truth, if there was a unitary truth, lay somewhere between the two poles: that there was an affinity between the individuals involved, which is not as unusual as it may appear, between the older man and the younger woman. Molly undoubtedly had her power, as he had his weakness. They played on each other.

And they played cat-and-mouse with Hermione Willetts.

She would be sitting at the meal table, with Willetts placed nearby. Into the room would come the naked Levaticus, on tiptoe. Winks were exchanged with Willetts. She would circle the room in a slow dance, hands above her head, showing her unshaven armpits, in a kind of *t'ai chi*, moving close to the blind woman.

Sensing a movement in the air, or a slight noise, Hermione would ask mildly, "Tomlin, dear, is there another person in the room?"

He would deny it.

Sometimes Hermione would strike out with her stick. Molly always dodged.

"Your behavior is very strange, Hermione," Willetts would say, severely. "Put down that stick. You are not losing your senses, are you?"

Or they would be in the living room. Hermione would be in her chair, reading a book in Braille. Molly would stick out her little curly pudendum almost in the lady's face. Hermione would sniff and turn the page. Molly would glide to Willetts' side, open his zip, and remove his erect penis, on which her fingers played like a musician with a flute. Then Hermione might lift her blind gaze and ask what her husband was doing.

"Just counting my medals, dearest," he would reply.

What was poor Hermione's perception of her world? How mistaken was it, or did she prefer not to suspect, being powerless?

But he was equally blind, disregarding the signals from MAW, urging an immediate decision on what to do to deflect or destroy the oncoming P-L6344.

Willetts was preoccupied with his private affairs, as I was preoccupied with my mentatropic meetings with Roslyn. As our bodies went on their courses, so too did the bodies of the solar system.

Apollo asteroids cross the Earth/Moon orbit. Of these nineteen small bodies, possibly the best known is Hermes, which at one time passed the Moon at a distance only double the Moon's distance from Earth. P-L6344 is a small rock, no more than one hundred and ninety meters across. On its previous crossing, the brave astronaut, Flavia da Beltrau do Valle, managed to anchor herself to the rock, planting there a metal replica of the Patagonian flag. At the period of which I am speaking, the asteroid was coming in fast at an inclination of five degrees to the plane of the ecliptic. Best estimations demonstrated that it would impact with the Moon at 23:03 on August 5th, 2208, just a few kilometers north of Ivy. But defensive action was delayed because of General Willetts' other interests.

So why were the computers not instructed by others, and the missiles not armed by subordinates? The answer must lie somewhere in everyone's absurd preoccupation with their own small universes, of which they form the perceived center. Immersed in Recreationals, they were in any case disinclined to act.

Perhaps we have a hatred of reality. Reality is too cold for us. Perceptions of all things are governed by our own selves. The French master Gustave Flaubert, when asked where he found the model for the central tragic figure of Emma in his novel, *Madame Bovary*, is said to have replied, "Madame Bovary? C'est moi." Certainly Flaubert's horror of life is embodied in his book. The novel stands as an example of a proto-recreational.

Even as the Apollo asteroid was rushing toward us, even as we were in mortal danger, I was looking—under Roslyn's direction—to find the meaning of my strange dream in the works of the German philosopher, Edmund Husserl. Husserl touched something in my soul, for he rejects all assumptions about existence, preferring the subjectivity of the individual's perceptions as a way in which we experience the universe.

A clever man, Husserl. But saying little about what things were really like if our perceptions turned out to be faulty. Or, for instance, if we did not perceive the crisis of an approaching asteroid soon enough.

Running promptly to timetable, P-L6344 struck. By a coincidence, it impacted in the Crater Copernicus, the very crater for which Joyce Bagreist had initially been aiming.

The Moon staggered in its orbit.

Everyone in Ivy fell down. Hermione, groping blindly for her stick, clutched Molly Levaticus's hairy little pudendum and shrieked, "There's a cat in here!"

Many buildings and careers were ruined, including General Willetts'.

Most lunarians took the nearest Bagreist home. Many feared that the Moon would swan off into outer space under the force of impact. I had my work to do. I disliked the squalid cities of Earth. But primarily I stayed on because Roslyn Staunton stayed, both she and I being determined to get to the bottom of my dream. Somehow, by magical transference, it had become her dream too. Our sessions together became more and more conspiratorial.

At one point I did consider marrying Roslyn, but kept the thought to myself.

After the strike, everyone was unconscious for at least two days. Sometimes for a week. The color red vanished from the spectrum.

Another strange effect was that my dream of the golf ball lying on its side faded away. I never dreamed it again. I missed it. I ceased visiting Roslyn as a patient. Since she no longer played a professional role in my life, I was able to invite her out to dine at the Earthscape Restaurant, where angelfish were particularly good, and later to drive out with her to inspect the impact site, once things had cooled down sufficiently.

Kilometers of gray ash rolled by as the car drove us westward. Plastic pine trees had been set up on either side of the road, in an attempt at scenery. They ceased a kilometer out of town, where the road forked. Distant palisades caught the slant of sun, transforming them into spires of an alien faith. Roslyn and I sat mute, side by side, pursuing our own thoughts as we progressed. We had switched off the radio. The voices were those of penguins.

"I miss Gauguins," she said suddenly. "His vivid expressionist color. The bloody Moon is so gray—I sometimes wish I had never come here. Bagreist made it all too easy. If it hadn't been for you . . . "

"I have a set of Gauguin paintings on slides. Love his work!"

"You do? Why didn't you say?"

"My secret vice. I have almost a complete set."

"You have? I thought he was the great forgotten artist."

"Those marvelous wide women, chocolate in their nudity. The dogs, the idols, the sense of a brooding presence . . ."

She uttered a tuneful scream. "Do you know *Vairaumati Tei Oa*? The woman smoking, a figure looming behind her?"

"And behind them a carving of two people copulating?"

"God, you do know it, Terry! The sheer color! The sullen joy! Let's stop and have a screw to celebrate."

"Afterward. Fine. His sense of color, of outline, of pattern. Lakes of red, forests of orange, walls of viridian . . ."

"His senses were strange. Gauguin learned to see everything new. Maybe he was right. Maybe the sand is pink."

"Funny he never painted the Moon, did he?"

"Not that I know of. It could be pink too."

We held hands. We locked tongues in each other's mouth. Our bodies forced themselves on each other. Craving, craving. Starved of color. Cracks appeared in the road. The car slowed.

My thoughts ran to the world Paul Gauguin had discovered and—a different matter—the one he opened up for others. His canvases were proof that there was no common agreement about how reality was. Gauguin was Husserl's proof. I cried my new understanding to Roslyn. "Reality" was a conspiracy, and Gauguin's images persuaded people to accept a new and different reality.

"Oh God, I am so happy!"

The road began to hump. The tracked vehicle went to dead slow. In a while it said, "No road ahead," and stopped. Roslyn and I clamped down our helmets, got out and walked.

No one else was about. The site had been cordoned off, but we climbed the wire. We entered Copernicus by the gap which had been built through its walls some years previously. The flat ground inside the crater was shattered. Heat of impact had turned it into glass. We picked our way across a treacherous skating rink. In the center of the upheaval was a new crater, the P-L6344 crater, from which a curl of smoke rose, to spread itself over the dusty floor.

Roslyn and I stood on the lip of this new crater, looking down. A crust of gray ash broke in one place, revealing a red glow beneath.

"Too bad the Moon got in the way . . . "

"It's the end of something . . . "

There was not much you could say.

She tripped as we made to turn back. I caught her arm and steadied her. Grunting with displeasure, Roslyn kicked at what she had tripped on. A stone gleamed dully.

She brought over her handling arm. Its long metal fingers felt in the churned muck and gripped the object—not a stone. It was rhomboidal—manufactured. In size, no bigger than a vacuum flask. Exclaiming, we took it back to the car.

The P-L6344 rhomboid! Dating techniques showed it to be something over two and a half million years old. It opened when chilled down to 185:333K.

From inside it emerged a complex thing which was at first taken for a machine of an elaborate, if miniature, kind. The machine moved slowly, retracting and projecting series of rods and corkscrew-like objects. Analysis showed it to be made of various semi-metal materials, such as were unknown to us, created from what we would have called artificial atoms, where semiconductor dots contained thousands of electrons. It emitted a series of light flashes.

This strange thing was preserved at 185:333K and studied.

Recreationals got in on the act because research was funded by treating this weird object from the remote past as a form of exhibition. I was often in the laboratory area. Overhearing what people said, as they shuffled in front of the one-way glass, I found that most of them thought it was pretty boring.

At night, Roslyn and I screamed at each other about "the

tourists." We longed for a universe of our own. Not here, not on the Moon. Her breasts were the most intelligent I ever sucked.

Talking to Roslyn about this strange signaling thing we owned, I must admit it was she who made the perception. "You keep calling it a machine," she said. "Maybe it is a kind of a machine. But it could be living. Maybe this is a survivor from a time when the universe did not support carbon-based life. Maybe it's a pre-biotic living thing!"

"A what?"

"A pre-life living thing. It isn't really alive because it has never died, despite being two million years in that can. Terry, you know the impossible happens. Our lives are impossible. This thing delivered to us is both possible and impossible."

My instinct was to rush about telling everyone. In particular, telling the scientists on the project. Roslyn cautioned me against doing so.

"There must be something in this for us. We may be only a day or two ahead of them before they too realize they are dealing with a kind of life. We have to use that time."

My turn to have a brainwave. "I've recorded all its flashes. Let's decode them, see what they are saying. If this little object has intelligence, then there's a meaning awaiting discovery . . . "

The universe went about its inscrutable course. People lived their inscrutable lives. But Roslyn and I hardly slept, slept only after her sharp little hips had ground into mine. We transformed the flickering messages into sound, we played them backward, we speeded them up and slowed them down. We even ascribed values to them. Nothing played.

The stress made us quarrelsome. Yet there were moments of calm. I asked Roslyn why she had come to the Moon. We had already read each other, yet did not know the alphabet.

"Because it was easy just to walk through the neighboring Bagreist, in a way my grandparents could never have imagined. And I wanted work. And—"

She stopped. I waited for the sentence to emerge. "Because of something buried deep within me."

She turned a look on me that choked any response I might make. She knew I understood her. Despite my job, despite my career, which hung on me like a loose suit of clothes, I lived for distant horizons.

"Speak, man!" she ordered. "Read me."

"It's the far perspective. That's where I live. I can say what you say, 'because of something buried deep within me.' I understand you with all my heart. Your impediment is mine."

She threw herself on me, kissing my lips, my mouth, saying, "God, I love you, I drink you. You alone understand—"

And I was saying the same things, stammering about the world we shared in common, that with love and mathematics we could achieve it. We became the animal with two backs and one mind.

I was showering after a night awake when the thought struck me. This pre-biotic semi-life we had uncovered, buried below the surface of the Moon for countless ages, did not require oxygen, anymore than did Roslyn's and my perceptions. What fuel, then, might it use to power its mentality? The answer could only be: *Cold!*

We sank the temperature of the flickering messages, using the laboratory machine when the place was vacated during the hours of night. At 185:332K, the messages went into phase. A degree lower, and they became solid, emitting a dull glow. We photographed them from several angles before switching off the superfrigeration.

What we uncovered was an entirely new mathematical mode. It was a mathematics of a different existence. It underpinned a phase of the universe which contradicted ours, which made our world remote from us, and from our concept of it. Not that it rendered ours obsolete: far from it, but rather that it demonstrated by irrefutable logic that we had not understood how small a part of totality we shared.

This was old gray information, denser by far than lead, more durable than granite. Incontrovertible.

Trembling, Roslyn and I took it—again at dead of night, when the worst crimes are committed—and fed its equations into the Crayputer which governed and stabilized Luna. It was entered and in a flash—

We climbed groaning out of the hole. Here was a much larger Bagreist. As we entered into the flabby light, we saw the far perspective we had always held embedded in us: that forlorn ocean, those leaden waves, and that desolate shore, so long dreamed about, its individual grains now scrunching under our feet.

Behind us lay the ball which had been the Moon, stranded from its old environment, deep in its venerable age, motionless upon its side.

We clasped each other's hands with a wild surmise, and pulled ourselves forth.

Creative Destruction

EDWARD M. LERNER

Edward M. Lerner [www.sfwa.org/members/lerner] is a physicist and computer scientist. He says he's paid to find "solutions for Internet service providers, satellite-based Earth observation, and other messy-but-fun problems. I like to think that background lends realism and depth to my fiction." He published his first story (in Analog, *where most of his fiction has appeared) in 1991. His novel* Probe *also came out in 1991. He has published only seven stories, including a series of four novelettes, in* Artemis *and* Analog, *that tell the story of an InterstellarNet, where interspecies dealings are radio-based. "In an Edward M. Lerner story," says Jay Kay Klein in Lerner's Biolog, "hi-tech never stands still. Computers continue to evolve, being still very new. Neural interfaces, AI, and ever-more-ubiquitous networks have to affect social and economic structures. A writer must take the exponential growth of technology into account—or explain what stopped it."*

"Creative Destruction," published in Analog, *is built like a compressed novel. The characterization is condensed; the story moves with a fast pace, and the illusion of a world much bigger than the story is created. The tale starts out in the noir detective mode—a man must investigate an old friend's mysterious death. It rapidly gets larger scale as it goes along, until it is full-blown hard SF space opera.*

1

There is no good way to learn that your best friend has died.

Justin Matthews stared at the now-blank screen of his personal digital assistant, numb from an overload of unwelcome information.

"Alice didn't suffer," Alicia's lawyer had said. Justin hoped the attorney had a better grasp of his other facts than he had of his client's name. "Hit and run. There hasn't been an arrest yet."

Dead at the age of thirty-seven—his age, too—in a senseless accident. In his mind's eye, Alicia Briggs remained twenty-three, their ages when they'd met at MIT. In truth, she hadn't changed much for as long as Justin had known her: short, wiry, and athletic. Mischievous. She was an extraordinarily accomplished software engineer who tackled projects with a tenacity that approached the mythical.

How could she be gone?

To the extent that, in his shock, his thoughts had focus, he wondered mostly how in an era of automated cars such an accident could have happened. He worried about how her sister was taking the awful news. He tried to grasp the notion of life without his longtime friend.

Those sad reflections left only one corner of his mind to consider an oddity: why on Earth had Alicia named him the executor of her estate?

Technomics: the synergistic combination of the engineering and economic sciences. Technomists seek to understand the economic impacts of major technological changes of the past and to predict the consequences of prospective new technologies. Technomists are employed in government and industry.

Xenotechnomics, a prominent sub-specialty within the discipline, focuses on the economic implications of possible radio-based technology exchanges with humanity's extra-terrestrial trading partners. See related entry, "Interstellar Commerce Union."

—Internetopedia

Countryside vanished past the express-train windows at 500 kph, too fast for details to be discernible even had Justin's attention been directed toward the scenery. It wasn't. He was focused instead on the screen of his personal digital assistant. The whisper-soft quiet of the maglev train was interrupted only by his occasional spoken requests to the PDA to navigate through data or download new files.

A spidery bridge caught his eye as the train whipped across. "Leo supersteel," he identified reflexively. As the staff xenotechnomist for ISI, Interplanetary Space Industries, he was highly attuned to applications of ET technology.

"Too broad a topic," answered the PDA. "Please refine your query."

"Cancel request." Justin smiled at his reflection in the train window. Far above the blur of farmland, sun glints from hundreds of aircraft caught his eye. The high-density, crisscrossing highways in the sky were made practical by—he managed not to vocalize this thought—Aquarian flight-control algorithms. The high-temp superconducting magnets that helped make this train possible: Centaur technology. The ultra-light, high-energy-density fuel cells that powered the train: another Leo innovation.

A discrete trill from the PDA announced an incoming e-mail, interrupting Justin's woolgathering. The tone pattern told him the communication was personal, rather than ISI-related. His mind wasn't on work today anyway. "Display new message."

"Request approval to decrypt." On the screen only the send and receive addresses were in plaintext. He knew who he was, and the indicated sender was a popular e-mail anonymizer service. The real sender's identity was, presumably, shown inside the encrypted message.

Strange. His business e-mail was often encrypted; his personal messages rarely were. Pressing his right index finger to a sensor pad, he enunciated softly, "Go for it." His words, fingerprint, and voiceprint together authorized the conversion.

"Justin . . . if you're not seated, find a chair," said Alicia's image on the PDA screen.

"Stop." Here he was, the reluctant executor, en route from his Richmond home to Boston for Alicia's funeral—and here was an e-mail purportedly from her. Although the nearest passenger was across the aisle and two rows away, Justin was uncomfortable airing on a public conveyance what might be Alicia's final words. He put in his earpiece. "Play from the beginning."

"Justin . . . if you're not seated, find a chair." She flashed a half-wry, half-weary smile. "Delivery of this e-mail means that something has gone badly wrong, that I've been unable to reset the timer that controls the message's release. The cause of my unavailability may be totally innocent, however unpleasant the implied mishap is for me. It may not. To help you decide which is true, I've attached some items that should be useful.

"I'm truly sorry to say this in so impersonal a manner, but I've always cherished our friendship. I know I can trust you to do the right thing, whatever this situation turns out to be."

He displayed the three attachments. The first was a net address that he recognized, that of a data archival service. She presumably kept backup files there. Next came a user ID/password pair for access to the archive.

The final, and by far the largest, item looked like gibberish. It was labeled as her private encryption key, and with it he could impersonate her, could legally obligate her, any-where on the net. If this really *was* her private key, and not some sort of sick joke.

All keys look alike, like random nonsense, so there was really only one way to be sure. He needed to test the key.

Security keys came in pairs. One key was called private and (normally) kept secret, under personalized biometric protection. Justin stored his private key on his PDA, accessi-ble only via a fingerprint scan, a code phrase, and a voice-print match. The second, or public, key was published to the net. Anyone could send Justin a confidential message by scrambling a plaintext using his public key; only someone who knew his private key could recover that message. It worked both ways: a message encrypted with a private key could be decrypted with the corresponding public key. In the latter case, the mechanism served as a digital signature.

Justin encoded a test message with Alicia's supposed pri-vate key. He had his PDA decode the result with Alicia's published public key. The resulting file matched the one with which he'd started. He repeated the decryption using several different public-key repositories. The outcome was unchanged.

Justin didn't much care for any of the logical explana-tions for his test findings. Once more he found himself staring at the countryside as it streamed by. Alicia was a hacker for hire, and one of the best in the solar system at that. Either the e-commerce infrastructure of the world had been compromised—and how was *that* for paranoid thinking?—or someone had sent him Alicia's private key.

It was simply not possible that his friend had innocently lost control of her private key. To take her message at face value meant believing that she'd implemented the fail-safe delivery of her private key. If so, something had had her very worried. To doubt the message but accept that the attach-ment was her private key would imply that the key had been coerced from her with intent to mislead him. Again, hard to believe.

What had she been up to?

Justin suspected that once he had the answer to that question he would also understand why she'd named him as her executor.

2

Alicia's memorial was held in the chapel of a funeral home, amid hushed whispers and sad, soft background music. Her parents had died years earlier in a plane crash; her only close relative was a sister, Barbara, who had flown in from L.A. Most of those in attendance seemed to be Alicia's neighbors or local friends; they chatted amongst themselves, leaving Barbara seated alone in the chapel's front row.

Barbara rose as Justin approached. Each gave the other a hug. "I'm so very sorry for your loss."

"Thank you, Justin." Subtract two inches of height and add some curl to her hair and the visual result would be Alicia. "And I'm sorry for you, too. I know how close you and my sister were."

"She was a special person." True, but hardly sufficient. Still, he didn't know what else to say.

The silence stretched awkwardly. "I'd like to ask you a question," she said finally. "How should I put this? Were you and Alicia more than just friends?"

His long-ago suitemates in the grad dorm had badgered him into wondering whether the relationship had any such potential. He'd asked Alicia if she felt any chemistry between them. Alicia's answer: "Yes, but it's all inorganic." She'd been right.

"No, Barbara. We were too much alike for anything beyond friendship to work for us."

"Then can you explain why Alicia went outside of the family for an executor?"

Outside the family meant: not her. Justin shook his head slowly. "I wish I did know."

Interstellar Commerce Union: the administrative body within the United Nations with responsibility for oversight of humanity's commercial communications with extraterrestrial species. The ICU reviews and must approve all candidate technologies for import, having as its primary goal the avoidance of unintended and unanticipated economic disruptions (such as the energy glut that followed the initial ET contact). See related entry, "Lalande Implosion." The ICU also authorizes all technology exports to other solar systems.

—Internetopedia

An armada of sail- and powerboats swarmed in Boston Harbor like so many bathtub toys in the eighteenth-floor perspective from Alicia's new condo. Justin had not been able to visit in person since she'd moved here; the VR tour he had gotten hadn't done the place justice. He'd known she was very good at what she did, but he had not realized quite how well it paid. Not that the money would do her any good now.

"Where's Allie's computer?"

Justin turned. Barbara used the childhood nickname that Alicia had hated. "I wouldn't know where she kept it."

"I *do* know where she had it," said Barbara, pointing. She had accepted his invitation to help inventory the things in the condo. "I used it the last time I visited. It's not here."

Justin rubbed his nose thoughtfully. Per Alicia's lawyer, her PDA had not been found at the accident scene. He didn't much care for the pattern. "Is anything else missing?"

Barbara walked from room to room. Drawers and cabinet doors squeaked and slammed. "That I notice, the living-room 3-V and an *objet d'art* or two."

"Jewelry? Silver?"

"They're here. Ditto an envelope with about fifty dollars in a kitchen drawer."

Alicia and her junk-food habit. She was always prepared for an emergency pizza delivery. Too wordy: she was always prepared, period . . . witness her postmortem e-mail. "It seems like someone broke in to steal the computer, then took a few other obvious things to make it look like an ordinary burglary. The net notice of Alicia's memorial service would have told whomever when the apartment was likely to be empty."

Barbara leaned against the dining room table. "But *why*, Justin?"

He thought again about Alicia's final e-mail. "I don't know yet . . . but I will."

The Boston police were quite disinterested in Justin's call. Nonviolent break-ins were far down their priority list. He was given a case number and the advice to change the lock and call Alicia's insurance company. They promised to dust for fingerprints, but would not commit to a date. If that visit was ever to happen, about which he had serious doubts, they would see the building superintendent for access to Alicia's unit.

He encountered business records in a filing cabinet before he found any insurance papers. The drawer held invoices and bill-collection histories, one hanging folder per company. The invoices were for unnamed "professional services rendered."

To his surprise, there was no ISI file. He knew for a fact that she'd consulted for his employer. Justin's PDA sat open from his inquiry to the unhelpful police. "Display twenty largest global megacorporations. List alphabetically." His eyes swiveled between the screen and the open file drawer. Within the top twenty, two were missing: ISI and Trans-Solar Corporation.

TSC, like ISI, was a wildly successful megaconglomerate with interplanetary scope. To call TSC an archenemy of ISI would be simplistic, since the two corporations partnered as often as they competed. The solar system was certainly big enough for the both of them.

The absence of an ISI file gave the false impression that she'd never consulted for ISI; he was equally skeptical that she'd never had dealings with TSC.

Alicia's computer and PDA were both gone. Given her last e-mail, he had hopes that her softcopy files were not.

Justin's Boston hotel catered to business travelers, providing fast wireless broadband capability to each suite. Around bites of room-service pepperoni pizza ordered in Alicia's honor, he directed his PDA to open a secure connection with her archival service. Unsurprisingly, even the names of the backed-up folders and files were encrypted.

"Number and size of files?"

"Thirty-seven folders, containing seven hundred forty-three files. Approximately eighty-four gigabytes."

"Decrypt folder names. Display the names of all folders in the archive, sorted by last modification date."

The most recently updated folders were named ISI and TSC.

Both folders had last been changed a week earlier, three days before Alicia's death. The next day, she'd seen her lawyer to execute a codicil to her will, replacing her sister's name with Justin's.

The PDA wasn't up to the task of decrypting gigabyte files, and he wasn't up to reviewing them. "Bridge in my home workstation, also on a secure link. Download Alicia's archive there. Leave everything encrypted for now."

3

It was almost midnight when Justin got home from the Richmond train station, but he was too keyed up to sleep. The number of questions about Alicia kept growing. Leaving his suitcase in the hall, he went directly to his den. Setting his PDA on the desk beside his workstation, he asked, "Have all files from Alicia's archive been downloaded?"

The two computers compared notes. "Yes," answered the PDA.

"Display archive configuration." A detailed structure of many files and folders spilled down the screen. "Show the content of the ISI folder in plaintext, newest files first." He got himself a Coke and some peanuts while the workstation cranked away. When this decryption was done he saw nothing unusual. Her last consulting assignment from ISI, work done two years earlier, was something he had himself arranged. The one recent entry was a current org chart, apparently hacked from ISI's intranet. Why had she wanted that information?

"Now show the content of the TSC folder in plaintext, newest files first."

Three months ago, TSC had received an unusual rush order from a small-fry wholesale trading company. The requisition included several expensive, and apparently very specialized, electronics assemblies that were identified only by part numbers. Alicia had been retained to do some basic commercial intelligence gathering: trace the goods to the ultimate end user, and understand how he was using these items. TSC was in part interested in basic market research, but reading between the lines they were more motivated by curiosity about the urgency implied by the contract's huge penalty for late delivery.

Crunching on peanuts, Justin continued to read. Alicia had hacked into the ordering company's mainframe, and identified another trading company that had earlier requested the TSC parts. She'd penetrated Company B, and they, too, were a front. He stopped chewing when he got to a third company: ISI secretly controlled Interplanetary Amalgamated Trading. He had himself, on occasion, bought a competitor's product through Amalgamated's auspices for analysis in ISI's labs. There was no indication that Alicia had gotten into Amalgamated's computers.

Did the soon-after change to her will mean that she'd known about the ISI/Amalgamated link?

An old photo of him and Alicia on a beach getaway sat on a bookshelf. He set it beside the workstation. "Background radio, WZAP." Sometimes soft music helped him think. Sometimes it put him to sleep. He guessed that tonight it would have the latter effect.

"Query: what are the electronics components identified by part number in the TSC folder? Order standard product literature via my personal e-mail account. Standard encryption."

Justin caught himself yawning, and realized that he'd

been doing so for a while. The clock in the corner of the PDA screen read 2:07 a.m. Time, and past time, for sleep. He deleted the decrypted files and went to bed.

4

Aquarians: the popular name for the intelligent species of the Luyten 789-6 solar system, approximately 10.5 light-years from Earth. The name comes from the constellation Aquarius, in which Luyten 789-6 is observed. Aquarians, like earlier-discovered ET species, engage in e-commerce with their interstellar neighbors.

Although Aquarians are well regarded for their advanced computational algorithms, it is interesting to note that they compute mentally rather than by computer. Their chief import from humanity is industrial technology.

—Internetopedia

When his PDA chimed to announce an ISI-internal call, Justin was working through the accumulated backlog from his Boston trip. Over the four-day weekend, his obedient filters had filed for his later attention twenty voice-mails and over three hundred business e-mails.

The top window on the PDA screen at that moment was the abstract of a report from ISI's atmospheric physics department. They were responding to his forwarding of a recently received Aquarian parallel-processing technique. He'd speculated that it might be adaptable to weather forecasting. From their initial results, the computational efficiencies made practical by the Aquarian algorithm would let ISI extend their predictions by up to a day. That would be a huge advantage in marketing forecasts to agribusinesses, fishing fleets, power companies, and commodities speculators.

The PDA chimed again. This time, he glanced at the caller ID: the incoming call was from Arlen Crawford, ISI's VP of Contracts and Justin's boss. ISI, like most large companies, had a single technomist on staff, and Justin had to report to someone. The two men often went weeks without speaking. They went far longer without face-to-face meetings, since Arlen's office was at ISI headquarters in Scotland. "Call accepted."

"Justin? Are you by yourself?" On the display screen, Arlen was wearing a suit jacket and tie. Why the formality?

"Hello, Arlen. Yes, I'm in my office and alone."

"Would you mind closing the door?"

How unusual, Justin thought to himself as he complied. "What can I do for you?"

"I have to ask about something that's rather irregular."

The xenotechnomist said nothing.

"Well, there's no graceful way to bring this up, so I'll just get right to it. Justin, the security department has informed me that you have been in contact with our TSC rivals."

"Oh?"

"I'm told that it was on your short leave of absence. Late last night, actually."

Justin considered. "It sounds like I have been under surveillance. Why is that, Arlen?"

His boss squirmed in his seat. "Nothing of the sort. I'm told that the security people use artificial intelligences to monitor all traffic on the corporate networks. They are curious about a message that you sent last night."

Justin's only recent message to TSC had been the request for product information, and that was via his private e-mail.

"I'd like to know why you contacted TSC."

"It was a personal matter, Arlen. There's no cause for security to be concerned."

"But they *are* concerned."

Anger mounting, Justin wondered if his face was flushed. "How does it happen that the company sees my private e-mail, composed at home using my *personal* digital assistant, and sent over the public network?"

At a loss for words, Arlen glanced off-camera. An unhappy, dark-haired man whom Justin didn't recognize stepped into view behind Arlen's chair. "As I'm sure you know, to transmit even personal messages requires accessing a net directory. Your PDA is apparently set to query an ISI directory server for address lookups."

So Arlen had asked whether Justin was alone while someone observed from an unviewable corner of his own office. What gall! "And you are?"

"Michael Zhang. Corporate security."

"So you would have me believe that security monitors every name lookup to see if any employee is in contact with another company?"

"Yes."

Justin shook his head. "I don't accept that. Ignoring innocent net surfing, I know of a dozen joint ventures that ISI has with TSC. Each such project is a reason for ISI employees to have regular contacts with TSC."

Zhang smiled, but it was not a pleasant expression. "Dr. Matthews, your beliefs are of very little interest to me. The fact that we did notice your message should, however, be important to *you*. Think about that.

"I will expect your prompt explanation as to why that message was sent."

Zhang's finger stabbed down to the top of Arlen's desk. The call window on Justin's PDA froze. "End of transmission."

"Save that call," said Justin. "Every last bit of it."

His PDA made no comment.

"And change your default setting for directory lookup to a public server."

What was going on?

Justin sat tipped back in a kitchen chair, his back against a wall of his dinette. The call from his boss and security made less sense each time he replayed it.

Technomics was a difficult subject; xenotechnomics was even tougher. Mastering his discipline, however, had ingrained in him a useful skill. When he couldn't make sense of what he was looking at, he knew to mentally step back and look at the bigger picture.

So what was the bigger picture here? TSC had retained

Alicia to identify the mysterious purchaser of what Justin now knew were ultra-sensitive radio receivers, items a well-funded radio astronomer might buy. She'd traced the sale to ISI, whether or not she recognized the fact, although his appointment as executor and the current ISI org chart in her archive suggested that she had. She was dead in what might truly be an accident—joyriding with a car's automatics turned off was not unheard of—but the timing was suspicious. The subsequent disappearances of her PDA and workstation were certainly suspicious. Then came the apparent theft of her billing records for TSC and ISI, as if to remove any suggestion that she'd ever had an involvement with either megacorp. Finally, Zhang's comments notwithstanding, Justin didn't accept that ISI could be monitoring every employee for possible access to the TSC net site. Which meant that he personally was under ISI surveillance.

Through metaphorical mists a picture was emerging, but he wasn't sure he believed it. Could he seriously contend that ISI, in which he'd been a happy employee since university, was involved in something so nefarious that it would kill to cover its tracks?

He'd brought the beach snapshot of himself and Alicia into the kitchen. Picking up the picture, he studied her face. "I *will* get to the bottom of this."

She wasn't impressed. Maybe one of the reasons they'd been such good friends was that she didn't impress easily. Most of his college acquaintances had not known how to deal with the near-celebrity of his modestly famous parents or his excess of competence, but Alicia had understood. "Bad luck," she'd once told him. "*Two* parents who played key roles in first contact with the Leos. What are you supposed to do for an encore?"

There was never any question that she'd be successful, if only in the tight-knit community of hackers—the only group whose opinion seriously mattered to her. She'd never approved of his decision to switch majors from computer science to technomics. "You're on the slippery slope to xenotechnomics, and back into the family's alien business."

She'd been right about his direction, wrong about his motivation . . . or at least so he still thought.

"So where did hacking get you?" he finally asked the photo.

An enigmatic smile was his only answer.

"Lock."

Recognizing Justin's voice, his car chirped in acknowledgment. The chirp and the louder sounds of door locks engaging echoed in the cavernous garage beneath his building.

"Dr. Matthews." The stranger stepped from behind a pillar. He was dressed in gangster chic: trenchcoat and fedora. One hand was in his coat pocket, the visible hand was gloved. "May I have a word with you?"

Justin nodded. If the aim of the visit was intimidation, he was duly concerned. He was not, however, too spooked to think. He sidled toward his car, and was rewarded when the stranger, turning to follow, presented a more face-on view to one of the security cameras.

"Dr. Matthews, it would be in your best interest to be expedient in wrapping up your executor duties."

Matthews leaned against his car. "I don't understand."

A humorless smile briefly manifested itself in the shadow of the hat. "Let's not waste time. The names of executors are matters of public record. So are burglary reports."

"I see."

"A certain corporation would prefer that one of its consulting assignments remain confidential. They feel very strongly about this point." The thug took his hand from his pocket. It held a thick envelope rather than the weapon Justin had been expecting. "Naturally the corporation wishes to reimburse the estate for past services rendered. We leave to your discretion the proper disposition of the funds."

Justin took the envelope, wondering as he did so about the etiquette of bribery. Was a verbal response expected? After a long silence, he decided that it wasn't.

"We appreciate your cooperation." With that his visitor turned and strode swiftly from the garage.

*   *   *

Barbara peered dubiously from Justin's living-room 3-V at the stack of hundred-dollar bills before him. The session was doubly encrypted, using his key and hers. The computational load from double decryption made the image jerky.

"I could use a little more input here," he said.

"This payoff is from TSC?"

"My visitor hinted as much, without making it explicit. I don't know that I believe it, though. The mystery is in ISI's clandestine use of the radio parts."

"Are there any hard facts beside the money?"

Alicia's long-ago annoyance at Justin's career change had come partially from the loss of a kindred spirit. Well, he may have decided not to program, let alone hack, for a living, but he'd never lost the knack. The security system in his apartment complex had proven to be no match for his skills.

Justin scanned backward through the garage's surveillance records to an earlier time that evening. His subterfuge in the garage hadn't worked: the thug's face was shadowed by the brim of the hat, his features indistinct. "Mr. X here is a fact, just not a useful one."

"I'm not so sure. Maybe I can do something with that. Send me copies?" She hummed to herself, toggling between the digital frames of his visitor. "I have software that can probably clean up the images."

To his puzzled look she explained, "You know I teach media studies at UCLA. Sometimes I recover old film, dusty reels no one has seen in decades, stuff that's shown up in Hollywood estate sales. That kind of old film is generally in horrible shape. Allie did up some image-enhancement software to my specs. Give me a sec."

The humming resumed, ending after a while in a satisfied, "Ah." She transferred an enhanced image file to Justin's workstation. The face of Justin's caller, slightly blurry but now fairly distinct, popped onto his 3-V.

"Good work." He studied the face, far clearer than it had been live in the dark garage. Would TSC care if their contract with Alicia became public? He saw no reason why they should. "Maybe it's time to play a hunch.

"Computer, log onto the ISI intranet. Download the group

directory for the security department. See if the enhancement from the apartment security system matches anyone there."

His suspect's face was still shadowed and blurry, so he wasn't surprised that the search took a while. He wasn't surprised either to learn that his visitor worked for Michael Zhang.

"There are too many odd circumstances surrounding Allie's death. I can't believe it's an accident," Barbara said.

"I don't know if we can be sure of that yet. What seems clear is that she had discovered something very embarrassing, if not illegal, at ISI. Something *major*. Even if Alicia's death was due only to a traffic accident, these people at ISI, whoever they are, still want to keep their actions secret."

"What actions?"

He shrugged. "I'm working on that."

5

So what was going on at ISI?

That wasn't an easy question. It was a big company, with hundreds, maybe thousands, of projects under way at any time. Justin couldn't possibly be aware of all of them, and surely Alicia had recognized that.

What Alicia *had* known with precision was the type of work he did at ISI: xenotechnomics. He pondered the technologies that the various ETs had disclosed, and how ISI might best leverage them. He tried to infer from what was already known what *else* of value the ETs might have, and then helped lobby the ICU to order that. He tried to anticipate ET responses, to get a jump on competitors who were more passively awaiting the next years-long interstellar messaging cycle.

Huge sums were involved in being first to market with new ET technologies, and in knowing ahead of time what markets to vacate because ET tech was about to make them obsolete. There was also gamesmanship: can you get the

ICU to order specific technologies that ISI might be able to exploit faster than its competitors?

What did ISI secretly ordering TSC radio receivers have to do with any of this?

Sigh. For absence of a better idea, he fell back onto one of his basic principles: if it can't hurt, try it. He was the only xenotechnomist at ISI, but he didn't exactly work alone. He worked routinely with a number of artificial intelligences—AIs. What with his computer-science background, before (as Alicia put it) he'd turned to the dark side, Justin had implemented several personal AIs. Maybe one of them would see what he was missing.

Only none of the AIs knew any more about ISI's interest in radio receivers than did Justin. Damn. To be thorough, he had them run self-diagnostics. All were fine. To be even more thorough, he made a final check. Every system he had ever built maintained a transaction history file, simply good programming practice in case of a system crash or subtle bug. As long as the programs ran smoothly, he had no need to check these files. He hadn't looked at some of the logs for years.

Perhaps he should have looked sooner.

One of his AIs did first-pass translations of messages from ETs. Over the decades, the intelligent species in the nearby solar systems had developed and continued to evolve a common trade language. It was very efficient at conveying mathematically or physically based information, less capable with regard to more abstract concepts like commercial terms. Most people found the language a nuisance to read and write.

"Decode" was, to his mind, still experimental. Certainly its automated translations were often quite curious, and needed his critical review. Justin had made no attempt to keep Decode a secret—it was just something he had written to work more efficiently. On the other hand, he'd not considered it ready for use by anyone other than himself. So who was this Kyle Fletcher whose name was all over Decode's history log?

He queried the company's on-line directory for the name. There were no matches. A consultant then, or a very recent hire. Only one way to find out surreptitiously came to mind. Even in death, Alicia seemed determined to keep him involved in hacking.

When you know you are under surveillance, you don't hack from your office or your home. Justin hit an ATM for cash, bought a calling card with cash at a convenience store three klicks away, then drove to the airport. He used the calling card to rent an hour on one of the net kiosks that catered to travelers. He was glad to see that the rent-a-computer had a keyboard, in part because he didn't care to articulate what he was up to, in part because the airport was so *noisy*.

One of computing's periodic crises, what Justin's father insisted on calling "Y2K, the sequel," had occurred earlier in Justin's career, on January 18, 2038. The venerable Unix operating system measured time's passage by counting the seconds from the onset of 1970—and on Unix Doomsday the seconds counter of the oldest Unix versions had run out of bits and rolled over to zero. The fear was that old Unix applications software would think the date was once more New Year's Day, 1970.

Like the Y2K crisis before it, Unix Doomsday had, for a while, briefly preempted some of the attention of virtually everyone who could spell "computer." At the height of the panic, Justin had been drafted to help validate some of ISI's fixes. In support of this temporary but urgent assignment, he'd been given sysadmin privileges. As sysadmin, he'd encountered several trap doors built into applications—gaping security holes that enabled the vendors to troubleshoot and upgrade their products remotely, over the net. The sysadmin password would surely have been changed many times since then, but Justin suspected that some of the trap doors were still there. He certainly hoped so.

He started with a payroll application that had provided an external interface to an outside paycheck service. No luck: the program must have been updated or replaced. He tried again with a system that he remembered had something to do with scheduling employee travel. That time he succeeded.

Once he had penetrated an ISI mainframe application at the maintenance programmer level, it was easy to gain access to other apps. Kyle Fletcher didn't show up in recruitment records, so he couldn't be a recent hire.

Fletcher did appear on an invoice in ISI's accounts payable. The consultancy doing the billing was not TSC . . . Justin wasn't lucky enough to have that sort of closure.

Fingers flying, he kept drilling down through linked files. At the end of the process, he'd encountered two interesting facts. First, Fletcher was a technology consultant with expertise in several fields, but notably in nanotech research. Second, the requester on the purchase order for Fletcher was the head of ISI security. Mike Zhang again.

ISI had for years shunned investments in nanotech. The company's executives had made it clear that they considered nanotech a laboratory curiosity, too fragile and unpredictable for commercial use. They'd coldly rejected Justin's periodic recommendations for pilot projects that might help nanotech graduate into production.

So why hadn't he been told of the renewed interest in nanotech? Why would security retain the consultant? And why was Fletcher secretly using Justin's ET translation program?

Ignoring the inexplicable security connection, Fletcher *could* conceivably be practicing with the Decode AI to prepare for an alien message. The TSC radio receivers that Alicia had been tracing *could* be of use in hearing an alien message.

It was the secrecy that was so puzzling. Even the most tightly focused ET signal beam became widely dispersed over interstellar distances. Such beam-casts could be received across the whole solar system. For that matter, listening to ET didn't take supersensitive receivers, just a bunch of satellite dishes in an array. That had been true even at first contact, in his parents' time. So, if an incoming ET message couldn't be a secret, why would ISI want to keep their one xenotechnomics expert—himself—out of the loop?

The more Justin learned, the thicker the fog he was trying to penetrate.

6

On the suborbital hop to visit his parents in Geneva, Justin had time to review more of Alicia's files. Most of her clients were Earth-based, but she had several with offices in Earth-orbiting habitats, four headquartered on the Moon, and one each on Mars and in the Belt. Each time a client folder passed muster as noncontroversial, he would send out a notification of Alicia's demise, with request for final payment as appropriate. Sad though this work was, it was a welcome change from the sleuthing in which he had become so unexpectedly mired.

His parents were loitering in their car at the spaceport arrivals area, and they whisked across town to his childhood home. "We're so sad about Alicia," were the first words from Mom's mouth. "Sorry we couldn't get to the funeral."

"I appreciate it. Thanks for sending the flowers, too; that meant a lot to her sister. I understand that you being there wasn't practical. So how was your trip?"

They took the hint that he didn't want to talk about Alicia. "The Moon's an amazing place to visit. We have a few hundred pictures that your father promised to inflict on you. Very nice hotel at Tycho City, too." Discussion of their dream vacation occupied the rest of the drive.

Justin tossed his travel bag into his old room, then started shifting cans in the pantry in search of a snack.

"Quit foraging," called Dad from the living room. "There's finger food on the coffee table, and you know where the bar is. We'll go out for dinner in a bit, though what with the time-zone difference, you're free to call it lunch."

He joined his parents. Munching on yogurt-covered pretzels, he glanced around the living room. Same old furniture. Same spectacular view of Lake Geneva. Lots of familiar framed photos and downloaded digital art, mostly of planets and moons spanning the solar system, plus not a few shots of Mom and/or Dad with renowned personages.

That wasn't fair. Mom and Dad were themselves famous—it was just hard to think of one's own parents in that way. Bridget Satterswaithe, not yet Matthews, had been Secretary-General of the International Telecommunications Union, the ITU, when humanity detected the initial message from the Leos and learned that we were not alone. She'd been tapped to form the Interstellar Commerce Union, a new UN agency, and been the ICU's first Secretary-General. Dean Matthews had ping-ponged between lead-technologist roles at aerospace and telecomm companies and senior positions at the ITU and ICU. Both elder Matthews still occasionally consulted for the ICU.

Amid the familiar images were some new ones. Justin gravitated toward a striking view of Jupiter with several of its moons in transit. For years, that large display unit had been dedicated to previews of the lunar vacation. "Your next jaunt?"

"One can dream," answered his mother. "These things take years of planning."

Jupiter and years of planning. . . . As he stared at the little marble that was Europa, the room seemed to recede.

ISI was the original winner of the base operations contract for Europa from the United Nations Aeronautics and Space Administration. The proposal from ISI had been so much lower than any other bidder that it had been a minor scandal within the company; Justin could never figure out why someone had wanted the UNASA contract that badly. ISI had serviced the base's environmental systems; flown shuttles between Earth and Europa with supplies and for staff rotations, managed the Earth/Europa comm link as a subset of the corporate interplanetary net; and overseen a fleet of robotic Jupiter probes. UNASA-funded scientists ran the labs at the base, researched Europa itself, and did most of the on-site data analysis.

A few years later, and just as inexplicably, ISI had asked for *way* too much when the UNASA contract was up for a recompete. Solar Services Corporation had held the contract for Europa base ever since. Almost to a man, the ISI staff on Europa had accepted the winner's employment offers—princely retention bonuses cost SSC much less than they would have paid to send new staff halfway across the solar system.

The ISI security goon in Justin's garage had posed as another company's representative. Was ISI's seemingly inexplicable bidding strategy toward the Europa base contract an elaborate way to plant disavowable staff on Europa? If so, might that long-range ploy relate somehow to the mysterious Kyle Fletcher and the multi-year nature of interstellar trade?

What had seemed to be unrelated facts started to form a pattern. On Earth, there was no need for especially sensitive components to build an ET radio receiver: collections of standard direct-to-home 3-V satellite dishes worked fine. Components like the ones Alicia had been tracing were designed for the largest radio telescopes. Hooked into an interplanetary dish antenna, though, a TSC receiver might well be the best way on Europa to listen clandestinely to ETs.

Who would pay attention to a few no doubt innocently labeled electronics modules on a Europa resupply ship? Upgrading the base's ninety-meter radio dish could be done quietly. That would certainly be less obvious than distributing an array of small antennas across the Europan landscape and doing the integration testing. Upgrading of the receiver electronics could be done with little risk of detection from UNASA scientists at the base.

Had the Europa dish been upgraded years ago? Was the rush order for parts because an in-use receiver had failed?

"Earth to Justin?"

"Sorry, Mom." He rested an arm across the shoulders of both parents. "You can take the boy out of the office. . . . Something you guys said helped me sort out a problem I've been wrestling with.

"Let's go eat. By the way, the schnitzel is on me."

The Europan tie-in for the Alicia situation made a sort of sense, but Justin was working more from inference than evidence.

He tossed and turned in his boyhood bed, feet dangling off the end. The only rationale for a clandestine receiving station was the expectation that a secret signal could be received. The xenotechnomist knew better than almost anyone how valuable ET messages could be. Such messages were the sole basis of the interstellar trade in intellectual property directed by the ICU.

If this theory held water, ISI's conspirators had placed an order with one of the ET species for to-be-determined technology. They'd ignored international law to do so. They might even have killed Alicia to protect their secret. It was an awful concept, but the immense profits to be made from xenotechnology made it credible.

Still, he couldn't get past one problem: the other side of the deal. The known ET species practiced a government-to-government trading policy. How could ISI have gotten ET cooperation with its plot?

The collective wisdom of the four known intelligent species had found no loopholes in the Einsteinian light-speed barrier. All interstellar interactions were by radio transmission.

The closest of the ET species was at Alpha Centauri, about four and a half light-years from Earth; a one-way communication between Sol system and the Centaurs took four and a half years. That meant that any unsolicited offer from the Centaurs of new technology was at least four and a half years old. Suppose that the Centaurs were responding to a secret ISI order, then that illegal request was at least nine years old. If a different set of aliens was involved, the plot had been hatched even longer ago.

Could Justin find evidence that old of the supposed conspiracy?

Lalande Implosion: the regional and industry-specific economic crisis of 2006–2009, during which the price of petroleum collapsed. The crisis was concurrent with, and caused by, the introduction of a practical electrical car. The new electric cars used fuel-cell technology derived from the first-contact message from Lalande 21185 (from the species popularly known as the Leos). Petroleum remains useful as a feedstock for the chemical industry, but production levels and prices never again approached their 2006 levels.

The reduced costs of transportation energy and chemical feedstocks were highly beneficial to most parts of the world economy. Major oil-producing countries and companies were, however, devastated by the rapid and unanticipated reduction in demand. In 2010, the United Nations enacted the Protocol on Interstellar Technology Commerce that established the Interstellar Commerce Union and gave it authority over matters of trans-species technology import and export. See related entry, "Proscribed Technology Transfers."

—Internetopedia

Trying to sleep was futile.

Justin left the elder Matthews a note that he had shopping to do—and he did intend to buy some Swiss chocolate while he was here—and headed for the Geneva spaceport and its net kiosks for travelers. ISI security had made clear that Justin was under observation, and he had no desire to bring his parents to their attention.

He once again used the compromised ISI employee-travel program to obtain sysadmin privileges. As a *faux* sysadmin, Justin easily retrieved the archive history of every ISI program in any way related to xenotechnomics. It seemed that the mysterious Kyle Fletcher had a longstanding relationship with ISI: he had used the Encode AI nine years earlier. The audit log pointed to the input file Encode had used and the output file it had produced.

The kiosk's computer, designed for checking e-mail and web-surfing, couldn't begin to handle the files about which Justin was now very curious. Muttering in frustration, he commanded the ISI system to copy the files to a net-based archive he had opened under an assumed name.

Souvenir candy in hand, he returned to his parents' house. His former bedroom was now normally his father's den; the workstation was more than adequate for his purposes. Trusting to the precautions he had already taken, he went on-line and accessed the talk-to-the-aliens files he'd just copied from ISI. The xenotechnomist was staring at the screen, mouth actually agape, when his parents walked silently up to him.

"I see two violations of UN protocol just on this screen," said his mother. "I'd sure like to know what's going on."

"That's not even the most interesting part," Justin replied. To the workstation, he added: "Scroll to beginning of file. Display new page every minute." Images flashed. His parents, each with decades of experience in interstellar commerce, read the *lingua franca* easily.

"Pause display." Bridget Matthews tapped the workstation screen. "My God. Does that passage say what I think it does?"

Justin swiveled his chair. "If you think the message purports to be from an alien species on Europa, then yes."

Fortified with a large mug of Swiss mocha, Justin brought his parents up to date. "So am I making sense?"

"Tell me if I have this right," said his mother. "ISI, through some fancy maneuvering, placed secret employees on Europa. Those agents surreptitiously upgraded the radio at Europa base to interstellar capability. Nine years ago they used one of your AIs to encode an unauthorized transmission to the Centaurs. In that message they claimed to be a separate species, to have monitored past Earth/Centaur dialogues, and to now be opening their own communications. The fake Europans were therefore able to explain knowing that the Centaurs wanted fusion technology, and that Earth did *not* want nanotech."

"They broadcast UN-proscribed fusion technology, including the design of the superpowerful lasers needed for inertial containment of deuterium/tritium fuel pellets. It's the lasers that the ICU has specifically embargoed, because of their potential use as weapons. And the conspirators requested in return that the Centaurs send Europa their mature industrial nanotech that the UN has refused to order."

To Justin's nod, his father added, "The claimed sensitivity to Earth's desire to avoid imported nanotech . . . oh, what a clever touch. It motivated the request that the Centaurs use a comparatively unattractive freq"—by which he meant a radio frequency with significantly more attenuation than commonly used for interstellar comm—"to reduce the likelihood that anyone but the plotters would hear the signal. ISI will not only obtain revolutionary technology, but they can claim it as indigenous. They'll be able to build patent walls here around the Centaurs' advanced nanotech, to supersede whole industries, and—unlike everything else we've ever learned from the ETs—ISI will be without competitors."

"There must be trillions of dollars at stake." Despite the plot just summarized, his nervous pacing, and his original intent *not* to involve his parents, Justin felt a sense of relief. Alicia had teased him about working in the family business, but there was truth to her jests. Drs. Dean and Bridget Matthews were among the world's top experts on commerce with the various ET races, having literally helped write the book on the subject. Their acceptance of his evidence and inferences meant that the worries preying on his mind were valid.

"Trillions of dollars. I believe they killed Alicia to protect their conspiracy. I can't help but think that they'd do so again."

7

"The horror of Alicia's death aside, might not the worst be over?" asked Bridget Matthews. "We know the frequency on which to listen, lest the Centaurs answer the fake Europans. I think it's time to turn over your findings to the Interstellar Commerce Union."

The question reflected a trust in government that was admirable in a public servant and ennobling in a parent. It seemed impractical in a counterconspirator. "I'm not convinced, Mom. Consider the deviousness involved in setting up Solar Services Corporation as a suspect in case the signal to the Centaurs is discovered . . . a bit of inspired misdirection that may yet protect the ISI masterminds if this goes to trial." Justin shook his head sadly. "No, what we've uncovered so far shows enough planning and chicanery that I suspect there's more to be found."

His mother got up to pace. "Such as?"

"Something more than an unusual frequency to keep from unintended ears the recipe for practical nanotech. Although I can't say how that could be done."

"Jamming," said his father.

"Jamming?"

"How many programmers does it take to change a light bulb?" Dad paused. "Can't be done—it's a hardware problem."

Not that Justin was a programmer any more, or that anyone had used light bulbs since Centaur ultrabright LEDs had been introduced twenty-some years ago. "What hardware problem?"

"I'm stretching a point. Orbital mechanics is the issue."

Dad had architected several satcom constellations and one interplanetary net; when Dean Matthews volunteered something about orbital mechanics or space-based comm systems, Justin took it as gospel—even when he didn't understand it.

"Even I know that interstellar receivers are very directional. To jam an incoming signal would take a space-based transmitter in the same direction as Alpha Centauri. But there are no such transmitters. Alpha Centauri is *way* off the plane of the ecliptic."

"Hence the matter of orbital mechanics."

"Dad . . . I'm running on no sleep, jet lag, and an ocean of coffee."

"Are you familiar with the Ulysses mission? Ancient stuff: launched by NASA in 1990." When no answer came, his father continued. "Isaac: display the mission trajectory for Ulysses." Presumably Isaac Newton, an orbital-mechanics program.

The Jupiter image that had dominated the wall was replaced by a 3-V solar-system cartoon. In that representation, a green thread arced out from Earth to Jupiter—where a bit of geometric magic occurred. The green bent sharply around

Jupiter, in the process twisting almost at right angles to the giant planet's orbit. The trajectory went on to become an elongated oval passing over the sun's polar regions. Dad pointed at the gas giant. "Through clever use of the gravity well, that 1992 Jupiter encounter changed Ulysses' path enough to reach eighty degrees solar latitude."

"Which is proof by example that someone can, if they choose to, put a transmitter into a stable orbit steeply inclined to the Earth's orbital plane." Justin followed some summary links about the displayed mission. "And Ulysses accomplished that maneuver almost purely by choice of the fly-by trajectory—think how much more could be done using a probe with a full load of fuel.

"The message I found in Encode requested a specific response date. ISI could easily have designed a mission to place a transmitter into jamming position. I mean, to put the spacecraft roughly between Earth and Alpha Centauri when the return message was expected."

Dad nodded agreement. "Of course even an orbit that grazes the sight line doesn't *stay* on it . . . especially as the Earth moves. When the time came, the spacecraft would use its engines to keep nudging itself back onto the Earth/Centaur line of sight. The typical ET broadcast lasts a few weeks, providing enough repetitions to assure complete reception—it shouldn't be a problem to carry enough fuel for that."

"You described ISI's probable defensive strategy as jamming. I think they could do better than that." Ignoring his stomach's explicit warning, Justin chugged another cup of now luke-tepid coffee. As the caffeine jolt cleared his thoughts, he went on. "This spacecraft we're imagining, ready to transmit over the Centaur signal . . . it has a receiver, too. To know when to send, when to maneuver, it needs either to hear a 'go' command from the conspirators' base or the Centauri signal directly. Instead of jamming with random noise, which risks detection by, say, an amateur radio astronomer, why not simply beamcast an out-of-phase version of the Centaur signal?"

"That's *good*. Cancel the signal, rather than jam it. That

would work like 'active stealth,' the radar countermeasure—except that the signal to be obscured is the original rather than a reflection. Although the Centaurs' beam will have dispersed to better than solar-system breadth, the cancellation signal need only spread to encompass the receivers on the Earth. From Earth's perspective the signal meant for the 'Europans' won't exist. All the while, the Centaurs' routine transmissions to us continue on the usual freqs."

Mom canted her head thoughtfully. "Are the people who you work for that shrewd?"

Justin strode over to the window and pulled open the drapes. Somehow, it had become midmorning. He gazed down to a slate-gray lake over which, appropriately, a squall was forming. "You can bet on it."

Too hyped and full of caffeine to sleep, Justin returned to the Geneva spaceport and its anonymous net connections. This research session required the exploration of unfamiliar systems and archives, but he persisted. His target: contractually required records from the years when ISI had run Europa base.

The UNASA scientists had initiated twenty-seven unmanned Jupiter missions during ISI's tenure. Exploration is a risky business: five of those probes had failed. Four of the failures were thoroughly documented. The dearth of information about the fifth disappointment stood out by comparison. Concurrent faults in the telemetry and main radio subsystems had left very little for the analysts to work with. The data shortfall from the probe was compounded by a base-side computer glitch that knocked the tracking radars off-line for forty minutes and overwrote many of the prelaunch records. The mainframe problem, at least, had an explanation: spectacularly poor timing for the installation of an operating-system upgrade.

All that could be said with certainty about the probe was that it had disappeared without a trace. ISI had recalled both its base executive and the failed mission's project manager in a futile attempt to placate UNASA.

That disgraced base executive was none other than ISI's current chief of security, Michael Zhang.

*   *   *

When Justin got back to his parents' house, his equally haggard-looking father was on the phone. Apparently Justin was not the only one unable to sleep.

Whoever was on the other end of the connection did most of the talking. "Uh-huh . . . yes . . . OK. You're sure? . . . Well, thanks, Vladimir. I owe you one." Dad stayed seated in a dinette chair, his head resting against the wall. He looked weary.

"Bad news?"

"There are advantages to having been around." Dad's eyes shut as he answered. "Good contacts, for example. I called an old friend—someone whose other friends might be able to do him a big favor. Vladimir Antinov, a Russian general who was a military liaison to the original Lalande task force."

Justin started measuring for one more pot of coffee. The technomist knew what question he would ask if he had had a high-level military connection, especially a retired general of the Russian strategic rocket forces. And Dad's reaction to Antinov's call had not been a happy one. "So military radar confirms an object in jamming position."

Dean Matthews opened his eyes. "This once I would have really liked to have been wrong."

8

Proscribed Technology Transfers: specific interspecies exchanges of technical data that have been barred by one or both parties. These proscriptions are generally justified on grounds of economics (that the introduction of a particular technology would be too disruptive) or public policy (that the technology could shift military/political balances). Each species is left to establish its own technology policy.

Human technology proscriptions are decided upon and enforced by the Interstellar Commerce Union. The ICU, as its name suggests, has jurisdiction only over interstellar

movements of technology. A technology that has been
banned by the ICU for import may be freely researched.

—Internetopedia

Dean and Bridget Matthews had semi-retired without re-
locating from Geneva, where the ICU was headquartered, so
naturally the current Secretary-General was out of town.
More precisely, she was off-planet.

Bridget Matthews had her own first-class connections. Dr.
Hanan al-Fraghani did not question her predecessor's request for an urgent face-to-face meeting, and al-Fraghani's
chief of staff pulled strings to get Justin on the next flight to
the L-5 habitat.

The habitat was located on the Moon's orbit, sixty degrees ahead of that orb. This position, one of two at which
the Earth's and the Moon's gravity fields meet in stable balance, provided a long-term fixed location for the colony. It
also made for a long trip.

Long after the transport's engines fell silent, Justin dozed
in his acceleration chair. Microgravity made him queasy,
and the medicine for space sickness made him groggy.
Vaguely aware that most of the other passengers were moving about the cabin and enjoying the spectacular views of
Earth and Moon, the xenotechnomist kept his eyes shut and
tried to sleep. He wanted to be rested for the upcoming
meeting.

When sleep came, it was troubled. The conspiracy dated
back at least to ISI's lowball bid on the initial Europa base
operations contract. That meant the skullduggery had been
going on throughout his entire tenure at ISI. How could he
have been so oblivious for so long?

Justin tossed and turned in his chair, kept from floating off
by loosely fastened straps. Arlen Crawford, his current boss,
had only been at ISI for four years. Arlen's boss, ISI's present Chief Operating Officer, was a long-term employee. The
COO was a competent but unimaginative administrator—
perhaps a member of a cabal, but unlikely to be its leader.

Justin's semiconscious mind turned to ISI's charismatic

Chief Executive Officer, Wayne LaPointe. One had only to chart ISI's growth during LaPointe's tenure as CEO to know that he was brilliant. He also had a reputation for ruthlessness, and an absolute lack of tolerance for anything short of his concept of perfection.

Despite the management layers that separated him from the CEO, Justin had been at many meetings with LaPointe. That had not seemed odd: xenotechnomics was a driving factor in setting corporate strategy for the aerospace giant. Should the CEO's interest have been a red flag?

A long-ago company party came to mind. How many years past? At least ten, Justin thought. He'd have to dig into some old files to be sure. LaPointe had been present, although at the time he hadn't yet taken the CEO job. About twelve years ago, then, not long after Justin finished school and joined ISI. The festivities were in recognition of a new product rollout. He couldn't exactly remember the project, some early exploitation of Leo superconducting technology.

LaPointe was holding forth about the state of ISI's business amid a gaggle of sycophants. Justin had sought other conversation, mildly turned off by the over-loud laughter at the executive's witticisms. Hearing his name called, he'd turned to see LaPointe gesturing him over.

"Justin. *Wunderkind.* Can we see you for a minute?"

"Sure." What other response could the new hire make?

"We were discussing protectionism. You're against that, right?"

The Matthews household sometimes had the atmosphere of a debating society. It was second nature to wonder about the question. "Are we discussing a specific situation?"

Two of the hangers-on exchanged looks of surprise. Imagine *not* reflexively agreeing to an exec's leading question.

"Old history, Justin. We're discussing old history. The Protocol on Interstellar Technology Commerce, to be precise. The proposal on the floor," and here LaPointe swept his arm grandly to encompass the group, "is that limiting imports of ET technology is protectionist and noncompetitive. As the company xenotechnomist, I felt certain you'd have an opinion."

How could Justin *not* have an opinion? Besides setting the policy that LaPointe had oversimplified, the protocol had also established the Interstellar Commerce Union. Justin's mother was the founding Secretary-General of the ICU. Was it possible that the exec didn't know that about Justin?

He picked his words carefully. "Protectionism has the right denotation but the wrong connotation. I would agree that the ICU charter includes import gatekeeping, to avoid any recurrence of something like the Lalande Implosion."

"Gatekeeping, exactly my point." LaPointe tapped Justin's chest for emphasis. "But, to reverse your phrase, the wrong denotation. The so-called 'Lalande Implosion' would be better described as the Lalande Expansion. Leo fuel cells made transportation *so* much less expensive, and the reduced demand for petroleum made petrochemicals that much cheaper. Introduction of Leo fuel cells was a good thing. The global economy benefited enormously. Only the petroleum companies think otherwise."

Justin didn't want to contradict the executive in a social setting, but intellectual honesty left him no other choice. "I suspect the citizens of many countries would have a different view." He had in mind the economic collapse of most of OPEC, plus significant recessions in Norway and the United Kingdom, during the Lalande Implosion.

Blind chance had just wrought simultaneous conversational pauses in all of the groups scattered across the ballroom. Justin's polite contradiction of LaPointe, ISI's rising star, seemed to hang out there—a most uncomfortable feeling. All eyes in the room now focused on the two debaters.

"What if ISI's labs had invented the new fuel cells? Would you still be in favor of suppressing that technology?"

LaPointe's scenario was hardly analogous. "The protocol says nothing about indigenous research, at ISI or any other human institution. The ICU was intended to consider possible unintended consequences from importing alien technology, something fully developed out there that might be revolutionary or disruptive here."

"The apple doesn't fall far from the tree, I see." The executive threw back his head and laughed. "Well no matter. It's always interesting to hear another opinion."

Hardly, thought Matthews. The protocol and what it stated were a matter of interplanetary law rather than of opinion.

That was the end of the conversation. With a motion that was half a pat on the arm and half a nudge, the executive was past Justin and on his way to another knot of employees.

Seat-back displays showed the approaching L-5 habitat, giving a pilot's-eye-view of the docking. Justin didn't notice the show. He'd awakened from his nap with a renewed memory of the long-ago conversation with the now-CEO of ISI, and an epiphany. LaPointe hadn't innocently fallen into conversation about the protocol and called the newly hired Justin over; the situation had been staged expressly to feel him out about participation in the conspiracy.

In retrospect, Justin's nonrecruitment was both a tribute and an affront. Continuing as ISI's xenotechnomist after failing LaPointe's test was presumably a compliment: it must have inconvenienced the cabal to keep him in the dark. The insult was that the plotters felt that they *could* keep Justin in the dark for year after year.

Sadly, Justin realized that the plotters had been right. Had he not been oblivious to the conspiracy going on around him, Alicia might be alive today. He could tell himself that he'd only been a naive and overachieving twenty-five-year-old on that night, but his conscience was not buying it.

He couldn't bring his friend back, but he could avenge her. And he would. . . .

9

What was now the L-5 habitat had once been an Earth-orbit-crossing, arguably Earth-threatening, nickel-iron asteroid. It had been tracked for eighteen years before space-mining techniques had advanced sufficiently to make it commercially exploitable.

In 2024, Solar Metals, Ltd, obtained the mining concession for the asteroid. The worldlet was permanently and safely parked at the L-5 point—which was as close to Earth as the UN would agree to aim such a massive object—in 2028. By 2036, the once-solid asteroid was a warren of played-out mining shafts.

In 2040, Solar Metals leased the husk of the asteroid to Interplanetary Resorts. Extraction techniques were turned to hollowing out the asteroid; the mining tunnels amounted to a good head start while also providing ready access to most of the interior. The asteroid was reduced to a more-or-less twenty-meter cylindrical shell balanced around its long axis and spun up to simulate a tenth of a gravity on its inner surface. The asteroid had just opened for business as a training facility for would-be Belters and as an extreme resort.

Using the facility in its second capacity, Dr. al-Fraghani was in an abandoned shaft playing at being a colonist when Justin arrived. She met him soon thereafter in the habitat's observation room, which the resort's management had discreetly cleared of all other guests but her aide. The assistant excused himself to leave Justin and the S-G completely alone.

After introductions and a modicum of small talk, al-Fraghani said, "Your mother suggested that I hear you out about something important. She is one of the few people whose advice I always consider seriously. What is on your mind?"

The observation lounge's spartan, lightweight furniture seemed somehow at odds with the stunning celestial display visible through its clear dome. Beyond the dome, a crescent Earth, a gibbous moon, and countless stars spun by each minute. The smartglass window eclipsed the sun on the same rotational schedule.

From his flight bag Justin removed a high-end commercial bug detector. "If you don't mind, I'd like to do a sweep first."

"My aide has done that already, with equipment you wouldn't be able to buy. Now what is so secret?"

He took a deep breath. "I have reason to believe that Interplanetary Space Industries has found a way to circumvent the Protocol on Interstellar Technology Commerce."

Her only answer was an arched eyebrow.

So he summarized the evidence that ISI, impersonating a Europa-based civilization, had ordered proscribed Centaur nanotech technology and paid with equally banned-for-export fusion technology.

She listened intently, whispering occasional comments to her PDA. When he had finished speaking, she settled back gingerly onto a chair—it was easy in the slight gravity of the habitat to bounce. "I understand the concern: that 'Europans' will obtain the nanotech information before the Centaurs could get a recall message from us. We can try to prosecute ISI, not that that's a very satisfying response. Can we prevent Europa base from receiving the signal?"

"I don't see how. The receiver is directional, so we can't jam the signal from anywhere that's not outsystem from Jupiter and close to a line between Jupiter and Alpha Centauri. The only transmitter anywhere near that position is the one I think will be used to keep Earth from hearing the signal.

"We have to assume that the interplanetary communications gear at Europa base is controlled by the conspirators. A radioed appeal for help to anyone on-base that the ICU or UNASA would trust would likely be intercepted and not delivered.

"We can't send in the 'cavalry' fast enough to matter: at maximum acceleration it would take Earth two months to get a ship there, and the nanotech message will likely have been received by then. I'm sorry," Justin concluded, "but we don't appear to have good options."

"You don't paint a pretty picture. I know this idea is draconian, and would inconvenience people who must mostly be innocent, but what about sending military police to enforce a quarantine of everyone on Europa? They would be empowered to impound all computers and data storage on the base."

Justin shook his head. "We'd never be sure we'd found all copies of the data. Remember, a standard one-terabyte archival cartridge is about a cubic centimeter. Copies of the Centaur message could easily be hidden outside the base, and we can hardly search that whole moon. Also, the nanotech information is *so* valuable that the conspirators could pay enormous bribes to any troops sent to enforce a theoretical embargo.

"In any event, I expect that the information will have been radioed from Europa long before a ship could get there to establish a quarantine. The plotters could retransmit the ET message to a Belter habitat or to a ship in space and we'd be none the wiser."

"So you can suggest no way to keep ISI from obtaining this knowledge." It was a summary statement, not a question. Falling silent, al-Fraghani stared out of the dome. At long last, she added, "I appreciate the warning, although it isn't clear yet what advantage that warning provides. This will take some thought."

"We've known for a long time that the Centaurs have nanotech, and the ICU consciously decided not to trade for that knowledge. Were records kept of those deliberations?"

The Secretary-General nodded.

"Those notes will name the countries and industries most opposed to the introduction of advanced nanotech. That should give the ICU a pretty good idea of whom to warn now. I suspect it's a long list."

10

Nanotechnology: the capability to build and control artifacts that are measured in, or have the ability to manipulate matter at, molecular dimensions. To accomplish macroscopically useful results, practical nanotech requires massive numbers of devices. It is generally thought that mass production of nanotech devices would be accomplished via self-replication.

Of the known intelligent species, only the Centaurs claim to have mastered nanotech. The ICU has opted not to import this capability, fearing that a mature nanotechnology could render whole industries obsolete in a short time. While indigenous research on nanotech is legal, and is being actively pursued, progress has been limited.

—Internetopedia

Hollywood Cemetery sits on a hill overlooking the James River, at the point where a massive jumble of rocks ended navigability. The cemetery was the final resting place of three presidents, if one included Jefferson Davis—and here in Richmond, the former capital of the Confederacy, people did. To the dismay of cemetery officials, the grounds had long been a popular rendezvous for students from the nearby campus of Virginia Commonwealth University, without much respect for the posted visiting hours.

Justin and Barbara were in no way associated with VCU, and they did not seek nighttime solitude for the same reason as the earnest young couple that was out of sight but not always out of earshot. The xenotechnomist and his friend sat leaning against the trunk of an ancient oak tree, not far from the iron-fenced enclosure of President Monroe's crypt, the inky blackness of the James spread out before them. Justin had simply found this to be a quiet place for thinking. A new, bright idea was called for: the best and brightest minds at the ICU had been unable to devise any way to counter ISI reception of the anticipated Centaur transmission.

Or more likely, judging by a rushed call from his mother, the now-in-progress transmission. Ten hours earlier, the suspicious object that the Russian space forces had first spotted had changed trajectories. Several course corrections to remain on the Earth-to-Alpha Centauri line of sight had already been observed by military radars.

There were also the barest suggestions of a signal in the suspected frequency band. Dad, who was once more consulting for the ICU, felt that the ISI spacecraft simply intercepted too small a sample of the Centaur signal to calculate an entirely accurate cancellation value. The countersignal was effective enough, however, that—had the ICU not known exactly what to look for—nothing would have been detected. The weakened and mostly canceled signal that remained was entirely unintelligible.

Stars glittered overhead in the crystalline air of Indian summer. One of the near-Earth orbiting habitats arced across the sky. The Moon beckoned.

ISI had, of course, denied knowledge of any unauthorized extrasolar transmissions. They were quick to point out that Solar Services ran the Europa base both when the supposed message had been sent to Alpha Centauri and now. And neither Solar Services nor government agencies seemed able to establish radio communications with Europa. Might the base's big dish be pointing elsewhere?

The limitless sky demanded Justin's attention. By profession he was sympathetic to change. Humanity had survived first contact and the Lalande Implosion, and then thrived. ISI's actions were unconscionable—and he would yet see the appropriate people punished for Alicia's death—but humanity would, once the disruptions had been recovered from, benefit enormously from Centaur nanotech.

Like the fusion technology for which it was being traded, nanotech had turned out to be an enormously complex technical challenge. Earth had needed more than seventy years to advance from the H-bomb to a commercial fusion power plant; human nanotech, after sixty years of lab research, was still forecast to be decades away from practical applications.

How would the new technology be used first? He imagined cell-sized cholesterol disassemblers scuttling around the human circulatory system. He mused about swarms of tiny machines digesting meteors directly into pure-metal ingots and steel I-beams. For whatever reason, neither application held his attention. Then, the Lalande Implosion freshly in his thoughts, and under a starry sky, the Oort Cloud came to mind.

Mankind had yet to visit the Oort Cloud, a vast region beyond Pluto, more for a lack of motivation than any inherent difficulty. Where as the asteroid belt was full of stony and metallic bodies, the cloud was made up of great snowballs of CHON: various compounds of carbon, hydrogen, oxygen, and nitrogen. CHON was the stuff of life, freeze-dried primordial soup, but the remoteness of the cloud had made its vast resources too expensive to exploit. Until now.

Self-replicating nanotech would be the ideal mechanism for converting those snowballs to petrochemicals. Mounting an expedition to the Oort Cloud, locating suitable planetesimals, and nudging them to Earth . . . all of that would take time. Still, a single large CHON body could be converted into petroleum on the scale of the now played-out Saudi oil fields. OPEC could be facing a rerun of the Lalande Implosion for its residual market in chemical feedstocks.

Another near-Earth habitat arced overhead. A shooting star followed. Justin's mind's eye began to visualize planetesimals and how easily they could be guided to the inner Solar System. Use a small fraction of the body itself for reaction mass, with a Leo fuel cell to provide initial power. It wasn't as if their orbits were that stable . . . gravitational perturbations, whether from the planets or passing unseen interstellar objects, often sent planetesimals plunging sunward. When that happened, the objects were called comets.

He pondered aloud. After a while, Barbara interrupted. "Of all of the applications for nanotech, this one seems the least imminent. How long will it take to catch a wannabe comet and do something useful with it? Why are you obsessing on that?"

"Good question." Something about comets had to be significant, had to be bugging his subconscious. What?

Comet-*watching*. NASA and the European Space Agency, before consolidation with their national and regional equivalents into UNASA, had had several comet-chasing missions.

He was both relieved and chagrined to find that even here in the depths of a cemetery his PDA had wireless net access. In deference to the necking couple downhill from them, Justin plugged in an earpiece. "Query: comet-related space probes," he whispered.

A few exchanges between man, digital assistant, and the net, and Justin knew what his subconscious had been yammering about. The last of the comet chasers, the Shoemaker probe, had been conceived of by NASA in 2009, had gone under contract in 2015, and was finally launched 2023. Its glory days were over by 2030, but with two low-budget mission extensions it had continued in limited use until only three years earlier. UNASA's decision to put Shoemaker into a low-energy safe mode had been purely financial.

"Display current position of Shoemaker relative to Earth, Sun, and Alpha Centauri. Superimpose an Alpha Centauri-to-Sol radio beam." An image filled the PDA's tiny screen. "Max brightness and contrast."

Wow. Shoemaker was out beyond Pluto, but still well within the forecast beam from the Centaurs. The probe was nowhere near the conspirators' jamming beam.

The mission profile had been base-lined in 2010. The spacecraft's design had been heavily constrained by the need to receive signals across the solar system from that era's comparatively low-powered transmitters. He retrieved an Internetopedia image of the probe and whistled. Shoemaker's body and instruments were dwarfed by the probe's parabolic antenna. The caption explained that the antenna was unfurled after launch, like a very large umbrella.

"A *very* good question, Barb."

Did Shoemaker have the sensitivity to receive the Centaur signal? Could it be reactivated?

It seemed impossible to keep the secrets of Centaur nanotech from ISI . . . but perhaps there was a way to keep that information from becoming the conspirators' monopoly.

"And I think Shoemaker is the answer."

Epilogue

". . . According to a spokesman for the Boston police, more arrests are anticipated. In other news, ..."

"3-V off," said Justin. The electronics complied. He

turned to Barbara Briggs, seated on the sofa across the room from his armchair. "Not that an arrest will bring back Alicia, but that report does my heart good."

"Me, too. Have you heard how high up ISI's management chain they expect to get?"

"Ex-management. Yesterday the Board of Directors voted in a new CEO, who is already cleaning house. According to usually informed sources," by which he meant the Secretary-General of the ICU, "the FBI and Interpol are now heavily involved. We can credit their encouragement for the sudden interest of the Boston police in investigating your sister's death as possibly something other than a traffic accident. The federal and UK cases for violating ICU protocols will take longer to prepare, but I hear there will be indictments for that, too.

"So, to finally answer your question, I wouldn't want to be Mr. LaPointe right now."

"I miss her, a lot." His guest went to gaze out of his apartment window. "What a damned shame."

Justin stood beside Barbara, a comforting arm around her shoulders. "What a damned shame, indeed."

The Earth spun beneath the space station, the terminator a racing wall of blackness. City lights sparkled across the night side of the planet. Much closer to the observation window, spacecraft ranging from planetary shuttles to deep-space tugs to free-flying microgravity factories to individual workers' vacuum suits sailed in and out of sight.

"It's a view I never tire of," said the Secretary-General of the ICU.

Justin nodded, wondering whether her summons had been in response to his e-mail. al-Fraghani's aide hadn't explained.

"*That*," and the S-G's gesture encompassed the vista spread before them, both earthly and space-based, "is what the ICU is here to protect. What ISI did, what you intervened in response to, put it all at risk. The worst possible outcome would have been the introduction of mature Centaur nanotech in the guise of an ISI monopoly. The industrial free-for-all we will now have instead, using the Centaur message as relayed by Shoemaker, is preferable only by comparison. It's still a nightmare."

The xenotechnomist remained silent.

Still admiring the view, al-Fraghani removed a piece of paper from a pocket. "I'll give you this, Justin. You don't think small thoughts."

Unfolded, he recognized the paper as a hardcopy of his e-mail. "Big problems call for big solutions."

"How ironic that the original manifestation of the big problem is nano-scaled."

She wasn't going to come out and ask, so Justin plunged ahead. "As outlined in my proposal, we have a problem that demands fixing: ICU no longer has a monopoly on interstellar transmitters. ISI has shown that. Other megacorps could be building more transmitters as we speak. The 'we are not human' gambit that ISI came up with could work again. The next time, we might not stumble upon the jammer."

"When we met, you had an equally interesting problem, but no solution." The Secretary-General gently waved his note. "This mentions that you have something to propose."

It irked him as a matter of principle that the best way he'd found to express this concept was an analogy. "Do you ever buy things over the net?"

"Of course . . . oh. *Oh*." She'd seen the dilemma. "So how can ET know which technology orders to honor?"

Justin patted his PDA. "The same way an e-tailer knows which orders to fill. Cryptography. Forgery-proof digital signatures. Public/private key technology.

"In short, we need to send basic e-commerce technology to the Leos, Centaurs, and Aquarians *immediately*. They need to know how to recognize which transmissions to ignore."

"A reasonable solution, but why did you emphasize 'immediately'?"

Engine ignition of a nearby shuttle caught his attention. After watching the spacecraft recede from sight, he answered. "We're in a race. If there *is* another megacorp out there with a transmitter, and it has this idea first, it could teach the ETs to honor only their requests. Or to always reply using encrypted messages that only it can decode."

"A terrible thought." Al-Fraghani shivered. "Yes, I see the need for urgency."

"There's one more tidbit I'd like to include in that urgent message, at least to the Centaurs."

"And what is that?"

Justin pointed out of the observation deck at Jupiter—Europa was too small to see with the naked eye. "I think we owe it to our Centaur friends to explain that there is not, and never has been, a native civilization on Europa."

Sometime in the course of discussing the xenotechnomist's proposal, Secretary-General al-Fraghani became simply Hanan. She insisted that Justin be her dinner guest at the space station's fabled four-star restaurant before taking a shuttle back to Earth. A good dinner was the least, she said, that the solar system owed him.

After oysters Rockefeller, while awaiting their lobster bisque, she said, "You said this morning, 'We have a problem' and again, 'We are in a race.' Does your choice of pronoun imply that you would be open to joining the ICU?"

"I think you'll understand that I felt I had to leave ISI, despite the arrests and the housecleaning that's under way. So, yes: it occurred to me to wonder if the ICU might have use for one more xenotechnomist."

"Hardly just one more xenotech." She paused while the tuxedoed waiter delivered the bisque. "So you've thought about joining the family business."

There was Alicia's recurring comment—accusation—again. She'd once teased Justin that attending grad school in Cambridge, MA, instead of Cambridge, UK, didn't qualify as a declaration of independence.

He tried to seem nonchalant. "If there happens to be a suitable role."

"An interesting new project has come to my attention, as

it happens. You've defined it," al-Fraghani smiled, "and it needs a leader. Are you ready to step up?"

To paraphrase: would Justin accept the challenge of making the solar system hacker-proof? "When can I start?"

He was certain that Alicia would have been proud.

Resurrection

DAVID MORRELL

David Morrell is a bestselling novelist whose first novel,
First Blood *(1972), introduced the character John Rambo,*
later played by Sylvester Stallone in a famous series of films.
Morrell taught at the University of Iowa, Iowa City, as a
professor of American literature, and his debut novel was
followed by other thrillers, filled with espionage, assassina-
tion, and worldwide terrorism, including The Brotherhood
of the Rose *(1984),* The Fraternity of the Stone *(1985),* The
League of Night and Fog *(1987), and* Desperate Measures
(1994). He also publishes occasional horror stories and has
one collection, Black Evening *(1984). While teaching and*
getting a graduate degree at Pennsylvania State University
in the 1960s, he learned a lot about writing from another
faculty member, Philip Klass (who is famous in SF as
William Tenn). So it is perhaps surprising that Morrell's first
SF story was published only this last year, 2001.

"Resurrection" was published in the original anthology
Red Shift, *an ambitious attempt to influence the direction of*
SF by presenting a flagship collection of new work, edited by
Al Sarrantonio. Part of the strength of Red Shift *is that Sar-*
rantonio solicited stories from famous writers new to SF,
such as Morrell and Joyce Carol Oates, and they wrote
them. This story is a strong character piece about people liv-
ing through decades of suspended animation and decades of
new life.

Anthony was nine when his mother had to tell him that his father was seriously ill. The signs had been there—pallor and shortness of breath—but Anthony's childhood had been so perfect, his parents so loving, that he couldn't imagine a problem they couldn't solve. His father's increasing weight loss was too obvious to be ignored, however.

"But . . . but what's wrong with him?" Anthony stared uneasily up at his mother. He'd never seen her look more tired.

She explained about blood cells. "It's not leukemia. If only it were. These days, that's almost always curable, but the doctors have never seen anything like this. It's moving so quickly, even a bone marrow transplant won't work. The doctors suspect that it might have something to do with the lab, with radiation he picked up after the accident."

Anthony nodded. His parents had once explained to him that his father was something called a maintenance engineer. A while ago, there'd been an emergency phone call, and Anthony's father had rushed to the lab in the middle of the night.

"But the doctors . . ."

"They're trying everything they can think of. That's why Daddy's going to be in the hospital for a while."

"But can't I see him?"

"Tomorrow." Anthony's mother sounded more weary. "Both of us can see him tomorrow."

When they went to the hospital, Anthony's father was too weak to recognize him. He had tubes in his arms, his mouth, and his nose. His skin was gray. His face was thinner than it had been three days earlier, the last time Anthony had seen him. If Anthony hadn't loved his father so much, he'd have been frightened. As things were, all he wanted was to sit next to his father and hold his hand. But after only a few minutes, the doctors said that it was time to go.

The next day, when Anthony and his mother went to the hospital, his father wasn't in his room. He was having "a procedure," the doctors said. They took Anthony's mother aside to talk to her. When she came back, she looked even more solemn than the doctors had. Everything possible had been done, she explained. "No results." Her voice sounded tight. "None. At this rate . . ." She could barely get the words out. "In a couple of days . . ."

"There's nothing the doctors can do?" Anthony asked, afraid.

"Not now. Maybe not ever. But we can hope. We can try to cheat time."

Anthony hadn't the faintest idea what she meant. He wasn't even sure that he understood after she explained that there was something called "cryonics," which froze sick people until cures were discovered. Then they were thawed and given the new treatment. In a primitive way, cryonics had been tried fifty years earlier, in the late years of the twentieth century, Anthony's mother found the strength to continue explaining. It had failed because the freezing method hadn't been fast enough and the equipment often broke down. But over time, the technique had been improved sufficiently that, although the medical establishment didn't endorse it, they didn't reject it, either.

"Then why doesn't everybody do it?" Anthony asked in confusion.

"Because . . ." His mother took a deep breath. "Because some of the people who were thawed never woke up."

Anthony had the sense that his mother was telling him more than she normally would have, that she was treating him like a grown-up, and that he had to justify her faith in him.

"Others, who did wake up, failed to respond to the new treatment," she reluctantly said.

"Couldn't they be frozen again?" Anthony asked in greater bewilderment.

"You can't survive being frozen a second time. You get only one chance, and if the treatment doesn't work . . ." She stared down at the floor. "It's so experimental and risky that insurance companies won't pay for it. The only reason we have it as an option is that the laboratory's agreed to pay for the procedure"—there was that word again—"while the doctors try to figure out how to cure him. But if it's going to happen, it has to happen now." She looked straight into his eyes. "Should we do it?"

"To save Daddy? We have to."

"It'll be like he's gone."

"Dead?"

Anthony's mother reluctantly nodded.

"But he *won't* be dead."

"That's right," his mother said. "We might never see him alive again, though. They might not ever find a cure. They might not ever wake him up."

Anthony had no idea of the other issues that his mother had to deal with. In the worst case, if his father died, at least his life insurance would allow his mother to support the two of them. In the unlikely event that she ever fell in love again, she'd be able to remarry. But if Anthony's father was frozen, in effect dead to them, they'd be in need of money, and the only way for her to remarry would be to get a divorce from the man who, a year after her wedding, might be awakened and cured.

"But it's the only thing we can do," Anthony said.

"Yes." His mother wiped her eyes and straightened. "It's the only thing we can do."

Anthony had expected that it would happen the next day or the day after that. But his mother hadn't been exaggerating that, if it were going to happen, it had to happen now. His unconscious father was a gray husk as they rode with him in an ambulance. At a building without windows, they walked next to his father's gurney as it was wheeled along a softly lit corridor and into a room where other doctors waited. There were glinting instruments and humming machines. A man in a suit explained that Anthony and his mother had to step outside while certain preparations were done to Anthony's father to make the freezing process safe. After that, they would be able to accompany him to his cryochamber.

Again, it wasn't what Anthony had expected. In contrast with the humming machines in the preparation room, the chamber was only a niche in a wall in a long corridor that had numerous other niches on each side, metal doors with pressure gauges enclosing them. Anthony watched his father's gaunt naked body being placed on a tray that went into the niche. But his father's back never actually touched the tray. As the man in the suit explained, a force field kept Anthony's father elevated. Otherwise, his back would freeze to the tray and cause infections when he was thawed. For the same reason, no clothes, not even a sheet, could cover him, although Anthony, thinking of how cold his father was going to be, dearly wished that his father had something to keep him warm.

While the man in the suit and the men who looked like doctors stepped aside, a man dressed in black but with a white collar arrived. He put a purple scarf around his neck. He opened a book and read, "I am the Way, the Truth, and the Life." A little later, he read, "I am the Resurrection."

Anthony's father was slid into the niche. The door was closed. Something hissed.

"It's done," the man in the suit said.

"That *quickly*?" Anthony's mother asked.

"It won't work if it isn't instantaneous."

"May God grant a cure," the man with the white collar said.

Years earlier, Anthony's father had lost his parents in a fire. Anthony's mother had *her* parents, but without much money, the only way they could help was by offering to let her and Anthony stay with them. For a time, Anthony's mother fought the notion. After all, she had her job as an administrative assistant at the laboratory, although without her husband's salary she didn't earn enough for the mortgage payments on their house. The house was too big for her and Anthony anyhow, so after six months she was forced to sell it, using the money to move into a cheaper, smaller town house. By then, the job at the lab had given her too many painful memories about Anthony's father. In fact, she blamed the lab for what had happened to him. Her bitterness intensified until she couldn't make herself go into the lab's offices any longer. She quit, got a lesser paying job as a secretary at a real-estate firm, persuaded a sympathetic broker to sell her town house but not charge a commission, and went with Anthony to live with her parents.

She and Anthony spent all their free time together, even more now than before the accident, so he had plenty of opportunity to learn what she was feeling and why she'd made those decisions. The times she revealed herself the most, however, were when they visited his father. She once complained that the corridor of niches reminded her of a mausoleum, a reference that Anthony didn't understand, so she explained it but so vaguely that he still didn't understand, and it was several years before he knew what she'd been talking about.

Visiting hours for the cryochambers were between eight and six during the day as long as a new patient wasn't being installed. At first, Anthony and his mother went every afternoon after she finished work. Gradually, that lessened to every second day, every third day, and once a week. But they didn't reach that point for at least a year. Sometimes, there were other visitors in the corridor, solitary people or incomplete families, staring mournfully at niches, sometimes leaving small objects of remembrance on narrow tables that the company had placed in the middle of the corridor: notes, photographs, dried maple leaves, and small candles shaped like pumpkins, to mention a few. The company placed no names on any of the niches, so visitors had used stick-on plaques that said who was behind the pressurized door, when he or she had been born, when they had gotten sick, of what, and when they had been frozen. Often there was a bit of a prayer or something as movingly simple as "We love you. We'll see you soon." Here and there, Anthony noticed just a name, but for the most part the plaques had acquired a common form, the same kind of information and in the same order as over the years a tradition had been established.

Over the years indeed. Some of the people in the niches had been frozen at least *twenty-five* years, he read. It made him fear that his father might never be awakened. His fear worsened each time his mother came back from visiting his father's doctors, who were no closer to finding a cure for his sickness. Eventually his mother took him along to see the doctors, although the visits grew wider apart, every other month, every six months, and then every year. The message was always depressingly the same.

By then, Anthony was fifteen, in his first year of high school. He decided that he wanted to become a doctor and find a way to cure his father. But the next year his grandfather had a heart attack, leaving a small life insurance policy, enough for his mother and his grandmother to keep the house going but hardly enough for Anthony's dreams of attending medical school.

Meanwhile, his mother began dating the sympathetic broker at the real-estate firm. Anthony knew that she couldn't be expected to be lonely forever, that after so much time it was almost as if his father were dead and not frozen, and that she had to get on with her life. But "as if his father were dead" wasn't the same as actually being dead, and Anthony had trouble concealing his unhappiness when his mother told him that she was going to marry the broker.

"But what about Dad? You're still married to *him*."

"I'm going to have to divorce him."

"No."

"Anthony, we did our best. We couldn't cheat time. It didn't work. Your father's never going to be cured."

"No!"

"I'll never stop loving him, Anthony. But I'm not betraying him. He's the same as dead, and I need to live."

Tears dripped from Anthony's cheeks.

"He'd have wanted me to," his mother said. "He'd have understood. He'd have done the same thing."

"I'll ask him when he wakes up."

When Anthony became eighteen, it struck him that his father had been frozen nine years, *half* of Anthony's life. If it hadn't been for pictures of his father, he feared that he wouldn't have been able to remember what his father had looked like. No, not *had* looked like, Anthony corrected himself. His father wasn't dead. Once a new treatment was discovered, once he was thawed and cured, he'd look the same as ever.

Anthony concentrated to remember his father's voice, the gentle tone with which his father had read bedtime stories to him and had taught him how to ride a bicycle. He remembered his father helping him with his math homework and how his father had come to his school every year on Career Day and proudly explained his job at the lab. He remembered how his father had hurried him to the emergency ward after a branch snapped on the backyard tree and Anthony's fall broke his arm.

His devotion to his father strengthened after his mother remarried and they moved to the broker's house. The broker turned out not to be as sympathetic as when he'd been courting Anthony's mother. He was bossy. He lost his temper if everything wasn't done exactly his way. Anthony's mother looked unhappy, and Anthony hardly ever talked to the man, whom he refused to think of as his stepfather. He stayed away from the house as much as possible, often lying that he'd been playing sports or at the library when actually he'd been visiting his father's chamber, which the broker didn't want him to do because the broker insisted it was disloyal to the new family.

The broker also said that he wasn't going to pay a fortune so that Anthony could go to medical school. He wanted Anthony to be a business major and that was the only education he was going to pay for. So Anthony studied extra hard, got nothing but A's, and applied for every scholarship he could find, eventually being accepted as a science major in a neighboring state. The university there had an excellent medical school, which he hoped to attend after his B.S., and he was all set to go when he realized how much it would bother him not to visit his father. That almost made him change his plans until he reminded himself that the only way his father might be cured was if he himself became a doctor and *found* that cure. So, after saying good-bye to his mother, he told the broker to go to hell.

He went to college, and halfway through his first year, he learned from his mother that the lab had decided that it was futile to hope for a cure. A number of recent deaths after patients were thawed had cast such doubt on cryonics that the lab had decided to stop the monthly payments that the cryocompany charged for keeping Anthony's father frozen. For his part, the broker refused to make the payments, saying that it wasn't his responsibility and anyway what was the point since the freezing process had probably killed Anthony's father anyhow.

Taking a job as a waiter in a restaurant, sometimes working double shifts even as he struggled to maintain his grades, Anthony managed to earn just enough to make the payments. But in his sophomore year, he received a notice that the cryocompany was bankrupt from so many people refusing to make payments for the discredited process. The contract that his mother had signed indemnified the company against certain situations in which it could no longer keep its clients frozen, and bankruptcy was one of those situations.

Smaller maintenance firms agreed to take the company's patients, but the transfer would be so complicated and hence so expensive that Anthony had to drop his classes and work full-time at the restaurant in order to pay for it. At school, he'd met a girl, who continued to see him even though his exhausting schedule gave him spare time only at inconvenient hours. He couldn't believe that he'd finally found some brightness in his life, and after he returned from making sure that his father was safely installed in a smaller facility, after he resumed his classes, completing his sophomore and junior year, he began to talk to her about marriage.

"I don't have much to offer, but . . ."

"You're the gentlest, most determined, most hardworking person I've ever met. I'd be proud to be your wife."

"At the start, we won't have much money because I have to pay for my father's maintenance, but . . ."

"We'll live on what *I* earn. After you're a doctor, you can take care of me. There'll be plenty enough for us and our children *and* your father."

"How many children would you like?"

"Three."

Anthony laughed. "You're so sure of the number."

"It's good to hear you laugh."

"You make me laugh."

"By the time you're a doctor, maybe there'll be a cure for your father and you won't have to worry about him anymore."

"Isn't it nice to think so?"

Anthony's mother died in a car accident the year he entered medical school. Her remarriage had been so unsatisfying that she'd taken to drinking heavily and had been under the influence when she veered from the road and crashed into a ravine. At the funeral, the broker hardly acknowledged Anthony and his fiancée. That night, Anthony cried in her arms as he remembered the wonderful family he had once been a part of and how badly everything had changed when his father had gotten sick.

He took his fiancée to the firm that now maintained his father. Since the transfer, Anthony had been able to afford returning to his home town to visit his father only sporadically. The distance made him anxious because the new firm didn't inspire the confidence that the previous one had. It looked on the edge of disrepair, floors not dirty but not clean, walls not exactly faded and yet somehow in need of painting. Rooms seemed vaguely underlit. The units in which patients were kept frozen looked cheap. The temperature gauges were primitive compared to the elaborate technology at the previous facility. But as long as they kept his father safe . . .

That thought left Anthony when he took another look at

the gauge and realized that the temperature inside his father's chamber had risen one degree from when he'd last checked it.

"What's wrong?" his fiancée asked.

Words caught in his throat. All he could do was point.

The temperature had gone up yet another degree.

He raced along corridor after corridor, desperate to find a maintenance worker. He burst into the company's office and found only a secretary.

"My father . . ."

Flustered, the secretary took a moment to move when he finished explaining. She phoned the control room. No one answered.

"It's almost noon. The technicians must have gone to lunch."

"For God's sake, where's the control room?"

At the end of the corridor where his father was. As Anthony raced past the niche, he saw that the temperature gauge had gone up fifteen degrees. He charged into the control room, saw flashing red lights on a panel, and rushed to them, trying to figure out what was wrong. Among numerous gauges, eight temperature needles were rising, and Anthony was certain that one of them was for his father.

He flicked a switch beneath each of them, hoping to reset the controls.

The lights kept flashing.

He flicked a switch at the end of their row.

Nothing changed.

He pulled a lever. Every light on the panel went out. "Jesus."

Pushing the lever back to where it had been, he held his breath, exhaling only when all the lights came back on. The eight that had been flashing were now constant.

Sweating, he eased onto a chair. Gradually, he became aware of people behind him and turned to where his fiancée and the secretary watched in dismay from the open door. Then he stared at the panel, watching the temperature needles gradually descend to where they had been. Terrified that the lights would start flashing again, he was still concentrating on the gauges an hour later when a bored technician returned from lunch.

It turned out that a faulty valve had restricted the flow of freezant around eight of the niches. When Anthony had turned the power off and on, the valve had reset itself, although it could fail again at any time and would have to be replaced, the technician explained.

"Then do it!"

He would never again be comfortable away from his father. It made him nervous to return to medical school. He contacted the cryofirm every day, making sure that there weren't any problems. He married, became a parent (of a lovely daughter), graduated, and was lucky enough to be able to do his internship in the city where he'd been raised and where he could keep a close watch on his father's safety. If only his father had been awake to see him graduate, he thought. If only his father had been cured and could have seen his granddaughter being brought home from the hospital . . .

One night, while Anthony was on duty in the emergency ward, a comatose patient turned out to be the broker who'd married his mother. The broker had shot himself in the head. Anthony tried everything possible to save him. His throat felt tight when he pronounced the time of death.

He joined a medical practice in his hometown after he finished his internship. He started earning enough to make good on his promise and take care of his wife after she'd spent so many years taking care of *him*. She had said that she wanted three children, and she got them sooner than she expected, for the next time she gave birth, it was to twins, a boy and a girl. Nonetheless, Anthony's work prevented him from spending as much time with his family as he wanted, for his specialty was blood diseases, and when he wasn't seeing patients, he was doing research, trying to find a way to cure his father.

He needed to know the experiments that the lab had conducted and the types of rays that his father might have been exposed to. But the lab was obsessed with security and refused to tell him. He fought to get a court order to force the lab to cooperate. Judge after judge refused. Meanwhile he was terribly conscious of all the family celebrations that his father continued to miss: the day Anthony's first daughter started grade school, the afternoon the twins began swimming lessons, the evening Anthony's second daughter played "Chopsticks" at her first piano recital. Anthony was thirty-five before he knew it. Then forty. All of a sudden, his children were in high school. His wife went to law school. He kept doing research.

When he was fifty-five and his eldest daughter turned thirty (she was married, with a daughter of her own), the laboratory made a mistake and released the information Anthony needed among a batch of old data that the lab felt was harmless. It wasn't Anthony who discovered the information, however, but instead a colleague two thousand miles away who had other reasons to look through the old data and recognized the significance of the type of rays that Anthony's father had been exposed to. Helped by his colleague's calculations, Anthony devised a treatment, tested it on computer models, subjected rats to the same type of rays, found that they developed the same rapid symptoms as his father had, gave the animals the treatment, and felt his pulse quicken when the symptoms disappeared as rapidly as they had come on.

With his wife next to him, Anthony stood outside his father's cryochamber as arrangements were made to thaw him. He feared that the technicians would make an error during the procedure (the word echoed from his youth), that his father wouldn't wake up.

His muscles tightened as something hissed and the door swung open. The hatch slid out.

Anthony's father looked the same as when he'd last seen him: naked, gaunt, and gray, suspended over a force field.

"You thawed him that *quickly*?" Anthony asked.

"It doesn't work if it isn't instantaneous."

His father's chest moved up and down.

"My God, he's alive," Anthony said. "He's actually . . ."

But there wasn't time to marvel. The disease would be active again, racing to complete its destruction.

Anthony hurriedly injected his father with the treatment. "We have to get him to a hospital."

He stayed in his father's room, constantly monitoring his father's condition, injecting new doses of the treatment precisely on schedule. To his amazement, his father improved almost at once. The healthier color of his skin made obvious what the blood tests confirmed—the disease was retreating.

Not that his father knew. One effect of being thawed was that the patient took several days to wake up. Anthony watched for a twitch of a finger, a flicker of an eyelid, to indicate that his father was regaining consciousness. After three days, he became worried enough to order another brain scan, but as his father was being put in the machine, a murmur made everyone stop.

". . . Where am I?" Anthony's father asked.

"In a hospital. You're going to be fine."

His father strained to focus on him. ". . . Who? . . ."

"Your son."

"No. . . . My son's . . . a child." Looking frightened, Anthony's father lost consciousness.

The reaction wasn't unexpected. But Anthony had his own quite different reaction to deal with. While his father hadn't seen him age and hence didn't know who Anthony was, Anthony's father *hadn't* aged and hence looked exactly as Anthony remembered. The only problem was that Anthony's memory came from when he was nine, and now at the age of fifty-five, he looked at his thirty-two-year-old father, who wasn't much older than Anthony's son.

"Marian's *dead*?"

Anthony reluctantly nodded. "Yes. A car accident."

"When?"

Anthony had trouble saying it. "Twenty-two years ago."

"No."

"I'm afraid it's true."

"I've been frozen *forty-six years*? No one told me what was going to happen."

"We couldn't. You were unconscious. Near death."

His father wept. "Sweet Jesus."

"Our house?"

"Was sold a long time ago."

"My friends?"

Anthony looked away.

With a shudder, his father pressed his hands to his face. "It's worse than being dead."

"No," Anthony said. "You heard the psychiatrist. Depression's a normal part of coming back. You're going to have to learn to live again."

"Just like learning to walk again," his father said bitterly.

"Your muscles never had a chance to atrophy. As far as your body's concerned, no time passed since you were frozen."

"But as far as my mind goes? Learn to live again? That's something nobody should have to do."

"Are you saying that Mom and I should have let you die? Our lives would have gone on just the same. Mom would have been killed whether you were frozen or you died. Nothing would have changed, except that *you* wouldn't be here now."

"With your mother gone . . ."

Anthony waited.

"With my son gone . . ."

"*I'm* your son."

"My son had his ninth birthday two weeks ago. I gave him a new computer game that I looked forward to playing with him. I'll never get to see him grow up."

"To see *me* grow up. But I'm here now. We can make up for lost time."

"Lost time." The words seemed like dust in his father's mouth.

"Dad"—it was the last time Anthony used that term—"this is your grandson, Paul. These are your granddaughters Sally and Jane. And this is *Jane's* son, Peter. Your *great*-grandson."

Seeing his father's reaction to being introduced to grandchildren who were almost as old as *he* was, Anthony felt heartsick.

"*Forty-six years?* But everything changed in a *second*," his father said. "It makes my head spin so much . . ."

"I'll teach you," Anthony said. "I'll start with basics and explain what happened since you were frozen. I'll move you forward. Look, here are virtual videos of—"

"What are virtual videos?"

"Of news shows from back then. We'll watch them in sequence. We'll talk about them. Eventually, we'll get you up to the present."

Anthony's father pointed toward the startlingly lifelike images from forty-six years earlier. "*That's* the present."

"Is there anything you'd like to do?"

"Go to Marian."

So Anthony drove him to the mausoleum, where his father stood for a long time in front of the niche that contained her urn.

"One instant she's alive. The next . . ." Tears filled his father's eyes. "Take me home."

But when Anthony headed north of the city, his father put a trembling hand on his shoulder. "No. You're taking the wrong direction."

"But we live at—"

"Home. I want to go *home*."

So Anthony drove him back to the old neighborhood, where his father stared at the run-down house that he had once been proud to keep in perfect condition. Weeds filled the yard. Windows were broken. Porch steps were missing.

"There used to be a lawn here," Anthony's father said. "I worked so hard to keep it immaculate."

"I remember," Anthony said.

"I taught my son how to do somersaults on it."

"You taught *me*."

"In an instant." His father sounded anguished. "All gone in an instant."

*　　*　　*

Anthony peered up from his breakfast of black coffee, seeing his father at the entrance to the kitchen. It had been two days since they'd spoken.

"I wanted to tell you," his father said, "that I realize you made an enormous effort for me. I can only imagine the pain and sacrifice. I'm sorry if I'm . . . No matter how confused I feel, I want to thank you."

Anthony managed to smile, comparing the wrinkle-free face across from him to the weary one that he'd seen in the mirror that morning. "I'm sorry, too. That you're having such a hard adjustment. All Mom and I thought of was, you were so sick. We were ready to do *anything* that would help you."

"Your mother." Anthony's father needed a moment before he could continue. "Grief doesn't last just a couple of days."

It was Anthony's turn to need a moment. He nodded. "I've had much of my life to try to adjust to Mom being gone, but I still miss her. You'll have a long hard time catching up to me."

"I . . ."

"Yes?"

"I don't know what to do."

"For starters, why don't you let me make you some breakfast." Anthony's wife was defending a case in court. "It'll be just the two of us. Do waffles sound okay? There's some syrup in that cupboard. How about orange juice?"

The first thing Anthony's father did was learn how to drive the new types of vehicles. Anthony believed this was a sign of improving mental health. But then he discovered that his father was using his mobility not to investigate his new world, but instead to visit Marian's ashes in the mausoleum and to go to the once-pristine house that he'd owned forty-six years previously, a time period that to him was yesterday. Anthony had done something similar when he'd lied to his mother's second husband about being at the library when actually he'd been at the cryofirm visiting his father. It worried him.

"I found a 'For Sale' sign at the house," his father said one evening at dinner. "I want to buy it."

"But . . ." Anthony set down his fork. "The place is a wreck."

"It won't be after I'm finished with it."

Anthony felt as if he were arguing not with his father but with one of his children when they were determined to do something that he thought unwise.

"I can't stay here," his father said. "I can't live with you for the rest of my life."

"Why not? You're welcome."

"A father and his grown-up son? We'll get in each other's way."

"But we've gotten along so far."

"I want to buy the house."

Continuing to feel that he argued with his son, Anthony gave in as he always did. "All right, okay, fine. I'll help you get a loan. I'll help with the down payment. But if you're going to take on this kind of responsibility, you'll need a job."

"That's something else I want to talk to you about."

His father used his maintenance skills to become a successful contractor whose specialty was restoring old-style homes to their former beauty. Other contractors tried to compete, but Anthony's father had an edge: he knew those houses inside and out. He'd helped build them when he was a teenager working on summer construction jobs. He'd maintained his when that kind of house was in its prime, almost a half century earlier. Most important, he loved that old style of house.

One house in particular—the house where he'd started to raise his family. As soon as the renovation was completed, he found antique furniture from the period. When Anthony visited, he was amazed by how closely the house resembled the way it had looked when he was a child. His father had arranged to have Marian's urn released to him. It sat on a shelf in a study off the living room. Next to it were framed pictures of Anthony and his mother when they'd been young, the year Anthony's father had gotten sick.

His father found antique audio equipment from back then. The only songs he played were from that time. He even found an old computer and the game that he'd wanted to play with Anthony, teaching his great-grandson how to play it just as he'd already taught the little boy how to do somersaults on the lawn.

Anthony turned sixty. The hectic years of trying to save his father were behind him. He reduced his hours at the office. He followed an interest in gardening and taught himself to build a greenhouse. His father helped him.

"I need to ask you something," his father said one afternoon when the project was almost completed.

"You make it sound awfully serious."

His father looked down at his callused hands. "I have to ask your permission about something."

"Permission?" Anthony's frown deepened his wrinkles.

"Yes. I . . . It's been five years. I . . . Back then, you told me that I had to learn to live again."

"You've been doing a good job of it," Anthony said.

"I fought it for a long time." His father looked more uncomfortable.

"What's wrong?"

"I don't know how to . . ."

"Say it."

"I loved your mother to the depth of my heart."

Anthony nodded, pained with emotion.

"I thought I'd die without her," his father said. "Five years. I never expected . . . I've met somebody. The sister of a man whose house I'm renovating. We've gotten to know each other, and . . . Well, I . . . What I need to ask is, Would you object, would you see it as a betrayal of your mother if . . ."

Anthony felt pressure in his tear ducts. "Would I object?" His eyes misted. "All I want is for you to be happy."

Anthony was the best man at his father's wedding. His stepmother was the same age as his daughters. The following summer, he had a half-brother sixty-one years younger than himself. It felt odd to see his father acting toward the baby in the same loving manner that his father had presumably acted toward him when *he* was a baby.

At the celebration when the child was brought home from the hospital, several people asked Anthony if his wife was feeling ill. She looked wan.

"She's been working hard on a big trial coming up," he said.

The next day, she had a headache so bad that he took her to his clinic and had his staff do tests.

The day after that, she was dead. The viral meningitis that killed her was so virulent that nothing could have been done to save her. The miracle was that neither Anthony nor anybody else in the family had caught it, especially the new baby.

He felt drained. Plodding through his house, he tried to muster the energy to get through each day. The nights were harder. His father often came and sat with him, a young man next to an older one, doing his best to console him.

Anthony visited his wife's grave every day. On the anniversary of her death, while picking flowers for her, he collapsed from a stroke. The incident left him paralyzed on his left side, in need of constant care. His children wanted to put him in a facility.

"No," his father said. "It's *my* turn to watch over *him*."

So Anthony returned to the house where his youth had been wonderful until his father had gotten sick. During the many hours they spent together, his father asked Anthony to fill in more details of what had happened as Anthony had grown up: the arguments he'd had with the broker, his double shifts as a waiter, his first date with the woman who would be his wife.

"Yes, I can see it," his father said.

The next stroke reduced Anthony's intelligence to that of a nine-year-old. He didn't have the capacity to know that the computer on which he played a game with his father came from long ago. In fact, the game was the same one that his father had given him on his ninth birthday, two weeks before his father had gotten sick, the game that he'd never had a chance to play with his son.

One morning, he no longer had a nine-year-old's ability to play the game.

"His neurological functions are decreasing rapidly," the specialist said.

"Nothing can be done?"

"I'm sorry. At this rate . . . In a couple of days . . ."

Anthony's father felt as if he had a stone in his stomach.

"We'll make him as comfortable here as possible," the specialist said.

"No. My son should die at home."

Anthony's father sat next to the bed, holding his son's frail hand, painfully reminded of having taken care of him when he'd been sick as a child. Now Anthony looked appallingly old for sixty-three. His breathing was shallow. His eyes were open, glassy, not registering anything.

His children and grandchildren came to pay their last respects.

"At least, he'll be at peace," his second daughter said.

His father couldn't bear it.

Jesus, he didn't give up on me. I won't give up on him.

"That theory's been discredited," the specialist said.

"It works."

"In isolated cases, but—"

"I'm one of them."

"Of the few. At your son's age, he might not survive the procedure."

"Are you refusing to make the arrangements?"

"I'm trying to explain that with the expense and the risk—"

"My son will be dead by tomorrow. Being frozen can't be worse than *that*. And as far as the expense goes, he worked hard. He saved his money. He can afford it."

"But there's no guarantee that a treatment will ever be developed for brain cells as damaged as your son's are."

"There's no guarantee it *won't* be developed, either."

"He can't give his permission."

"He doesn't need to. He made me his legal representative."

"All the same, his children need to be consulted. There are issues of estate, a risk of a lawsuit."

"*I'll* take care of his children. *You* take care of the arrangements."

They stared at him.

Anthony's father couldn't tell if they resisted his idea because they counted on their inheritance. "Look, I'm begging. He'd have done this for you. He did it for *me*. For God's sake, you can't give up on him."

They stared harder.

"It's not going to cost you anything. I'll work harder and pay for it myself. I'll sign control of the estate over to you. All I want is, don't try to stop me."

Anthony's father stood outside the cryochamber, studying the stick-on plaque that he'd put on the hatch. It gave Anthony's name, his birthdate, when he'd had his first stroke, and when he'd been frozen. "Sweet dreams," it said at the bottom. "Wake up soon."

Soon was a relative word, of course. Anthony had been frozen six years, and there was still no progress in a treatment. But that didn't mean there wouldn't be progress tomorrow or next month. There's always hope, Anthony's father thought. You've got to have hope.

On a long narrow table in the middle of the corridor, there were tokens of affection left by loved ones of other patients: family photographs and a baseball glove, for example. Anthony's father had left the disc of the computer game that he and Anthony had been playing. "We'll play it again," he'd promised.

It was Anthony's father's birthday. He was forty-nine. He had gray in his sideburns, wrinkles in his forehead. I'll soon look like Anthony did when I woke up from being frozen and saw him leaning over me, he thought.

He couldn't subdue the discouraging notion that one of these days he'd be the same age as Anthony when he'd been frozen. But now that he thought about it, maybe that notion wasn't so discouraging. If they found a treatment that year, and they woke Anthony up, and the treatment worked . . . We'd both be sixty-six. We could grow old together.

I'll keep fighting for you, Anthony. I swear you can count on me. I couldn't let you die before me. It's a terrible thing for a father to outlive his son.

The Cat's Pajamas

JAMES MORROW

---

*James Morrow [www.sff.net/people/Jim.Morrow] lives in
State College, Pennsylvania, according to his website, "with
his wife, Kathryn, his twelve-year-old son, Christopher, and
two enigmatic dogs: Pooka, a Border collie, and Amtrak, a
stray Doberman that Jim and Kathy rescued from a train
station in Orlando, Florida. He devotes his leisure hours to
his family, his Lionel toy electric trains, and his video collection of vulgar Biblical spectacles." Morrow's novels include* This Is the Way the World Ends *(1986), a Nebula
finalist,* Only Begotten Daughter *(1990), winner of the
World Fantasy Award, and* Towing Jehovah *(1994), the first
of a trilogy about the death of God and winner of the World
Fantasy Award and the Grand Prix de l'Imaginaire. Much of
his short fiction is collected in* Bible Stories for Adults
*(1996), including the Nebula Award-winning fable, "The
Deluge." His next book is an historical novel,* The
Witchfinder General, *due out in 2002.*

"The Cat's Pajamas" was published in F&SF *and in the
anthology* Embrace the Mutation; *a man and a woman set
out on a car trip, leaving New Jersey to look for adventure;
they find more than they bargained for across the state line
in Pennsylvania. The story is both an homage to H. G. Wells'*
The Island of Dr. Moreau, *and to George Orwell's* Animal
Farm. *But Morrow's is absurdist SF, funny and hyperbolic.*

> *"All politics is local politics."*
> —Tip O'Neill

The Eighteenth-Century Enlightenment was still in our faces, fetishizing the rational intellect and ramming technocracy down our throats, so one day I said to Vickie, "Screw it. This isn't for us. Let's hop in the car and drive to romanticism, or maybe even preindustrial paganism, or possibly all the way to hunter-gatherer utopianism." But we only got as far as Pennsylvania.

I knew that the idea of spending all summer on the road would appeal to Vickie. Most of her affections, including her unbridled *wanderlust*, are familiar to me. Not only had we lived together for six years, we also worked at the same New Jersey high school—Vickie teaching American history, me offering a souped-up eleventh-grade Humanities course—with the result that both our screaming matches and our flashes of rapport drew upon a fund of shared experiences. And so it was that the first day of summer vacation found us rattling down Route 80 in our decrepit VW bus, listening to Crash Test Dummies CDs and pretending that our impulsive westward flight somehow partook of political subversion, though we sensed it was really just an extended camping trip.

Despite being an *épater le bourgeois* sort of woman, Vickie had spent the previous two years promoting the idea of holy matrimony, an institution that has consistently failed to enchant me. Nevertheless, when we reached the Delaware

Water Gap, I turned to her and said, "Here's a challenge for us. Let's see if we can't become man and wife by this time tomorrow afternoon." It's important, I feel, to suffuse a relationship with a certain level of unpredictability, if not outright caprice. "Vows, rings, music, all of it."

"You're crazy," she said, brightening. She's got a killer smile, sharp at the edges, luminous at the center. "It takes a week just to get the blood-test results."

"I was reading in *Newsweek* that there's a portable analyzer on the market. If we can find a technologically advanced justice of the peace, we'll meet the deadline with time to spare."

"Deadline?" She tightened her grip on the steering wheel. "Jeez, Blake, this isn't a *game*. We're talking about a *marriage*."

"It's a game and a gamble—I know from experience. But with you, sweetheart, I'm ready to bet the farm."

She laughed and said, "I love you."

We spent the night in a motel outside a pastoral Pennsylvania borough called Greenbriar, got up at ten, made distracted love, and began scanning the yellow pages for a properly outfitted magistrate. By noon we had our man, District Justice George Stratus, proud owner of a brand new Sorrel-130 blood analyzer. It so happened that Judge Stratus was something of a specialist in instant marriage. For a hundred dollars flat, he informed me over the phone, we could have "the nanosecond nuptial package," including blood test, license, certificate, and a bottle of Taylor's champagne. I told him it sounded like a bargain.

To get there, we had to drive down a sinuous band of dirt and gravel called Spring Valley Road, past the asparagus fields, apple orchards, and cow pastures of Pollifex Farm. We arrived in a billowing nimbus of dust. Judge Stratus turned out to be a fat and affable paragon of efficiency. He immediately set about pricking our fingers and feeding the blood to his Sorrel-130, which took only sixty seconds to endorse our DNA even as it acquitted us of venereal misadventures. He faxed the results to the county courthouse, signed the marriage certificate, and poured us each a glass of champagne. By three o'clock, Vickie and I were legally entitled to partake of connubial bliss.

I think Judge Stratus noticed my pained expression when I handed over the hundred dollars, because he suggested that if we were short on cash, we should stop by the farm and talk to Andre Pollifex. "He's always looking for asparagus pickers this time of year." In point of fact, my divorce from Irene had cost me plenty, making a shambles of both my bank account and my credit record, and Vickie's fondness for upper-middle-class counterculture artifacts, solar-powered trash compacters and so on, had depleted her resources as well. We had funds enough for the moment, though, so I told Stratus we probably wouldn't be joining the migrant worker pool before August.

"Well, sweetheart, we've done it," I said as we climbed back into the bus. "Mr. and Mrs. Blake Meeshaw."

"The price was certainly right," said Vickie, "even though the husband involved is a fixer-upper."

"You've got quite a few loose shingles yourself," I said.

"I'll be hammering and plastering all summer."

Although we had no plans to stop at Pollifex Farm, when we got there an enormous flock of sheep was crossing the road. Vickie hit the brakes just in time to avoid making mutton of a stray lamb, and we resigned ourselves to watching the woolly parade, which promised to be as dull as a passing freight train. Eventually a swarthy man appeared gripping a silver-tipped shepherd's crook. He advanced at a pronounced stoop, like a denizen of Dante's Purgatory balancing a millstone on his neck.

A full minute elapsed before Vickie and I realized that the sheep were moving in a loop, like wooden horses on a carousel. With an impatience bordering on hysteria, I leaped from the van and strode toward the obnoxious herdsman. What possible explanation could he offer for erecting this perpetual barricade?

Nearing the flock, I realized that the scene's strangest aspect was neither the grotesque shepherd nor the tautological roadblock, but the sheep themselves. Every third or fourth animal was a mutant, its head distinctly humanoid, though the facial features seemed melted together, as if they'd been cast in wax and abandoned to the summer sun. The sooner we were out of here, I decided, the better.

"What the hell do you think you're doing?" I shouted. "Get these animals off the road!"

The shepherd hobbled up to me and pulled a tranquilizer pistol from his belt with a manifest intention of rendering me unconscious.

"Welcome to Pollifex Farm," he said.

The gun went off, the dart found my chest, and the world turned black.

Regaining consciousness, I discovered that someone—the violent shepherd? Andre Pollifex?—had relocated my assaulted self to a small bright room perhaps twelve feet square. Dust motes rode the sunlit air. Sections of yellow wallpaper buckled outward from the sheetrock like spritsails puffed with wind. I lay on a mildewed mattress, elevated by a box-spring framed in steel. A turban of bandages encircled my head. Beside me stood a second bed, as uninviting as my own, its bare mattress littered with artifacts that I soon recognized as Vickie's—comb, hand mirror, travel alarm, ankh earrings, well-thumbed paperback of *Zen and the Art of Motorcycle Maintenance*.

It took me at least five minutes, perhaps as many as ten, before I realized that my brain had been removed from my cranium and that the pink, throbbing, convoluted mass of tissue on the nearby customized library cart was in fact my own thinking apparatus. Disturbing and unorthodox as this arrangement was, I could not deny its actuality. Every time I tapped my skull, a hollow sound came forth, as if I were knocking on an empty casserole dish. Fortunately, the physicians responsible for my condition had worked hard to guarantee that it would entail no functional deficits. Not only was my brain protected by a large plexiglass jar filled with a clear, acrid fluid, it also retained its normal connection to my heart and spinal cord. A ropy mass of neurons, interlaced with augmentations of my jugular vein and my two carotid arteries, extended from beneath my orphaned medulla and stretched across four feet of empty space before disappearing into my reopened fontanel, the whole arrangement shielded from microbial contamination by a flexible plastic tube. I was thankful for my surgeons' conscientiousness, but also—I don't mind telling you—extremely frightened and upset.

My brain's extramural location naturally complicated the procedure, but in a matter of minutes I managed to transport both myself and the library cart into the next room, an unappointed parlor bedecked in cobwebs, and from there to an enclosed porch, all the while calling Vickie's name. She didn't answer. I opened the door and shuffled into the putrid air of Pollifex Farm. Everywhere I turned, disorder prospered. The cottage in which I'd awoken seemed ready to collapse under its own weight. The adjacent windmill canted more radically than Pisa's Leaning Tower. Scabs of leprous white paint mottled the sides of the main farmhouse. No building was without its unhinged door, its shattered window, its sunken roof, its disintegrating wall—a hundred instances of entropy mirroring the biological derangement that lay within.

I did not linger in the stables, home to six human-headed horses. Until this moment, I had thought the centaurial form intrinsically beautiful, but with their bony backs and twisted faces these monsters soon deprived me of that supposition. Nor did I remain long in the chicken coop, habitat of four gigantic human-headed hens, each the size of a German shepherd. Nor did the pig shed detain me, for seven human-headed hogs is not a spectacle that improves upon contemplation. Instead I hurried toward an immense barn, lured by a spirited performance of Tschaikovsky's Piano Concerto No. 1 wafting through a crooked doorway right out of *The Cabinet of Dr. Caligari*.

Cautiously I entered. Spacious and high-roofed, the barn was a kind of agrarian cathedral, the Chartres of animal husbandry. In the far corner, hunched over a baby grand piano, sat a humanoid bull: blunt nose, gaping nostrils, a long tapering horn projecting from either side of his head. Whereas his hind legs were of the bovine variety, his forelegs ended in a pair of human hands that skated gracefully along the keyboard. He shared his bench with my wife, and even at this distance I could see that the bull man's virtuosity had brought her to the brink of rapture.

Cerebrum in tow, I made my way across the barn. With each step, my apprehension deepened, my confusion increased, and my anger toward Vickie intensified. Apprehension, confusion, anger: while I was not yet accustomed to experiencing such sensations in a location other than my head, the phenomenon now seemed less peculiar than when I'd first returned to sentience.

"I know what you're thinking," said Vickie, acknowledging my presence. "Why am I sitting here when I should be helping you recover from the operation? Please believe me: Karl said the anesthesia wouldn't wear off for another four hours."

She proceeded to explain that Karl was the shepherd who'd tranquilized me on the road, subsequently convincing her to follow him onto the farm rather than suffer the identical fate. But Karl's name was the least of what Vickie had learned during the past forty-eight hours. Our present difficulties, she elaborated, traced to the VD screening we'd received on Wednesday. In exchange for a substantial payment, Judge Stratus had promised to alert his patrons at Pollifex Farm the instant he happened upon a blood sample bearing the deoxyribonucleic acid component known as QZ-11-4. Once in possession of this gene—or, more specifically, once in possession of a human brain whose *in utero* maturation had been influenced by this gene—Dr. Pollifex's biological investigations could go forward.

"Oh, Blake, they're doing absolutely *wonderful* work here." Vickie rose from the bench, came toward me, and, taking care not to become entangled in my spinal cord, gave me a mildly concupiscent hug. "An external brain to go with your external genitalia—very sexy."

"Stop talking nonsense, Vickie!" I said. "I've been *mutilated!*"

She stroked my bandaged forehead and said, "Once you

hear the whole story, you'll realize that your bilateral hemispherectomy serves a greater good."

"Call me Maxwell," said the bull man, lifting his fingers from the keyboard. "Maxwell Taurus." His voice reminded me of Charles Laughton's. "I must congratulate you on your choice of marriage partner, Blake. Vickie has a refreshingly open mind."

"And I have a depressingly vacant skull," I replied. "Take me to this lunatic Pollifex so I can get my brain put back where it belongs."

"The doctor would never agree to that." Maxwell fixed me with his stare, his eyes all wet and brown like newly created caramel apples. "He requires round-the-clock access to your anterior cortex."

A flock of human-headed geese fluttered into the barn, raced toward a battered aluminum trough full of grain, and began to eat. Unlike Maxwell, the geese did not possess the power of speech—either that, or they simply had nothing to say to each other.

I sighed and leaned against my library cart. "So what, exactly, does QZ-11-4 *do*?"

"Dr. Pollifex calls it the integrity gene, wellspring of decency, empathy, and compassionate foresight," said Maxwell. "Francis of Assisi had it. So did Charles Darwin, Clara Barton, Mahatma Gandhi, Florence Nightingale, Albert Schweitzer, and Susan B. Anthony. And now—now that Dr. Pollifex has started injecting me with a serum derived from your hypertrophic superego—now *I've* got it too."

Although my vanity took a certain satisfaction in Maxwell's words, I realized that I'd lost the thread of his logic. "At the risk of sounding disingenuously modest, I'd have to say I'm not a particularly ethical individual."

"Even if a person inherits QZ-11-4, it doesn't necessarily enjoy expression. And even if the gene enjoys expression—" Maxwell offered me a semantically freighted stare—"the beneficiary doesn't always learn to use his talent. Indeed, among Dr. Pollifex's earliest discoveries was the fact that complete QZ-11-4 actualization is impossible in a purely human species. The serum—we call it Altruoid—the serum reliably engenders ethical superiority only in people who've been genetically melded with domesticated birds and mammals."

"You mean—you used to be . . . human?"

"For twenty years I sold life insurance under the name Lewis Phelps. Have no fear, Blake. We are not harvesting your cerebrum in vain. I shall employ my Altruoid allotment to bestow great boons on Greenbriar."

"You might fancy yourself a moral giant," I told the bull man, "but as far as I'm concerned, you're a terrorist and a brain thief, and I intend to bring this matter to the police."

"You will find that strategy difficult to implement." Maxwell left his piano and, walking upright on his hooves, approached my library cart. "Pollifex Farm is enclosed by a barbed-wire fence twelve feet high. I suggest you try making the best of your situation."

The thought of punching Maxwell in the face now occurred to me, but I dared not risk uprooting my arteries and spinal cord. "If Pollifex continues pilfering my cortex, how long before I become a basket case?"

"Never. The doctor happens to be the world's greatest neurocartographer. He'll bring exquisite taste and sensitivity to each extraction. During the next three years, you'll lose only trivial knowledge, useless skills, and unpleasant memories."

"Three years?" I howled. "You bastards plan to keep me here *three years?*"

"Give or take a month. Once that interval has passed, my peers and I shall have reached the absolute apex of vertebrate ethical development."

"See, Blake, they've thought of *everything*," said Vickie. "These people are *visionaries*."

"These people are Nazis," I said.

"Really, sir, name calling is unnecessary," said Maxwell with a snort. "There's no reason we can't all be friends." He rested an affirming hand on my shoulder. "We've given you a great deal of information to absorb. I suggest you spend tomorrow afternoon in quiet contemplation. Come evening, we'll all be joining the doctor for dinner. It's a meal you're certain to remember."

My new bride and I passed the night in our depressing little cottage beside the windmill. Much to my relief, I discovered that my sexual functioning had survived the bilateral hemispherectomy. We had to exercise caution, of course, lest we snap the vital link between medulla and cord, with the result that the whole encounter quickly devolved into a kind of slow-motion ballet. Vickie said it was like mating with a china figurine, the first negative remark I'd heard her make concerning my predicament.

At ten o'clock the next morning, one of Karl's human-headed sheep entered the bedroom, walking upright and carrying a wicker tray on which rested two covered dishes. When I asked the sheep how long she'd been living at Pollifex Farm, her expression became as vacant as a cake of soap. I concluded that the power of articulation was reserved only to those mutants on an Altruoid regimen.

The sheep bowed graciously and left, and we set about devouring our scrambled eggs, hot coffee, and buttered toast. Upon consuming her final mouthful, Vickie announced that she would spend the day reading two scientific treatises she'd received from Maxwell, both by Dr. Pollifex: *On the Mutability of Species* and *The Descent of Morals*. I told her I had a different agenda. If there was a way out of this bucolic asylum, I was by-God going to find it.

Before I could take leave of my wife, Karl himself appeared, clutching a black leather satchel to his chest as a mother might hold a baby. He told me he deeply regretted Wednesday's assault—I must admit, I detected no guile in his apology—then explained that he'd come to collect the day's specimen. From the satchel he removed a glass-and-steel syringe, using it to suck up a small quantity of anterior cortex and transfer it to a test tube. When I told Karl that I felt nothing during the procedure, he reminded me that the human brain is an insensate organ, nerveless as a stone.

I commenced my explorations. Pollifex's domain was

vaster than I'd imagined, though most of its fields and pastures were deserted. True to the bull man's claim, a fence hemmed the entire farm, the barbed-wire strands woven into a kind of demonic tennis net and strung between steel posts rising from a concrete foundation. In the northeast corner lay a barn as large as Maxwell's concert hall, and it was here, clearly, that Andre Pollifex perpetrated his various crimes against nature. The doors were barred, the windows occluded, but by staring through the cracks in the walls I managed to catch glimpses of hospital gurneys, surgical lights, and three enormous glass beakers in which sallow, teratoid fetuses drifted like pickles in brine.

About twenty paces from Pollifex's laboratory, a crumbling tool shed sat atop a hill of naked dirt. I gave the door a hard shove—not too hard, given my neurological vulnerability—and it pivoted open on protesting hinges. A shaft of afternoon sunlight struck the interior, revealing an assortment of rakes, shovels, and pitchforks, plus a dozen bags of fertilizer—but, alas, no wire cutters.

My perambulations proved exhausting, both mentally and physically, and I returned to the cottage for a much-needed nap. That afternoon, my brain tormented me with the notorious "student's dream." I'd enrolled in an advanced biology course at my old alma mater, Rutgers, but I hadn't attended a single class or handed in even one assignment. And now I was expected to take the final exam.

Vickie, my brain, and I were the last to arrive at Andre Pollifex's dinner party, which occurred in an airy glass-roofed conservatory attached to the back of the farmhouse. The room smelled only slightly better than the piano barn. At the head of the table presided our host, a disarmingly ordinary-looking man, weak of jaw, slight of build, distinguished primarily by his small black mustache and complementary goatee. His face was pale and flaccid, as if he'd been raised in a cave. The instant he opened his mouth to greet us, though, I apprehended something of his glamour, for he had the most majestic voice I've ever heard outside of New York's Metropolitan Opera House.

"Welcome, Mr. and Mrs. Meeshaw," he said. "May I call you Blake and Vickie?"

"Of course," said Vickie.

"May I call you Joseph Mengele?" I said.

Pollifex's white countenance contracted into a scowl. "I can appreciate your distress, Blake. Your sacrifice has been great. I believe I speak for everyone here when I say that our gratitude knows no bounds."

Karl directed us into adjacent seats, then resumed his place next to Pollifex, directly across from the bull man. I found myself facing a pig woman whose large ears flopped about like college pennants and whose snout suggested an oversized button. Vickie sat opposite a goat man with a tapering white beard dangling from his chin and two corrugated horns sprouting from his brow.

"I'm Serge Milkovich," said the goat man, shaking first Vickie's hand, then mine. "In my former life I was Bud Frye, plumbing contractor."

"Call me Juliana Sowers," said the pig woman, enacting the same ritual. "At one time I was Doris Owens of Owens Real Estate, but then I found a higher calling. I cannot begin to thank you for the contribution you're making to science, philosophy, and local politics."

"Local politics?" I said.

"We three beneficiaries of QZ-11-4 form the core of the new Common Sense Party," said Juliana. "We intend to transform Greenbriar into the most livable community in America."

"I'm running for Borough Council," said Serge. "Should my campaign prove successful, I shall fight to keep our town free of Consumerland discount stores. Their advent is inevitably disastrous for local merchants."

Juliana crammed a handful of hors d'oeuvres into her mouth. "I seek a position on the School Board. My stances won't prove automatically popular—better pay for elementary teachers, sex education starting in grade four—but I'm prepared to support them with passion and statistics."

Vickie grabbed my hand and said, "See what I mean, Blake? They may be mutants, but they have terrific ideas."

"As for me, I've got my eye on the Planning Commission," said Maxwell, releasing a loud and disconcerting burp. "Did you know there's a scheme afoot to run the Route 80 Extension along our northern boundary, just so it'll be easier for people to get to Penn State football games? Once construction begins, the environmental desecration will be profound."

As Maxwell expounded upon his anti-extension arguments, a half-dozen sheep arrived with our food. In deference to Maxwell and Juliana, the cuisine was vegetarian: tofu, lentils, capellini with meatless marinara sauce. It was all quite tasty, but the highlight of the meal was surely the venerable and exquisite vintages from Pollifex's cellar. After my first few swallows of Brunello di Montalcino, I worried that Pollifex's scalpel had denied me the pleasures of intoxication, but eventually the expected sensation arrived. (I attributed the hiatus to the extra distance my blood had to travel along my extended arteries.) By the time the sheep were serving dessert, I was quite tipsy, though my bursts of euphoria alternated uncontrollably with spasms of anxiety.

"Know what I think?" I said, locking on Pollifex as I struggled to prevent my brain from slurring my words. "I think you're trying to turn me into a zombie."

The doctor proffered a heartening smile. "Your discomfort is understandable, Blake, but I can assure you all my interventions have been innocuous thus far—and will be in the future. Tell me, what two classroom pets did your second-grade teacher, Mrs. Hines, keep beside her desk, and what were their names?"

"I have no idea."

"Of course you don't. That useless memory vanished with the first extraction. A hamster and a chameleon. Florence and Charlie. Now tell me about the time you threw up on your date for the senior prom."

"That never happened."

"Yes it did, but I have spared you any recollection of the event. Nor will you ever again be haunted by the memory of forgetting your lines during the Cransford Community Theater production of *A Moon for the Misbegotten*. Now please recite Joyce Kilmer's 'Trees.' "

"All right, all right, you've made your point," I said. "But you still have no right to mess with my head." I swallowed more wine. "As for this ridiculous Common Sense Party—okay, sure, these candidates might get *my* vote—I'm for better schools and free enterprise and all that—but the average Greenbriar citizen. . . ." In lieu of stating the obvious, I finished my wine.

"What *about* the average Greenbriar citizen?" said Juliana huffily.

"The average Greenbriar citizen will find us morphologically unacceptable?" said Serge haughtily.

"Well . . . yes," I replied.

"Unpleasantly odiferous?" said Maxwell snippily.

"That too."

"Homely?" said Juliana defensively.

"I wouldn't be surprised."

The sheep served dessert—raspberry and lemon sorbet—and the seven of us ate in silence, painfully aware that mutual understanding between myself and the Common Sense Party would be a long time coming.

During the final two weeks of June, Karl siphoned fourteen additional specimens from my superego, one extraction per day. On the Fourth of July, the shepherd unwound my bandages. Although I disbelieved his assertion to be a trained nurse, I decided to humor him. When he pronounced that my head was healing satisfactorily, I praised his expertise, then listened intently as he told me how to maintain the incision, an ugly ring of scabs and sutures circumscribing my cranium like a crown of thorns.

As the hot, humid, enervating month elapsed, the Common Sense candidates finished devising their strategies, and the campaign began in earnest. The piano barn soon overflowed with shipping crates full of leaflets, brochures, metal buttons, T-shirts, bumper stickers, and pork-pie hats. With each passing day, my skepticism intensified. A goat running for Borough Council? A pig on the School Board? A bull guiding the Planning Commission? Pollifex's menagerie didn't stand a chance.

My doubts received particularly vivid corroboration on July 20th, when the doctor staged a combination cocktail party and fund-raiser at the farmhouse. From among the small but ardent population of political progressives inhabiting Greenbriar, Pollifex had identified thirty of the wealthiest. Two dozen accepted his invitation. Although these potential contributors were clearly appalled by my bifurcation, they seemed to accept Pollifex's explanation. (I suffered from a rare neurological disorder amenable only to the most radical surgery.) But then the candidates themselves sauntered into the living room, and Pollifex's guests immediately lost their powers of concentration.

It wasn't so much that Maxwell, Juliana, and Serge looked like an incompetent demiurge's roughest drafts. The real problem was that they'd retained so many traits of the creatures to which they'd been grafted. Throughout the entire event, Juliana stuffed her face with canapés and petits fours. Whenever Serge engaged a potential donor in conversation, he crudely emphasized his points by ramming his horns into the listener's chest. Maxwell, meanwhile, kept defecating on the living-room carpet, a behavior not redeemed by the mildly pleasant fragrance that a vegetarian diet imparts to bovine manure. By the time the mutants were ready to deliver their formal speeches, the pledges stood at a mere fifty dollars, and every guest had manufactured an excuse to leave.

"Your idea is never going to work," I told Pollifex after the candidates had returned to their respective barns. We were sitting in the doctor's kitchen, consuming mugs of French roast coffee. The door stood open. A thousand crickets sang in the meadow.

"This is a setback, not a catastrophe," said Pollifex, brushing crumbs from his white dinner jacket. "Maxwell is a major Confucius scholar, with strong Kantian credentials as well. He can surely become housebroken. Juliana is probably the finest utilitarian philosopher since John Stuart Mill. For such a mind, table manners will prove a snap. If you ask

Serge about the Sermon on the Mount, he'll recite the King James translation without a fluff. Once I explain how uncouth he's being, he'll learn to control his butting urge."

"Nobody wants to vote for a candidate with horns."

"It will take a while—quite a while—before Greenbriar's citizens appreciate this slate, but eventually they'll hop on the bandwagon." Pollifex poured himself a second cup of French roast. "Do you doubt that my mutants are ethical geniuses? Can you imagine, for example, how they responded to the Prisoner's Dilemma?"

For three years running, I had used the Prisoner's Dilemma in my Introduction to Philosophy class. It's a situation-ethics classic, first devised in 1951 by Merrill Flood of the RAND Corporation. Imagine that you and a stranger have been arrested as accomplices in manslaughter. You are both innocent. The state's case is weak. Even though you don't know each other, you and the stranger form a pact. You will both stonewall it, maintaining your innocence no matter what deals the prosecutor may offer.

Each of you is questioned privately. Upon entering the interrogation room, the prosecutor lays out four possibilities. If you and your presumed accomplice hang tough, confessing to nothing, you will each get a short sentence, a mere seven months in prison. If you admit your guilt and implicate your fellow prisoner, you will go scot free—and your presumed accomplice will serve a life sentence. If you hang tough and your fellow prisoner confesses-and-implicates, *he* will go scot free—and *you* will serve a life sentence. Finally, if you and your fellow prisoner both confess-and-implicate, you will each get a medium sentence, four years behind bars.

It doesn't take my students long to realize that the most logical course is to break faith with the stranger, thus guaranteeing that you won't spend your life in prison if he also defects. The uplifting-but-uncertain possibility of a short sentence must lose out to the immoral-but-immutable fact of a medium sentence. Cooperation be damned.

"Your mutants probably insist that they would keep faith regardless of the consequences," I said. "They would rather die than violate a trust."

"Their answer is subtler than that," said Pollifex. "They would tell the prosecutor, 'You imagine that my fellow prisoner and I have made a pact, and in that you are correct. You further imagine that you can manipulate us into breaking faith with one another. But given your obsession with betrayal, I must conclude that you are yourself a liar, and that you will ultimately seek to convert our unwilling confessions into life sentences. I refuse to play this game. Let's go to court instead.' "

"An impressive answer," I said. "But the fact remains. . . ." Reaching for the coffee pot, I let my voice drift away. "Suppose I poured some French roast directly into my jar? Would I be jolted awake?"

"Don't try it," said Pollifex.

"I won't."

The mutant maker scowled strenuously. "You think I'm some sort of mad scientist."

"Restore my brain," I told him. "Leave the farm, get a job at Pfizer, wash your hands of politics."

"I'm a sane scientist, Blake. I'm the last sane scientist in the world."

I looked directly in his eyes. The face that returned my gaze was neither entirely mad nor entirely sane. It was the face of a man who wasn't sleeping well, and it made me want to run away.

The following morning, my routine wanderings along the farm's perimeter brought me to a broad, swiftly flowing creek about twelve feet wide and three deep. Although the barbed-wire net extended beneath the water, clear to the bottom, I suddenly realized how a man might circumvent it. By redirecting the water's flow via a series of dikes, I could desiccate a large section of the creek bed and subsequently dig my way out of this hellish place. I would need only one of the shovels I'd spotted in the tool shed—a shovel, and a great deal of luck.

Thus it was that I embarked on a secret construction project. Every day at about eleven A.M., right after Karl took the specimen from my superego, I slunk off to the creek and spent a half-hour adding rocks, logs, and mud to the burgeoning levees, returning to the cottage in time for lunch. Although the creek proved far less pliable than I'd hoped, I eventually became its master. Within two weeks, I figured, possibly three, a large patch of sand and pebbles would lie exposed to the hot summer sun, waiting to receive my shovel.

Naturally I was tempted to tell Vickie of my scheme. Given my handicap, I could certainly have used her assistance in building the levees. But in the end I concluded that, rather than endorsing my bid for freedom, she would regard it as a betrayal of the Common Sense Party and its virtuous agenda.

I knew I'd made the right decision when Vickie entered our cottage late one night in the form of a gigantic mutant hen. Her body had become a bulbous mass of feathers, her legs had transmuted into fleshy stilts, and her face now sported a beak the size of a funnel. Obviously she was running for elective office, but I couldn't imagine which one. She lost no time informing me. Her ambition, she explained, was to become Greenbriar's next mayor.

"I've even got an issue," she said.

"I don't want to hear about it," I replied, looking her up and down. Although she still apparently retained her large and excellent breasts beneath her bikini top, their present context reduced their erotic content considerably.

"Do you know what Greenbriar needs?" she proclaimed. "Traffic diverters at certain key intersections! Our neighborhoods are being suffocated by the automobile!"

"You shouldn't have done this, Vickie," I told her.

"My name is Eva Pullo," she clucked.

"These people have brainwashed you!"

"The Common Sense Party is the hope of the future!"

"You're talking like a fascist!" I said.

"At least I'm not a coward like you!" said the chicken.

For the next half-hour we hurled insults at each other— our first real post-marital fight—and then I left in a huff, eager to continue my arcane labors by the creek. In a peculiar way I still loved Vickie, but I sensed that our relationship was at an end. When I made my momentous escape, I feared, she would not be coming with me.

Even as I redirected the creek, the four mutant candidates brought off an equally impressive feat—something akin to a miracle, in fact. They got the citizens of Greenbriar to listen to them, and the citizens liked what they heard.

The first breakthrough occurred when Maxwell appeared along with three other Planning Commission candidates—Republican, Democrat, Libertarian—on Greenbriar's local-access cable channel. I watched the broadcast in the farmhouse, sitting on the couch between Vickie and Dr. Pollifex. Although the full-blooded humans on the podium initially refused to take Maxwell seriously, the more he talked about his desire to prevent the Route 80 Extension from wreaking havoc with local ecosystems, the clearer it became that this mutant had charisma. Maxwell's eloquence was breathtaking, his logic impeccable, his sincerity sublime. He committed no fecal faux pas.

"That bull was on his game," I admitted at the end of the transmission.

"The moderator was *enchanted*," enthused Vickie.

"Our boy is going to win," said Pollifex.

Two days later, Juliana kicked off her campaign for School Board. Aided by the ever-energetic Vickie, she had outfitted the back of an old yellow school bus with a Pullman car observation platform, the sort of stage from which early twentieth-century presidential candidates campaigned while riding the rails. Juliana and Vickie also transformed the bus's interior, replacing the seats with a coffee bar, a chat lounge, and racks of brochures explaining the pig woman's ambition to expand the sex education program, improve services for special-needs children, increase faculty awareness of the misery endured by gay students, and—most audacious of all—invert the salary pyramid so that first-grade teachers would earn more than high-school administrators. Day in, day out, Juliana tooled around Greenbriar in her appealing vehicle, giving out iced cappuccino, addressing crowds from the platform, speaking to citizens privately in the lounge, and somehow managing to check her impulse toward gluttony, all the while exhibiting a caliber of wisdom that eclipsed her unappetizing physiognomy. The tour was a fabulous success—such, at least, was the impression I received from watching the blurry, jerky coverage that Vickie accorded the pig woman's campaign with Pollifex's camcorder. Every time the school bus pulled away from a Juliana Sowers rally, it left behind a thousand tear-stained eyes, so moved were the citizens by her commitment to the glorious ideal of public education.

Serge, meanwhile, participated in a series of "Meet the Candidates" nights along with four other Borough Council hopefuls. Even when mediated by Vickie's shaky videography, the inaugural gathering at Greenbriar Town Hall came across as a powerful piece of political theater. Serge fully suppressed his impulse to butt his opponents—but that was the smallest of his accomplishments. Without slinging mud, flinging innuendo, or indulging in disingenuous rhetoric, he made his fellow candidates look like moral idiots for their unwillingness to stand firm against what he called "the insatiable greed of Consumerland." Before the evening ended, the attending voters stood prepared to tar-and-feather any discount chain executive who might set foot in Greenbriar, and it was obvious they'd also embraced Serge's other ideas for making the Borough Council a friend to local business. If Serge's plans came to fruition, shoppers would eventually flock to the downtown, lured by parking-fee rebates, street performers, bicycle paths, mini-playgrounds, and low-cost supervised day care.

As for Vickie's mayoral campaign—which I soon learned to call Eva Pullo's mayoral campaign—it gained momentum the instant she shed her habit of pecking hecklers on the head. Vickie's commitment to reducing the automobile traffic in residential areas occasioned the grandest rhetorical flights I'd ever heard from her. "A neighborhood should exist for the welfare of its children, not the convenience of its motorists," she told the local chapter of the League of Women Voters. "We must not allow our unconsidered veneration of the automobile to mask our fundamental need for community and connectedness," she advised the Chamber of Commerce. By the middle of August, Vickie had added a dozen other environmentalist planks to her platform, including an ingenious proposal to outfit the town's major highways with underground passageways for raccoons, badgers, woodchucks, skunks, and possums.

You must believe me, reader, when I say that my conversion to the Common Sense Party occurred well before the *Greenbriar Daily Times* published its poll indicating that the entire slate—Maxwell Taurus, Juliana Sowers, Serge Milkovich, Eva Pullo—enjoyed the status of shoo-ins. I was not simply trying to ride with the winners. When I abandoned my plan to dig an escape channel under the fence, I was doing what I thought was right. When I resolved to spend the next three years nursing the Pollifex Farm candidates from my cerebral teat, I was fired by an idealism so intense that the pragmatists among you would blush to behold it.

I left the levees in place, however, just in case I had a change of heart.

The attack on Pollifex Farm started shortly after eleven P.M. It was Halloween night, which means that the raiders probably aroused no suspicions whatsoever as, dressed in shrouds and skull masks, they drove their pickup trucks through the streets of Greenbriar and down Spring Valley Road. To this day, I'm not sure who organized and paid for the atrocity. At its core, I suspect, the mob included not only yahoos armed with torches but also conservatives gripped by fear, moderates transfixed by cynicism, liberals in the pay of the *status quo*, libertarians acting out anti-government fantasies, and a few random anarchists looking for a good time. Whatever their conflicting allegiances, the vigilantes stood united in their realization that Andre Pollifex, sane scientist, was about to unleash a reign of enlightenment on Greenbriar. They were having none of it.

I was experiencing yet another version of the student's dream—this time I'd misconnected not simply with one class but with an entire college curriculum—when shouts, gunshots, and the neighing of frightened horses awoke me. Taking hold of the library cart, I roused Vickie by ruffling her feathers, and side by side we stumbled into the parlor. By the time we'd made our way outside, the windmill, tractor shed, corn crib, and centaur stables were all on fire. Although I could not move quickly without risking permanent paralysis, Vickie immediately sprang into action. Transcending her spheroid body, she charged into the burning stables and set the mutant horses free, and she proved equally unflappable when the vigilantes hurled their torches into Maxwell's residence. With little thought for her personal safety, she ran into the flaming piano barn, located the panicked bull man and the equally discombobulated pig woman—in recent months they'd entered into a relationship whose details needn't concern us here—and led them outside right before the roof collapsed in a great red wave of cascading sparks and flying embers.

And still the arsonists continued their assault, blockading the main gate with bales of burning hay, setting fire to the chicken coop, and turning Pollifex's laboratory into a raging inferno. Catching an occasional glimpse of our spectral enemies, their white sheets flashing in the light of the flames, I saw that they would not become hoist by their own petards, for they had equipped themselves with asbestos suits, scuba regulators, and compressed air tanks. As for the inhabitants of Pollifex Farm, it was certain that if we didn't move quickly, we would suffer either incineration, suffocation, or their concurrence in the form of fatally seared lungs.

Although I had never felt so divided, neither the fear spasms in my chest nor the jumbled thoughts in my jar prevented me from realizing what the mutants must do next. I told them to steal shovels from the tool shed, make for the creek, and follow it to the fence. Thanks to my levees, I explained, the bed now lay in the open air. Within twenty minutes or so, they should be able to dig below the barbed-wire net and gouge a dry channel for themselves. The rest of my plan had me bringing up the rear, looking out for Karl, Serge, and Dr. Pollifex so that I might direct them to the secret exit. Vickie kissed my lips, Juliana caressed my cheek,

Maxwell embraced my brain, and then all three candidates rushed off into the choking darkness.

Before that terrible night was out, I indeed found the other Party members. Karl lay dead in a mound of straw beside the sheep barn, his forehead blasted away by buckshot. Serge sat on the rear porch of the farmhouse, his left horn broken off and thrust fatally into his chest. Finally I came upon Pollifex. The vigilantes had roped the doctor to a maple tree, subjected him to target practice, and left him for dead. He was as perforated as Saint Sebastian. A mattock, a pitchfork, and two scythes projected from his body like quills from a porcupine.

"Andre, it's me, Blake," I said, approaching.

"Blake?" he muttered. "Blake? Oh, Blake, they killed Serge. They killed Karl."

"I know. Vickie got away, and Maxwell too, and Juliana."

"I was a sane scientist," said Pollifex.

"Of course," I said.

"There are some things that expediency was not meant to tamper with."

"I agree."

"Pullo for Mayor!" he shouted.

"Taurus for Planning Commission!" I replied.

"Milkovich for Borough Council!" he shouted. "Sowers for School Board!" he screamed, and then he died.

There's not much more to tell. Although Vickie, Juliana, Maxwell, and I all escaped the burning farm that night, the formula for the miraculous serum died with Dr. Pollifex. Deprived of their weekly Altruoid injections, the mutants soon lost their talent for practical idealism, and their political careers sputtered out. Greenbriar now boasts a mammoth new Consumerland. The Route 80 extension is almost finished. High school principals still draw twice the pay of first-grade teachers. Life goes on.

The last time I saw Juliana, she was the opening act at Caesar's Palace in Atlantic City. A few songs, some impersonations, a standup comedy routine—mostly vegetarian humor and animal-rights jokes leavened by a sardonic feminism. The crowd ate it up, and Juliana seemed to be enjoying herself. But, oh, what a formidable School Board member she would've made!

When the Route 80 disaster occurred, Maxwell was devastated—not so much by the extension itself as by his inability to critique it eloquently. These days he plays piano at Emilio's, a seedy bar in Newark. He is by no means the weirdest presence in the place, and he enjoys listening to the customers' troubles. But he is a broken mutant.

Vickie and I did our best to make it work, but in the end we decided that mixed marriages entail insurmountable hurdles, and we split up. Eventually she got a job hosting a preschool children's television show on the Disney Channel, *Arabella's Barnyard Band*. Occasionally she manages to insert a satiric observation about automobiles into her patter.

As for me, after hearing the tenth neurosurgeon declare that I am beyond reassembly, I decided to join the world's eternal vagabonds. I am brother to the Wandering Jew, the Flying Dutchman, and Marley's Ghost. I shuffle around North America, dragging my library cart behind me, exhibiting my fractured self to anyone who's willing to pay. In the past decade, my employers have included three carnivals, four roadside peep shows, two direct-to-video horror movie producers, and an artsy off-Broadway troupe bent on reviving *Le Grand Guignol*.

And always I remain on the lookout for another Andre Pollifex, another scientist who can manufacture QZ-11-4 serum and use it to turn beasts into politicians. I shall not settle for any sort of Pollifex, of course. The actual Pollifex, for example, would not meet my standards. The man bifurcated me without my permission, and I cannot forgive him for that.

The scientist I seek would unflinchingly martyr himself to the Prisoner's Dilemma. As they hauled him away to whatever dungeon is reserved for such saints, he would turn to the crowd and say, "The personal cost was great, but at least I have delivered a fellow human from an unjust imprisonment. And who knows? Perhaps his anguish over breaking faith with me will eventually transform him into a more generous friend, a better parent, or a public benefactor."

Alas, my heart is not in the quest. Only part of me—a small part, I must confess—wants to keep on making useful neurological donations. So even if there is a perfect Pollifex out there somewhere, he will probably never get to fashion a fresh batch of Altruoid. Not unless I father a child—and not unless the child receives the gene—and not unless the gene finds expression—and not unless this descendent of mine donates his superego to science. But as the bull man told me many years ago, QZ-11-4 only rarely gets actualized in the humans who carry it.

I believe I see a way around the problem. The roadside emporium in which I currently display myself also features a llama named Loretta. She can count to ten and solve simple arithmetic problems. I am enchanted by Loretta's liquid eyes, sensuous lips, and splendid form—and I think she has taken a similar interest in me. It's a relationship, I feel, that could lead almost anywhere.

The Dog Said Bow-Wow

MICHAEL SWANWICK

Michael Swanwick [www.michaelswanwick.com] has two
stories in this book (see "Under's Game"). This is in part
because he has mastered the form of the short short story,
and has published twenty or more of them in each of the last
three years. The other reason is that he is unquestionably
one of the finest writers currently working in SF and fantasy,
and each year publishes at least one story that is among the
year's best, sometimes two. Every four or five years he publishes a new novel, and 2002 is the year of Bones of the
Earth.

"The Dog Said Bow-Wow" was published in Asimov's,
and is set in a fantastic Cordwainer Smithian future in which
the Queen of England is in Buckingham Labyrinth, the
world has somewhat recovered from the destruction of the
ancient civilization of the Utopians, and biotechnology
rules. A human, Aubrey, and a genetically engineered thief,
lover, and dog, Sir Blackthorpe Ravenscairn de Plus Preci-
uex, also known as "Surplus," plan a complex scam. But
Swanwick is the most engaging con man of all.

The Dog Said Bow-Wow
MICHAEL SWANWICK

The dog looked as if he had just stepped out of a children's book. There must have been a hundred physical adaptations required to allow him to walk upright. The pelvis, of course, had been entirely reshaped. The feet alone would have needed dozens of changes. He had knees, and knees were tricky.

To say nothing of the neurological enhancements.

But what Darger found himself most fascinated by was the creature's costume. His suit fit him perfectly, with a slit in the back for the tail, and—again—a hundred invisible adaptations that caused it to hang on his body in a way that looked perfectly natural.

"You must have an extraordinary tailor," Darger said.

The dog shifted his cane from one paw to the other, so they could shake, and in the least affected manner imaginable replied, "That is a common observation, sir."

"You're from the States?" It was a safe assumption, given where they stood—on the docks—and that the schooner *Yankee Dreamer* had sailed up the Thames with the morning tide. Darger had seen its bubble sails over the rooftops, like so many rainbows. "Have you found lodgings yet?"

"Indeed I am, and no I have not. If you could recommend a tavern of the cleaner sort?"

"No need for that. I would be only too happy to put you up for a few days in my own rooms." And, lowering his voice, Darger said, "I have a business proposition to put to you."

235

"Then lead on, sir, and I shall follow you with a right good will."

The dog's name was Sir Blackthorpe Ravenscairn de Plus Precieux, but "Call me Sir Plus," he said with a self-denigrating smile, and "Surplus" he was ever after.

Surplus was, as Darger had at first glance suspected and by conversation confirmed, a bit of a rogue—something more than mischievous and less than a cut-throat. A dog, in fine, after Darger's own heart.

Over drinks in a public house, Darger displayed his box and explained his intentions for it. Surplus warily touched the intricately carved teak housing, and then drew away from it. "You outline an intriguing scheme, Master Darger—"

"Please. Call me Aubrey."

"Aubrey, then. Yet here we have a delicate point. How shall we divide up the . . . ah, *spoils* of this enterprise? I hesitate to mention this, but many a promising partnership has foundered on precisely such shoals."

Darger unscrewed the salt cellar and poured its contents onto the table. With his dagger, he drew a fine line down the middle of the heap. "I divide—you choose. Or the other way around, if you please. From self-interest, you'll not find a grain's difference between the two."

"Excellent!" cried Surplus and, dropping a pinch of salt in his beer, drank to the bargain.

It was raining when they left for Buckingham Labyrinth. Darger stared out the carriage window at the drear streets and worn buildings gliding by and sighed. "Poor, weary old London! History is a grinding-wheel that has been applied too many a time to thy face."

"It is also," Surplus reminded him, "to be the making of our fortunes. Raise your eyes to the Labyrinth, sir, with its soaring towers and bright surfaces rising above these shops and flats like a crystal mountain rearing up out of a ramshackle wooden sea, and be comforted."

"That is fine advice," Darger agreed. "But it cannot comfort a lover of cities, nor one of a melancholic turn of mind."

"Pah!" cried Surplus, and said no more until they arrived at their destination.

At the portal into Buckingham, the sergeant-interface strode forward as they stepped down from the carriage. He blinked at the sight of Surplus, but said only, "Papers?"

Surplus presented the man with his passport and the credentials Darger had spent the morning forging, then added with a negligent wave of his paw, "And this is my autistic."

The sergeant-interface glanced once at Darger, and forgot about him completely. Darger had the gift, priceless to one in his profession, of a face so nondescript that once someone looked away, it disappeared from that person's consciousness forever. "This way, sir. The officer of protocol will want to examine these himself."

A dwarf savant was produced to lead them through the outer circle of the Labyrinth. They passed by ladies in bioluminescent gowns and gentlemen with boots and gloves cut from leathers cloned from their own skin. Both women and men were extravagantly bejeweled—for the ostentatious display of wealth was yet again in fashion—and the halls were lushly clad and pillared in marble, porphyry, and jasper. Yet Darger could not help noticing how worn the carpets were, how chipped and sooted the oil lamps. His sharp eye espied the remains of an antique electrical system, and traces as well of telephone lines and fiber optic cables from an age when those technologies were yet workable.

These last he viewed with particular pleasure.

The dwarf savant stopped before a heavy black door carved over with gilt griffins, locomotives, and fleurs-de-lis. "This is a door," he said. "The wood is ebony. Its binomial is *Diospyros ebenum*. It was harvested in Serendip. The gilding is of gold. Gold has an atomic weight of 197.2."

He knocked on the door and opened it.

The officer of protocol was a dark-browed man of imposing mass. He did not stand for them. "I am Lord Coherence-Hamilton, and this—" he indicated the slender, clear-eyed woman who stood beside him—"is my sister, Pamela."

Surplus bowed deeply to the Lady, who dimpled and dipped a slight curtsey in return.

The Protocol Officer quickly scanned the credentials. "Explain these fraudulent papers, sirrah. The Demesne of Western Vermont! Damn me if I have ever heard of such a place."

"Then you have missed much," Surplus said haughtily. "It is true we are a young nation, created only seventy-five years ago during the Partition of New England. But there is much of note to commend our fair land. The glorious beauty of Lake Champlain. The gene-mills of Winooski, that ancient seat of learning the *Universitas Viridis Montis* of Burlington, the Technarchaeological Institute of—"' He stopped. "We have much to be proud of, sir, and nothing of which to be ashamed."

The bearlike official glared suspiciously at him, then said, "What brings you to London? Why do you desire an audience with the queen?"

"My mission and destination lie in Russia. However, England being on my itinerary and I a diplomat, I was charged to extend the compliments of my nation to your monarch." Surplus did not quite shrug. "There is no more to it than that. In three days I shall be in France, and you will have forgotten about me completely."

Scornfully, the officer tossed his credentials to the savant, who glanced at and politely returned them to Surplus. The small fellow sat down at a little desk scaled to his own size and swiftly made out a copy. "Your papers will be taken to Whitechapel and examined there. If everything goes well—which I doubt—and there's an opening—not likely—you'll be presented to the queen sometime between a week and ten days hence."

"Ten days! Sir, I am on a very strict schedule!"

"Then you wish to withdraw your petition?"

Surplus hesitated. "I . . . I shall have to think on't, sir."

Lady Pamela watched coolly as the dwarf savant led them away.

The room they were shown to had massively framed mirrors and oil paintings dark with age upon the walls, and a generous log fire in the hearth. When their small guide had gone, Darger carefully locked and bolted the door. Then he tossed the box onto the bed, and bounced down alongside it. Lying flat on his back, staring up at the ceiling, he said, "The Lady Pamela is a strikingly beautiful woman. I'll be damned if she's not."

Ignoring him, Surplus locked paws behind his back, and proceeded to pace up and down the room. He was full of nervous energy. At last, he expostulated, "This is a deep game you have gotten me into, Darger! Lord Coherence-Hamilton suspects us of all manner of blackguardry."

"Well, and what of that?"

"I repeat myself: We have not even begun our play yet, and he suspects us already! I trust neither him nor his genetically remade dwarf."

"You are in no position to be displaying such vulgar prejudice."

"I am not *bigoted* about the creature, Darger, I *fear* him! Once let suspicion of us into that macroencephalic head of his, and he will worry at it until he has found out our every secret."

"Get a grip on yourself, Surplus! Be a man! We are in this too deep already to back out. Questions would be asked, and investigations made."

"I am anything but a man, thank God," Surplus replied. "Still, you are right. In for a penny, in for a pound. For now, I might as well sleep. Get off the bed. You can have the hearth-rug."

"I! The rug!"

"I am groggy of mornings. Were someone to knock, and I to unthinkingly open the door, it would hardly do to have you found sharing a bed with your master."

The next day, Surplus returned to the Office of Protocol to declare that he was authorized to wait as long as two weeks for an audience with the queen, though not a day more.

"You have received new orders from your government?" Lord Coherence-Hamilton asked suspiciously. "I hardly see how."

"I have searched my conscience, and reflected on certain subtleties of phrasing in my original instructions," Surplus said. "That is all."

He emerged from the office to discover Lady Pamela waiting outside. When she offered to show him the Labyrinth, he agreed happily to her plan. Followed by Darger, they strolled inward, first to witness the changing of the guard in the forecourt vestibule, before the great pillared wall that was the front of Buckingham Palace before it was swallowed up in the expansion of architecture during the mad, glorious years of Utopia. Following which, they proceeded toward the viewer's gallery above the chamber of state.

"I see from your repeated glances that you are interested in my diamonds, 'Sieur Plus Precieux,'" Lady Pamela said. "Well might you be. They are a family treasure, centuries old and manufactured to order, each stone flawless and perfectly matched. The indentures of a hundred autistics would not buy the like."

Surplus smiled down again at the necklace, draped about her lovely throat and above her perfect breasts. "I assure you, madame, it was not your necklace that held me so enthralled."

She colored delicately, pleased. Lightly, she said, "And that box your man carries with him wherever you go? What is in it?"

"That? A trifle. A gift for the Duke of Muscovy, who is the ultimate object of my journey," Surplus said. "I assure you, it is of no interest whatsoever."

"You were talking to someone last night," Lady Pamela said. "In your room."

"You were listening at my door? I am astonished and flattered."

She blushed. "No, no, my brother . . . it is his job, you see, surveillance."

"Possibly I was talking in my sleep. I have been told I do that occasionally."

"In accents? My brother said he heard two voices."

Surplus looked away. "In that, he was mistaken."

England's queen was a sight to rival any in that ancient land. She was as large as the lorry of ancient legend, and surrounded by attendants who hurried back and forth, fetching food and advice and carrying away dirty plates and signed legislation. From the gallery, she reminded Darger of a queen bee, but unlike the bee, this queen did not copulate, but remained proudly virgin.

Her name was Gloriana the First, and she was a hundred years old and still growing.

Lord Campbell-Supercollider, a friend of Lady Pamela's met by chance, who had insisted on accompanying them to the gallery, leaned close to Surplus and murmured, "You are impressed, of course, by our queen's magnificence." The warning in his voice was impossible to miss. "Foreigners invariably are."

"I am dazzled," Surplus said.

"Well might you be. For scattered through her majesty's great body are thirty-six brains, connected with thick ropes of ganglia in a hypercube configuration. Her processing capacity is the equal of many of the great computers from Utopian times."

Lady Pamela stifled a yawn. "Darling Rory," she said, touching the Lord Campbell-Supercollider's sleeve. "Duty calls me. Would you be so kind as to show my American friend the way back to the outer circle?"

"Or course, my dear." He and Surplus stood (Darger was, of course, already standing) and paid their compliments. Then, when Lady Pamela was gone and Surplus started to turn toward the exit, "Not that way. Those stairs are for commoners. You and I may leave by the gentlemen's staircase."

The narrow stairs twisted downward beneath clouds of gilt cherubs-and-airships, and debouched into a marble-floored hallway. Surplus and Darger stepped out of the stairway and found their arms abruptly seized by baboons.

There were five baboons all told, with red uniforms and matching choke collars with leashes that gathered in the hand of an ornately mustached officer whose gold piping identified him as a master of apes. The fifth baboon bared his teeth and hissed savagely.

Instantly, the master of apes yanked back on his leash and said, "There, Hercules! There, sirrah! What do you do? What do you say?"

The baboon drew himself up and bowed curtly. "Please come with us," he said with difficulty. The master of apes cleared his throat. Sullenly, the baboon added, "Sir."

"This is outrageous!" Surplus cried. "I am a diplomat, and under international law immune to arrest."

"Ordinarily, sir, this is true," said the master of apes courteously. "However, you have entered the inner circle without her majesty's invitation and are thus subject to stricter standards of security."

"I had no idea these stairs went inward. I was led here by—" Surplus looked about helplessly. Lord Campbell-Supercollider was nowhere to be seen.

So, once again, Surplus and Darger found themselves escorted to the Office of Protocol.

"The wood is teak. Its binomial is *Tectonia grandis*. Teak is native to Burma, Hind, and Siam. The box is carved elaborately but without refinement." The dwarf savant opened it. "Within the casing is an archaic device for electronic intercommunication. The instrument chip is a gallium-arsenide ceramic. The chip weighs six ounces. The device is a product of the Utopian end-times."

"A modem!" The protocol officer's eyes bugged out. "You dared bring a *modem* into the inner circle and almost into the presence of the queen?" His chair stood and walked around the table. Its six insectile legs looked too slender to carry his great, legless mass. Yet it moved nimbly and well.

"It is harmless, sir. Merely something our technarchaeologists unearthed and thought would amuse the Duke of Muscovy, who is well known for his love of all things antiquarian. It is, apparently, of some cultural or historical significance, though without re-reading my instructions, I would be hard pressed to tell you what."

Lord Coherence-Hamilton raised his chair so that he loomed over Surplus, looking dangerous and domineering. "*Here* is the historic significance of your modem: The

Utopians filled the world with their computer webs and nets, burying cables and nodes so deeply and plentifully that they shall never be entirely rooted out. They then released into that virtual universe demons and mad gods. These intelligences destroyed Utopia and almost destroyed humanity as well. Only the valiant worldwide destruction of all modes of interface saved us from annihilation!" He glared.

"Oh, you lackwit! Have you no history? These creatures hate us because our ancestors created them. They are still alive, though confined to their electronic netherworld, and want only a modem to extend themselves into the physical realm. Can you wonder, then, that the penalty for possessing such a device is—" he smiled menacingly—"death?"

"No, sir, it is not. Possession of a *working* modem is a mortal crime. This device is harmless. Ask your savant."

"Well?" the big man growled at his dwarf. "Is it functional?"

"No. It—"

"Silence." Lord Coherence-Hamilton turned back to Surplus. "You are a fortunate cur. You will not be charged with any crimes. However, while you are here, I will keep this filthy device locked away and under my control. Is that understood, Sir Bow-Wow?"

Surplus sighed. "Very well," he said. "It is only for a week, after all."

That night, the Lady Pamela Coherence-Hamilton came by Surplus's room to apologize for the indignity of his arrest, of which, she assured him, she had just now learned. He invited her in. In short order they somehow found themselves kneeling face-to-face on the bed, unbuttoning each other's clothing.

Lady Pamela's breasts had just spilled delightfully from her dress when she drew back, clutching the bodice closed again, and said, "Your man is watching us."

"And what concern is that to us?" Surplus said jovially. "The poor fellow's an autistic. Nothing he sees or hears matters to him. You might as well be embarrassed by the presence of a chair."

"Even were he a wooden carving, I would his eyes were not on me."

"As you wish." Surplus clapped his paws. "Sirrah! Turn around."

Obediently, Darger turned his back. This was his first experience with his friend's astonishing success with women. How many sexual adventuresses, he wondered, might one tumble, if one's form were unique? On reflection, the question answered itself.

Behind him, he heard the Lady Pamela giggle. Then, in a voice low with passion, Surplus said, "No, leave the diamonds on."

With a silent sigh, Darger resigned himself to a long night. Since he was bored and yet could not turn to watch the pair cavorting on the bed without giving himself away, he was perforce required to settle for watching them in the mirror.

They began, of course, by doing it doggy-style.

The next day, Surplus fell sick. Hearing of his indisposition, Lady Pamela sent one of her autistics with a bowl of broth and then followed herself in a surgical mask.

Surplus smiled weakly to see her. "You have no need of that mask," he said. "By my life, I swear that what ails me is not communicable. As you doubtless know, we who have been remade are prone to endocrinological imbalance."

"Is that all?" Lady Pamela spooned some broth into his mouth, then dabbed at a speck of it with a napkin. "Then fix it. You have been very wicked to frighten me over such a trifle."

"Alas," Surplus said sadly, "I am a unique creation, and my table of endocrine balances was lost in an accident at sea. There are copies in Vermont, of course. But by the time even the swiftest schooner can cross the Atlantic twice, I fear me I shall be gone."

"Oh, dearest Surplus!" The Lady caught up his paws in her hands. "Surely there is some measure, however desperate, to be taken?"

"Well . . ." Surplus turned to the wall in thought. After a very long time, he turned back and said, "I have a confession to make. The modem your brother holds for me? It is functional."

"Sir!" Lady Pamela stood, gathering her skirts, and stepped away from the bed in horror. "Surely not!"

"My darling and delight, you must listen to me." Surplus glanced weakly toward the door, then lowered his voice. "Come close and I shall whisper."

She obeyed.

"In the waning days of Utopia, during the war between men and their electronic creations, scientists and engineers bent their efforts toward the creation of a modem that could be safely employed by humans. One immune from the attack of demons. One that could, indeed, compel their obedience. Perhaps you have heard of this project."

"There are rumors, but . . . no such device was ever built."

"Say rather that no such device was built *in time*. It had just barely been perfected when the mobs came rampaging through the laboratories, and the Age of the Machine was over. Some few, however, were hidden away before the last technicians were killed. Centuries later, brave researchers at the Technarchaeological Institute of Shelburne recovered six such devices and mastered the art of their use. One device was destroyed in the process. Two are kept in Burlington. The others were given to trusted couriers and sent to the three most powerful allies of the Demesne—one of which is, of course, Russia."

"This is hard to believe," Lady Pamela said wonderingly. "Can such marvels be?"

"Madame, I employed it two nights ago in this very room! Those voices your brother heard? I was speaking with my principals in Vermont. They gave me permission to extend my stay here to a fortnight."

He gazed imploringly at her. "If you were to bring me the device, I could then employ it to save my life."

Lady Coherence-Hamilton resolutely stood. "Fear nothing, then. I swear by my soul, the modem shall be yours tonight."

*   *   *

The room was lit by a single lamp that cast wild shadows whenever anyone moved, as if of illicit spirits at a witch's Sabbath.

It was an eerie sight. Darger, motionless, held the modem in his hands. Lady Pamela, who had a sense of occasion, had changed to a low-cut gown of clinging silks, dark-red as human blood. It swirled about her as she hunted through the wainscoting for a jack left unused for centuries. Surplus sat up weakly in bed, eyes half-closed, directing her. It might have been, Darger thought, an allegorical tableau of the human body being directed by its sick animal passions, while the intellect stood by, paralyzed by lack of will.

"There!" Lady Pamela triumphantly straightened, her necklace scattering tiny rainbows in the dim light.

Darger stiffened. He stood perfectly still for the length of three long breaths, then shook and shivered like one undergoing seizure. His eyes rolled back in his head.

In hollow, unworldly tones, he said, "What man calls me up from the vasty deep?" It was a voice totally unlike his own, one harsh and savage and eager for unholy sport. "Who dares risk my wrath?"

"You must convey my words to the autistic's ears," Surplus murmured. "For he is become an integral part of the modem—not merely its operator, but its voice."

"I stand ready," Lady Pamela replied.

"Good girl. Tell it who I am."

"It is Sir Blackthorpe Ravenscairn de Plus Precieux who speaks, and who wishes to talk to . . ." She paused.

"To his most august and socialist honor, the mayor of Burlington."

"His most august and socialist honor," Lady Pamela began. She turned toward the bed and said quizzically, "The mayor of Burlington?"

" 'Tis but an official title, much like your brother's, for he who is in fact the spy-master for the Demesne of Western Vermont," Surplus said weakly. "Now repeat to it: I compel thee on threat of dissolution to carry my message. Use those exact words."

Lady Pamela repeated the words into Darger's ear.

He screamed. It was a wild and unholy sound that sent the Lady skittering away from him in a momentary panic. Then, in mid-cry, he ceased.

"Who is this?" Darger said in an entirely new voice, this one human. "You have the voice of a woman. Is one of my agents in trouble?"

"Speak to him now, as you would to any man: forthrightly, directly, and without evasion." Surplus sank his head back on his pillow and closed his eyes.

So (as it seemed to her) the Lady Coherence-Hamilton explained Surplus's plight to his distant master, and from him received both condolences and the needed information to return Surplus's endocrine levels to a functioning harmony. After proper courtesies, then, she thanked the American spy-master and unjacked the modem. Darger returned to passivity.

The leather-cased endocrine kit lay open on a small table by the bed. At Lady Pamela's direction, Darger began applying the proper patches to various places on Surplus's body. It was not long before Surplus opened his eyes.

"Am I to be well?" he asked and, when the Lady nodded, "Then I fear I must be gone in the morning. Your brother has spies everywhere. If he gets the least whiff of what this device can do, he'll want it for himself."

Smiling, Lady Pamela hoisted the box in her hand. "Indeed, who can blame him? With such a toy, great things could be accomplished."

"So he will assuredly think. I pray you, return it to me."

She did not. "This is more than just a communication device, sir," she said. "Though in that mode it is of incalculable value. You have shown that it can enforce obedience on the creatures that dwell in the forgotten nerves of the ancient world. Ergo, they can be compelled to do our calculations for us."

"Indeed, so our technarchaeologists tell us. You must. . . ."

"We have created monstrosities to perform the duties that were once done by machines. But with *this*, there would be no necessity to do so. We have allowed ourselves to be ruled by an icosahexadexal-brained freak. Now we have no need for Gloriana the Gross, Gloriana the Fat and Grotesque, Gloriana the Maggot Queen!"

"Madame!"

"It is time, I believe, that England had a new queen. A human queen."

"Think of my honor!"

Lady Pamela paused in the doorway. "You are a very pretty fellow indeed. But with this, I can have the monarchy and keep such a harem as will reduce your memory to that of a passing and trivial fancy."

With a rustle of skirts, she spun away.

"Then I am undone!" Surplus cried, and fainted onto the bed.

Quietly, Darger closed the door. Surplus raised himself from the pillows, began removing the patches from his body, and said, "Now what?"

"Now we get some sleep," Darger said. "Tomorrow will be a busy day."

The master of apes came for them after breakfast, and marched them to their usual destination. By now, Darger was beginning to lose track of exactly how many times he had been in the Office of Protocol. They entered to find Lord Coherence-Hamilton in a towering rage, and his sister, calm and knowing, standing in a corner with her arms crossed, watching. Looking at them both now, Darger wondered how he could ever have imagined that the brother outranked his sister.

The modem lay opened on the dwarf-savant's desk. The little fellow leaned over the device, studying it minutely.

Nobody said anything until the master of apes and his baboons had left. Then Lord Coherence-Hamilton roared, "Your modem refuses to work for us!"

"As I told you, sir," Surplus said coolly, "it is inoperative."

"That's a bold-arsed fraud and a goat-buggering lie!" In his wrath, the Lord's chair rose up on its spindly legs so high that his head almost bumped against the ceiling. "I know of your activities—" he nodded toward his sister—"and demand that you show us how this whoreson device works!"

"Never!" Surplus cried stoutly. "I have my honor, sir."

"Your honor, too scrupulously insisted upon, may well lead to your death, sir."

Surplus threw back his head. "Then I die for Vermont!"

At this moment of impasse, Lady Hamilton stepped forward between the two antagonists to restore peace. "I know what might change your mind." With a knowing smile, she raised a hand to her throat and denuded herself of her diamonds. "I saw how you rubbed them against your face the other night. How you licked and fondled them. How ecstatically you took them into your mouth."

She closed his paws about them. "They are yours, sweet 'Sieur Precieux, for a word."

"You would give them up?" Surplus said, as if amazed at the very idea. In fact, the necklace had been his and Darger's target from the moment they'd seen it. The only barrier that now stood between them and the merchants of Amsterdam was the problem of freeing themselves from the Labyrinth before their marks finally realized that the modem was indeed a cheat. And to this end they had the invaluable tool of a thinking man whom all believed to be an autistic, and a plan that would give them almost twenty hours in which to escape.

"Only think, dear Surplus." Lady Pamela stroked his head and then scratched him behind one ear, while he stared down at the precious stones. "Imagine the life of wealth and ease you could lead, the women, the power. It all lies in your hands. All you need do is close them."

Surplus took a deep breath. "Very well," he said. "The secret lies in the condenser, which takes a full day to recharge. Wait but—"

"Here's the problem," the savant said unexpectedly. He poked at the interior of the modem. "There was a wire loose."

He jacked the device into the wall.

"Oh, dear God," Darger said.

A savage look of raw delight filled the dwarf savant's face, and he seemed to swell before them.

"I am free!" he cried in a voice so loud it seemed impos-

sible that it could arise from such a slight source. He shook as if an enormous electrical current were surging through him. The stench of ozone filled the room.

He burst into flames and advanced on the English spymaster and her brother.

While all stood aghast and paralyzed, Darger seized Surplus by the collar and hauled him out into the hallway, slamming the door shut as he did.

They had not run twenty paces down the hall when the door to the Office of Protocol exploded outward, sending flaming splinters of wood down the hallway.

Satanic laughter boomed behind them.

Glancing over his shoulder, Darger saw the burning dwarf, now blackened to a cinder, emerge from a room engulfed in flames, capering and dancing. The modem, though disconnected, was now tucked under one arm, as if it were exceedingly valuable to him. His eyes were round and white and lidless. Seeing them, he gave chase.

"Aubrey!" Surplus cried. "We are headed the *wrong way!*"

It was true. They were running deeper into the Labyrinth, toward its heart, rather than outward. But it was impossible to turn back now. They plunged through scattering crowds of nobles and servitors, trailing fire and supernatural terror in their wake.

The scampering grotesque set fire to the carpets with every footfall. A wave of flame tracked him down the hall, incinerating tapestries and wallpaper and wood trim. No matter how they dodged, it ran straight toward them. Clearly, in the programmatic literalness of its kind, the demon from the web had determined that having early seen them, it must early kill them as well.

Darger and Surplus raced through dining rooms and salons, along balconies and down servants' passages. To no avail. Dogged by their hyper-natural nemesis, they found themselves running down a passage, straight toward two massive bronze doors, one of which had been left just barely ajar. So fearful were they that they hardly noticed the guards.

"Hold, sirs!"

The mustachioed master of apes stood before the doorway, his baboons straining against their leashes. His eyes widened with recognition. "By gad, it's you!" he cried in astonishment.

"Lemme kill 'em!" one of the baboons cried. "The lousy bastards!" The others growled agreement.

Surplus would have tried to reason with them, but when he started to slow his pace, Darger put a broad hand on his back and shoved. "Dive!" he commanded. So of necessity the dog of rationality had to bow to the man of action. He tobogganed wildly across the polished marble floor between two baboons, straight at the master of apes, and then between his legs.

The man stumbled, dropping the leashes as he did.

The baboons screamed and attacked.

For an instant, all five apes were upon Darger, seizing his limbs, snapping at his face and neck. Then the burning dwarf arrived, and, finding his target obstructed, seized the nearest baboon. The animal shrieked as its uniform burst into flames.

As one, the other baboons abandoned their original quarry to fight this newcomer who had dared attack one of their own.

In a trice, Darger leaped over the fallen master of apes, and was through the door. He and Surplus threw their shoulders against its metal surface and pushed. He had one brief glimpse of the fight, with the baboons aflame, and their master's body flying through the air. Then the door slammed shut. Internal bars and bolts, operated by smoothly oiled mechanisms, automatically latched themselves.

For the moment, they were safe.

Surplus slumped against the smooth bronze, and wearily asked, "Where did you *get* that modem?"

"From a dealer of antiquities." Darger wiped his brow with his kerchief. "It was transparently worthless. Whoever would dream it could be repaired?"

Outside, the screaming ceased. There was a very brief silence. Then the creature flung itself against one of the metal doors. It rang with the impact.

A delicate girlish voice wearily said, "What is this noise?"

They turned in surprise and found themselves looking up at the enormous corpus of Queen Gloriana. She lay upon her pallet, swaddled in satin and lace, and abandoned by all, save her valiant (though doomed) guardian apes. A pervasive yeasty smell emanated from her flesh. Within the tremendous folds of chins by the dozens and scores was a small human face. Its mouth moved delicately and asked, "What is trying to get in?"

The door rang again. One of its great hinges gave.

Darger bowed. "I fear, madame, it is your death."

"Indeed?" Blue eyes opened wide and, unexpectedly, Gloriana laughed. "If so, that is excellent good news. I have been praying for death an extremely long time."

"Can any of God's creations truly pray for death and mean it?" asked Darger, who had his philosophical side. "I have known unhappiness myself, yet even so life is precious to me."

"Look at me!" Far up to one side of the body, a tiny arm— though truly no tinier than any woman's arm—waved feebly. "I am not God's creation, but Man's. Who would trade ten minutes of their own life for a century of mine? Who, having mine, would not trade it all for death?"

A second hinge popped. The doors began to shiver. Their metal surfaces radiated heat.

"Darger, we must leave!" Surplus cried. "There is a time for learned conversation, but it is not now."

"Your friend is right," Gloriana said. "There is a small archway hidden behind yon tapestry. Go through it. Place your hand on the left wall and run. If you turn whichever way you must to keep from letting go of the wall, it will lead you outside. You are both rogues, I see, and doubtless deserve punishment, yet I can find nothing in my heart for you but friendship."

"Madame. . . ." Darger began, deeply moved.

"Go! My bridegroom enters."

The door began to fall inward. With a final cry of "Farewell!" from Darger and "Come *on!*" from Surplus, they sped away.

By the time they had found their way outside, all of Buckingham Labyrinth was in flames. The demon, however, did not emerge from the flames, encouraging them to believe that when the modem it carried finally melted down, it had been forced to return to that unholy realm from whence it came.

The sky was red with flames as the sloop set sail for Calais. Leaning against the rail, watching, Surplus shook his head. "What a terrible sight! I cannot help feeling, in part, responsible."

"Come! Come!" Darger said. "This dyspepsia ill becomes you. We are both rich fellows, now! The Lady Pamela's diamonds will maintain us lavishly for years to come. As for London, this is far from the first fire it has had to endure. Nor will it be the last. Life is short, and so, while we live, let us be jolly!"

"These are strange words for a melancholiac," Surplus said wonderingly.

"In triumph, my mind turns its face to the sun. Dwell not on the past, dear friend, but on the future that lies glittering before us."

"The necklace is worthless," Surplus said. "Now that I have the leisure to examine it, free of the distracting flesh of Lady Pamela, I see that these are not diamonds, but mere imitations." He made to cast the necklace into the Thames.

Before he could, though, Darger snatched away the stones from him and studied them closely. Then he threw back his head and laughed. "The biters bit! Well, it may be paste, but it looks valuable still. We shall find good use for it in Paris."

"We are going to Paris?"

"We are partners, are we not? Remember that antique wisdom that whenever a door closes, another opens? For every city that burns, another beckons. To France, then, and adventure! After which, Italy, the Vatican Empire, Austro-Hungary, perhaps even Russia! Never forget that you have yet to present your credentials to the Duke of Muscovy."

"Very well," Surplus said. "But when we do, *I'll* pick out the modem."

The Building

URSULA K. LE GUIN

Ursula K. Le Guin [www.ursulakleguin.com] is one of the finest living SF and fantasy writers. She also writes poetry, mainstream fiction, children's books, and literary essays, has published a good book on how to write narrative fiction and nonfiction, and co-edited the Norton Book of Science Fiction, *an influential anthology. She has published seventeen novels and eight short story collections to date. She is one of the leading feminists in SF, and in recent years a supporter of the James Tiptree, Jr. Awards, named in honor of Le Guin's peer and friend Alice Bradley Sheldon's SF pseudonym. Le Guin's work is widely read outside the SF field, and she is taken seriously as a contemporary writer. In recent years she has published a number of distinguished short stories, and in 2000 not only did she continue to do that, but also published her first SF novel in more than ten years,* The Telling. *Recent publications include two books of* Earthsea, Tales from Earthsea *and a novel,* The Other Wind *(both 2001), and a collection of science fiction,* The Birthday of the World *(2002).*

"The Building," from Red Shift, *is a Le Guin fictional ethnography along the lines of her classic, "The Author of the Acacia Seeds." The "unteachable" humanoid race, the Aq, is compelled by unknown forces to build, by hand, an enormous stone building over the course of three or four thousand years.*

On Qoq there are two rational species. The Adaqo are stocky, greenish-tan-colored humanoids who, after a period of EEPT (explosive expansion of population and technology) four to five thousand years ago, barely survived the ensuing ecocastrophe. They have since lived on a modest scale, vastly reduced in numbers and more interested in survival than dominion.

The Aq are taller and a little greener than the Adaqo. The two species diverged from a common simioid ancestor, and are quite similar, but cannot interbreed. Like all species on Qoq, except a few pests and the insuperable and indifferent bacteria, the Aq suffered badly during and after the Adaqo EEPT.

Before it, the two species had not been in contact. The Aq inhabited the southern continent only. As the Adaqo population escalated, they spread out over the three land masses of the northern hemisphere, and as they conquered their world, they incidentally conquered the Aq.

The Adaqo attempted to use the Aq as slaves for domestic or factory work, but failed. The historical evidence is shaky, but it seems the Aq, though unaggressive, simply do not take orders from anybody. During the height of the EEPT, the most expansive Adaqo empires pursued a policy of slaughtering the "primitive" and "unteachable" Aq in the name of progress. Less bloody-minded civilizations of the equatorial zone merely pushed the remnant Aq populations into the deserts and barely habitable canebrakes of the coast. There a

thousand or so Aq survived the destruction and final crash of
the planet's life-web.

Descent from this limited genetic source may help explain the prevalence of certain traits among the Aq, but the
cultural expression of these tendencies is inexplicable in its
uniformity. We don't know much about what they were like
before the crash, but their reputed refusal to carry out the
other species' orders might imply that they were already, as
it were, working under orders of their own.

As for the Adaqo, their numbers have risen from perhaps
a hundred thousand survivors of the crash to about two million, mostly on the central north and the south continents.
They live in small cities, towns, and farms, and carry on
agriculture and commerce; their technology is efficient but
modest, limited both by the exhaustion of their world's resources and by strict religious sanctions.

The present-day Aq number about forty thousand, all on
the south continent. They live as gatherers and fishers, with
some limited, casual agriculture. The only one of their domesticated animals to survive the die-offs is the boos, a
clever creature descended from pack-hunting carnivores.
The Aq hunted with boos when there were animals to hunt.
Since the crash, they use the boos to carry or haul light
loads, as companions, and in hard times as food.

Aq villages are movable; their houses, from time imme-
morial, have consisted of fabric domes stretched on a frame
of light poles or canes, easy to set up, dismantle, and transport. The tall cane which grows in the swampy lakes of the
desert and all along the coasts of the equatorial zone of the
southern continent is their staple; they gather the young
shoots for food, spin and weave the fiber into cloth, and
make rope, baskets, and tools from the stems. When they
have used up all the cane in a region they pick up the village
and move on. The caneplants regenerate from the root system in a few years.

They have kept pretty much to the desert-and-canebrake
habitat enforced upon them by the Adaqo in earlier millennia. Some, however, camp around outside Adaqo towns and
engage in a little barter and filching. The Adaqo trade with

them for their fine canvas and baskets, and tolerate their thievery to a surprising degree.

Indeed the Adaqo attitude to the Aq is hard to define. Wariness is part of it; a kind of unease that is not suspicion or distrust; a watchfulness that, surprisingly, stops short of animosity or contempt, and may even become conciliating, as if the uneasiness were located in the Adaqo conscience.

It is even harder to say what the Aq think of the Adaqo. They communicate in a pidgin or jargon containing elements from both Adaqo and Aq languages, but it appears that no individual ever learns the other species' language. The two species seem to have settled on coexistence without relationship. They have nothing to do with each other except for these occasional, slightly abrasive contacts at the edges of Adaqo settlements—and a certain limited, strange collaboration having to do with what I can only call the specific obsession of the Aq.

I am not comfortable with the phrase "specific obsession," but "cultural instinct" is worse.

At about two and a half or three years old, Aq babies begin building. Whatever comes into their little greeny-bronze hands that can possibly serve as a block or brick they pile up into "houses." The Aq use the same word for these miniature structures as for the fragile cane-and-canvas domes they live in, but there is no resemblance except that both are roofed enclosures with a door. The children's "houses" are rectangular, flat-roofed, and always made of solid, heavy materials. They are not imitations of Adaqo houses, or only at a very great remove, since most of these children have never seen an Adaqo building or a representation of one.

It is hard to believe that they imitate one another with such unanimity that they never vary the plan; but it is harder to believe that their building style, like that of insects, is innate.

As the children get older and more skillful they build larger constructions, though still no more than knee-high, with passages, courtyards, and sometimes towers. Many children spend all their free time gathering rocks or making mud bricks and building "houses." They do not populate their buildings with toy people or animals or tell stories about them. They just build them, with evident pleasure and satisfaction. By the age of six or seven some children begin to leave off building, but others go on working together with other children, often under the guidance of interested adults, to make "houses" of considerable complexity, though still not large enough for anyone to live in. The children do not play in them.

When the village picks up and moves to a new gathering-ground or canebrake, these children leave their constructions behind without any sign of distress, and as soon as they are settled begin building again, often cannibalizing stones or bricks from the "houses" of a previous generation left on the site. Popular gathering sites are marked by dozens or hundreds of solidly built miniature ruins, populated only by the joint-legged gikoto of the marshes or the little ratlike hikiqi of the desert.

No such ruins have been found in areas where the Aq lived before the Adaqo conquest—an indication that their propensity to build was less strong, or didn't exist, before the conquest or before the crash.

Two or three years after their ceremonies of adolescence some of the young people, those who went on building "houses" until they reached puberty, will go on their first stone faring.

A stone faring sets out once a year from the Aq territories. The complete journey takes from two to three years, after which the travelers return to their natal village for five or six years. Some Aq never go stone faring, others go once, some go several or many times in their life.

The route of the stone farings is to the coast of Riqim, on the northeast continent, and back to the Mediro, a rocky plateau far inland from the southernmost canebrakes of the great south continent.

The Aq stone farers gather in spring, coming overland or by caneraft from their various villages to Gatbam, a small port near the equator on the west coast of the south continent. There a fleet of cane-and-canvas sailboats awaits them. The sailors and navigators are all Adaqo, most of them from towns of the northwest coast. They are professional sailors, mostly fishermen; some of them "sail the faring" every year for decades. The Aq pilgrims have nothing to pay them with, arriving with provisions for the journey but nothing else. While at Riqim, the Adaqo sailors will net and salt fish from those rich waters, a catch which makes their journey profitable. But they never go to fish off Riqim except with the stone-faring fleet.

The journey takes several weeks. The voyage north is the dangerous one, made early in the year so that the return voyage, carrying the cargo, may be made at the optimal time. Now and then boats or even whole fleets are lost in the wild tropical storms of that wide sea.

As soon as they disembark on the stony shores of Riqim, the Aq get to work. Under the direction of senior stone farers, the novices set up domed tents, store their sparse provisions, take up the tools left there by the last pilgrimage, and climb the steep green cliffs to the quarries.

Riqimite is a lustrous, fine-textured, greenish stone with a tendency to cleave along a plane. It can be sawed in blocks or split into stone "planks" or smaller "tiles" and even into sheets so thin they are translucent. Though relatively light, it is stone, and a ten-meter canvas sailboat can't carry great quantities of it; so the stone farers carefully gauge the amount they quarry. They roughshape the blocks at Riqim and even do some of the fine cutting, so that the boats carry as little waste as possible. They work fast, since they want to start home in the calm season around the solstice. When their work is complete they run up a flag on a high pole on the cliffs to signal the fleet, which comes in boat by boat over the next few days. They load the stone aboard under the tubs of salted fish and set sail back south.

The boats put in at various Adaqo ports, usually the crew's home port, to unload and sell their fish; then they all sail on several hundred kilometers down the coast to Gazt, a long, shallow harbor in the hot marshlands south of the canebrake country. There the sailors help the Aq unload the stone. They receive no payment for or profit from this part of the trip. I asked a shipmaster who had "sailed the faring" many times why she and her sailors were willing to make the trip to Gazt. She shrugged. "It's part of the agreement," she said, evidently not having thought much about it, and after thinking, added, "Be an awful job to drag that stone overland through the marshes."

Before the boats have sailed halfway back to the harbor mouth, the Aq have begun loading the stone onto wheeled flatbed carts left on the docks of Gazt by the last stone faring.

Then they get into harness and haul these carts five hundred kilometers inland and three thousand meters upward.

They go at most three or four kilometers a day. They encamp before evening and fan out from the trails to forage and set snares for hiqiki, since by now their supplies are low. The cart train tends to follow the least recently used of the several winding trails, because the hunting and gathering will be better along it.

During the sea voyages and at Riqim the mood of the stone farers tends to be solemn and tense. They are not sailors, and the labor at the quarries is hard and driven. Hauling carts by shoulder-harness is certainly not light work either, but the pilgrims take it merrily; they talk and joke while hauling, share their food and sit talking around their campfires, and behave like any group of people engaged willingly in an arduous joint enterprise.

They discuss which path to take, and wheel-mending techniques, and so on. But when I went with them I never heard them talk in the larger sense about what they were doing, their journey's goal.

All the paths finally have to surmount the cliffs at the edge of the plateau. As they come up onto the level after that terrible last grade, the stone farers stop and gaze to the southeast. One after another the long, flat carts laden with dusty stone buck and jerk up over the rim and stop. The haulers stand in harness, gazing silent at the Building.

After a thousand years or so of the long, slow recovery of the shattered ecosystem, enough Aq began to have enough food to have enough energy for activities beyond forage and storage. It was then, when bare survival was still chancy, that they began the stone faring. So few, in such an inimical world, the atmosphere damaged, the great cycles of life not yet reestablished in the poisoned and despoiled oceans, the lands full of bones, ghosts, ruins, dead forests, deserts of salt, of sand, of chemical waste—how did the inhabitants of such a world think of undertaking such a task? How did they know the stone they wanted was at Riqim? How did they know where Riqim was? Did they originally make their way there somehow without Adaqo boats and navigators? The origins of the stone faring are absolutely mysterious, but no more mysterious than its object. All we know is that every stone in the Building comes from the quarries of Riqim, and that the Aq have been building it for over three thousand, perhaps four thousand years.

It is immense, of course. It covers many acres and contains thousands of rooms, passages, and courts. It is certainly one of the largest edifices, perhaps the largest single one, on any world. And yet declarations of size, counts and measures, comparisons and superlatives, are meaningless, the fact being that a technology such as that of contemporary Earth, or the ancient Adaqo, could have built a building ten times bigger in ten years.

It is possible that the ever-increasing vastness of the Building is a metaphor or illustration of precisely such a moral enormity.

Or its size may be purely, simply, a result of its age. The oldest sections, far inside its outermost walls, show no indication that they were—or were not—seen as the beginning of something immense. They are exactly like the Aq children's "houses" on a larger scale. All the rest of the Building has been added on, year by year, to this modest beginning, in much the same style. After perhaps some centuries the builders began to add stories onto the flat roofs of the early Building, but have never gone above four stories, except for towers and pinnacles and the airy barrel-domes that reach a height of perhaps sixty meters. The great bulk of the Building is no more than five to six meters high. Inevitably it has kept growing outward laterally, by way of ells and wings and joining arcades and courtyards, until it covers so vast an area that from a distance it looks like a fantastic terrain, a low mountain landscape all in silvery green stone.

Although not dwarfed like the children's structures, curiously enough the Building is not quite full scale, taking the average height of an Aq as measure. The ceilings are barely high enough to allow them to stand straight, and they must stoop to pass through the doors.

No part of the Building is ruined or in disrepair, though occasional earthquakes shake the Mediro plateau. Damaged areas are repaired annually, or furnished stone to rebuild with.

The work is fine, careful, sure, and delicate. No material is used but riqimite, mortised and tenoned like wood, or set in exquisitely fitted blocks and courses. The indoor surfaces are mostly finished satin smooth, the outer faces left in contrasting degrees of roughness and smoothness. There is no carving or ornamentation other than thin moldings or incised lines repeating and outlining the architectural shapes.

Windows are unglazed stone lattices or pierced stone sheets cut so thin as to be translucent. The repetitive rectangular designs of the latticework are elegantly proportioned; a ratio of four to five runs through many though not all of the Building's rooms and apertures. Doors are thin stone slabs so well balanced and pivoted that they swing lightly and smoothly open and shut. There are no furnishings.

Empty rooms, empty corridors, miles of corridors, endlessly similar, stairways, ramps, courtyards, roof terraces, delicate towers, vistas over the roofs of roof beyond roof, tower beyond tower, dome beyond dome to the far distance; high rooms lighted by great lacework windows or only by the dim, greenish, mottled translucency of windowpanes of stone, corridors that lead to other corridors, other rooms, stairs, ramps, courtyards, corridors. . . . Is it a maze, a labyrinth? Yes, inevitably; but is that what it was built to be?

Is it beautiful? Yes, in a way, wonderfully beautiful; but is that what it was built to be?

The Aq are a rational species. Answers to these questions must come from them. The troubling thing is that they have many different answers, none of which seems quite satisfying to them or anyone else.

In this they resemble any reasonable being who does an unreasonable thing and justifies it with reasons. War, for example. My species has a great many good reasons for making war, though none of them is as good as the reason for not making war. Our most rational and scientific justifications—for instance, that we are an aggressive species—are perfectly circular: we make war because we make war. This is not really satisfying to the reasonable mind. Our justifications for making a particular war (such as: our people must have more land and more wealth, or: our people must have more power, or: our people must obey our deity's orders to crush the heinous sacrilegious infidel) all come down to the same thing: we must make war because we must. We have no choice. We have no freedom. This is not ultimately satisfactory to the reasoning mind, which desires freedom.

In the same way the efforts of the Aq to explain or justify their building and their Building all invoke a necessity which doesn't seem all that necessary and use reasons which meet themselves coming around. We go stone faring because we have always done it. We go to Riqim because the best stone is there. The Building is on the Mediro because the ground's good and there's room for it there. The Building is a great undertaking, which our children can look forward to and our finest men and women can work together on. The stone faring brings people from all our villages together. We were only a poor scattered people in the old days, but now the Building shows that there is a great vision in us.—All these reasons make sense but don't quite convince, don't satisfy.

Perhaps the questions should be asked of those Aq who never have gone stone faring. They don't themselves question the stone faring. They speak of the stone farers as people doing something brave, difficult, worthy, perhaps sacred. So why have you never gone yourself?—Well, I never felt the need to. People who go, they have to go, they're called to it.

What about the other people, the Adaqo? What do they

think about this immense structure, certainly the greatest enterprise and achievement on their world at this time? Very little, evidently. Even the sailors of the stone faring never go up onto the Mediro and know nothing about the Building except that it is there and is very large. Adaqo of the northwest continent know it only as rumor, fable, travelers' tales—the Palace of the Mediro on the Great South Continent. Some tales say the King of the Aq lives there in unimaginable splendor; others that it is a tower taller than the mountains, in which eyeless monsters dwell; others that it is a maze where the unwary traveler is lost in endless corridors full of bones and ghosts; others say that the winds blowing through it moan in huge chords like a vast aeolian harp, which can be heard for hundreds of miles; and so on. To the Adaqo it is a legend, like their own legends of the Ancient Times when their mighty ancestors flew in the air and drank rivers dry and turned forests into stone and built towers taller than the sky, and so on. Fairy tales.

Now and then an Aq who has been stone faring will say something different about the Building. If asked about it, some of them reply: "It is for the Adaqo."

And indeed the Building is better proportioned to the short stature of the Adaqo than to the tall Aq. The Adaqo, if they ever went there, could walk through the corridors and doorways upright.

An old woman of Katas, who had been five times a stone farer, was the first who gave me that answer.

"For the Adaqo?" I said, taken aback. "But why?"

"Because of the old days."

"But they never go there."

"It isn't finished," she said.

"A retribution?" I asked, puzzling at it. "A recompense?"

"They need it," she said.

"The Adaqo need it, but you don't?"

"No," the old woman said with a smile. "We build it. We don't need it."

Gray Earth

STEPHEN BAXTER

Stephen Baxter (www.sam.math.ethz.ch/%7Epkeller/Baxter-Page.html) is now one of the big names in hard SF, the author of a number of highly regarded novels (he has won the Philip K. Dick Award, the John W. Campbell Memorial Award, the British SF Association Award, and others for his novels) and many short stories. He published four books in 2000, including a collaboration with Arthur C. Clarke, The Light of Other Days, *and* Space: Manifold 2 *(titled Manifold: Space in the U.S.), and won the Philip K. Dick Award for his collection,* Vacuum Diagrams *(1999). The third volume,* Origin: Manifold 3, *was published in 2001, as was* Icebones, Deep Time, *and a collection,* Ormegatropic: Non-Fiction & Fiction. *In the mid and late 1990s, he produced five or ten short stories a year in fantasy, SF, and horror venues, and did so again in 2001. He appeared in most of the major magazines, sometimes twice.*

"Gray Earth" appeared in Asimov's, and although complete in itself, is an outtake from his novel Manifold: Origin. *Filled with SF ideas, it is about a dying human woman living among Neanderthals on an alternate Earth, coming to terms with her death in the context of an orchestrated human evolution. It feels like Baxter is emulating Ursula K. Le Guin here, with respectable results.*

She was old now. The cold dug into her joints and her scars, and the leg she had fractured long ago, more than it used to.

She still called herself Mary. But she was one of the last to use the old names. And the people no longer called themselves Hams—for there were no Skinnies here who could call them that, none save Nemoto—and they were no longer called the People of the Gray Earth, for they had come home to the Gray Earth, and had no need to remember it.

There came a day, when they put old Saul in the ground, when Mary found herself the last to remember the old place, the Red Moon where she had been born.

Outside the cave that day there was only darkness, the still darkness of the Long Night, broken by the stars that sprinkled the cloudless black sky. Mary's deep past was a place of dark green warmth. But her future lay in the black cold ground, where so many had gone before her: Ruth, Joshua, Saul, even one of her own children.

But it didn't matter.

All that mattered were her skins, and the fug of gossip and talk that filled the cave, and the warm sap that bled from the root of the blood-tree that pierced the cave roof, on its way to seek out the endless warmth that dwelled in the belly of this earth, this Gray Earth.

All that mattered was today. Comparisons with misty other times—with past and future, with a girl who had fought and laughed and loved on a different world, with the bones that would soon rot in the ground—were without meaning.

Nemoto was not so content, of course.

> *Day succeeds empty day.*
>
> *At first, on arriving here, I dreamed of physical luxuries:running hot water, clean, well-prepared food, a soft bed. But now it is as if my soul has been eroded down to an irreducible core. To sleep in the open on a bower of leaves no longer troubles me. To have my skin coated in slippery grime is barely noticeable.*
>
> *But I long for security. And I long for the sight of another human face.*
>
> *Sometimes I rage inwardly. But I have no one to blame for the fact that I have become lost between worlds, between realities.*
>
> *And when I become locked inside my own head, when my inner distress becomes too apparent, it disturbs the Hams, as if I am becoming a danger to them.*
>
> *So I have learned not to look inward.*
>
> *I watch the Hams as they shamble about their various tasks, their brute bodies wrapped up in tied-on animal skins like Christmas parcels. All I see is their strangeness, fresh every day. They will complete a tool, use it once, drop it where they stand, and move on. It is as if every day is the very first day of their lives, as if they wake up to a world created anew.*
>
> *It is obvious that their minds, housed in those huge skulls, are powerful, but they are not like humans'. But then they are not human. They are Neandertal.*
>
> *This is their planet. A Neandertal planet.*
>
> *Still, I try to emulate them. I try to live one day at a time. It is comforting.*
>
> *My name is Nemoto. If you find this diary, if you understand what I have to say, remember me.*

Nemoto was never content. Even in the deepest dark of the Long Night, she would bustle about the cave, arguing with herself, agitated, endlessly making her incomprehensible objects. Or else she would blunder out into the dark, heavily wrapped in furs, perhaps seeking her own peace in the frozen stillness beyond.

Few watched her come and go. To the younger folk, Nemoto had been here all their lives, a constant, unique, somewhat irritating presence.

But Mary remembered the Red Moon, and how its lands had run with Skinnies like Nemoto.

Mary understood. Mary was of the Gray Earth, and she had come home. But Nemoto was of the Red Moon—or perhaps of another place, a Blue Earth of which she sometimes spoke—and now it was Nemoto who had been stranded far from her home.

And so Mary made space for Nemoto. She would protect Nemoto when the children were too boisterous with her, or when an adult challenged her, or when she fell ill or injured herself. She would even give her meat to eat. But Nemoto's thin, pointed jaw could make no impression on the deep-frozen meat of the winter store, nor could her shining tools. So Mary would soften the meat for her with her own strong jaws, chewing it as she would to feed a child.

But one day Nemoto spat out her mouthful of meat on the floor of the cave. She raged and shouted in her jabbering Skinny tongue, expressing disgust. She pulled on her furs and gathered her tools, and stamped out of the cave.

Time did not matter during the Long Night, nor during its bright twin, the Long Day. Nemoto was gone, as gone as if she had been put in the ground, and she began to soften in the memory.

But at last Nemoto returned, as if from the dead. She was staggering and laughing, and she carried a bundle under her arms. The children gathered around to see.

It was a bat, still plump with its winter fat, its leathery wings folded over. The bat had tucked itself into a tree hollow to endure the Long Night. But Nemoto had dug it out, and now she put it close to a warm root of the blood-tree to let it thaw. She jabbered about how she would eat well of fresh meat.

The bat revived briefly, flapping its broad wings against

the cave floor. But Nemoto briskly slit its throat with a stone knife, and began to butcher it.

Nemoto consumed her bat, giving warm tidbits to the children who clustered around to see. She sucked marrow from its thread-thin bones, and gave that to the children as well. But when she offered the children bloated, pink-gray internal organs, mothers pulled the children away.

That was the last time Nemoto was ever healthy.

Mary eats her meat raw, tearing at it with her shovel-shaped teeth and cutting it with a flake knife; every so often she scrapes her teeth with the knife. And as her powerful jaw grinds at the meat, great muscles work in her cheeks.

Mary is short, robust, heavily built. She is barrel-chested, and her arms and massive-boned legs are slightly bowed. Her feet are broad, her toes fat and bony. Her massive hands, with their long powerful thumbs, are scarred from stone chips. Her skull, under a thatch of dark brown hair, is long and low, with a pronounced bulge at the rear. Her face is pulled forward into a great prow fronted by her massive, fleshy nose; her cheeks sweep back as if streamlined, but her jaw, though chinless, is massive and thrust forward. From her lower forehead a great ridge of bone thrusts forward, masking her eyes. There is a pronounced dip above the ridges, before her shallow brow leads back into a tangle of hair.

She is Neandertal. There can be no doubt.

She lives—I live—in a system of caves. There is an overpowering stench of people, of sweat, wood smoke, excrement, and burning fur, and a musty, disagreeable odor of people who don't wash.

Every move the Hams make, every act they complete, from cracking open a bone to bouncing a child in the air, is suffused with strength. They suffer a large number of injuries bone fractures and crushing injuries and gouged and scarred skin. But then, their favored hunting technique is to wrestle their prey to the ground. It is like living with a troupe of rodeo riders.

The Hams barely notice me. They are utterly wrapped up in each other. Some of the children pluck at the remnants of my clothing with their intimidatingly strong fingers. But otherwise the Hams step around me, their eyes sliding away, as if I am a rock embedded in the ground. I sometimes theorize that they are only truly conscious in social interactions; everything else—eating, making tools, even hunting—is done in a rapid blur, as I used to drive a car, without thinking. Certainly, to a Neandertal, by far the most fascinating things in the world are other Neandertals.

They are not human. But they care for their children, and for their ill and elderly. However coolly the Hams treat me, they have not expelled me, which is why I survive.

I brought them here, from the Red Moon. This tipped-up Earth is their home. They remembered it during the time of their exile on another world. Remembered it for forty thousand years, an unimaginable time.

I imagined I would be able to get away from here, to home. It did not happen that way.

There was a time of twilights, blue-purple shading to pink. And then, at last, the edge of the sun was visible over the horizon: just a splinter of it, just for an hour, but it was the first time the sun had shown at all for sixty-eight days.

When the people saw the light they came bursting out of the cave.

They scrambled onto the low bluff over the cave, where the blood-tree stood: leafless and gaunt now, but its blood-red sap coursed with the warmth it had drawn from the Gray Earth's belly, the warmth that had sustained the people through the Long Night. The people danced and capered and threw off their furs. Then they retreated to the warmth of the cave, where there was much chatter, much eating, much joyous sex.

Though it would be some time yet before the frozen lakes

and rivers began to thaw, there was already a little meltwater to be had. And the first hibernating animals—birds and a few large rats—were beginning to stir, sluggish and vulnerable to hunting. The people enjoyed the first thin fruits of the new season.

But Nemoto's illness was worse.

She suffered severe bouts of diarrhea and vomiting. She steadily lost weight, becoming, in the uninterested eyes of the people, even more gaunt than she had seemed before. And her skin grew flaky and sore. The children would watch in horrified fascination as she shucked off her furs and her clothes, and then peeled off bits of her skin, as if she would keep on until nothing was left but a heap of bones.

Mary tried to treat the diarrhea. She brought water, brine from the ocean diluted by meltwater. But she did not know how to treat the poisoning that was working its way through Nemoto's system.

> *The key incident in the formation of the Earth was the collision of proto-Earth with a wandering planetesimal larger than Mars. This is known as the Big Whack.*
>
> *It is hard to envisage such an event. The projectile that ended the Cretaceous era, sending the dinosaurs to extinction, was perhaps six miles across. The primordial impactor was some four thousand miles across. It was a fully formed planet in its own right. And the collision released two hundred million times as much energy as the Cretaceous impact.*
>
> *The proto-Earth's oceans were boiled away. About half of Earth's crust was demolished by the impact. A tremendous spray of liquid rock was hurled into space. The impactor was stripped of its own mantle material, and its core sank into the interior of the Earth. Much of the plume fell back to Earth. Whatever was left of the atmosphere was heated to thousands of degrees.*
>
> *The remnant plume settled into a ring around the Earth, glowing white hot. As it cooled, it solidified into a swarm of moonlets. It was like a replay of the forma-*

tion of the solar system itself. The largest of the moonlets won out. The growing Moon swept up the remnant particles, and, under the influence of tidal forces, rapidly receded from Earth.

Earth itself, meanwhile, was afflicted by huge tides, a molten crust, and savage rains as the ocean vapor fell back from space. It took millions of years before the rocks had cooled enough for liquid water to gather once more.

Everything was shaped in those moments of impact: Earth's spin, the tilt of the axis that gives us seasons, the planet's internal composition, the Moon's composition and orbit.

But it didn't have to be that way.

Such immense collisions are probably common in the formation of any planetary system. But the impact itself was a random event: chaotic, in that small differences could have produced large, even unpredictable consequences. The impactor might have missed Earth altogether—but that would have left Earth with its original atmosphere, a crushing Venus-like blanket of carbon dioxide. Or the impactor might have hit at a subtly different angle. A single Moon isn't necessarily the most likely outcome; many collision geometries would produce two twin Moons, or three or four, or ring systems like Saturn's. And so on.

Many possibilities. All of which, somewhere in the infinite manifold of universes, must have come to pass.

I know this because I have visited several of those possibilities.

The days lengthened rapidly.

The ice on the lakes and rivers melted, causing splintering crashes all over the landscape, like a long, drawn-out explosion. Soon the lakes were blue, though pale cores of unmelted ice lingered in their cores.

Life swarmed. In this brief temperate interval between deadly cold and unbearable heat, plants and animals alike engaged in a frenzied round of fighting, feeding, breeding, dying.

The people moved rapidly about the landscape. They gathered the fruit and shoots that seemed to burst out of the ground. They hunted the small animals and birds that emerged from their hibernations to seek mates and nesting places.

And soon a distant thunder sounded across the land: relentless, billowing day and night across the newly green plains, echoing from green-clad mountains. It was the sound of hoofed feet, the first of the migrant herds.

The men and women gathered their weapons, and headed toward the sea.

It turned out to be a herd of giant antelopes. They were slim and streamlined, the muscles of their legs and haunches huge and taut, the bucks sporting large folded-back antlers. And they ran like the wind. Since most of this tilted world was, at any given moment, freezing or baking through its long seasons, migrant animals were forced to travel across thousands of kilometers, spanning continents in their search for food, water, and temperate climes. Speed and endurance were of the essence for survival.

But predators came too, sleek hyenas and cats stalking the vast herds. Though the antelopes were mighty runners—fueled by high-density fat, able to race for days without a break—there were always outliers who could not keep up: the old, the very young, the injured, mothers gravid with young. And it was on these weaker individuals that the predators feasted.

Those predators included the people, who inhabited a neck of land between two continents, a funnel down which the migrant herds were forced to swarm.

The antelope herd was huge. But it passed so rapidly that the great river of flesh was gone in a couple of days. And after another day, the predator packs that stalked it had gone too.

The people ate their antelope meat and sucked rich marrow, and gathered their fruit and nuts and shoots, and waited for their next provision to come to them, delivered up by the tides of the world.

But the next group of running animals to come by was

small—everyone could sense that—and everybody knew what they were, from their distinctive, high-pitched cries.

Everybody lost interest. Everybody but Nemoto.

The Hams are aware of the coming and going of the herds of migrating herbivores on which they rely for much of their meat, and are even able to predict them by the passage of the seasons. But Hams do not plan. They seem to rely on the benison of the world to provision them, day to day. It means they sometimes go hungry, but not even that dents their deep, ancient faith in the world's kindness.

I remember a particular hunt. I followed a party of Hams along a trail through the forest.

They stopped by a small tree, thick with hanging fibers, and with dark hollows showing beneath its prop roots. White lichen was plastered over its trunk, and a parasitic plant with narrow, dark-green leaves dangled from a hollow in its trunk. A Ham cut a sapling and pushed it into one deep dark hollow, just above the muddy mush of leaves and detritus at the base of the tree.

A deep growling emerged from beneath the roots of the tree.

Excited, the Hams gathered around the tree and began to haul at it, shaking it back and forth. To my amazement they pulled the tree over by brute force, just ripping the roots out of the ground. Out squirmed a crocodile, a meter long, jaws clamped at the end of the pole. It was dark brown with a red-tinged head, huge eyes, and startlingly white teeth.

It was a forest crocodile. These creatures come out at night. They eat frogs, insects, flightless birds, anything they can find. They have barely changed in two hundred million years.

This world is full of such archaisms and anachronisms—like the Hams themselves. Of course it is. For it is not my world, my Earth. It is not my universe.

The Hams fell on the crocodile in their brutal, un-

compromising way. They rolled it onto its back. One woman took a stone hand-axe and sliced off the right front leg, then the left. The animal, still alive, struggled feebly; its screams were low, like snoring. When the woman opened its chest it slumped at last.

I confronted Abel. "Why didn't you kill it before starting the butchering?"

The big man just looked back at me, apparently bemused.

These are not pet-owners. They aren't even farmers. They are hunter-gatherers. They have no reason to be sentimental about the animals, to care about them. My ancestors were like this once.

Not only that: the Hams do not anthropomorphize. They could not imagine how it would be to suffer like the animal, for it was a crocodile, not a person.

I turned away from the blood, which was spreading over the ground.

Sickly, gaunt, enfeebled, her clothing stained with her own shit and piss, her eyes so weak she had to wear slitted skins over her face, Nemoto seemed enraged by the approach of these new arrivals. She gathered up her tools of stone and metal, and hurried out of the cave toward the migrants.

Mary followed Nemoto, catching her easily.

Soon they saw the Running-folk.

There were many of them, men, women, children. They had broken their lifelong trek at a river bank. They were splashing water into their mouths, and over their faces and necks. The children were paddling in the shallows. They were all naked, all hairless save for thatches on their scalps and in their groins and arm-pits.

They would never have been considered beautiful by a human, for their legs were immensely long and their chests expanded behind huge rib cages, giving them something of the look of storks. But they had the faces of their *Homo erectus* ancestors, small and low-browed with wide, flat nostrils.

And Nemoto was stalking toward this gathering, waving

her arms and brandishing her weapons. "Get away! Get away from there, you brutes!"

Some of the adults got to their feet, their legs unfolding, bird-like. Mary could hear their growls, though she and Nemoto were still distant. The first rock—crudely chipped, as if by a child—landed in the dirt at their feet.

Mary grabbed Nemoto's arm. Nemoto struggled and cursed, but Mary held her effortlessly. She dragged Nemoto back out of range of the stones.

The Runners settled again to their bathing and drinking. They stayed where they were for most of that long day, and so did Nemoto, squatting in the dirt with scarcely a motion, staring at the Runners.

Mary stayed with her, growing increasingly hot and thirsty.

At last, as the evening drew in, the Runners got to their feet, one by one, picking up their long hinged legs. And then they began to move off along the river. They became lanky silhouettes against the setting sun, and the river gleamed gold.

Nemoto stalked down toward the river.

Here, just where the Runners had settled, there was a shell of white and black, cracked open. It was the thing Nemoto called a *lander*. Once, Nemoto had used it to bring the Hams here, to the Gray Earth, to home. Nemoto clambered inside the shattered hull. After so many cycles of the Gray Earth's ferocious seasons, there was little left of the interior equipment now. Mary saw how birds and wasps and spiders had made their home here, and grass and herbs had colonized the remnants of the softer materials.

Mary thought she understood. Though it had been broken open the moment it had fallen to the ground, Nemoto had done her best to protect and preserve the wreck of the lander. Perhaps she wanted it to take her home.

But the lander remained resolutely smashed and broken, and Nemoto could not even persuade the people to get together to haul it away from the river.

As the light seeped out of the sky, Nemoto, at last, came away from the wreck. Mary took her arm, and shepherded her quickly toward the security of the cave, for the predators hunted at sunset.

It proved to be the last time Nemoto ever left the community.

I do not know how this came to be, this manifold, this cosmic panoply, this proliferation of realities.

There is a theory that our universe grew from a seed, a tiny piece of very-high-density material that then inflated into a great volume of spacetime, with planets and stars and galaxies. This was the Big Bang. But perhaps that seed was not unique. Perhaps there is a sea of primordial high-density matter-energy—a sea where temperatures and densities and pressures exceed anything in our universe, where physics operates according to different laws—and within this sea universes inflate, one after another, like bubbles in foam. These bubble-universes would have no connection with each other. Their inhabitants would see only their own bubble, not the foam itself.

That is my legend. The Hams' legend is that the Old Ones created it all. Who is to say who is right? How could we ever know?

Whatever the origin of the manifold, within it there could be an infinite number of universes. And in an infinite ensemble, everything that is logically possible must—somewhere, somehow—come to pass.

Thus there must be a cluster of bubble-spaces with identical histories up to the moment of Earth's formation, the Big Whack—and differing after that only in the details of the impact itself, and their consequences. I imagine the possible universes arrayed around me in a kind of probability space. And universes differing only in the details of the Earth-Moon impact must somehow be close to ours in that graph of the possible.

I know this from personal experience.

For me it began when a new Moon appeared in Earth's sky: a fat Moon, a Red Moon, replacing poor dead Luna. I traveled to that Moon on a quixotic jaunt with Reid Malenfant, ostensibly in search of his lost wife, Emma Stoney. There we encountered many hominid forms—some more or less human, some not—all refugees from different reality strands, swept away by that Red Moon, which slides in sideways knight's moves between universes.

Just as Malenfant and I were swept away, when my own Earth, Blue Earth, disappeared from the Moon's sky. I knew immediately that I could never go home.

To fulfil a pledge foolishly made to these Hams by Emma Stoney, I agreed to use our small Earth-Moon ferry spacecraft to carry the Hams back to their Gray Earth—when the opportunity presented itself, as our wandering Moon happened that way. Once I was off the Red Moon, with a spacecraft, I vaguely imagined that I would be able to go further, to get away from the deadening menticulture that rapidly emerged among the stranded on the Red Moon. But it was not to be; I crashed here, and when the Red Moon wandered away from the sky, I was left doubly stranded.

The Red Moon is an agent of human evolution. That is why it wanders. Its interstitial meandering is a mixing device, an artifact of the Old Ones, who may even have manufactured this vast mesh of realities.

So I believe.

But whatever the purpose of that Moon's wandering, it destroyed my own life.

For the Hams, for Mary, the Gray Earth is home. For me, this entire universe is a vast prison.

The air grew hotter yet, approaching its most violent peak of temperature, even though the sun still lingered beneath the horizon for part of its round, even though night still touched the Gray Earth. Soon the fast-growing grasses and herbs were dying back, and the migrant animals and birds had fled, seeking the temperate climes.

The season's last rain fell. Mary closed her eyes and raised her open mouth to the sky, for she knew it would be a long time before she felt rain on her face again.

The ground became a plain of baked and cracked mud.

The people retreated to their cave. Just as its thick rock walls had sheltered them from the most ferocious cold of the winter, so now the walls gave them coolness. And just as the people had drawn warmth from the sap of the blood-tree, pumped up from the ground, now the tree let its sap carry its excess heat down into the ground, and its tangle of roots cooled the cave further.

The people ate the meat they had dried out and stored in the back of their cave, and they drank water from the drying rivers and lakes, and dug up hibernating frogs, fat sacks of water and meat that croaked resentfully as they were briskly killed.

Nemoto could not leave the cave, of course. Long before the heat reached its height, her relentless illness had driven her to her pallet, where she remained, unable to rise, with a strip of skin tied across her eyes. But Mary brought her water and food.

At length, there came a day when the sun failed even to brush the horizon at its lowest point. From now on, for sixty-eight days, it would not rise or set, but would make meaningless circles in the sky, circles that would grow smaller and more elevated.

The Long Day had begun.

And still the great blood-tree grew, drinking in the endless light of the sun and the water it found deep beneath the ground, so that sometimes the roots that pierced the cave writhed like snakes.

Here is how, or so I have come to believe, this Red Moon has played a key role in human evolution.

Consider. How do new species arise, of hominids or any organism?

Isolation is the key. If mutations arise in a large and freely mixing population, any new characteristic is diluted and will disappear within a few generations. But when a segment of the population becomes isolated from the rest, dilution through interbreeding is prevented. Thus the isolated group may, quite rapidly, di-

verge from the base population. And when those barriers to isolation are removed, the new species finds itself in competition with its predecessors. If it is more fit, in some sense, it will survive by out-competing the parent stock. If not, it declines.

When our scientists believed there was only one Earth, they developed a theory of how the evolution of humanity occurred. The ape-like bipeds called Australopithecines gave rise to tool users, who in turn produced tall erect hairless creatures capable of walking on the open plain, who gave rise to various species of Homo sapiens—*the genus that includes myself. It is believed that at some points in history there were many hominid species, all derived from the base Australopithecine stock, extant together on the Earth. But my kind*—Homo sapiens sapiens—*proved the fittest of them all. By out-competition, the variant species were removed.*

Presumably, each speciation episode was instigated by the isolation of a group of the parent stock. We assumed that the key isolating events were caused by climate changes: rising or falling sea levels, the birth or death of forests, the coming and going of glaciation. It was a plausible picture—before we knew of the Red Moon, of the Gray Earth, of other Moons and Earths.

Assume that the base Australopithecine stock evolved on Earth—my Earth. Imagine that some mechanism scooped up handfuls of undifferentiated Australopithecines, and, perhaps some generations later, deposited them on a variety of subtly different Earths.

It is hard to imagine a more complete isolation. And the environments in which they were placed might have had no resemblance to those from which they were taken. In that case, our Australopithecines would have had to adapt or die.

And later, samples of those new populations were swept up in their turn, and handed on to other Earths, where they were shaped again. Thus the Hams, with *their power and conservatism, have been shaped by the brutal conditions of this Gray Earth.*

This is my proposal: that hominid speciation has been driven by the transfer of populations between parallel Earths. It is fantastic, but logical. If this is true, then everything about us—everything about me—has been shaped by the meddling of the Old Ones, these engineers of worlds and hominids, for their own unrevealed, unfathomable purpose. Just as my own life story—too complicated to set out here—has become a scrawl across multiple realities.

What remains unclear is why the Old Ones, if they exist, should wish to do this. Perhaps their motives were somehow malicious, or somehow benevolent; perhaps they wished to give the potential of humankind its fullest opportunity of expression.

But their motive is scarcely material.

What power for mortals to hold.

What arrogance to wield it.

Nemoto said she would not go into the ground until she saw another night. But she grew steadily weaker, until she could not raise her body from its pallet of moss, or clean herself, or even raise her hands to her mouth.

Mary cared for her. She would give Nemoto water in sponges of mashed-up leaf, and when Nemoto fouled herself Mary cleaned her with bits of skin, and she bathed her body's suppurating sores with blood-tree sap.

But Nemoto's skin continued to flake away, as the slow revenge of the bat disturbed from its hibernation took its gruesome course.

There came a day when the sun rolled along the horizon, its light shimmering through the trees that flourished there. Mary knew that soon would come the first night, the first *little* night, since the spring. So she carried Nemoto to the mouth of the cave—she was light, like a thing of twigs and dried leaves—and propped her up on a bundle of skins, so that her face was bathed in the sunlight.

But Nemoto screwed up her face. "I do not like the light,"

she said, her voice a peevish husk. "I can bear the dark. But not these endless days. I have always longed for tomorrow. For tomorrow I will understand a little more. I have always wanted to *understand*. Why I am here. Why the world is as it is. Why there is something, rather than nothing."

"Lon' for tomorrow," Mary echoed, seeking to comfort her.

"Yes. But *you* do not dream of the future, do you? For you there is only today. Here especially, with your Long Day and your Long Night, as if a whole year is made of one tremendous day."

Overhead, a single bright star appeared.

Nemoto gasped. "The first star since the spring. How marvelous, how beautiful, how fragile." She settled back on her bundle of skins. "You know, the stars here are the same—I mean the same as those that surround the world where I grew up, the Blue Earth. But the way they swim around the sky is not the same." She was trying to raise her arm, perhaps to point, but could not. "You have a different pole star here. It is somewhere in Leo, near the sky's equator. I cannot determine which . . . your world is tipped over, you see, like Uranus, like a top lying on its side; that is how the Big Whack shaped it here. And so for six months, when your pole points at the sun, you have endless light; and for six months endless dark. . . . Do you follow me? No, I am sure you do not." She coughed, and seemed to sink deeper into the skins. "All my life I have sought to understand. I believe I would have pursued the same course whichever of our splintered worlds I had been born into. And yet, and yet—" She arched her back, and Mary laid her huge hands on Nemoto's forehead, trying to soothe her. "And yet I die alone."

Mary took her hand. It was delicate, like a child's. "Not alone," she said.

"Ah. I have you, don't I, Mary? I have a friend. That is something, isn't it? That is an achievement. . . ." Nemoto tried to squeeze Mary's hand; it was the gentlest of touches.

And the sun, as if apologetically, slid beneath the horizon. Crimson light towered into the sky.

*   *   *

There are no books here. There is nothing like writing of any kind. And there is no art: no paintings on animal skins or cave walls, no tattoos, not so much as a dab of crushed rock on a child's face.

As a result, the Hams' world is a startlingly drab place, lacking art and story.

To me, a beautiful sunset is a comforting reminder of home, a symbol of renewal, a sign of hope for a better day tomorrow. But to the Hams, I believe, a sunset is just a sunset. But every sunset is like the first they have ever seen.

They are clearly aware of past and future, of change within their lives. They care for each other. They will show concern over another's wounds, and lavish attention on a sickly infant. They show pain, and fear, a great sense of loss when a loved one dies—and a deep awareness of their own mortality.

But they are quite without religion.

Think what that means. Every morning Mary must wake up, as alert and conscious as I am, and she must face the horror of life full in the face—without escape, without illusion, without consolation.

As for me, I have never abandoned my shining thread of hope that someday I will get out of here—without that I would fear for my sanity. But perhaps that is just my Homo sapiens *illusion, my consolation.*

Before the sun disappeared again, Mary had placed her friend in the ground, the ground of this Gray Earth.

The memory of Nemoto faded, as memories will.

But sometimes, sparked by the scent of the breeze that blew off the sea—a scent of different places—she would think of Nemoto, who had died far from home, but who had not died alone.

The Lagan Fishers

TERRY DOWLING

*Terry Dowling [eidolon.net/homesite.html?section_name=
terry_dowling] lives in Australia and is one of the best prose
stylists in Australian science fiction and fantasy. His short
fiction is widely published in Australia and has appeared in*
F & SF *and* Interzone. *Although he has never written a
novel, his SF stories have been collected in eight volumes in
Australia since 1990, most famously in the Tom Rynosseros
series, and his influences are most saliently the stories of
J. G. Ballard, Ray Bradbury, and Jack Vance. Most recently,
he was presented with the special Convenor's Award for Excellence at the 1999 Aurealis Awards for* Antique Futures:
The Best of Terry Dowling. *A critic and reviewer, and an an-
thologist, Dowling is also a musician and songwriter, with
eight years of appearances on Australia's longest-running
television program, ABC's* Mr Squiggle & Friends. *And he
currently teaches a Communications course at a large Syd-
ney college.*

*"The Lagan Fishers," like the Ings story in this collection,
first appeared online at the SciFiction website, and is also a
story of alien invasion, though of an extremely different
sort—here the alien is a mysterious crystalline plant incur-
sion (that echoes Ballard's* The Crystal World).

In the first week of September, a lagan bloom appeared in the south meadow below Sam Cadrey's kitchen window, and that was the day it felt real at last.

Something glinting in the morning sunlight caught his eye as he stood making coffee—dislodged hubcap, plastic drum lid, discarded garbage bag, he couldn't be sure—something close to the road but definitely on his property. When he hurried down to see what it was, there was no mistaking the glossy quatrefoil of tartarine pushing up through the lucerne like an old bore cover made of fused glass. He kicked at the shell of opalescent stuff, beat on it a few times, then stood wondering how much his life would change.

Sam knew his rights. They couldn't take his farm back, he was sure of that. When that small container of mioflarin—MF—illegally buried in the Pyrenees had leaked in 2029, poisoning so much of Europe, then the rest of the world, he'd become that rare and wondrous thing, a true global hero: one of the twenty-two volunteers sent in to cap it, one of the five who had survived Site Zero and made it out again. Sam had freehold in perpetuity, and the World Court in Geneva had decreed that lagan blooms were land-title pure and simple. Sure, there were local magistrates, local ordinances and local prejudices to reckon with, but the Quarantine was officially over, the last of the embargoes lifted—both made a laughingstock by the sheer extent of the bloom outbreaks and their consistently benign nature. A disfigured, forty-nine-year-old MF veteran and widower on a

UN life pension had recourse to legal aid as well. Looking down at the four-lobed curving hump of the bloom, Sam knew he was king of all that he surveyed and that, in all probability, his kingdom would be an alien domain for the next year or so.

Within fourteen minutes, orbiting spysats had logged it. Within forty, Mayor Catherine was in her living room with their local Alien Influences Officer, Ross Jimmins, to log the official registration, and a dozen lagan fishers were at the end of his drive waiting to bid for trawling rights. Protection agents and insurance reps were at his door too, offering assistance against the usual: everything from highly organized looters to salting by disgruntled neighbors. But Sam was a UN vet. Within the hour, there were two AIO lagan custodians at his front gate wearing blue armbands, and the usually strident hucksters pacing up and down the gravel drive had become unusually courteous.

"How soon before the hedges form?" Sam asked Mayor Catherine, sounding both cautious and eager, still not sure about the whole thing. Catherine was the closest thing to a rocket scientist Tilby had, a handsome, middle-aged woman with steel-gray hair, looking the perfect, latter-day *nasa*-chik in her navy-blue jumpsuit. The NASA look. The imprimatur of discipline and professional responsibility. Who would have thought?

"It's still three to four days," she said, taking the AIO notepad from Jimmins and adding her verification code. "Latest count, fourteen percent of blooms don't hold. Remember that, Sam. They sink back."

"That's not many though," Ross Jimmins said, reassuring him, wishing Sam well with every puff on his lagan-dross day-pipe. The pipe was carved from lagan horn, a length of hollowed lattice from a "living" hedge. As well as the wonderful fragrance the slow-combusting dross gave off, somewhere between gardenia and the finest aromatic tobaccos of the previous four centuries, there was a welter of other positive side effects, and the molecularly atrophying horn itself scattered its own immune-enhancing dusting of euphorines on the warm morning air.

"It is like some intelligence is behind it," Sam said, looking out through the big view window, and knew how inane it sounded coming from him, the Tilby Tiger, the great skeptic.

Catherine gave a wry smile. "It's good to have you back in the world. We lost you there for a while."

"At least Jeanie didn't see me like this." Sam had resolved he wouldn't say it, but there it was.

The Mayor looked off at the fields and hills, out to where a tiny orange bus was bringing more science students from the local high school to do a real-time, hands-on site study of early bloom effect. "Jeanie didn't and it's not what I meant, Sam." She changed her tone. "So, what are you going to do about it? Lease it out?"

Sam was grateful. "You think I should? Let them wall it off, rig up processing gantries? Put storage modules down there?" *Stop me seeing it*, he didn't add.

"Best way. Nothing is lost but spindrift through the flumes. You get the hedges; they get the lagan. There's no poaching and none of the hassles."

"You representing anybody?" Sam asked. He'd always been a wary and even harsh critic where the lagan was concerned. It had always been someone else's experience, the reality of others, thus easy to comment on. This had changed him—what was the quaint old *fin-de-siècle* saying?—had made it "up close and personal."

"I had a dozen phone calls before I left the office, but no. Hope you believe it, Sam."

"Ross?"

"Eight calls. Nope."

Sam needed to believe them. They were his friends. They'd been with him when Jeanie died. He needed to brave it out. "Cat, I want to see it. I've gone revisionist *pro tem*, okay? If it's alien invasion, let's have it. I *want* hedges to form. I want them stretching along the road all the way to town. People should be able to poach stuff. Break bits off."

Cat answered right on cue. This was an area of major personal concern. "A lot of wildcat lagan owners agree with you. I've always said it. Keep the cartels out."

"I've got control, right?"

She gave a little frown. "Your property, Sam."

"What about outside options?"

"Some control. It's an official thing. What's on your mind?"

"I want it all hands-on. No remotes. None of those little science doovers. No aerostats."

"That's tricky, Sam," she said. "It's standard nowadays. Every general access unit means a thousand global onlines and probably a thousand research facilities. A fortune from sponsors to you. Even if you could close 'em out, you'd just get thousands more people coming in. You don't want that."

"Then only for part of the day. Only in the afternoon. Say, 1300 till sundown. None at night. Can we do that?"

"We can try," Jimmins said and keyed in the request, waited less than a minute, nodded. "You've got it for now, flagged for renegotiation later. Bless your MF, Sam. You'll get rogues slipping in, but we'll put up a burn field. Fry 'em in the sky."

Cat nodded, confirming how easy it was going to be. "They'll stop when they lose a few. So, what will you do?"

Talking the talk was easy, Sam found. "I'll fish it myself. See what comes up."

"Great idea. Can we help?"

It all happened quickly once the Mayor and Jimmins left. The waiting fishers at the gate drove off the moment they learned Sam was going to wildcat it himself, all but one, the craggy-looking, gray-haired older man perched on the bonnet of his truck. When Sam went down to quiz him on why he stayed, he saw that it was Howard Dombey, the proprietor of the Lifeways produce market on the far side of Tilby. He was a part-time lagan fisher, and people said he did some lagan brokering as well.

"It's Howard Dombey, isn't it?" Sam said.

"Right on, Mr. Cadrey. Like to help if you're a mind." His idioms were straight from Life Studies Online, all very PC, optimally relaxing, maximally community building.

Sam found himself matching them. "Doing it myself. And it's Sam."

"Like to help just the same, Sam. Don't figure profit margins too well anymore. Just like working with it. Seeing it come to."

"Why?"

Howard Dombey shrugged, going with the role beautifully. "Just do. Watching the spin. Seeing it all flicky-flashy with lagan, pretty as the day. Give me five percent and I'll do the scut work. Give me ten and I'll fence the bounty you clear as well. Save you the grief."

"There'll be slow days, Howard."

"Counting on it. At my age, they're the ones I like."

They made quite a team—a vet skeptic with a face ruined by MF, a town mayor looking like a shuttle-butt spaceways groupie from the nineties, a pipe-smoking AIO officer, and a small-time entrepreneur who did the culture-speak of mid-twentieth rural USA.

They started early each morning and left off around 1300, with Howard often as not staying on at the sorting trays till sunset when the last of the afternoon's tek and spec groups had gone—whichever AIO officials were rostered for that day's site check.

It was funny how much of an unspoken routine it all was. By the time Sam had disengaged the perimeter sensors and AIO alarms around 0700, the four of them were there, ready to set off in pairs, carefully locating the newbies and keying spot and spec codes into notepads for their own constantly updating operations program and the AIO global master.

It was on a spell during one of these start-up checks, after Sam had pointed to a perfect cloudform lagan building on one of the hedges, that Howard told him about the name.

"You know what lagan originally was?"

Sam just stared; it seemed such an odd question. "I thought it was named after the river in that old Irish song. You know, *My Lagan Love*. They're always playing it."

"Most people think that. No. It's from the language of shipwreck. Flotsam, jetsam and lagan. Flotsam is wreckage that floats when a ship goes down. Jetsam is what's thrown overboard to lighten her. Jetsam when it's jettisoned, see. If it floats, it's flotsam. If it sinks, it's lagan. A lot of valuable stuff was marked with buoys so they could retrieve it later. There were salvage wars over it. Deliberate wrecking, especially on the coast of Cornwall and around the Scillies. Lights set during storms to lure ships onto rocks. Lamps tied to the horns of cows—'horn beacons' they called 'em. Whole families involved. Whole communities."

"So why that name now? Lagan?"

"Some scientist came up with it. These are floats from somewhere else, aren't they? Buoys poking through. Lines leading down to stuff."

"I've never heard this."

Howard looked at him as if to say: *You've been out of it for quite a while.*

"Lots of folks haven't. But it's true. We get whatever comes up from the 'seabed.' "

"But—"

"Okay, don't say it! There's no line. No seabed. It's how the whole thing goes—first the shelltop like yours last week, then the bounty is hauled up."

"But it's not *down* is it, Howard? And it isn't *hauled* up. Words hide it. Tidy it up too much."

"Okay, but they help us live with it."

"And hide it. How's the weather? How's the lagan? Geologists and seismologists doing their tests all the time, finding nothing. No pressure variables under the caps. None of the expected physics. It's all so PC."

"See my point, Sam. The blooms link to somewhere else, somewhere out of sight, to something worth waiting for. Stuff comes up; you get the hedges with bits of lagan in them like fish in a net. At the very least, you get chunks of molybdenum and diamond-S and those funny little spindles of—what're those new words?—crowfenter and harleybine? Now and then there's the gold and silver."

"But no Nobel Prizes yet."

"What? Oh, right. No, no Nobel Prizes in those hedges so far. No real answers."

"See, there's another word. Hedges."

"They follow roads and field lines, Sam. That's what hedges do. Hedges is what they are."

"Hides it, Howie."

"Hasn't stopped you."

Which was too close to the truth and too soon in their friendship right then, so they both gladly changed the subject. It was made easier by Mayor Catherine dumping her sample bag on the sorting table.

"New tally," she said. "Eighty-two viable. Sixteen fallow."

Howard keyed the totals into his notepad. "Sounds right. Everyone gets twenty percent that are empty."

"Looted?" Sam asked.

"Don't see how. Just empty. Nothing when the hedges form. Air pockets."

Sam kept at it. "Looted elsewhere?"

Howard watched him for a few moments. "Hadn't thought of that. Looted on the other side. You better watch 'im, Cat. Sounds like we got ourselves a new rocket scientist."

Howard knew well enough to take up a sample bag then and set off for the hedges.

By the end of the fifth week, their four major branchings had become seven, and what started as an ordinary watchtower lofting on one of them swelled, brachiated and buttressed first into a classic "salisbury point," then—over another twenty days—a full-blown "chartres crown," finally a true "notre dame." It meant endless media fly-bys, countless tek visits, even more busloads of tourists and school groups, but so few blooms became cathedral that Sam couldn't blame them. It was the appropriate response. He would have been worried if there hadn't been the extra attention, though it made it harder to live with what his world was becoming. Having the lagan was one thing; now it was becoming too strikingly alien.

Again it was genial, friendly Howard who triggered the next outburst, dumping his bag on the sorting table, then coming over to stand with his newfound friend to admire the towering structure.

"How about it, Sam? A cathedral. Makes you believe in the mirroring, don't it?"

"What's that, Howie?" The word mirror often caught him like that. The Tilby Tiger lived in a house without mirrors. (But full of reflections, he sometimes quipped on better days, making the tired old joke.)

"The online spiel. That it's mimicry. Skeuomorphism. The lagan sees clouds; it tries to make clouds. Sees trees and roads, does its best to give trees and roads."

"You believe that?"

Howard shrugged. "Makes sense. Has a certain appeal. This stuff pushes through, looks around, imitates what it sees."

"Sees! Sees! Sees! Where the hell has my bloom *seen* a cathedral, Howard, tell me that!"

Again Howard shrugged. "Dunno. It goes into the sky; it blows in the air; it feels the sun and gets in among the flowers. Maybe ancient cathedrals were just imitations of high places too. Maybe other lagan blooms have seen cathedrals and pass on the knowledge. Anyway, Sam, I figure why resist what's as natural as what nature's already doin'. Why resist it? Why do you?"

Because, Sam wanted to say. Just because. Then, needing reasons, needing reason, gave himself: There's my face, there's the other MF impairment, my infertility, there's Jeanie lost (not MF-related, no, but more old sayings covered it: "collateral damage," "friendly fire"). This is too new, too fast, too change-everything insistent. For someone keeping someone lost as alive as possible in what had *been*, simply *been* for them—views, routines, sugars in coffee, favorite songs, the spending of days, the very form and nature of days—how dare this brutal new lagan change it so. As Jeanie-bright, as Jeanie-fresh as Sam tried to make it, the lagan more than anything was always saying *that* time has gone. Jeanie is gone. Let them go.

Sam found himself trying so hard. Jeanie would have loved the lagan, arranged picnics, invited friends. Jeanie would have liked Howard and the others getting together, liked the little-kid thrill of them bringing in the bounty—grown-ups acting like kids acting like grown-ups.

But try as he might, Sam always found himself on both

sides of it, and his words kept coming out a bit crazy. He couldn't help himself.

"Look at what's happened. First the MF outbreak in '29, then the lagan five years later."

"They're not related," Howard said. "It's not cause and effect."

"Maybe. Experts in nineteenth century London didn't see the connection between smog and tuberculosis either."

"Between what and what?"

Sam was careful not to smile. For all his smarts, Howard was an aging child of the times, a true citizen of the age, lots of compartmentalized knowledge, but no true overview. He knew all about shipwrecks and 1930s Hudson locomotives and Napoleon Bonaparte and vintage CD-ROM games, but lacked the larger cultural horizon for such things. For him the old term PC still meant "Politically Correct" not "Pre-Copernican," though who remembered Copernicus these days, or Giordano Bruno, or William Tyndale, or the Library at Alexandria or, well, the economic conditions that had led to horn beacons and shipwrecking and the original lagan, all the other things that were lost? Things eroded, worn smooth and featureless by too much time.

It sobered him having Howard to measure himself by. It brought him back, made him remember to be smarter. Kinder. Set him in the present as much as anything could.

"But Howie, what if it's real lagan? In the shipwreck sense?"

"What, marked with a buoy?"

"Or sent up *as* a buoy."

"What! Why do you say that?"

"I have no idea. Just should be said, I guess."

At 0140 on 15th October, Sam woke and lay there in the dark, listening to the wind stir in the dream hedges. He was surprised that he could sleep at all, that he didn't wake more often. It was almost as if the soughing and other hedge sounds were deliberately there to lull the lagan-blessed. Like the dross, the spindrift, the honey-balm, it too was benign. The hedges breathing, thriving, being whatever they were.

Even as he drowsed, settled back toward sleep, that slipping, dimming thought made Sam rouse himself, leave his bed and go out onto the verandah. Of course it was deliberate. Look at how everyone accepted the phenomenon now, built it into their lives.

Sam regarded the fields picked out by the half-phase spring moon. He smelled the honey-balm wind that blew up from the hedgerows and made himself listen to the "croisie," not just hear it—that mysterious, oscillating tone produced by nearly all lagan blooms, a barely there, modulating drone set with what one moment sounded for all the world like someone shaking an old spray can, the next jingling bangles together on a waving arm. Never enough to annoy or intrude. Oh no. Not the croisie. Lulling. A welcome and welcoming thing. Always better than words made it seem. Something that would be missed like birdsong and insect chorus when the bloom ended and the hedges were left to dry out and rattle and fall to slow dust on the ordinary wind.

Sam left the verandah and walked down to the road. The hedges stretched away like screens of coral in the moonlight or, better yet, like frames, nets and trellises of moonlight, all ashimmer—all "flicky-flashy" as Howard would say—yes, like blanched coral or weathered bone robbed of their day colors but releasing a flickering, deep, inner light, an almost-glow. Better still—fretted cloudforms, heat-locked, night-locked, calcined, turned to salt like Lot's wife, turned to stone by the face of this world meeting the Gorgon-stare of some other.

The croisie murmured. The honey-balm blew. Spindrift lofted and feather-danced in the bright dark. The air smelled wonderful.

What a wondrous thing, he thought. What a special time. If only Jeanie were here to see it. The different world. The dream hedges and lagan. The spindrift dancing along the road and across the fields. His own MF legacies too, though she wouldn't have cared.

There are enough children in the world, she would've said. Who needs more than six in ten to be fertile anyway? The world is the birthright, not people. It doesn't need more peo-

ple. Hasn't for more than a century. Can't have too many people or people stop caring for each other. Only common sense.

She would never have mentioned his face—or perhaps
only to quip: "My Tiger. You were always too handsome
anyway."

She would have made it—easier.

Sam watched the ghostly palisades in their warps and
woofs, their herringbones and revetments, found himself
counting visible towerheads till he reached the riot of the
notre dame. Then he shut his eyes and listened to the ever-
shifting, ever-the-same voice of the croisie and tried to find,
beyond it, the rush of the old night wind in the real-trees. He
could, he was sure he could, anchoring himself in the other,
larger, older world by it.

But he wouldn't let it take his thoughts from Jeanie. No.
He kept her there in the questing—most vividly by adding to
the list of things he would have said to her, imagining what
she might have said to him. Like how you did start to count
your life more and more as doors closed to you, that was a
Jeanie line. How it took the MF pandemic damaging much
of the genetic viability first of Europe, then Africa and Asia,
on and on, to close some important doors for everyone, to
unite the world, make them finally destroy the old weapons.
The destroyable ones.

Jeanie would have put her spin on it. Her spindrift.

Sam grinned at the night. More language from the sea.
More shipwreck talk. Spindrift blew along the road, the
skeins and eddies of spores and hedge-dust, the "moonsilk,"
the "flit," the "dross"—there were so many names—but,
whatever it was, all safely moribund, *sufficiently* chemically
inert, they said, though still finely, subtly psychoactive just
by being there. Had to be. Part of the night. This night. His.

Theirs. Jeanie keenly there. His lagan love. Still.

Sam breathed in the bounty, filled his lungs with all the
changed nature. Howard was right. Blooms and hedges. Lagan. Watchtowers, thunderheads, cathedrals and hutches. So
much better than crystalline molecular skeuomorphs with
key attributes of long-chain polymer-calcinite hybrids or
whatever they were touting in the net journals.

Then the cathedral sighed, the only word for it. A single falling note swelled against the croisie, a distinct sad trailing-away sound that left the alien lagan-tone, the honey-balm and the night-wind beyond like a strange silence when it had gone.

From the cathedral?

Sam accepted that it was, knowing that almost all the logged lagan anomalies were around the big cloudform and cathedral loftings. The hutches and nestings, the basements and even stranger subbasements were always silent, but the loftings sometimes belled and breathed and sounded like this, like great whales of strangeness making their song.

The mikes would have tracked it. Nearby stats had to be homing in, risking burn. Tomorrow there'd be extra flybys and spec groups.

Sam walked closer to the looming thirty-meter structure, looked up into the interstices of the triple spire, the converging, just-now braiding salisbury points, then down to where the portal and narthex would be in a true cathedral. He began a circuit. There was only the croisie now and the distant wind if you listened for it.

There were no doors in the logged salisburys, chartres and notre dames. There were outcroppings like porches and lintels, but no doors, no chambers. The loftings were always solid lagan.

But here was a door—rather a shadowing, a doorness beneath such an outcropping, a cleft between buttress swellings that held darkness like one.

Why now? Why mine? Sam thought, but came back, Jeanie-wise, with: Why not? If not now, when?

Still he resisted. He'd finally—mostly—accepted the lagan. He'd welcomed the wealth, but mainly the companionship the lagan had brought, a new set of reasons for people doing things together. But he wanted nothing more, no additional complications. Another old *fin-de-siècle* saying from Life Studies covered it: "not on my watch."

Had to be—ready, the words came, bewildering him till he realized they answered his two unspoken questions.

A sentient, talking, telepathic cathedral? It was too much. It was bathos.

But it made him move in under the overhang, the lip of the porch, whatever it was, made him step into the darkness.

He found her there, found her by the darkness lightening around her; the final corner of the narthex, apse or niche ghost-lighting this latest, incredible lagan gift.

She would never be beautiful, if *she* were even the right word. The eyes were too large, the face too pinched, the ears and nose too small, like something half-made, a maquette, a Y99 Japanese *animé* figure, a stylized, waxy, roswell mannequin. The naked body too doll-smooth, too androgynous, with not even rudimentary genitalia or breasts that he could tell, yet somehow clearly not meant to be a child.

He knew who she was meant to be.

"You're not Jeanie." He had to say it.

No. It sounded in his mind.

"You're something like her. A bit."

"It was—your thoughts—there." Spoken words this time. The creature enunciated them so carefully, seemed to agonize over each one, fiercely concentrating, being so careful. Could it be, did he imagine it or was there perspiration on the forehead, the sheen of stress or panic? "I know—Jeanie."

"You do!"

The mannequin frowned, desperately confused, clearly alarmed if the twisting of the face were any indication. "It was—there. There. The—anchor?" The final word was a question.

"Ah." Sam felt hope vanish, felt fascination empty out and drain away, then refill from what truly, simply was on this strangest, most magical night.

"*Who* are you?" he said, gentler, easier now. "What are you?"

"Yours?" Again, it was almost a question. This creature seemed in shock, far more troubled than he was, but a shock almost of rapture as well as panic. At the wonder of being here. Being lost, bereft, but here. Somewhere. Anywhere.

Sam couldn't help himself. He stepped back, did so again

and again, moved out of the chamber, out from under the porch. He had to anchor himself too. He looked around at the night, at the rising laganform looming over him, at the spread of coral barricades sweeping away in the vivid dark. No wonder they called them dream hedges. He saw it all now. Others had had these visitations. That's what the official Alien Influence spec groups were *really* looking for. Motile manifestations. Lifesign. The cathedrals were concentrations for hiding passengers, for delivering them into this world.

What to do? Tell the others? Share this latest, strangest, most important discovery—not the word!—this benefice, this gift? The orbitals were nightsighted, but Sam and this creature, this—*Kyrie?*—the name was just there—*Kyrie!*—just was, were *in* the lagan, with the croisie at full song and the honey-balm strengthening, both caught in the richest rush of spindrift he'd seen in weeks, with the most vivid runs of ghost-light making the hedges all flicky-flashy. Flickers of lagan dance, lagan blush. Semaphores of dream. The tides of this other sea bringing up its bounty.

He made himself go back into the darkness. He had to. It was a chance, a chance for something. He barely understood, but he *knew*.

"Kyrie?" He named it. Named her. What else could he do?

She was standing out from the chamber wall, just standing there naked and waiting.

"Kyrie?" he said again, then gave her his dressing gown, moved in and draped it about her shoulders. How could he not?

Before he quite knew he was doing so, he was leading her out into the night, holding her, steadying her. She walked stiff-legged, with a strange and stilted gait, new to walking, new to everything, but flesh-warm and trembling under his hands. She was hurting, panicking, desperately trying to do as he did. Sam guided her up the path and into the house. It was all so unreal, yet so natural. It was just what you did, what was needed.

Because it seemed right, because he needed it, Sam put

her in Jeanie's room, in Jeanie's bed, in the room and bed Jeanie had used in her final days before hospitalization was necessary and she had gone away forever. He did that and more. Though he balked at it, he couldn't help himself. He left the photos and quik-sims of Jeanie he'd put there when she'd left, made himself do that, hating it, needing it, needing it knowing what this brand-new Kyrie was trying to become.

She was still there the next morning and, yes, hateful and wonderful both, there did seem more of Jeanie in the drawn, minimalist face. Did he imagine it? Yearn for it too much? Was it the light of day playing up the tiniest hint?

Sam felt like a ghoul, like something cruel and perverse when he brought in more pictures of Jeanie and set them on the sideboard, even put one in the en suite.

It was mainly curiosity, he kept telling himself. But need too, though too dimly considered to be allowed as such. He just had to see.

No one had observed their meeting. Or, rather, no queries came, no AIO agents, no officials quizzing him about an overheard conversation, about a late-night lagan-gift from the cathedral. It seemed that the lagan had masked it; the croisie had damped it down; the honey-balm had blurred the words to nothing—perhaps their intended function all along. Misleading. Deceiving. Hiding the passengers. Working to let this happen privately, secretly. Who could say?

He helped her become human.

It was hard to work in the hedges in the days that followed, so hard to chat and make small-talk knowing that she was up in the house with the books and the sims, learning his world, learning to be human, eating and drinking mechanically but unassisted now, if without evident pleasure, being imprinted. Becoming. The only word for it.

They saw that he was distracted, took it as an allowable relapse by their MF recluse, the famous Tilby Tiger. Becoming was an appropriate word for Sam too. Though he made himself work at doing and saying the right things, remaining courteous and pleasant, it was like doing the compulsory Life Studies modules all over again, all those mandatory re-altime, facetime *têtes* and citizenship dialogues for getting along. Comfortable handles for the myriad, net-blanded, on-line, PC global villagers. Words, words and words. Sam hated it but managed.

He had Jeanie back in a way he hadn't expected. Like a flower moving with the sun or a weathervane aligning with the wind, he just found himself responding to what was natural in his life. Kyrie was of *this* time, *this* place, *this* moment, but with something of Jeanie, just as the old song had it. *My Lagan Love* indeed.

Sam cherished the old words anew, and sang them as he worked in the hedgerows below her window.

> *Where Lagan stream sings lullaby*
> *There blows a lily fair;*
> *The twilight gleam is in her eye,*
> *The night is on her hair.*
> *And, like a love-sick lenanshee,*
> *She hath my heart in thrall;*
> *Nor life I owe, nor liberty,*
> *For Love is lord of all.*
>
> *And often when the beetle's horn*
> *Hath lulled the eve to sleep,*
> *I steal unto her shielding lorn*
> *And thro' the dooring peep.*
> *There on the cricket's singing stone*
> *She spares the bog wood fire.*
> *And hums in sad sweet undertone*
> *The song of heart's desire.*

But Sam remained the skeptic too, was determined not to become some one-eyed Love's Fool. Even as he guided Kyrie, added more photos, ran the holos, he tried to fit this visitation into the science of lagan.

It was a cycle, a pendulum swing. One moment he'd be sitting with his alien maquette in her window-shaded room, singleminded, determined, perversely searching for new traces of Jeanie. The next, he was touring the online lagan sites—scanning everything from hard science briefs to the wildest theories, desperately seeking anything that might give a clue.

There was so much material, mostly claims of the "I know someone who knows someone" variety, and Sam was tempted to go the exophilia route and see the World Government muddying up the informational waters, hiding the pearls of truth under the detritus.

Finally, inevitably, he went back to his bower-bird friend, brought up the subject during a morning tour of the hedges.

"Howie, official findings aside, you ever hear of anything found alive in the lagan?"

"Apart from the lagan itself? Nothing above the microbial."

"But unofficial."

"Well, the rumors are endless. People keep claiming things; the UN keeps saying it's reckless exophilia. And I tell myself, Sam, if something was found, how could they keep a lid on it? I mean, statistically, there'd be so many visitations, passengers, whatever, word would get out."

"What if people are hiding them?"

Howie shook his head. "Doesn't follow. Someone somewhere would go for the gold and the glory instead, bypass the authorities and go to the media direct. You'd only need one."

Sam didn't press it too closely, didn't say: unless they were loved ones. Returnees. Things of the heart. He kept it casual, made it seem that he was just—what was Howie's saying?—shooting the breeze.

"Ever meet anyone who claims to have seen someone?"

"Sure. Bancroft, but he's always claiming one thing or another about the lagan. Sally Joule's neighbor, Corben, had a stroke, but she won't buy it. Reckons the lagan did it to him because he discovered something."

"Would he mind if I visited?"

"Probably not. I know Corben. He's two counties over, an hour's drive or more. But I go sit with him sometimes. Talk's ninety-eight percent one-sided these days, but that's okay.

And you've got things in common. He wildcatted his field too, just as you've done. I can take you out."

Ben Corben seemed pleased to see them. At least he tracked their approach from his easy chair on the front porch and gave a lopsided smile when Howie greeted him and introduced Sam. He couldn't speak well anymore, and took ages to answer the same question Sam had put to Howie: had he ever heard of anything found alive in the lagan.

"Sum-thin," Corben managed. "Stor-ees."

And that was it for a time. The live-in nurse served afternoon tea, helped Corben with his teacup and scones.

Which was fine, Sam found. It gave him time to look out over Corben's lapsed domain, let him see what his own bloom would one day become.

Finally Howard brought them back to the question as if it hadn't been asked.

"Ever find anything out there, Corb? Anything alive?" He gestured at what remained of Corben's hedges, stripped and wasted now, the towers and barricades fallen, the basements collapsed in on themselves, just so many spike-fields, kite-frames and screens of wind-torn filigree, rattling and creaking and slowly falling to dust.

"No," Corben said, so so slowly, and his skewed face seemed curiously serene, alive with something known.

"It's important, Ben," Sam said. "It's just—it's really important. I've got hedges now. Never expected it. Never did. But I think something's out there. Calling at night." He didn't want to give too much away. And Howie had gone with it, bless him, hadn't swung about and said: hey, what's this? Good friend.

Corben blinked, looked out across the ruin of his own lagan field, now two years gone, so Howie had said.

Again Sam noticed the peace in the man, what may have been a result of the stroke or even some medication stupor, but seemed for all the world like uncaring serenity, as if he'd seen sufficient wonders and was content, as if—well, as if—

And there it was. Of course. Like Kyrie. Corben was like

Kyrie. Slow and careful. Minimalist. Just like Kyrie. Of course.

It was all so obvious once Sam saw it like that. Back home, he removed the photos, sims and mirrors, left Kyrie to be what she—what "it" had tried to be all along. He saw what he thought to be relief in the maquette's suffering eyes as he removed the last of the distractions, then brought a chair and sat in front of it.

Finish your job, he thought, but didn't speak it. Finish being what you already are.

And Sam found it such a relief to sit there and let it happen. Kyrie had never tried to be Jeanie, had never been a gift from the lagan to ease a broken heart.

Not Kyrie. Cadrey.

Sam saw how he'd been: thinking of Jeanie by day, not thinking of her—blessedly forgetting her—at night when he slept. Escaping in dreams, his only true time of self. Swaying Kyrie this way and that in its Becoming—by day toward Jeanie, by night back toward its intended form all along.

Poor agonized thing. Here from somewhere else, now beautified by Jeanie-thought, now showing the ruin of his own MF tiger mask, coping, copying. Poor ugly, beautiful, languishing thing. Trying all the while.

Then, like looking through doors opened and aligned, he saw the rest. Its message, its purpose. I will be you to free you so you can have your turn. Moving on. Taking it with you.

What a clumsy, awkward method, Sam decided. What a flawed—no! What a natural and fitting way to do it, more like a plant in a garden, some wild and willful, wayward garden, some natural, blundering, questing thing, trying again and again to push through. Stitching it up. Linking the worlds.

What it was, never the issue. Only *that* it was.

He had to help. Do sittings. Leave photos of his red-demon, tiger-faced self (how the others would smile!), try not to think of Jeanie for now, just for now.

For Kyrie. Oh, the irony. So many times he stood before the mirrors and laughed, recalling that old story of desperate choice: the Lady or the Tiger. Well, now he played both parts—showing the Tiger but being *like* Jeanie for Kyrie.

Giving of himself. Giving self. Generous. The Lady *and* the Tiger.

Two weeks later, at brightest, deepest midnight, he stood before the notre dame, bathed in the honey-balm and the spindrift, letting the croisie take him, tune him, bring him in. They were all part of it—transition vectors, carrier modes.

Kyrie was in place back in the house, maimed, shaped, pathetic and wonderful both. Sam Cadrey enough. Would seem to have had a stroke when they found *him*. That would cover the slips, the gaffes and desperate gracelessness. His friends would find, would impose, the bits of Sam Cadrey no time or training could provide. Friendship allowing, they would find him in what was left, never knowing it was all there was.

Sam looked around at his world, at the fullness of it, the last of it, then stepped into the narrow chamber.

The cathedral did what it had to do, blindly or knowing, who could say, but naturally.

Sam felt himself changing, becoming—why, whatever it needed him to be this time, using what was in the worlds. And as he rose, he had the words, unchanged in all that changing. *Nor life I know, nor liberty.* Had his self, his memories to be enough of self around. *For Love is lord of all.*

Sam held Jeanie to him, as firm and clear as he could make her, and rose from the troubled seabed to the swelling, different light of someone else's day.

In Xanadu

THOMAS M. DISCH

Thomas M. Disch is among the finest living writers of fantasy and science fiction. His prominence in SF was founded in the 1960s upon such novels as The Genocides *(1965),* The Puppies of Terra *(1966), and* Camp Concentration *(1968), and enhanced in the 1970s by the novels* 334 *(1972), and* On Wings of Song *(1979), and by his powerful short stories, collected in five volumes. He is now more famous outside the genre as a poet, critic, and novelist. His connection to SF since the 1970s might reasonably be described as a love-hate relationship. His most recent SF book is a work of criticism, the sometimes strikingly uncomplimentary* The Dreams Our Stuff Is Made Of: How Science Fiction Conquered the World *(1998), which won the Hugo Award for Best Related Book (1999). In 2001 he returned to genre publications with a number of excellent stories. His tribute website [www.michaelscycles.freeserve.co.uk/tmd.htm] is a model of what such a site should be, with a wonderful literary biography.*

"In Xanadu," a tribute to Disch's old friend, black humorist John Sladek, who died recently, is from Red Shift. *In a digital afterlife run by Disney-Mitsubishi, the protagonist is notified that his bills are unpaid, and so he is resurrected and invited to sign new agreements by which he becomes an employee serving the paying customers. Black humor indeed, and of high quality.*

IN MEMORY OF JOHN SLADEK,
WHO DIED MARCH 10, 2000

And all should cry, Beware! Beware!
His flashing eyes, his floating hair!
Weave a circle round him thrice,
And close your eyes with holy dread,
For he on honey-dew hath fed,
And drunk the milk of Paradise.
                              —Samuel Taylor Coleridge

PART ONE

Xanadu

His awareness was quite limited during the first so-long. A pop-up screen said WELCOME TO XANADU, [Cook, Fran]. YOUR AFTERLIFE BEGINS NOW! BROUGHT TO YOU BY DISNEY-MITSUBISHI PRODUCTIONS OF QUEBEC! A VOTRE SANTE TOUJOURS! Then there was a choice of buttons to click on, **Okay** or **Cancel**. He didn't have an actual physical mouse, but there was an equivalent in his mind, in much the way that amputees have ghostly limbs, but when he clicked on **Okay** with his mental mouse there was a dull *Dong!* and nothing happened. When he clicked on **Cancel** there was a trembling and the smallest flicker of darkness and then the pop-up screen greeted him with the original message.

This went on for an unknowable amount of time, there being no means by which elapsed time could be measured. After he'd *Dong!*ed on **Okay** enough times, he stopped bothering. The part of him that would have been motivated, back when, to express impatience or to feel resentment or to worry just wasn't connected. He felt an almost supernatural passivity. Maybe this is what people were after when they took up meditation. Or maybe it *was* supernatural, though it seemed more likely, from the few clues he'd been given, that it was cybernetic in some way.

He had become lodged (he theorized) in a faulty software program, like a monad in a game of JezzBall banging around inside its little square cage, ricocheting off the same four points on the same four walls forever. Or as they say in Quebec, *toujours*.

And oddly enough that was **Okay**. If he were just a molecule bouncing about, a lifer rattling his bars, there was a kind of comfort in doing so, each bounce a proof of the mass and motion of the molecule, each rattle an SOS dispatched to someone who might think, Ah-ha, there's someone there!

State Pleasure-Dome 1

And then—or, as it might be, once upon a time—**Cancel** produced a different result than it had on countless earlier trials, and he found himself back in some kind of real world. There was theme music ("Wichita Lineman") and scudding clouds high overhead and the smell of leaf mold, as though he'd been doing push-ups out behind the garage, with his nose grazing the dirt. He had his old body back, and it seemed reasonably trim. Better than he'd left it, certainly.

"Welcome," said his new neighbor, a blond woman in a blouse of blue polka dots on a silvery rayonlike ground. "My name is Debora. You must be Fran Cook. We've been expecting you."

He suspected that Debora was a construct of some sort, and it occurred to him that he might be another. But whatever she was, she seemed to expect a response from him beyond his stare of mild surmise.

"You'll have to fill me in a little more, Debora. I don't really know where we are."

"This is Xanadu," she said with a smile that literally flashed, like the light on top of a police car, with distinct, pointed sparkles.

"But does Xanadu exist anywhere except in the poem?"

This yielded a blank look but then another dazzling smile. "You could ask the same of us."

"Okay. To be blunt: Am I dead? Are you?"

Her smile diminished, as though connected to a rheostat. "I think that might be the case, but I don't know for sure. There's a sign at the entrance to the pleasure-dome that says 'Welcome to Eternity.' But there's no one to ask, there or anywhere else. No one who knows anything. Different people have different ideas. I don't have any recollection of dying, myself. Do you?"

"I have no recollections, period," he admitted. "Or none that occur to me at this moment. Maybe if I tried to remember something in particular . . ."

"It's the same with me. I can remember the plots of a few movies. And the odd quotation. 'We have nothing to fear but fear itself.' "

"Eisenhower?" he hazarded.

"I guess. It's all pretty fuzzy. Maybe I just wasn't paying attention back then. Or it gets erased when you come here. I think there's a myth to that effect. Or maybe it's so blurry because it never happened in the first place. Which makes me wonder, are we really people here, or what? And where is here? This isn't anyone's idea of heaven that *I* ever heard of. It's kind of like Disney World, only there's no food, no rides, no movies. Nothing to do, really. You can meet people, talk to them, like with us, but that's about it. Don't think I'm complaining. They don't call it a pleasure-dome for nothing. That part's okay, though it's not any big deal. More like those Magic Finger beds in old motels."

He knew just what she meant, though he couldn't remember ever having been to an old motel or lain down on a Magic Fingers bed. When he tried to reach for a memory of his earlier life, any detail he could use as an ID tag, it was like drawing a blank to a clue in a crossword. Some very simple word that just wouldn't come into focus.

Then there was a fade to black and a final, abject *Dong!* that didn't leave time for a single further thought.

Alph

"I'm sorry," Debora said, with a silvery shimmer of rayon, "that was my fault for having doubted. Doubt's the last thing either of us needs right now. I *love* the little dimple in your chin."

"I'm not aware that I *had* a dimple in my chin."

"Well, you do now, and it's right—" She traced a line up the center of his chin with her finger, digging into the flesh with the enameled tip as it reached. "—here."

"Was I conked out long?"

She flipped her hair as though to rid herself of a fly, and smiled in a forgiving way, and placed her hand atop his. At that touch he felt a strange lassitude steal over him, a deep calm tinged somehow with mirth, as though he'd remembered some sweet, dumb joke from his vanished childhood. Not the joke itself but the laughter that had greeted it, the laughter of children captured on a home video, silvery and chill.

"If we suppose," she said thoughtfully, tracing the line of a vein on the back of his hand with her red fingertip, "that our senses *can* deceive us, then what is there that *can't?*" She raised her eyebrows italic-wise. "I mean," she insisted, "my body might be an illusion, and the world I *think* surrounds me might be another. But what of that 'I think'? The very act of doubting is a proof of existence, right? I think therefore I am."

"Descartes," he footnoted.

She nodded. "And who would ever have supposed that

that old doorstop would be relevant to real life, so-called? Except I think it would be just as true with any other verb: I *love* therefore I am."

"Why not?" he agreed.

She squirmed closer to him until she could let the weight of her upper body rest on his as he lay there sprawled on the lawn, or the illusion of a lawn. The theme music had segued, unnoticed, to a sinuous trill of clarinets and viola that might have served for the orchestration of a Strauss opera, and the landscape was its visual correlative, a perfect Puvis de Chavannes—the same chalky pastels in thick impasto blocks and splotches, but never with too painterly panache. There were no visible brush strokes. The only tactile element was the light pressure of her fingers across his skin, making each least hair in its follicle an antenna to register pleasure.

A pleasure that need never, could never cloy, a temperate pleasure suited to its pastoral source, a woodwind pleasure, a fruity wine. Lavender, canary yellow. The green of distant mountains. The ripple of the river.

Caverns Measureless to Man

The water that buoyed the little skiff was luminescent, and so their progress through the cave was not a matter of mere conjecture or kinesthesia. They could see where they were going. Even so, their speed could only be guessed at, for the water's inward light was not enough to illumine either the ice high overhead or either shore of the river. They were borne along into some more unfathomable darkness far ahead as though across an ideal frictionless plane, and it made him think of spaceships doing the same thing, or of his favorite screen saver, which simulated the white swirl-by of snowflakes when driving through a blizzard. One is reduced at such moments (he was now) to an elemental condition, as near to being a particle in physics as a clumsy, complex mammal will ever come.

"I shall call you Dynamo," she confided in a throaty whisper. "Would you like that as a nickname? The Dynamo of Xanadu."

"You're too kind," he said unthinkingly. He had become careless in their conversations. Not a conjugal carelessness: he had not talked with her so very often that all her riffs and vamps were second nature to him. This was the plain unadorned carelessness of not caring.

"I used to think," she said, "that we were all heading for hell in a handbasket. Is that how the saying goes?"

"Meaning, hastening to extinction?"

"Yes, meaning that. It wasn't my *original* idea. I guess everyone has their own vision of the end. Some people take it straight from the Bible, which is sweet and pastoral, but maybe a little dumb, though one oughtn't to say so, not where they are likely to overhear you. Because is that really so different from worrying about the hole in the ozone layer? That was my apocalypse of choice, how we'd all get terrible sunburns and cancer, and then the sea level would rise, and everyone in Calcutta would drown."

"You think this is Calcutta?"

"Can't you ever be serious?"

"So, what's your point, Debora?" When he wanted to be nice, he would use her name, but she never used his. She would invent nicknames for him, and then forget them and have to invent others.

It was thanks to such idiosyncrasies that he'd come to believe in her objective existence as something other than his mental mirror. If she were no more than the forest pool in which Narcissus gazed adoringly, their minds would malfunction in similar ways. Were they mere mirror constructs, he would have known by now.

"It's not," she went on, "that I worry that the end is near. I suppose the end is always near. Relative to Eternity. And it's not that I'm terribly curious *how* it will end. I suppose we'll hurtle over the edge of some immense waterfall, like Columbus and his crew."

"Listen!" he said, breaking in. "Do you hear that?"

"Hear what?"

"The music. It's the score for *Koyaanisqatsi*. God, I used to watch the tape of that over and over."

She gave a sigh of polite disapproval. "I can't bear Philip Glass. It's just as you say, the same thing over and over."

"There was this one incredible pan. It must have been taken by a helicopter flying above this endless high-rise apartment complex. But it had been abandoned."

"And?" she insisted. "What is your point?"

"Well, it was no simulation. The movie was made before computers could turn any single image into some endless quilt. We were really seeing this vast deserted housing project, high-rise after high-rise with the windows boarded up. The abandoned ruins of some ultra-modern city. It existed, but until that movie nobody *knew* about it. It makes you think."

"It doesn't make *me* think."

There was no way, at this moment, they were going to have sex. Anyhow, it probably wouldn't have been safe. The boat would capsize and they would drown.

A Sunless Sea

It was as though the whole beach received its light from a few candles. A dim, dim light evenly diffused, and a breeze wafting up from the water with an unrelenting coolness, as at some theater where the air-conditioning cannot be turned off. They huddled within the cocoon of a single beach towel, thighs pressed together, arms crisscrossed behind their backs in a chaste hug, trying to keep warm. The chill in the air was the first less than agreeable physical sensation he'd known in Xanadu, but it did not impart that zip of challenge that comes with October weather. Rather, it suggested his own mortal diminishment. A plug had been pulled somewhere, and all forms of radiant energy were dwindling synchronously, light, warmth, intelligence, desire.

There were tears on Debora's cheek, and little sculptures of sea foam in the shingle about them. And very faint, the scent of nutmeg, the last lingering trace of some long-ago lotion or deodorant.

The ocean gray as aluminum.

The Wailing

Here were the high-rises from the movie, but in twilight now, and without musical accompaniment, though no less portentous for that. He glided past empty benches and leaf-strewn flower beds like a cameraman on roller skates, until he entered one of the buildings, passing immaterially through its plate-glass door. Then there was, in a slower pan than the helicopter's but rhyming to it, a smooth iambic progression past the doors along the first-floor corridor.

He came to a stop before the tenth door, which stood ajar. Within he could hear a stifled sobbing—a wailing, rather. He knew he was expected to go inside, to discover the source of this sorrow. But he could not summon the will to do so. Wasn't his own sorrow sufficient? Wasn't the loss of a world enough?

A man appeared at the end of the corridor in the brown uniform of United Parcel Service. His footsteps were inaudible as he approached.

"I have a delivery for Cook, Fran," the UPS man announced, holding out a white envelope.

At the same time he was offered, once again, the familiar, forlorn choice between **Okay** and **Cancel**.

He clicked on **Cancel**. There was a trembling, and the smallest flicker of darkness, but then the corridor reasserted itself, and the wailing behind the door. The UPS man was gone, but the envelope remained in his hand. It bore the return address in Quebec of Disney-Mitsubishi.

There was no longer a **Cancel** to click on. He had to read the letter.

Dear [Name]:

The staff and management of Xanadu International regret to inform you that as of [date] *all services in con-*

*nection with your contract [Number] will be canceled
due to new restrictions in the creation and maintenance of posthumous intelligence. We hope that we
will be able to resolve all outstanding differences with
the government of Quebec and restore the services
contracted for by the heirs of your estate, but in the
absence of other communications you must expect the
imminent closure of your account. It has been a pleasure to serve you. We hope you have enjoyed your time
in Xanadu.*

*The law of the sovereign state of Quebec requires us
to advise you that in terminating this contract we are
not implying any alteration in the spiritual condition
of [Name] or of his immortal soul. The services of
Xanadu International are to be considered an esthetic
product offered for entertainment purposes only.*

When he had read it, the words of the letter slowly faded
from the page, like the smile of the Cheshire cat.

The wailing behind the door had stopped, but he still
stood in the empty corridor, scarce daring to breathe. Any
moment, he thought, might be his last. In an eyeblink the
world might cease.

But it didn't. If anything the world seemed solider than
heretofore. People who have had a brush with death often
report the same sensation.

He reversed his path along the corridor, wondering if anyone lived behind any of them, or if they were just a facade, a
Potemkin corridor in a high-rise in the realm of faerie.

As though to answer his question Debora was waiting for
him when he went outside. She was wearing a stylishly tailored suit in a kind of brown tweed, and her hair was swept
up in a way that made her look like a French movie star of
the 1940s.

As they kissed, the orchestra reintroduced their love
theme. The music swelled. The world came to an end.

PART TWO

Xanadu

But then, just the way that the movie will start all over again
after The End, if you just stay in your seat, or even if you go
out to the lobby for more popcorn, he found himself back at
the beginning, with the same pop-up screen welcoming him
to Xanadu and then a choice of **Okay** or **Cancel**. But there
was also, this time, a further choice: a blue banner that
pulsed at the upper edge of consciousness and asked him if
he wanted expanded memory and quicker responses. He
most definitely did, so with his mental mouse he accepted
the terms being offered without bothering to scroll through
them.

He checked off a series of **Yeses** and **Continues**, and so,
without his knowing it, he had become, by the time he was
off the greased slide, a citizen of the sovereign state of Quebec, an employee of Disney-Mitsubishi Temps E-Gal, and—
cruelest of his new disadvantages—a girl.

A face glimmered before him in the blue gloaming. At
first he thought it might be Debora, for it had the same tentative reality that she did, like a character at the beginning of
some old French movie about railroads and murderers, who
may be the star or only an extra on hand to show that this is
a world with people in it. It was still too early in the movie to
tell. Only as he turned sideways did he realize (the sound
track made a samisen-like *Twang!* of recognition) that he
had been looking in a mirror, and that the face that had been
coalescing before him—the rouged cheeks, the plump lips,
the fake lashes, the mournful gaze—had been his own! Or
rather, now, her own.

As so many other women had realized at a similar point in
their lives, it was already too late and nothing could be done
to correct the mistake that Fate, and Disney-Mitsubishi, had
made. Maybe he'd always been a woman. [Cook, Fran] was
a sexually ambiguous name. Perhaps his earlier assumption
that he was male was simply a function of thinking in En-

glish, where *one* may be mistaken about *his* own identity (but not about hers). I think; therefore I am a guy.

He searched through his expanded memory for some convincing evidence of his gender history. Correction: *her* gender history. Her-story, as feminists would have it. Oh, dear—would he be one of *them* now, always thinking in italics, a grievance committee of one in perpetual session?

But look on the bright side (she told herself). There might be advantages in such a change of address. Multiple orgasms. Nicer clothes (though she couldn't remember ever wanting to dress like a woman when she was a man). Someone else paying for dinner, assuming that the protocols of hospitality still worked the same way here in Xanadu as they had back in reality. This was supposed to be heaven and already she was feeling nostalgic for a life she couldn't remember, an identity she had shed.

Then the loudspeaker above her head emitted a dull *Dong!*, and she woke up in the Women's Dormitory of State Pleasure-Dome 2. "All right, girls!" said the amplified voice of the matron. "Time to rise and shine. *Le temps s'en va, mesdames, le temps s'en va.*"

State Pleasure-Dome 2

"*La vie,*" philosophized Chantal, "*est une maladie dont le sommeil nous soulagons toutes les seize heures. C'est un palliative. La morte est un remède.*" She flicked the drooping ash from the end of her cigarette and made a move of chic despair. Fran could understand what she'd said quite as well as if she'd been speaking English: Life is a disease from which sleep offers relief every sixteen hours. Sleep is a palliative—death a remedy.

They were sitting before big empty cups of café au lait in the employee lounge, dressed in their black E-Gal minis, crisp white aprons, and fishnet hose. Fran felt a positive fever of chagrin to be seen in such a costume, but she felt nothing otherwise, really, about her entire female body, especially the breasts bulging out of their casings, breasts that quivered visibly at her least motion. It was like wearing a T-shirt with some dumb innuendo on it, or a blatant sexual invitation. Did every girl have to go through the same torment of shame at puberty? Was there any way to get over it except to get into it?

"Mon bonheur," declared Chantal earnestly, *"est d'augmenter celle des autres."* Her happiness lay in increasing that of others. A doubtful proposition in most circumstances, but not perhaps for Chantal, who, as an E-Gal was part geisha, part rock star, and part a working theorem in moral calculus, an embodiment of Francis Hutcheson's notion that that action is best which procures the greatest happiness for the greatest numbers. There were times— Thursdays, in the early evening—when Chantal's bedside/Website was frequented by as many as two thousand admirers, their orgasms all bissfully synchronized with the reels and ditties she performed on her dulcimer, sometimes assisted by Fran (an apprentice in the art) but usually all on her own. At such times (she'd confided to Fran) she felt as she imagined a great conductor must feel conducting some choral extravaganza, the *Missa Solemnis* or the Ninth Symphony.

Except that the dulcimer gave the whole thing a tinge and twang of hillbilly, as of Tammy Wynette singing "I'm just a geisha from the bayou." Of course, the actual Tammy Wynette had died ages ago and could sing that song only in simulation, but still it was hard to imagine it engineered with any other voice-print: habit makes the things we love seem inevitable as arithmetic.

"Encore?" Chantal asked, lifting her empty cup, and then, when Fran had nodded, signaling to the waiter.

Coffee, cigarettes, a song on the jukebox. Simple pleasures, but doubled and quadrupled and raised to some astronomical power, the stuff that industries and gross national products are made of. Fran imagined a long reverse zoom away from their table at the café, away from the swarming hive of the city, to where each soul and automobile was a mere pixel on the vast monitor of eternity.

The coffees came, and Chantal began to sing, *"Le bon-*

heur de la femme n'est pas dans la liberté, mais dans l'acceptation d'un devoir."

A woman's happiness lies not in liberty, but in the acceptance of a duty.

And what was that duty? Fran wondered. What could it be but love?

In a Vision Once I Saw

There were no mirrors in Xanadu, and yet every vista seemed to be framed as by those tinted looking glasses of the eighteenth century that turned everything into a Claude Lorrain. Look too long or too closely into someone else's face, and it became your own. Chantal would tilt her head back, a flower bending to the breeze, and she would morph into Fran's friend of his earlier afterlife, Debora. Debora, whose hand had caressed his vanished sex, whose wit had entertained him with Cartesian doubts.

They were the captives (it was explained, when Fran summoned **Help**) of pirates, and must yield to the desires of their captors in all things. That they were in the thrall of copyright pirates, not authentic old-fashioned buccaneers, was an epistomological quibble. Subjectively their captors could exercise the same cruel authority as any Captain Kidd or Hannibal Lecter. Toes and nipples don't know the difference between a knife and an algorithm. Pirates of whatever sort are in charge of pain and its delivery, and that reduces all history, all consciousness, to a simple system of pluses and minuses, do's and don'ts. Suck my dick or walk the plank. That (the terrible simplicity) was the downside of living in a pleasure-dome.

"Though, if you think about it," said Debora, with her hand resting atop the strings of her dulcimer, as though it might otherwise interrupt what she had to say, "every polity is ultimately based upon some calculus of pleasure, of apportioning rapture and meting out pain. The jukebox and the slot machine, what are they but emblems of the Pavlovian bargain we all must make with that great dealer high in the sky?" She lifted a little silver hammer and bonked her dulcimer a triple bonk of do-sol-do.

"The uncanny thing is how easily we can be programmed to regard mere symbols—" Another do-sol-do. "—as rewards. A bell is rung somewhere, and something within us resonates. And music becomes one of the necessities of life. Even such a life as this, an ersatz afterlife."

"Is there some way to escape?" Fran asked.

Debora gave an almost imperceptible shrug, which her dulcimer responded to as though she were a breeze and it a wind chime hanging from the kitchen ceiling. "There are rumors of escapees—E-Men, as they're called. But no one *I've* ever known has escaped, or at least they've never spoken of it. Perhaps they do, and get caught, and then the memory of having done so is blotted out. Our memories are not exactly ours to command, are they?"

The dulcimer hyperventilated.

Debora silenced it with a glance and continued: "Some days I'll flash on some long-ago golden oldie, and a whole bygone existence will come flooding back. A whole one-pound box of madeleines, and I will be absolutely convinced by it that I *did* have a life once upon a time, where there were coffee breaks with doughnuts bought at actual bakeries and rain that made the pavements speckled and a whole immense sensorium, always in flux, which I can remember now only in involuntary blips of recall. And maybe it really was like that once, how can we know, but whether we could get back to it, that I somehow can't believe."

"I've tried to think what it would be like to be back there, where we got started." Fran gazed into the misty distance, as though her earlier life might be seen there, as in an old home video. "But it's like trying to imagine what it would be like in the thirteenth century, when people all believed in miracles and stuff. It's beyond me."

"Don't you believe in miracles, then?" The dulcimer twanged a twang of simple faith. "I do. I just don't suppose they're for us. Miracles are for people who pay full price. For us there's just Basic Tier programming—eternal time and infinite space."

"And those may be no more than special effects."

Debora nodded. "But even so . . ."

"Even so?" Fran prompted.

"Even so," said Debora, with the saddest of smiles, a virtual flag of surrender, "if I were you, I would try to escape."

Those Caves of Ice!

Ebay was a lonely place, as holy and enchanted as some underwater cathedral in the poem of a French symbolist, or a German forest late at night. If you have worked at night as a security guard for the Mall of America, or if you've seen Simone Simon in *Cat People* as she walks beside the pool (only her footsteps audible, her footsteps and the water's plash), only then can you imagine its darkling beauty, the change that comes over the objects of our desire when they are flensed of their purveyors and consumers and stand in mute array, aisle after aisle. Then you might sweep the beam of your flashlight across the waters of the recirculating fountain as they perpetually spill over the granite brim. No silence is so large as that where Muzak played, but plays no more.

Imagine such a place, and then imagine discovering an exit that announces itself in the darkness by a dim red light and opening the door to discover a Piranesian vista of a further mall, no less immense, its tiers linked by purring escalators, the leaves of its potted trees shimmering several levels beneath where you are, and twinkling in the immensity, the signs of the stores—every franchise an entrepreneur might lease. Armani and Osh-Kosh, Hallmark, Kodak, Disney-Mitsubishi, American Motors, Schwab. A landscape all of names, and yet if you click on any name, you may enter its portal to discover its own little infinity of choices. Shirts of all sizes, colors, patterns, prices; shirts that were sold, yesterday, to someone in Iowa; other shirts that may be sold tomorrow or may never find a taker. Every atom and molecule in the financial continuum of purchases that might be made has here been numbered and cataloged. Here, surely, if anywhere, one might become if not invisible then scarcely noticed, as in some great metropolis swarming with illegal aliens, among whom a single further citizen can matter not a jot.

Fran became a mote in that vastness, a pip, an alga, unaware of his own frenetic motion as the flow of data took him from one possible purchase to the next. Here was a CD of Hugo Wolf lieder sung by Elly Ameling. Here a pair of Lucchese cowboy boots only slightly worn with western heels. Here six interesting Japanese dinner plates and a hand-embroidered black kimono. This charming pig creamer has an adorable French hat and is only slightly chipped. These Viking sweatshirts still have their tags from Wal-Mart, $29.95. Sabatier knives, set of four. A 1948 first edition of *The Secret of the Old House*. Hawaiian Barbie with hula accessories. *"Elly Ameling Sings Schumann!"* Assorted rustic napkins from Amish country.

There is nothing that is not a thought away, nothing that cannot be summoned by a wink and a nod to any of a dozen search engines. But there is a price to pay for such accessibility. The price is sleep, and in that sleep we buy again those commodities we bought or failed to buy before. No price is too steep, and no desire too low. Cream will flow through the slightly chipped lips of the charming pig creamer in the adorable hat, and our feet will slip into the boots we had no use for earlier. And when we return from our night journeys, like refugees returning to the shells of their burned homes, we find we are where we were, back at Square One. The matron was bellowing over the PA, *"Le temps s'en va, mesdames! Le temps s'en va!"* and Fran wanted to die.

Grain Beneath the Thresher's Flail

She was growing old in the service of the Khan, but there was no advantage to be reaped from long service, thanks to the contract she'd signed back when. She had become as adept with the hammers of the dulcimer as ever Chantal had been (Chantal was gone now, no one knew whither), but in truth the dulcimer is not an instrument that requires great skill—and its rewards are proportional. She felt as though she'd devoted her life—her afterlife—to the game of Parcheesi, shaking the dice and moving her tokens around the board forever. Surely this was not what the prospectus promised those who signed on.

She knew, in theory (which she'd heard, in various forms, from other denizens), that the great desideratum here, the magnet that drew all its custom, was beauty, the rapture of beauty that poets find in writing poetry or composers in their music. It might not be the Beatific Vision that saints feel face-to-face with God, but it was, in theory, the next best thing, a bliss beyond compare. And perhaps it was all one could hope for. How could she be sure that this bliss or that, as it shivered through her, like a wind through Daphne's leaves, wasn't of the same intensity that had zapped the major romantic poets in their day?

In any case, there was no escaping it. She'd tried to find an exit that didn't, each day, become the entrance by which she returned to her contracted afterlife and her service as a damsel with a dulcimer. Twang! Twang! *O ciel! O belle nuit!* Not that she had any notion of some higher destiny for herself, or sweeter pleasures—except the one that all the poets agreed on: Lethe, darkness, death, and by death to say we end the humdrum daily continuation of all our yesterdays into all our tomorrows.

The thought of it filled her with a holy dread, and she took up the silver hammers of her dulcimer and began, once again, to play such music as never mortal knew before.

The Go-Between

LISA GOLDSTEIN

Lisa Goldstein [www.brazenhussies.net/goldstein] is a distinguished fantasy writer who occasionally writes SF. Her first fantasy novel, The Red Magician *(1982) won the American Book Award for Best Paperback.* Tourists *(1989),* Strange Devices of the Sun and Moon *(1993), and* Dark Cities Underground *(1999) are among her other distinguished novels, and her stories are collected in* Daily Voices *(1989) and* Travellers in Magic *(1994). In an era when most writers fill their novels with lavish description and dramatize every minor scene, Goldstein is notable for her precise and concise novels, lapidary prose, psychological insight, and condensation—the hallmark of Goldstein's writing is no wasted words.*

"The Go-Between," published in Asimov's, *is a traditional SF problem-solving story, set in an alien world, with dogs. It has some of the gentle passion and social insight of the classic City stories of Clifford D. Simak, and a similar love and respect for man's best, first friend.*

The car moved through the dim streets of Port City, the driver slowing every so often to point out the sights. Here was a good bar, there the hospital, that huge building across the street a military barracks.

Majli looked out the rear window and tried to fix it all in her mind. Everything looked vaguely familiar, the same concrete prefabs SpaceAdmin threw up on every planet she had ever been posted to. But this one was different. This was her first plum assignment, an ambassadorship. If she did well here on Malku—if her negotiations were successful—there was no telling how high she could climb.

She strained to see through the indistinct light. They passed squat trees with right-angle branches and soft furry leaves, blue-green, gray-green, pale purple. Fog rolled down the mountains like a wave, further obscuring the view outside. She switched on the interior light and took her notes out of her briefcase.

When she looked up next, the car was pulling up to the embassy compound, an imposing building compared to the surrounding prefabs. She caught a glimpse of her face in the rearview mirror, level gray eyes, thick light-brown hair. Tendrils of hair had already come free of the tight bun she had fixed this morning, and she sighed and pushed them back.

She opened the door and stepped out. "This way, Madam Ambassador," the guard out front said, ushering her though the front door. She was not yet used to the title; it gave her an absurd feeling of importance and she shook her head to dispel it. She needed to be clear headed, especially now, for her first meeting.

She walked through the huge foyer, her heels echoing off the green marble floor, and presented her credentials to the guard at the front desk. "Yes, of course, Ms. Iris," the guard said. "The conference room is down the hall, the first door to your left."

Nearly everyone was in the conference room already, ranged around the metal table. She sat at the head and bent over her notes again. After the soft light outside, the room seemed harsh, too bright, though it was only what she was used to back on Earth.

When the last person arrived, she looked up. Of all the people there, she knew only the vice-ambassador, a fussy young woman who had met her late last night when her ship touched down. She took a deep breath. Okay.

"Hello," she said. "I'm the new ambassador, Majli Iris. I'd like you all to introduce yourselves, please."

She met, in turn, the Chief of Protocol, the anthropologist and two members of his team, the vice-ambassador again, the base commander and his adjutant, and a few others. Her memory for faces was poor, a bad trait in a diplomat. Fortunately, she had a dossier with all their names in her briefcase.

"Thank you," she said when they had finished, looking around the table. "As you probably know, I've been sent here to renegotiate the terms under which we lease Port City from the Hwaru. We want—we need—more space. This location is crucial if we're going to expand into the neighboring systems. If the estimates are right, we'll need as many as twenty ships taking off from this port every day."

She looked at each of them again, slower this time. "So what I want from you is your best behavior. We have to prove to the Hwaru that we'll make good neighbors. That means no socializing, except at officially sponsored events. No insults or slurs, even if you're just talking among yourselves. No fighting with them, of course, and no sex."

A few of the men smirked at that last. And she knew that it would prove impossible to enforce; she just hoped she could keep the incidents down to a minimum.

"All right," she said. "What do I need to know that wasn't covered in the briefings?"

The muted roar of a ship taking off sounded outside the building, and the windows rattled in their frames. "Madam Ambassador," the anthropologist said. Delgado, his name was, Delgado something or something Delgado. She nodded at him.

He switched on the holo display on the table. An image of a Hwaru appeared. The figure was shrouded in a voluminous hooded robe, but the robe opened at the front and she could see how lean it was, the bones showing in odd places. The thin ones are the males, she remembered. He was blacker than anyone she had ever seen on Earth, a reflecting black like onyx or coal, and his robe matched his skin. Gems glinted at his neck and wrists. His nose and jaw thrust forward to form a snout.

"This is a male," Delgado said. "He's about seven feet tall—you can't really see the scale in this picture. There is pronounced sexual dimorphism among the Hwaru—the females are shorter and rounder. They are organized into clans, with something like a king at the top. . . ."

"Yes, yes, I know all that," Majli thought. She forced herself to look as though she were paying attention. Delgado was short and stocky, with a face that could have come directly from a Mayan frieze: slanted forehead, straight aristocratic nose, full wide mouth. She would have to stop him soon; she would meet the Hwaru the next morning, and she still had a great deal of reading to get through.

". . . and he has a dog," Delgado said.

"I'm sorry. Who has a dog?"

"The one who calls himself Go-Between, or the Go-Between. He's the one you'll be dealing with. The king is present at all the meetings, of course, but he never says anything and we're working on the hypothesis that he's just a figurehead. We think it's Go-Between who makes the policy. Anyway, he brings a dog to all the meetings."

"Where did he get it?"

"It's probably one of the strays at the port. People bring

them from Earth and then find out they don't have the time or energy to take care of them."

"Well, that's interesting. What else can you tell me about the meetings?"

"Well." Delgado hesitated; she saw that she had derailed the lecture he had prepared. "There's a lot of silence. It's a little nerve-wracking at first—you start to think they're never going to say anything at all. You just have to wait it out."

"They have a funny smell, too," the commander's adjutant said. Everyone turned to look at him. "The Sheepfaces. They smell funny."

Majli's head jerked up. "The what?" she said.

"The Sheepfaces. I'm sorry, but everyone calls them that."

"You're more than sorry," Majli said. "You just disobeyed a direct order. Or weren't you listening when I said no slurs?"

"I'm sorry, I said. I won't do it again. Everyone says it, though. They say worse things."

"No, you certainly won't do it again. You'll report to the personnel office, collect two weeks' pay, and leave on the next ship out."

The adjutant opened his mouth to say something, closed it, then stood and walked stiffly to the door. A few people watched him go; the rest pretended to study their notes or look out the window.

Her heart was beating fast. She waited for someone to mutter one of the words she hated, "bitch" or "slag," but no one said anything. She had to do it, though; she had to make an example of the man, to demonstrate that she took her authority seriously and that they had damned well better take her seriously too. God, and she didn't even know the man's name.

They talked for another hour about what she might expect from the Hwaru, and then she adjourned the meeting.

The car arrived the next day to take her to the Hwaru's dwelling. They drove in the opposite direction from the embassy, stopped at the checkpoint on the outskirts of Port City, and were waved through.

Once they passed the checkpoint, the car bumped along dirt roads, some of them barely wide enough to accommodate it. Mountains loomed ahead of them in the indistinct light. As they came closer, she saw low rambling structures built along the foothills, barely distinguishable from the mountains behind them.

No, it was just one building. The Hwaru's dwelling, made of dark gray stone, seemed to run for miles along the base of the mountain. They pulled up before a section slightly higher than the rest and she got out.

Majli was a tall woman, but the Hwaru who stood at the door to greet her was far taller, a male. None of the briefings had mentioned his eyes, which were as onyx-black as his skin, with no whites. They were disconcerting in that night-dark face, and very difficult to read, especially in the vague light.

And, as Delgado said, he had a dog. A very ordinary-looking dog, a medium-sized mutt with shaggy black fur and an even bushier tail. It trotted forward to sniff at her politely.

She was surprised to feel a twinge of annoyance, almost jealousy. Dogs and people had kept each other company for tens of thousands of years; dogs had willingly, even eagerly, thrown their lot in with humans. Would they do the same for any sentient being? Did the ancient bond between dogs and humans mean nothing to them after all?

"My name is Go-Between," the Hwaru said. "I am honored to invite you to our hearth." He bowed and she followed him inside.

As her eyes adjusted to the gloom, she saw that he meant the word "hearth" literally. Fires glowed in two opposite walls, their flames golden; they and the smoky candles in sconces along the walls provided the only light in the room. A tall stone chair stood at the end of the room, a throne. She squinted to make out the figure seated there, but she already knew who it must be.

"I have the honor to present my king," Go-Between said.

His voice sounded overly loud; were the Hwaru slightly deaf? "King Darhu, this is Ambassador Majli Iris."

She bowed to the other Hwaru. Now she could see that he wore jewelry at his neck and wrists, more than Go-Between, and a circlet of gems bound his forehead. Even the jewels were dim, deep red and dark gold. "I'm honored, my lord," she said.

The king said nothing. She became aware of the smell the adjutant had mentioned. She could not put a name to it but it was not unpleasant, a warm, sweet odor, slightly spicy. Cinnamon?

Several Hwaru children chased each other through the room, shouting and making a noise that sounded like growling. The children were small and plump: were they females, or did the sexual differences only show up at puberty? Dogs played at their feet. Two women came in and lit candles from the fire.

"He is honored to meet you as well, Ambassador Iris," Go-Between said.

Majli forced her attention away from the chaos in the room. Delgado had mentioned this in one of his reports; he called it "lack of separation between public and private spheres."

Go-Between indicated a chair at the base of the throne for her. As she sat, the others arrived, the anthropology team and the vice-ambassador, and Go-Between ushered them to seats as well. The dog came and nuzzled at Go-Between's hands, then curled up and went to sleep on a pile of blankets by one of the fires. Majli marveled at how well-trained it was.

The Hwaru's skin glittered in the light from the fires. They were the color of coffee beans, of polished black shoes, of cockroaches. As her eyes grew accustomed to the light she noticed a tapestry worked in gold thread behind the throne, a complex tracery of curves and lines. Gold flashed as the fire played over it.

"King Darhu wishes to know how you like our country," Go-Between said.

"I like it a great deal," Majli said. In fact, she had not seen very much of it. SpaceAdmin placed top priority on expanding Port City, and she had been rushed to the negotiations without any time for sightseeing. Fortunately, she had read enough to be able to say a few complimentary things about the planet.

Go-Between said nothing for a long time. Children played, dogs barked, the life of the hearth went on loudly around them. Majli felt a strong urge to fill the pause with trifles, to say anything at all, but she restrained herself: this was just one of the silences Delgado had mentioned. Finally, Go-Between said, "The king is very pleased."

As the conversation went on, Go-Between continued to do all the talking while Darhu remained silent. Was Delgado right then, was Darhu a figure-head and Go-Between the true power on this part of the planet?

She found herself talking directly to Go-Between instead of the king, and had to force herself to include Darhu in the conversation. It was difficult, though, to focus on either of the Hwaru; because their black eyes had no whites, she couldn't tell half the time what they were looking at.

They made small talk for the next hour, each side feeling the other out. Majli felt disappointed that they were not making better progress, but she knew from experience that negotiations like this one took time.

Finally, Go-Between stood; apparently, the meeting was over for now. The dog woke up and stretched and went over to Go-Between. Once again, she felt a sort of betrayal that humanity's oldest friend should attach itself to this alien being.

"What's his name?" she asked.

"She is a she," Go-Between said, then added something in his own language. The dog looked up eagerly, and Go-Between scratched her behind the ears. "Loyalty is very important to us," he said. "The name means something like 'Loyal' or 'Faithful.'"

"Fido," Majli said, trying not to laugh.

"What?"

"It is a name we have given to dogs for many years," she said. "Loyalty is very important to us too."

"I am glad to hear it," Go-Between said.

*   *   *

It was mid-afternoon by the time they left the meeting but the planet's shadowy light made it seem like evening; Majli had to shake off a feeling that night would fall any minute. The fog had burned off, though, and the temperature felt almost pleasant.

She got in the waiting car and they returned to the city. When they passed the checkpoint, she leaned forward and said to the driver, "I think I'll walk from here."

"My orders were to drive you," the driver said.

"Well, I'm giving you new orders." She opened the door. "Take the afternoon off."

"I can't let you do that! What if something happens to you?"

"What could happen? No one's allowed into Port City unless they're cleared beforehand."

She stepped out. The driver glanced at the guards on the checkpoint as if seeking their assistance, but they said nothing and he shrugged and pulled away.

She wanted—needed—the walk for several reasons. She had to be alone, to clear her head after the strange sights and smells of the hearth. And she wanted to see Port City up close, so that she could talk about it with Go-Between, show him the benefits that SpaceAdmin could bring to his planet.

She could have explained all this to the driver, of course. "Never explain," her father used to say. "Your subordinates don't need to know, and your superiors will ask if they don't understand."

She had thought about her father a great deal since she came to Malku and Port City. "If someone disobeys an order, you make an example of him immediately," he had said. "No one will disobey you after that." And she had; she had fired the adjutant. She wondered if he would have approved.

Her father had died three years ago, before she received her promotion to ambassador. Since then, the things he had taught her seemed more important than ever; she found herself remembering them at odd times, relying on them to find her way through the complex maze of interplanetary diplomacy. After all, he had negotiated the Peace of Altair, single-handedly ending a war that had cost millions of lives and nearly destroyed an entire planet. Would anything she did ever match that?

She sighed; she missed him very much. She wished she could tell him about her new posting. So much rested on her shoulders. Would he be proud of her?

She passed ugly gray buildings, groups of soldiers in uniform, dockworkers getting off their shift. A noisy crowd came out of a tavern, laughing and shouting. Streetlights glowed every dozen yards or so, casting a little light before the gloom closed in again.

She saw a few Hwaru, not very many. Once, she saw a male part his robe and relieve himself against the corner of a building; she had heard about this in the briefings but she still felt a shudder of disgust to see it. Another example of Delgado's "lack of separation between public and private spheres," probably. The urine left a dark stain against the concrete.

The buildings thinned and she began to pass clusters of trees like the ones she had seen that morning. Their right-angle branches, turning left and right, up and down, made them look like intricate puzzles. They smelled like pencil shavings, that same odor of wood and graphite combined.

Far off, she saw the lights of a ship as it lifted into the air; a loud rumbling came to where she stood a moment later. She hurried home, eager to write up her notes and impressions.

A few days later, she arrived at the hearth to find everything in chaos—children crying, adults racing back and forth, dogs barking. Delgado sat in his customary chair, looking as if he would rather be anywhere else. Of all the people from the base, only he continued to attend the talks; he needed to be there to study the Hwaru, and to explain some of the nuances of their behavior if Majli failed to understand anything.

"What's wrong?" she asked.

"A child is sick," Go-Between said.

Now she realized that only one child was crying, though it

made enough noise for a whole roomful of them. It was bedded down by one of the fires; an adult held a clay cup to its mouth, trying to make it drink. A dog, fluffy and golden as a chrysanthemum, lay on the bed with the child and whined anxiously.

"I can send a doctor from the hospital," she said. "They might be able to find out what's wrong."

One of the long nerve-wracking silences passed. "We would like that very much," Go-Between said finally. "There is suspicion, you know—some people think that you brought the disease."

"That I—"

"Your people. Though the disease existed for a few years before you arrived. I am sorry to say that there is some distrust of you."

"Oh, no," she said, appalled. "We would never do anything like that. I assure you that you can trust us."

Delgado's head jerked toward her; she could not make out his expression in the dim smoky light.

"I hope we can put to rest all your suspicion," she said into the silence. "We are here to help you."

"That's the first time I've heard you lie," Delgado said. Their briefings after the negotiations had evolved into something more informal, dinner or coffee at the embassy cafeteria. And Delgado himself seemed more at ease with her, less inclined to launch into a lecture on any pretext.

"Lie? What do you mean?" She poured coffee from the urn and headed toward a free table. He got his own cup and followed.

"When you said we would never intentionally bring disease." He sat. "Earth's history is full of examples where we did just that. People gave blankets infected with smallpox to Native Americans, for example."

"Oh, but that was a long time ago! I remember that story now, but I certainly wasn't thinking of it during the negotiations."

Delgado looked at her silently, his full lips curled up in a smile.

"Look," she said. "I'm not here to fill the Hwaru in on every terrible thing we've done throughout our history. I have to put the best face on things. My father used to say, 'An ambassador is an honest man sent to lie abroad for the good of his country.' He was quoting someone, I don't remember who—"

"I've heard of your father. He negotiated the Peace of Altair, didn't he?"

She smiled wryly. "Everyone's heard of him."

"How old were you then?"

"About five. I don't remember much, just sitting on the floor and playing with my glow-gun while my father had long conversations with something that looked like a giant green lobster."

"So you were there at the talks themselves?"

"Oh, yeah. My father wanted me to learn everything I could, for when I joined SpaceAdmin myself. I remember that I was under strict orders not to point my gun at the lobster and make him glow."

"Did you go with him on every posting, then?"

"Sure. That was my whole childhood, moving from planet to planet, going wherever my father was needed. My mother couldn't take it—she finally left us and went back to Earth. What about you? Where did you grow up?"

"Merida, in Mexico. I never went anywhere, just stayed in the same town until I left for college."

She shook her head. "I can't imagine that. What was it like? Did you have a big family?"

"Huge. Aunts and uncles and brothers and sisters and cousins and dogs—"

"You had dogs?"

"Lots. Why?"

"Well, I'm wondering about the dogs here. I still can't get over it. I mean, wouldn't the Hwaru, well, *look* wrong to the dogs somehow?"

"Smell wrong, more likely. Dogs rely on smell more than any other sense."

"You sound like you've been researching this."

"I have been, yes. The thing about dogs—they're pack animals. They're happiest when they're in a group, and when they know what everyone's place is in that group. Someone has to be the pack leader, the alpha dog, and if you want your dog to obey you, that has to be you, the owner. It doesn't bother them that their pack includes another species. I never thought about it when I was a kid, but it's amazing, really, that it doesn't, that they're so open to animals that act and smell different from them, that aren't dogs. They're the opposite of bigoted. There are stories of gorillas in captivity keeping dogs as pets, and race horses that won't run if their dogs aren't there. Dogs seem to accept *any* species joining the pack, anyone that has the presence to become pack leader. Even aliens, apparently."

"Yes, but humans grew up with dogs. We evolved with them. So did gorillas and horses, for that matter. You said it yourself—anyone not from Earth would smell wrong. Have dogs ever accepted any other alien species?"

"There's no record of it happening. But it does make a sort of sense that they would. If they can join other non-dog species, why not aliens?" He finished his coffee and grinned at her. "There's a paper to be written here."

The negotiations went on. She met with Go-Between nearly every day, with time off for the Hwaru's holidays. (She, of course, had no holidays.) She talked about the technology the humans could give the Hwaru, the medical advances that could be theirs as soon as scientists had a chance to study Hwaru biology, the knowledge the two cultures could exchange.

The negotiations moved slowly; in the maddening silences between conversation, time seemed to crawl, almost stop altogether. Sometimes, she sensed resistance from Go-Between, but she told herself that she was imagining it, that it was only a function of the slow pace of the talks.

She wondered once or twice what would happen if she did not succeed, if the Hwaru did not agree to the port expansion. Her upward climb in SpaceAdmin would come to an abrupt end; she would be sent to some backwater planet with no chance for advancement. "Never think about failure," her father used to say. "Keep your goal ahead of you at all times."

She took to wandering Port City whenever she had a spare moment, trying to become familiar with every corner and crevice, looking for any possible advantage in the talks. And she could not help but be fascinated by the city: the sweet lingering odor, strongest in the Hwaru hearth but present everywhere, the beautiful colors of the leaves, the tall angular males and the round fat females, headed on unguessable errands of their own. They walked so gracefully, as if in a stately procession. And what did the females do? She would have to ask Delgado.

One afternoon, she heard a commotion up ahead, and strained to see in the murky light. A group of soldiers were laughing and shouting. "Hey, Sheepface!" one of them called.

"Baaa! Baaa!"

"Hey, Shitface! Look at us when we're talking to you!"

The soldiers had surrounded a Hwaru male and were backing him against a wall; she could see his dark muzzle looming above the crowd. "Stop that!" she said, hurrying forward. "Stop it right now!"

"Don't let the dog escape!" one of the soldiers said. "Here, doggie!"

A dog? Oh, God, it wasn't Go-Between, was it? She broke into a run.

"Sheep shouldn't have dogs!"

"It's a sheepdog!"

Harsh laughter rose up at this. She ran faster. She sensed other people hurrying after her but she had no time to stop.

"Baaa, baaa, black sheep!" someone said.

"Get away from him," she called, breathing hard. No one paid her any attention. Louder, she said, "Right *now*. That's an *order*, soldiers!"

Some of the men turned away from the Hwaru and looked at her, befuddled. They were drunk, she saw. Anger filled her. She would discharge their sorry asses and get them off-planet before they had a chance to sober up.

Other men closed in around the Hwaru. She heard a dog

yelp. Suddenly, she realized where she was, a lone woman in a crowd of hostile, raucous men, all of them armed, most too drunk to understand the damage she could do to their careers.

Then Hwaru surrounded her on all sides, a dozen of them, maybe more, males and females. And more dogs, dogs swarming between the legs of the Hwaru, barking urgently, growling, baring their teeth at the soldiers.

The soldiers slowly became aware of the crowd around them. They stopped and backed away, then ran off into the dark. Should she tell them to stay? "Never give an order you know won't be obeyed," her father had said. She let them go.

A dog whimpered. A Hwaru male bent over it. His scent was very strong, something like burning metal. Oh, God, it *was* Go-Between. He would never deal with her after this; the negotiations had failed. "Go-Between?" she said.

"Yes?" said a voice behind her.

She turned quickly. A tall Hwaru stood there. She recognized the gems glimmering at his neck and wrists and flushed with embarrassment. She couldn't even tell one Hwaru from another; she was screwing up in all kinds of ways today. "I want to assure you that this will never happen again," she said to Go-Between. "These men will be disciplined."

"Let's not worry about that for the moment," Go-Between said in his loud voice. "We need to get the dog back to the hearth."

The other Hwaru—the dog's owner—moved aside, and now she could see that the dog looked nothing like Fido; it had short brown fur, pointed ears, and a strange crooked tail. It lay on its side, panting heavily.

The headlights of an embassy car cut through the gloom. Thank God, she might still be able to salvage something from this situation. She waved it down. It came to a stop and two soldiers got out.

"We need to get to the hearth, fast," she said to them. "This Hwaru here and the dog, who's injured, and Go-Between and I."

The two men responded quickly to the emergency. One of

them took off his coat and maneuvered the dog onto it; the dog whimpered quietly. The other opened the car door and helped lift the makeshift bed onto the backseat. The two Hwaru got in with the dog; Majli crowded in with the soldiers in the front.

"I'm very sorry this happened," she said, twisting in her seat to look at the Hwaru. The car turned around and headed toward the checkpoint. "And I'm sorry I didn't recognize you, but it was dark. . . ."

Never apologize unless you absolutely have to, her father had said. What would he think of her behavior today? But she was in the wrong, she and the people under her command. Surely he would understand that.

"I am not offended," Go-Between said. "It is very hard for us to distinguish you humans by sight, one from another. You all look alike to us, even your males and females the same."

She nearly grinned at hearing the ancient cliché come from Go-Between's strange muzzle. But she had to concentrate, had to save something from this debacle. Amazingly, Go-Between and the other Hwaru did not seem angry. Perhaps they had misunderstood, perhaps they had taken the soldiers' hostility for high spirits. The other Hwaru did not look hurt, thank God.

"This is Hiraz, one of our hearth," Go-Between said, indicating the other Hwaru. "Hiraz, this is Ambassador Majli Iris."

"I am very pleased to meet you," Majli said. She searched for a neutral topic. "Why do you like dogs so much?"

"Dogs?" Go-Between's muzzle opened; she knew by now that that meant he was smiling. "Dogs are amazing animals. They are so happy, they live in the moment. Look at this one—" He nodded to the dog on the seat next to him, its eyes closed, its breathing regular now. "He's asleep. After everything that happened, he's asleep. They are so uncomplicated. It is good to be uncomplicated, sometimes."

His eyes met hers. For the first time in their negotiations, they shared a moment of pure communication; she knew exactly what he was thinking. He was telling her that the two of them were doing a complicated dance, that he understood all the reasons why the dance had to continue, but that he regretted the necessity for it all the same.

She nodded. She regretted it too, sometimes. Once or twice during the talks she had wondered what would happen if she simply said, "Okay. You have the land—we want it. Yes or no?"

Go-Between ran his hand lightly over the dog's flank. "He seems not to be hurt, merely frightened. But look—" He indicated the dog's crooked tail, then gently parted the fur on its side to show her an ugly scar, a long pale gash. "He was injured badly once. I wonder what happened. Well, there's no way of telling now."

"Maybe a car accident?" she suggested.

The car pulled up to the checkpoint and the guards waved them through. She faced forward, needing to hold on to the door handle as they jounced along the rutted roads.

When they arrived at the hearth, the soldiers jumped out and opened the doors, then lifted the dog between them and carried it inside. In the main room, the familiar confusion swirled around them, children yelling and growling, dogs playing, someone calling across the room, someone else hurrying through with a platter of food.

A dog separated from the pack and ran up to them, tail wagging wildly. It was Fido, she saw, thrilled that her owner had come home. "How can you not like dogs?" Go-Between said, smiling.

He turned to the soldiers. "Put the dog down over here," he said, indicating a spot by the fire. The soldiers settled it gently on a pile of blankets. Fido padded toward the blankets, ears down, legs stiff, hackles raised, prepared to fight this interloper in her spot. Then, suddenly, she backed away and returned to the pack. Once again, Majli was amazed at how well-behaved the dog was.

The other dog opened its eyes and then, to Majli's surprise, wagged its misshapen tail feebly, clearly happy to be home and safe and warm. "You can communicate with dogs," someone said behind her.

Majli turned. Hiraz stood behind her. "You asked why we

like dogs," he said. His accent was stronger than Go-Between's; the words came from deeper within his muzzle and sounded close to a growl. "It is partly because you can communicate with them."

Go-Between looked at Hiraz quickly, a complex expression that Majli couldn't interpret. "You can communicate with cats, too, probably," Hiraz said. "But they seem not to want to."

"Thank you for all your help," Go-Between said. "We can take care of everything from here."

Should she ask whether the talks would continue after this? No, best to act as if nothing had changed. "I'll see you tomorrow, then."

"Tomorrow," Go-Between said.

She breathed a sigh of relief and headed back to the car.

A few days later, the base commander reported that Hiraz had identified one of the soldiers who had surrounded him, and that, acting on Hiraz's information, they had arrested Private Tully Walter. "He says he didn't do it, though," the commander said. "And we can't hold him much longer—we'll have to let him go if there's no evidence."

Majli arranged for an interview with Walter at the stockade. The interview room consisted of a table and several chairs. She took one facing the soldier. A guard sat between them.

"What exactly was the idea of attacking one of the Hwaru?" she asked with no preliminaries.

"I didn't do anything," Walter said. "I wasn't even there."

"That's not what our informant says. We have a witness who puts you right at the scene."

"A witness? Who?"

A Hwaru, Majli thought. Suddenly she remembered Go-Between saying, "You all look alike to us," and she wondered exactly how Hiraz had identified this man.

She forced the thought aside; she could not afford to let her doubt show. "Look," she said, leaning forward. "These talks are critical. SpaceAdmin needs this port. If someone

interferes with the negotiations here—and that includes ha-
rassing the Hwaru, giving them the idea we won't make
good neighbors—well, that could be grounds for court mar-
tial."

Walter went very pale. "I didn't do it," he said. "I never
touched him."

"Who *did* touch him?" Majli asked softly. "Give me a
name, and I'll see that you get off fairly lightly."

"A guy named San Corio," Walter said reluctantly. "It was
his idea. He saw the Sh—the Hwaru, walking all by himself,
just him and the dog, and he said—well, the dog made him
angry. I mean, they're *our* dogs."

"And then what happened?"

"Well, then he started yelling. He said that—excuse me,
but he said that sheep shouldn't own dogs. He said it was up
to us to rescue it. We didn't mean to hurt him, we just
wanted to get the dog back. And then it all got out of control.
I didn't touch him, though, I swear. I was at the back. I may
have yelled a few things, but I never touched him."

"All right. We'll talk to Corio, see what he has to say."

"What about me? What's going to happen to me now?"

"I can't promise anything. It depends on whether you
were telling me the truth. You'll be discharged, of course,
and sent off-planet, but that might be the worst of it. The
discharge might not even be dishonorable."

Walter seemed to relax a little. She stood and nodded to
the guard to unlock the interview room, then headed for
home.

She thought that she knew now how Hiraz had identified
Walter: his dog had sniffed him out. Thank God they had the
right person, and that the people responsible would be punished, just as she had promised Go-Between.

She hated to admit it, though, but she understood how
Walter felt. "Dammit," she thought, "they are our dogs!"

In the days that followed, Walter came forward with the
names of others in the crowd, and they and San Corio were
arrested. Corio denied everything at first, but when several

people identified him as the instigator, he broke down and confessed.

Meanwhile, the talks dragged on. One day, during a particularly long pause, a dog came over and sniffed at her hands. It was Hiraz's dog; she recognized the crooked tail and sharp pointed ears. She patted him carefully. "I'm glad to see he's well enough to go outside," she said.

"He's not well at all, I'm sorry to say," Go-Between said. "He turned out to have suffered several broken ribs."

"You mean he hasn't left the hearth?"

"Not since that night."

"But—" Majli hesitated. "Think twice about everything you say," her father had said. "Then think once more."

The hell with that. She shut her father out. There was something strange here, something these people were hiding from her, and she had to get to the bottom of it. She could no longer afford diplomacy.

"How did Hiraz recognize the person in the crowd that night?" she asked bluntly. "I thought the dog recognized his smell, but you said the dog hasn't been out. And we all look alike to you; you said that too."

Go-Between was silent for a long moment. "There are things we do not tell you," he said finally. "Just as I am certain there are things you do not tell us."

The dog lowered his nose to her shoes, apparently finding a fascinating scent there. Suddenly, a good many puzzles came together. The long silences, and the friendship with dogs, and the fact that King Darhu never spoke. . . .

"Hiraz recognized Walter by *smell*," she said. "You communicate by smell, don't you? You translate what I say for the king, and he answers you, all by scent. That's why you talk so loudly—because normally, when you're close to each other, you don't use your voice at all. Speech is only for long distances, isn't that right?" She didn't wait for an answer. "I thought *you* were the power here, but you're only the translator."

"The Go-Between. We have never lied to you."

"And dogs—they communicate by smell too," she said,

thinking quickly. God, it was worse than she'd thought; the implications were devastating. "You—somehow you can talk to dogs, actually *speak* to them. Hiraz even told me so, but I didn't listen. That's why the dogs here are so well-behaved."

Delgado took out his notebook and stylus and began to write furiously. *Great*, she thought, *he's going to get a paper out of this. I'm going to be posted to some backwater, and he's going to be famous!* She shook her head; she had to concentrate.

"Is that true?" Delgado asked. "Do dogs have language? How much can they communicate?"

"More than you suspect," Go-Between said.

"But what do they talk about? Can they understand abstract concepts?"

"Enough of this," Majli said, snapping at Delgado. "You can interview him later." She turned to Go-Between. "You said—you said that there was no way of knowing now how Hiraz's dog got injured. The important word was 'now,' and I missed it. What you meant was, you'd ask him when he woke up. Isn't that right? And what did he tell you? How was he hurt?"

"A car accident. As you thought."

"And the broken ribs?" She held her breath.

"A man in the crowd kicked him. Kicked him several times."

She slumped. "And so you know—"

"Know what?" Go-Between said. His muzzle opened; he was smiling, though she could not imagine what he found so amusing.

"Know that we are not the way we represented ourselves," Majli said. "That we are crueler than you thought."

Delgado gave her a warning look. She shook her head. There was nothing she could salvage from this situation; she might as well tell the truth. She stood, ready to leave if Go-Between dismissed her.

"Sit down, please," Go-Between said. He said nothing for a long moment; she thought she might scream from the tension, then realized that he and the king were communicating, just as she had guessed. The spicy scent around her grew stronger.

"On the contrary," Go-Between said finally. "We would like to accept your offer and lease the port to you. We are eager to share all the learning you have promised us."

"You—you are? But *why?*"

"The dogs told us. They said that you could be cruel, yes, but that you were rarely so. They said that they have loved you for years uncountable. That you are good, and worthy of our trust."

She grabbed an armful of her clothes from the closet and thrust them into her suitcase, the hangers still attached. A knock came at her door. She didn't answer.

"Hello?" someone said. Delgado stepped inside. "My God, what are you doing? Are you leaving?"

She faced him, still feeling the anger that had driven her to start packing. "Do you know how my father negotiated the Peace of Altair?"

Delgado said nothing.

"He did it by lying to them. Over and over, until he came up with lies each side wanted to hear. Beautiful lies, all of them. Beautiful, worthless lies."

"Are you drunk?"

"No. No, I'm fine."

"Listen, you wouldn't believe what I'm learning about dogs! This is amazing. Do you know why they wag their tails? It's to spread their scent around—it's like shouting. And when they're frightened and they tuck their tails beneath them—that's to make sure that no one can smell them out, can hear them, if you like, and find them."

Majli plucked the hangers from her clothes. "That's nice."

"And when they urinate, that's like writing. They can pack enormous amounts of meaning into it. Go-Between says it's almost like epic poetry, one vast poem that every dog adds to. All this communication going on around us, and we never knew."

Majli said nothing.

"What's wrong?" Delgado asked. "*Are* you leaving?"

"Yes."

"But why? You did a great job here. You got us the port. Sure, you went a little crazy toward the end there, told them that stuff about us being cruel, but no one back at SpaceAdmin has to know that. I won't mention it in my report, if that's what's worrying you."

"What's wrong is that we're misrepresenting ourselves to the Hwaru. The dogs told them that we're wonderful people. Well, dogs are saps, you know that! You can kick them and kick them and they still come back, they still love you. Dogs don't know anything!"

She turned toward him. "We're *not* wonderful. Look at those soldiers, ready to riot just because they saw a Hwaru with a dog. And here I was, trying to pretend we were something else, kind, generous people who wouldn't hurt a flea. Wouldn't hurt a dog. I was lying, just like you said. All I thought about was getting that port, was winning. It never occurred to me that if we won, the Hwaru might lose. We haven't changed—we'll never change. We're still the same people who gave the Native Americans those blankets."

"Well, but we're trying. We're more careful now. That's what I'm here for, that's why they send anthropologists to these talks. To make sure we understand who we're dealing with, that we don't screw it up this time."

"And we won't? Can you promise me that? We're going to have thousands of people coming here to work on the port. Can you promise me the Hwaru won't be attacked again?"

"No, of course not. Of course not. But—"

"All my life, I wanted to be an ambassador. *Thought* I wanted to be an ambassador. But it was just my father, pushing me and pushing me. You know, there was a part of me that was glad when he died. Glad I wouldn't have to hear any of those stupid homilies again. I didn't know that I'd be hearing them for the rest of my life, that I'd never get rid of them. That they'd play on an infinite loop in my brain."

"You *are* drunk."

"Maybe. Maybe a little. But I'm not changing my mind. I'm quitting. I can't go on telling these—these lies about us to everyone we meet. You didn't see those soldiers, that mob, when they attacked Hiraz. It was horrible. *We're* horrible."

"Maybe," Delgado said. "But you know, the *dogs* like us. That's got to count for something."

Viewpoint

GENE WOLFE

Gene Wolfe lives in Barrington, Illinois, and is widely considered the most accomplished writer in the fantasy and science fiction genres; his four-volume Book of the New Sun *is an acknowledged masterpiece. Although his novels are most often science fiction, his richly textured far-future worlds often feel like fantasy. His most recent book is* Return to the Whorl, *the third volume of* The Book of the Short Sun *(really a single huge novel), which some of his most attentive readers feel is his best book yet. He has published many fantasy, science fiction, and horror stories over the last thirty years and more, and has been given the World Fantasy Award for Life Achievement. Collections of his short fiction include* The Island of Dr. Death and Other Stories and Other Stories, Storeys from the Old Hotel, Endangered Species, *and* Strange Travelers.

"Viewpoint," from Red Shift, *is a Gene Wolfe adventure in social satire mode, reminiscent of Robert Sheckley's classic "The Prize of Peril." Here, a backcountry man becomes a contestant on a TV show that gives him $100,000 in cash and sends the public (and the government) to try to rob him.*

"**I** have one question and one only," Jay declared. "How do I know that I will be paid? Answer it to my satisfaction and give your orders."

The youngish man behind the desk opened a drawer and pulled out a packet of crisp bills. It was followed by another and another, and they by seven more. The youngish man had brown-blond hair and clear blue eyes that said he could be trusted absolutely with anything. Looking at them, Jay decided that each had cost more than he had ever had in his entire life to date.

"Here's the money," the youngish man told Jay softly. "These are hundreds, all of them. Each band holds one hundred, so each bundle is ten thousand. Ten bundles make a hundred thousand. It's really not all that much."

"Less than you make in a year."

"Less than I make in three months. I know it's a lot to you." The youngish man hesitated as though groping for a new topic. "You've got a dramatic face, you know. Those scars. That was your edge. Did you really fight a bobcat?"

Jay shrugged. "The bullet broke its back, and I thought it was dead. I got too close."

"I see." The youngish man pushed the packets of bills toward him. "Well, you don't have to worry about getting paid. That's the full sum, and you're getting it up front and in cash." He paused. "Maybe I shouldn't tell you this."

Jay was looking at the money. "If it's confidential, say so and I'll keep it that way."

"Will you?"

Jay nodded. "For a hundred thousand? Yes. For quite a bit less than that."

The youngish man sighed. "You probably know anyway, so why not? You can't just go out and stick it in a bank. You understand that?"

"They'll say it's drug money."

For a moment the youngish man looked as if he were about to sigh again, although he did not. "They'll say it's drug money, of course. They always do. But they really don't care. You have a lot of money, and if it gets into a bank Big Daddy will have it in a nanosecond. It'll take you years to get it back, and cost a lot more than a hundred thousand."

Though skeptical, Jay nodded. "Sure."

"Okay, I didn't want to give you this and have them grab it before five. They'll take a big cut of anything you spend it on anyway, but we've all got to live with that."

Jay did not, but he said nothing.

"Count it. Count it twice and look carefully. I don't want you thinking we cheated you for a lousy hundred thou."

Jay did, finding it impossible to think of what so much money could buy. He had needed money so badly that he could no longer calculate its value in terms of a new rifle or a canoe. It was money itself he hungered for now, and this was more than he had dared dream of.

"You want a bag? I can give you one, but that jacket's got plenty of pockets. It's for camping, right?"

"Hunting."

The youngish man smiled the smile of one who knows a secret. "Why don't you put it in there? Should be safer than a bag."

Jay had begun to fill them already—thirty thousand in the upper right inside pocket, twenty more in the upper left, behind his wallet. Twenty in the left pocket outside.

"You're BC, right?"

"Sure." Jay tapped the empty screen above his eyes.

"Okay." The youngish man opened another drawer. "As a bonus you get a double upgrade. Couple of dots. Sit still."

Jay did.

When the youngish man was back behind his desk, he said, "I bet you'd like to look at yourself. I ought to have a mirror, but I didn't think of it. You want to go to the men's? There's a lot of mirrors in there. Just come back whenever you've seen enough. I've got calls to make."

"Thanks," Jay said.

In the windowless office beyond the youngish man's, his secretary was chatting with a big security bot. Jay asked where the rest rooms were, and the bot offered to show him, gliding noiselessly down the faux-marble corridor.

"Tell me something," Jay said when the bot had come to a stop before the door. "Suppose that when I got through in there I went down to the lobby. Would there be anything to stop me from going out to the street?"

"No, sir."

"You're going to be standing out here waiting for me when I come out, right? I'd never make it to the elevators."

"Will you need a guide at that point, sir?"

The blank metal face had told Jay nothing, and the pleasant baritone had suggested polite inquiry, and nothing else. Jay said, "I can find my way back all right."

"In that case, I have other duties, sir."

"Like talking to that girl?"

"Say *woman*, sir. To that young woman. They prefer it, and Valerie is an excellent source of intelligence. One cultivates one's sources, sir, in police work."

Jay nodded, conceding the point. "Can you answer a couple more questions for me? If it's not too much trouble?"

"If I can, sir. Certainly."

"How many dots have I got?"

"Are you referring to IA stars, sir?"

Jay nodded.

"Two, sir. Are you testing my vision, sir?"

"Sure. One more, and I'll let you alone. What's the name of the man I've been talking to? There's no nameplate on his desk, and I never did catch it."

"Mr. Smith, sir."

"You're kidding me."

"No, sir."

"John Smith? I'll bet that's it."

"No, sir. Mr. James R. Smith, sir."

"Well, I'll be damned."

Scratching his chin, Jay went into the men's room. There were at least a dozen mirrors there, as the youngish man had said. The little augmentation screen set into his forehead, blank and black since he had received it between the fourth and the fifth grades, showed two glimmering stars now: five- or six-pointed, and scarlet or blue depending on the angle from which he viewed them.

For ten minutes or more he marveled at them. Then he relieved himself, washed his hands, and counted the money again. One hundred thousand in crisp, almost-new hundreds. Logically, it could be counterfeit. Logically, he should have shown one to the security bot and asked its opinion.

Had the bot noticed his bulging pockets? Security bots would undoubtedly be programmed to take note of such things, and might well be more observant than a human officer.

He took out a fresh bill and examined it, riffling it between his fingers and holding it up to the light, reading its serial number under his breath. Good.

If the bot had called it bad, it would have been because the bot had been instructed to do so, and that was all.

Furthermore, someone had been afraid he would assault the youngish man the bot called James R. Smith, presumably because metal detectors had picked up his hunting knife; but Smith had not asked him to remove it, or so much as mentioned it. Why?

Jay spent another fifteen or twenty seconds studying the stars in his IA screen and three full minutes concentrating before he left the rest room. There was no bot in the hall. A middle-aged man who looked important passed him without a glance and went in.

Jay walked to the elevators, waved a hand for the motion detector, and rode a somewhat crowded car to the lobby. So far as he could see, no one was paying the least attention to him. There was another security bot in the lobby (as there had been when he had come in), but it appeared to pay no particular attention to him either.

Revolving doors admitted him to Sixth Avenue. He elbowed his way for half a block along a sidewalk much too crowded, and returned to the Globnet Building.

The security bot was chatting with the young woman in her windowless room again. When she saw Jay she nodded and smiled, and the doors to Smith's office swung open.

Smith, who had said that he would be making calls, was standing at one of his floor-to-ceiling windows staring out at the gloomy December sky.

"I'm back," Jay said. "Sorry I took so long. I was trying to access the new chips you gave me."

"You can't." Smith turned around.

"That's what I found out."

Smith's chair rolled backwards, and he seated himself at his desk. "Aren't you going to ask me what they're for?"

Jay shook his head.

"Okay, that will save me a lot of talking. You've still got the hundred thousand?"

Jay nodded.

"All right. In about forty-seven minutes we're going to announce on all our channels that you've got it. We'll give your name, and show you leaving this building, but that's all. It will be repeated on every newscast tonight, name, more pictures, a hundred thou in cash. Every banger and grifter in the city will be after you, and if you hide it, there's a good chance they'll stick your feet in a fire."

Smith waited, but Jay said nothing.

"You've never asked me what we're paying you to do, but I'll tell you now. We're paying you to stay alive and get some good out of your money. That's all. If you want to stay here and tough it out, that's fine. If you want to run, that's fine, too. As far as we're concerned, you're free to do whatever you feel you have to do."

Smith paused, studying Jay's scarred face, then the empty, immaculate surface of his own desk. "You can't take those chips out. Did you know that?"

Jay shook his head.

"It's easy to put them in to upgrade, but damned near impossible to take them out without destroying the whole unit and killing its owner. They do that to make it hard to rob people of their upgrades. I can't stop you from trying, but it won't work and you might hurt yourself."

"I've got it." Jay counted the stars on Smith's screen. Four.

"The announcement will go out in forty-five minutes, and you have to leave the building before then so we can show you doing it."

The doors behind Jay swung open, and the security bot rolled in.

"Kaydee Nineteen will escort you." Smith sounded embarrassed. "It's just so we can get the pictures."

Jay rose.

"Is there anything you want to ask me before you go? We'll have to keep it brief, but I'll tell you all I can."

"No." Jay's shoulders twitched. "Keep the money and stay alive. I've got it."

As they went out, Smith called, "Kaydee Nineteen won't rob you. You don't have to worry about that."

Kaydee Nineteen chuckled when Smith's doors had closed behind them. "I bet you never even thought of that, sir."

"You're right," Jay told him.

"Are you going to ask where the holo cameras are, sir?"

"In the lobby and out in the street. They have to be."

"That's right, sir. Don't go looking around for them, though. It looks bad, and they'll have to edit it out."

"I'd like to see the announcement they're going to run," Jay said as they halted before an elevator. "Can you tell me where I might be able to do that?"

"Certainly, sir. A block north and turn right. They call it the Studio." The elevator doors slid back, moving less smoothly than Smith's; Kaydee Nineteen paused, perhaps to make certain the car was empty, then said, "Only you be careful, sir. Just one drink. That's plenty."

Jay stepped into the elevator.

"They've got a good holo setup, I'm told, sir. Our people go there all the time to watch the shows they've worked on."

When the elevator doors had closed, Jay said, "I don't suppose you could tell me where I could buy a gun?"

Kaydee Nineteen shook his head. "I ought to arrest you, sir, just for asking. Don't you know the police will take care of you? As long as we've police, everybody's safe."

The elevator started down.

"I just hoped you might know," Jay said apologetically.

"Maybe I do, sir. It doesn't mean I tell."

Slipping his hand into his side pocket, Jay broke the paper band on a sheaf of hundreds, separated two without taking the sheaf from his pocket, and held them up. "For the information. It can't be a crime to tell me."

"Wait a minute, sir." Kaydee Nineteen inserted the fourth finger of his left hand into the STOP button, turned it, and pushed. The elevator's smooth descent ended with shocking abruptness.

"Here, take it." Jay held out the bills.

Kaydee Nineteen motioned him to silence. A strip of paper was emerging from his mouth; he caught it before it fell. "Best dealer in the city, sir. I'm not saying she won't rip you off. She will. Only she won't rip you off as badly as the rest, and she sells quality. If she sells you home-workshop, she tells you home-workshop."

He handed the slip to Jay, accepted the hundreds, and dropped them into his utility pouch. "You call her up first, sir. There's an address on that paper, too, but don't go there until you call. You say Kincaid said to. If she asks his apartment number or anything like that, you have to say number nineteen. Do you understand me, sir?"

Jay nodded.

"It's all written out for you, and some good advice in case you forget. Only you chew that paper up and swallow it once you got your piece, sir. Are you going to do that?"

"Yes," Jay said. "You have my word."

"It better be good, sir, because if you get arrested, you're going to need friends. If they find that paper on you, you won't have any."

Jay walked through the lobby alone, careful not to look for the holo camera. Those outside would be in trucks or vanettes, presumably, but might conceivably be in the upper windows of buildings on the other side of Sixth. He turned north, as directed. Glancing to his right at the end of the next block, he saw the Studio's sign, over which virtual stagehands moved virtual lights and props eternally; but he continued to walk north for two more blocks, then turned toward Fifth and followed the side street until he found a store in which he bought a slouch hat and an inexpensive black raincoat large enough to wear over his hunting coat.

Returning to the Studio, he approached it from both west and east, never coming closer than half a block, without spotting anyone watching the entrance. It was possible—just possible, he decided reluctantly—that Kaydee Nineteen had been as helpful as he seemed. Not likely, but possible.

In a changing booth in another clothing store, he read the slip of paper:

Try Jane MacKann, Bldg. 18 Unit 8 in Greentree Gardens. 1028 7773-0320. Call her first and say Kincaid. Say mine if she asks about any number. She will not talk to anybody nobody sent, so you must say mine. She likes money, so say you want good quality and will pay for it. When you get there, offer half what she asks for and go from there. You should get ten, twenty percent off her price. Do not pay her asking price. Do not take a cab. Walk or ride the bus. Do not fail to phone first. Be careful.

It took him the better part of an hour to find a pay phone in the store that looked secure. He fed bills—the change from the purchase of his raincoat—into it and keyed the number on Kaydee Nineteen's paper slip.

Three rings, and the image of a heavyset frowning woman in a black plastic shirt and a dark skirt appeared above the phone; she had frizzy red hair and freckles, and looked as though she should be smiling. "Hello. I'm not here right now, but if you'll leave a message at the tone I'll call you back as soon as I can."

The tone sounded.

"My name's Skeeter." Jay spoke rapidly to hide his nervousness. "I'm a friend of Kinkaid's. He said to call you when I got into the city, but I'm calling from a booth, so you can't call me. I'll call again when I get settled."

None of the clerks looked intelligent. He circled the store slowly, pretending to look at cheap electric razors and souvenir shirts until he found a door at the back labeled DO NOT ENTER. He knocked and stepped inside.

The manager flicked off his PC, though not before Jay had seen naked women embracing in the dark window behind him. "Yes, sir. What's the problem?"

"You don't have one," Jay told him, "but I do, and I'll pay a hundred"—he held up a bill—"to you to help me with it. I want to rent this office for one half hour so that I can use your phone. I won't touch your papers, and I won't steal anything. You go out in your store and take care of business. Or go out and get a drink or a sandwich, whatever you want. After half an hour you come back and I leave."

"If it's long distance . . ."

Jay shook his head. "Local calls, all of them."

"You promise that?" The manager looked dubious.

"Absolutely."

"All right. Give me the money."

Jay handed the bill over.

"Wait a minute." The manager switched on his computer, studied the screen, moved his mouse and clicked, studied the result, and clicked again. Jay was looking at the phone. As he had expected, its number was written on its base.

"All right," the manager repeated. "I've blocked this phone so it won't make long distance calls. To unblock it, you'd have to have my password."

"I didn't know you could do that," Jay said.

"Sure. You want out of the deal?"

Jay shook his head.

"Okay, you've got the place for half an hour. Longer if you need it, only not past three-thirty. Okay?"

"Okay."

The manager paused at the door. "There's a booth out here. You know about that?"

Jay nodded. "It won't accept incoming calls."

"You let them take calls and the dealers hang around and won't let anybody use it. You a dealer?"

Jay shook his head.

"I didn't think so." The manager shut the door.

One oh two eight. Seven seven seven three. Oh three two oh. Three rings as before, and the image of the heavyset redhead appeared. "Hello. I'm not here right now, but if you'll leave a message at the tone I'll call you back as soon as I can."

The tone sounded.

"This is Skeeter again," Jay said. "I've got money, and Kincaid said you and I could do some business." He recited the number from the base of the manager's phone. "If you can give me what I want, this is going to be a nice profitable deal for you." Hoping that she would not, he added, "Ask Kincaid," and hung up.

He had slept in a bod mod at the Greyhound station, had left his scant luggage in a storage locker; that luggage was worth nothing, and seemed unlikely to furnish clues to his whereabouts when a criminal gang came looking for him and his hundred thousand.

The forty-five minutes Smith had mentioned had come and gone. His image had appeared in the Studio and millions of houses and apartments.

They might be looking for him already—at the bus station, at the Studio, at any other place they could think of. At the MacKann woman's.

The phone rang and he picked it up. "Skeeter."

"This's Jane, Skeeter." The loose shirt was the same, but the dark skirt had given way to Jeens, and her hair was pulled back by a clip. "Kincaid said to call me?"

"That's right," Jay told her. "He said we might be able to do business, and he gave me your number."

"He must be getting to be a big boy now, that Kincaid."

"He's bigger than I am," Jay said truthfully.

"How old is Kincaid these days anyway?"

"Nineteen."

"He gave you my address? Or was it just this number?"

"He gave me an address," Jay said carefully. "I can't say whether it's right or not. Have you moved recently?"

"What is it?"

Jay hesitated. "All right to read it over the phone?"

"I don't see why not."

The door opened, and the manager looked in. Jay waved him away.

"What address did he give you?"

Kaydee Nineteen's paper lay on the desk. Jay held it up so the small woman seated above the telephone could read it.

"The print's too small," she told him. "You'll have to say it."

"It doesn't bother you?"

"Why should it?"

Jay sighed. "I don't know. When I was in college, I used to play chess. Now I feel like I'm playing chess again and I've forgotten how." He reversed the slip of paper. "Building Eighteen, Unit Eight in the Greentree Gardens?"

"That's it. When will you be here?"

The black raincoat had slits above its pockets that let Jay reach the pockets of the camouflage hunting coat under it. Extracting a bill, he held it up. "Can you read this?"

"Sure."

"I'll give it to you if you'll pick me up. You've seen me and how I'm dressed. I'll be in that little park at the corner of Sixth and Fortieth."

"No," she said.

"I'll be there, and I'll buy. I'll pay you this just for the ride." He hung up, rose, and left the store, waving to the manager.

There was a hotel down the street; he went in and stood at the front desk, a vast affair of bronze and marble. After five minutes a black woman in a transparent plastic blouse asked, "You checkin' in?"

"I'd like to." Jay laid two hundreds on the counter.

"We can't take those." She eyed them as though they were snakes. "Got a credit card?"

Jay shook his head.

"You got no bags either."

Jay did not deny it.

"You can't check in here."

He indicated the hundreds. "I'll pay in advance."

The black woman lowered her voice. "They don't let us take anybody like you, even if you got two dots."

In a department store a block away, Jay cornered a clerk. "I want a lightweight bag, about this long."

The clerk yawned. "Three feet, sir?"

"More than that." Jay separated his hands a bit.

The clerk (who probably called himself an associate) shook his head and turned away.

"Three and a half, anyway. Forty-two inches."

"Soft-sided?" The clerk clearly hoped Jay would say no.

"Sure," Jay said, and smiled.

"Wait right here." Briefly, the clerk's fingers drummed the top of a four-suiter. "I'll be gone a while, you know?"

Jay removed his slouch hat and wiped his forehead with his fingers. The hat had been a comfort in the chill air of the street, but the store was warm.

None of the milling shoppers nearby were giving him any attention, as far as he could judge; but, of course, they would not. If he was being watched, it would be by someone some distance away, or by an electronic device of some kind. Looking around for the device, he found three cameras, none obtrusive but none even cursorily concealed. City cops, store security, and somebody else—for a minute or two Jay tried to think who the third watchers might be, but no speculation seemed plausible.

Men's Wear was next to Luggage. He wandered over.

"What do you want?" The clerk was young and scrawny and looked angry.

With your build, you'd better be careful, Jay thought; but he kept the reflection to himself. Aloud he said, "I had to buy this raincoat in a hurry. I thought I might get a better one here."

"Black?"

Jay shook his head. "Another color. What've you got?"

"Blue and green, okay?"

"Green," Jay decided, "if it's not too light."

The clerk stamped over to a rack and held up a coat. "Lincoln green. Okay?"

"Okay," Jay said.

"Only if you turn it inside out, it's navy. See?"

Jay took the coat from him and examined it. "There are slits over the pockets. I like that."

"Same pockets for both colors," the clerk sounded as if he hoped that would kill the sale.

"I'll take it."

The clerk glanced at a tag. "Large-tall. Okay?"

"Okay," Jay said again.

"You want a bag?"

Jay nodded. A stout plastic bag might prove useful.

The clerk was getting one when the clerk from Luggage returned. He frowned until Jay hurried over.

"This's what we call a wheeled duffel," the luggage clerk explained. "You got a handle there. You can carry it, or you got this handle here that pops out, and wheels on the other end. Forty-four inches, the biggest we've got. You got a store card?"

"Cash," Jay told him.

"You want a card? Ten percent off if you take it."

Jay shook his head.

"Up to you. Hear about that guy with all the cash?"

Jay shook his head again. "What guy?"

"On holo. They gave him a wad so somebody'll rip him off. Only they see what he sees, so I don't think it's going to work. They'd have a description."

"They see what he sees?"

"Sure," the clerk said. "It's his augment, you know? Anytime he sees you they see you."

"Can they spy on people like that?"

"They don't give a rat's ass," the clerk said.

The angry Men's Wear clerk had vanished. Jay's new reversible raincoat lay on a counter in a plastic bag. He unzipped his new wheeled duffel and put the raincoat inside.

Outside it was growing dark; beggars wielding plastic broomhandles and pieces of conduit were working the shopping crowd, shouting threats at anyone who appeared vulnerable.

The little park was an oasis of peace by comparison. Jay sat down on a bench, the wheeled duffel between his knees, and waited. Traffic crawled past, largely invisible behind the hurrying, steam-breathing pedestrians. Some of the drivers looked as angry as the Men's Wear clerk; but most were empty-faced, resigned to driving their cubical vanettes and hulking CUVs at four miles per hour or less.

"Ain't you cold?" An old man with a runny nose had taken the other end of Jay's bench.

Jay shook his head.

"I am. I'm damned cold."

Jay said nothing.

"They got shelters down there," the old man pointed, "ta keep us off the streets. Only you get ripped off soon's you go to sleep. Right. An' they don't give you nothin' ta eat, either. So if you was ta give me somethin', I could get me somethin' an' go down there an' sleep without bein' hungry. Right."

"You could get a bottle of wine, too," Jay said.

"They won't sell it 'less you got the card." The old man was silent for a moment, sucking almost toothless gums. "Only you're c'rect, I'd like to."

"Sure," Jay said.

"I used ta get Social Security, only it don't come no more. There's some kind a problem with it."

"You could get yourself a sweater, too," Jay suggested. "Winter's just getting started."

"If there was enough I could," the old man agreed. "I could sleep in one a them boxes, too, 'stead a the shelter."

"A bod mod."

"Yeah, right."

"I slept in one last night." Jay considered. "I didn't like it, but they're probably better than the shelter."

"Right."

"You said you were cold. Would you like my coat?"

The old man appeared to hesitate. "You said you wasn't. You will be if you give it."

Jay stood up, pressing rubberoid buttons through plastic buttonholes.

On Fortieth someone leaned down on the horn, a muted keening that suggested a dying whale.

"You're givin' it?"

"I am," Jay said. He held it out by the shoulders. "Put it on."

The old man pushed an arm into one of the capacious sleeves. "Lady over there wants you, is what I think."

"Those cars aren't moving anyhow." Jay waited until the old man's other arm was in the other sleeve, then fished a hundred out of his hunting coat. "If I give you this, are you going to tell those beggars with the sticks?"

"Hell, no," the old man said. "They'd take it."

"Right." Jay put the hundred in his hand and sprinted out of the park, thrust shoppers aside with the duffel, and strode out into the motionless traffic.

A red-haired woman in a dark gray vanette was waving urgently. He opened the right front door and tossed in the duffel, got in, and sat down, smelling dusty upholstery and stale perfume.

"Don't look at me," she said. "Look straight ahead."

Jay did.

"Anytime you're with me, you don't look at me. You got that? Never. No matter what I say, no matter what I do, don't look."

Assuming that she was looking at him, Jay nodded.

"That's the first thing. They've already seen me on the phone, but the less they see of me the better."

"Thank you for coming to get me," Jay said.

"I wasn't going to," the woman told him bitterly, "but you knew I would. You knew I'd have to."

Jay shook his head again, still without looking in her direction. "I hoped you would, that's all. You said you wouldn't, but after I'd hung up I decided that if I were you

I'd have said the same thing, so they wouldn't be waiting for us if they were listening in."

"They were listening. They're listening now. They can hear everything you hear and see everything you see."

Mostly to himself, Jay nodded. "I should have known it would be something like that."

"They put our call on the news. That dump in Greentree? There's a mob there. I went there thinking I'd wait for you, and there must have been five hundred people, and more coming all the time."

"I'm sorry," Jay said, and meant it.

"I'll have to get a new dump, that's all." The woman fell silent; he sensed that her jaw was clenched. "Anyway, I came. I probably shouldn't have, but I did. Did you see my license plate?"

He searched his memory. "No."

"That's good. Don't look at it when you get out, okay?"

"Okay."

"Did you think Jane MacKann was my real name?"

"It isn't?" The thought had not occurred to him.

"Hell, no. This isn't even my car, but the guy I borrowed it from is kind of a friend, and he'd have to steal new plates. So all they know is a green car, and there are lots of them."

"My color vision's a little off," Jay told her.

"Yeah, sure. A lot of guys have that." The woman paused to blow the vanette's horn, futilely, at the semibus ahead of her. "Anyway, I came and got you. So you owe me."

Jay fished a hundred from a pocket and gave it to her.

"This isn't for your heat. This's just for the ride. You tell me where, and I'll take you there and drop you, okay? That's what you're paying me for now."

"If I tell you, I'll be telling them as well?"

"I guess so. I didn't watch it, but that's what the people I talked to said."

"Suppose I were to write it on a piece of paper without looking at the paper. Then I could pass it to you without looking at you, and you could look at it."

The woman considered. "That ought to work. I've got a pen in my purse, if you've got paper."

"I do." Jay hesitated. "You said heat. I want a gun."

"Sure. That's heat."

"Slang."

"No, it's just what everybody says. Or it's tons if you got more than one. Like, I got fifteen tons stashed around now. So immediate delivery on them. What kind you want?"

Jay stroked his jaw, trying to reduce a hundred dreams to the pinpoint of a single gun small enough to fit into his wheeled duffel.

"Lemme explain my pricing structure to you while you're thinking it over," the woman said, sounding very professional indeed. "Top of the line, I got submachine guns and machine pistols. That's mostly nine millimeter, but there's some other stuff, too. Like right now, on hand, I've got this very cool little machine pistol that's seven sixty-five."

She had paused to see whether he was interested; he sensed her scrutiny.

"It's what we used to call a thirty-two, only this one's got seven point sixty-five on the slide."

He shook his head and said, "I understand."

"Okay, under that is your high-cap autos. Only they're not really full auto, they're semi. One I got's a nine that holds seventeen rounds. Honest to God. Twenty-five hundred for any of those."

Jay did not speak.

"Where you draw the line is eleven, okay? If it holds eleven or under, it's low cap. Twelve or better is high."

"These are handguns you're talking about."

"Yeah. Sure. Low cap is two thousand. Or eighteen hundred if it only holds eight. There's a lot of these single-stack forty-fives around, and eight is all they'll take. So eighteen hundred for one in good shape. Then if you want a real buy, you get a revolver. I've seen some that hold eight, but it's mostly six, and nine times out of ten six will do it if you're careful. Twelve, thirteen hundred and you can get two, so that gives you twelve rounds and you got two guns in case one breaks. It's a really good deal, because most people are too dumb to see that it is."

"I need a rifle," Jay told her. "Don't you have any rifles?"

"The feds melted them down, or most of them," the woman said dubiously.

"I know. But I hunt my food, for the most part." Jay cleared his throat. "I'm not from around here at all. I'm from Pennsylvania."

"So you don't really want to shoot anybody?"

"Deer," he told her. "Deer and black bear. Rabbits and so forth now and then. Birds. A shotgun would be better for those, but I can't carry both back with me, and if I had a rifle I could shoot birds sitting sometimes." Doubting her comprehension, he added, "Ducks on the water. That sort of thing."

"I don't have one in my stock. I don't have a shotgun, either, and the shells are really hard to get these days."

He nodded sadly. "I suspected that they would be."

"Listen, we're just sitting here in this traffic. Would it bother you too much if I banged on my laptop some? Maybe I can find something for you."

"No. Go ahead."

"Okay, turn around the other way. Not toward me, away from me. Push slow against the harness."

He did, and the vanette announced, "I am required by law to caution you that your chance of survival in a high-speed crash has been reduced by sixty-two percent."

The woman said, "We're not even crawling, you idiot."

"The vehicle that strikes me may be traveling at a high rate of speed, however," the vanette replied primly.

Jay had contrived to turn 180 degrees, so that he was kneeling in his seat and peering into the immensely cluttered rear of the vanette.

"Chinese red," the woman said.

He picked up the only red object he saw and held it up, careful not to look at her. "Is this it?"

"Sure."

Turning away from her again, he resumed a normal posture. "Would you like me to open it for you?"

"You can't. There's a thumbprint lock." She took it, and

from the corner of his eye he saw her prop it against the wheel and plug a wire into the instrument panel. "You watch traffic, okay? If the car in front moves, tell me."

"All right," he said, and added, "Where are we going?"

"Nowhere." She sounded abstracted, and he heard the quick, hard tapping of her fingers on the keys. "We're going nowhere, Skeeter." More taps, and a little sound of disgust.

"They know that name already, huh? From when you phoned." The woman appeared to hesitate. "Yeah, I guess they have to. You can call me Mack."

"All right. Can't you find me a rifle, Mack?"

"Not so far. I got one more place I can try, though." She tapped keys again.

He said, "The car in front's moving."

"About time."

"Can I ask a question?"

"Sure. You can ask me a thousand, only I might not answer any."

"Who is *they*?"

He felt her incomprehension.

"You said they probably know my name. Did you mean the holovid people who gave me the upgrade?"

"Globnet."

"Yes, Globnet. Was that who you meant, Mack?"

"No. The feds. Big Daddy."

"So they can collect taxes on my money? I haven't refused to pay them. I haven't even been asked to pay."

Traffic had stopped again. Jay heard the rattle of its hard plastic case as the woman shifted her laptop back to the steering wheel. "They know you won't pay. Say, would you like a carbine? He's got a carbine."

Jay felt his heart sink. "Not as much as a rifle. Hasn't anybody got a rifle?"

"Not now. They might have something later, but maybe not. You never know."

Unwilling to surrender the new rifle he needed, Jay changed the subject. "How could the government possibly know I won't pay the tax?"

"How much did they give you? The holovid people?"

"That's my affair."

"Okay. Whatever it was? Have you still got it all?"

"No," Jay said. "I gave you a hundred."

"So you don't. So you wouldn't pay the whole tax because you couldn't."

He felt her hand on his arm.

"They want it all. The works. You'll find out. Not all you've got now, the most you ever had. Traffic like this—how many choppers do you think we ought to hear?"

He shook his head.

"About one every hour, maybe a little more. Three in an hour, tops. They been goin' over every three or four minutes lately. I just timed the last two on the dash clock. About three minutes."

From the corner of his eye he saw her hand reach out to rap the instrument panel. "Hey, you! Wake up there. I want you to open the sunroof."

The sunroof slid smoothly back, and the interior of the vanette was abruptly frigid. "Watch them awhile," the woman told Jay, "it'll keep you from looking at me."

He did, craning his neck to see the bleak winter sky where the towering office buildings had failed to obscure it. "Won't our open roof attract their attention?"

"I don't think so. There must be a couple of thousand people stuck in this mess who're wondering why they're flying over all the time."

"Black helicopters." Jay spoke half to himself. "Out where I live, way out in the country, people make jokes about black helicopters. Somebody in town did once, that's what I'm trying to say, one time when I came into town. He said the black helicopters would get me, and laughed, and I've remembered it for some reason."

"Sure."

"It's supposed to be like flying saucers, something crazy people see. But here in the city it's real. I caught sight of one a moment ago."

"Sure," the woman repeated. "They're looking for drugs out there is what we hear. Flying over the farmers' fields to see if they're growing pot in the middle of the cornfield.

They're not really black, I guess. People who've seen them up close say they're UPS brown, really. But they sure look black, up there."

"They must have binoculars—no, something better than binoculars. Isn't there a chance they'll see me down here and recognize me?"

"Mmm," the woman said.

"If the government is really after me at all, I mean. The holovid people said it would be criminals." Jay paused, recalling his conversations with Smith. "Mostly criminals, unless I put the money in a bank."

"Okay, close it," the woman told the vanette, and the sunroof slid shut as smoothly as it had opened. "You're right about the binoculars," she told Jay. "They'll have something better, something they won't let us own. But I'm right about the feds being after you. Ten minutes after the broadcast, they'll have had a dozen people on it, and by this time there could be a couple of hundred. They'll be another news tonight at eleven, and we'd better watch it."

Jay nodded. "If we can."

"We can. The big question's how good a look they've had at you. Been looking in any mirrors lately?"

"Since I got the upgrade?" Certain already that he knew the answer, he squirmed in his seat. "Let me think. Yes, once. In a rest room in the Globnet Building. I was looking at the new stars in my screen, though. Not at my own face."

"You will have seen your face, though," the woman said thoughtfully. "I'd like to know if they broadcast that. In a toilet? Maybe not."

"I'd like to watch the news tonight. I know how silly this sounds, but I can't visualize it." Apologetically he added, "I haven't watched much holovid."

"I'd like to, too," the woman said, "because I haven't seen this either, just had people tell me. I'll fix it."

"Thanks."

"What about this carbine? Do you want it?"

"I don't know. Perhaps I'd better take it, if there's nothing else. No rifles."

"They're harder to hide, so the feds have about cleaned them out, and there's not much call for them. Later I might be able to find one for you."

"Later I won't be here. What caliber is it?"

"Forty. Same as a forty-caliber pistol is what he says, and uses the same magazine." She pressed more buttons. "It folds up, too."

"A folding stock?"

"Doesn't say. Just that it's thirty inches long to shoot and sixteen folded. What are you grinning about?"

Jay patted the duffel. "I was afraid this wouldn't be long enough to hold the rifle I was hoping to get."

She grunted. "Well, you could carry this under that coat. Put a loop of string over your shoulder and fold it over the string. It wouldn't be as handy as a pistol, but you could do it."

"I'd rather hang it by the butt, if it will stay folded." Jay was silent for a moment, thinking. "I'll have to see it first. I don't suppose that gadget gives an effective range?"

More buttons. "A hundred and fifty meters is what he says."

"Huh."

"Probably got a lot of barrel. Twelve, fourteen inches. Something like that, and even out of a pistol barrel a forty travels pretty fast."

"I imagine he's stretching it," Jay said slowly, "even so, most of the shots I get are under a hundred yards, and those that are longer aren't a lot longer."

"Going to take it?"

He nodded. "I've been using a bow. A bow I made myself and arrows I made myself, too. Did I tell you?"

"I don't think so. I thought maybe you had a shotgun already. You hunt a lot."

He nodded again. When ten minutes had passed, and they were crawling along steadily, he asked, "Where are we going?"

"Dump I got. You know that address? Greentree?"

"There were people there, you said."

"We're not going there. I just wanted to say I don't live there. It's a place I got where I make sales sometimes, that's all. Where we're going now's like that, only uptown."

The sunroof slid smoothly back, and a woman in an orange jumpsuit dropped into the rear seat. Jay released his seat harness to turn and look at her, and the vanette said, "I am required by law to caution you that your chance of survival in a high-speed crash has been reduced by seventy percent."

The woman who sold guns snapped, "Shut your sunroof!"

The woman in the orange jumpsuit had cleared a space for herself on the seat. She removed her helmet, shook out long, dark hair, and smiled at Jay. "I'm sure you know who I am."

He tried to return the smile. "I have no idea."

"Who I represent, I mean. My name is Hayfa, Hayfa Washington." She ran her finger down the front seam of her jumpsuit, reached inside, and produced a sparkling business card. "Look at this, please. Read it carefully."

Captain H. Washington
Fifth Airborne Brigade
Federal Revenue & Security Services
0067 5667-1339
www.hayfawings.gov

"You may keep the card, of course."

"I'd like to," Jay told her. "I've never seen such a beautiful one."

She smiled again. "You have a great deal of money belonging to our Federal Government. One hundred thousand, if not more."

The other woman said, "He thinks it belongs to him."

"I do," Jay said. "It was paid me by Globnet."

"Which didn't own it either," Hayfa Washington told him.

Jay said, "They ran advertisements, as I understand it, and included it in a lot of their news broadcasts. I was at a friend's house and saw one. My rifle's broken, and I need a new ax and—" For a moment, her expression silenced him. "And other things. You don't care about that, do you?"

"Not really."

"So I wrote a letter and my friend e-mailed it, with some pictures of me and my cabin. They said that if I'd come here and talk to them, they might give me the money."

"A hundred thousand."

"Yes, one hundred thousand. I borrowed money for bus fare, and I came. And they talked to me and gave it to me."

"No, they didn't." The woman in the orange jumpsuit looked sincere and somewhat troubled; she leaned toward Jay as she spoke. "They couldn't, you see. It didn't belong to them. All money belongs to the Federal Government, Jay. People—people who own small businesses, particularly—speak of making money. Quite often they use those exact words. But if you'll think about it, you'll see that they are not true. All money is made by Government, and so all money belongs to Government, which allows citizens like you and me to have some, sometimes, so we can buy the things we need. But Government keeps title to all of it, and by the very nature of things it can't lose title to any of it. I've most of last month's pay on me right now." She paused, extracting a hard plastic portemoney from an interior pocket of her jumpsuit.

"You're saying that what they paid isn't mine at all."

"Correct. Because no money really belongs to anyone except Government, which issued it." The woman in the orange jumpsuit opened her portemoney, took out bills, and fanned them. "Here's mine. You see? Eleven five-hundreds, three one-hundreds, and some twenties, tens, fives, and singles. This is what our Government lets me have, because my taxes were already deducted from my check."

The other woman said, "Except sales tax."

"Correct, although sales tax is actually paid by the seller. There's a pretense that the buyer pays, but we needn't get into that. The point is that I have this money, although it's not mine, and I'm showing it to you. This is what I've got, Jay. Now will you, in an act of good faith, show what you have to me?"

"No," Jay said.

"I'm sorry to hear that, very sorry." The woman in the orange jumpsuit paused as though expecting her expression of regret to change his answer. He said nothing more; neither did the other woman.

"There's an easy, painless way to handle this," the woman in the orange jumpsuit said. "You could turn the money over to me now. I'd count it and give you a receipt for it that would be backed by the full faith and credit of the Federal Government. When the Government had decided how much should be returned to you, it would be sent to you. I'm sure there would be enough for a new ax. Not for a rifle, though. The danger a rifle would pose to you and your family would far outweigh any possible benefit to you."

"They're against the law," the other woman remarked a little dryly.

"Yes, they are, for that very reason." The woman in the orange jumpsuit spoke to Jay again. "You wouldn't have to do prison time. I think I can promise you that. There probably wouldn't even be a trial. Won't you please hand that money—the Government's money—to me to count? Now?"

He shook his head.

"You want to think it over. I understand." The woman in the orange jumpsuit tapped the other woman's shoulder. "Where are we? Ninety-fifth? You can let me out now. Just stop anywhere."

The vanette stopped, causing several vehicles behind it to blow their horns, and the woman in the orange jumpsuit opened its sliding door and stepped out. "You've got my card, Jay. Call anytime."

He nodded and shut the door, the vanette lurched forward, and the woman driving it said, "Thank you for appearing on our show tonight."

Jay nodded, although he could not be sure she was looking at him. "That was for the holovid, wasn't it? She was so pretty."

"Prettier than me?" There was a half-humorous challenge in the question.

"I don't know," Jay told her. "You don't want me to look at you."

"Well, she was, and she wasn't just pretty, she was beautiful, the way the Government wants you to think all the feds look, beautiful women and good-looking men. She'll make the next news for sure. I wouldn't be surprised if they run everything she said. You still want to see it?"

"Yes," he said. "Certainly."

"Okay, we will. I've got a place a couple of blocks from here."

"What about my carbine? I'd like to buy it tonight."

"He's got to get it from wherever he's got it stashed. Ammo, too. I said fifty rounds."

"More," Jay told her. He considered. "Five hundred, if he has them."

"Okay, I'll tell him." The vanette pulled into an alley, and the laptop returned to the steering wheel. When the woman who sold guns had closed it again, she said, "Ten years ago I could have stood up to her. I was a knockout. You don't have to believe me, but I was."

He said he believed her.

"But I had two kids. I put on some weight then and I've never got it off, and I quit taking care of my complexion for a while. You haven't been looking at me."

"No," he said.

"That's good, but now don't look at anything else either, okay? I want you to shut your eyes and keep them shut. Just lean back and relax."

He nodded, closed his eyes, and leaned back as she had suggested, discovering that he was very tired.

As if it were in another room, her fingers tapped the instrument panel. Softly she said, "Hey, you. Open your sunroof."

Cold poured over him like water, and he shivered. She grunted, the vanette shook, and the seat he had shared with her sagged; after a little thought, he decided that she was standing on it with her head and shoulders thrust up through the open sunroof.

Sometime after that, the sunroof closed again and she left the vanette, got into the rear seat, and rummaged among her possessions there.

"Okay," she said. "Only don't open your eyes."

He said that he would not.

"I figured she might have planted some sort of bug, you know? Something to tell the feds where we went. Only it would have to be on the roof or in back, and I couldn't find it, so probably they figure you're all the bug they need. We're going to drive around some now, and I want you to keep your eyes shut the whole time. We'll be turning corners and doubling back and all that, but don't look."

They "drove around" for what seemed an hour; but though there were indeed a number of turns, Jay got the impression that the point at which they stopped was miles from the one at which he had closed his eyes.

"All right." She tapped the instrument panel. "No lights." The engine died; the soft *snick* he heard was presumably the ignition key backing out. It rattled against other keys as she removed it and dropped it into her purse. "You can look around. Just don't look at me."

He did. "It's dark."

"Yeah. Well, it gets dark early this time of year. But it's about eight o'clock. You don't have a watch."

"No," he said.

"Me neither. There's the dash clock if I'm driving, and the holovid will give it if I'm inside. Come on."

There was no doorman, but the lobby into which she led him was fairly clean. He said, "You don't really live here."

"Hell, no. But sometimes I sleep here, and I'm going to sleep here tonight. We both are."

He wondered whether she meant together. Aloud, he said, "You don't really live in Greentree Gardens, either. That's what you told me."

"Nope."

"I would think it would be horribly expensive to rent so many places."

The doors of an elevator shook and groaned, and at last rattled open. They stepped inside.

"It costs, but not nearly as much as you'd think. These old twentieth-century buildings are all rent controlled."

He said, "I didn't know that."

"So what it is, is the grease you've got to pay the agent to get in. That can be quite a chunk. You don't understand grease, do you?"

"No," he said.

"I could see you didn't. It's under-the-counter money, money the agent can put in his pocket and not pay taxes on. Money's like three, four times more without taxes."

The elevator ground to a halt, and they got out.

"So I pay that—I've got to—and the first month's rent. I buy used furniture, not very much, and move in. Then I don't pay anything else for as long as I can get by with it."

The keys were out again, jangling in her hand.

"That could be six months. It could be a year. When I get the feeling they're about ready to take me to court, I pay another month, maybe, or half a month. It's rent controlled, like I said, so it's not much."

She opened a door that had long ago been damaged by water. "My utility bills aren't much because I'm hardly ever here, and I don't complain or cause trouble. See? And they know if they go to court the judge will find out I just paid something and tell them to give me more time. So they don't. You want to turn that thing on? It's almost time for the nine o'clock."

He did, fumbling with the controls until he found the right control.

"It's an old one," she said apologetically.

A shimmering beach half filled the stale air of the dingy room; on it, young women with spectacular figures tossed a multicolored ball, at last throwing it into the ocean and swimming out to retrieve it.

"You were expecting voice control, right? I got it at the Salvation Army store. They fixed it up so it would work again."

He nodded. A brunette with flashing eyes had gotten the ball. She threw it to a blonde, tracing a high arc of red, green, and yellow against the clear blue sky.

"This's a commercial," the woman who sold guns told him. "See how their makeup stays on and their hair stays nice even in the water? That's what you're supposed to be looking at."

He nodded again.

An elderly sofa groaned as she sat down. "You want the sound? It's the next knob up, only they're going to be talking about hair spray and stuff."

He shook his head.

"Fine with me. Only we better turn it on when the news comes on."

He did, and by the time he had taken a seat next to her, a handsome black man and a beautiful Chinese woman faced them across a polished double desk. Both smiled in friendly fashion. "Thank you for inviting us into your living room," the black man said.

The Chinese woman added, "There's a lot of news tonight. What do you say we get to it, Phil?"

Phil nodded, abruptly serious. "There certainly is, Lee-Anne. Johns Hopkins has a new artificial heart so small you can have it implanted before your present heart gives out."

Lee-Anne said, "There's the cat in the mayor's Christmas tree, too. I like that story. The firemen way up on their little ladders look like ornaments."

Phil smiled. "You're right, they do. We've got a review of the new Edward Spake film, too. *The Trinidad Communiqué*. It got raves at Cannes."

"Aunt Betsy's going to show us how to make cranberry flan for the holidays."

"Almost live coverage of the big parade in Orlando."

"And a peek in on the Hundred Thousand Man. He's had a little visit from FR&SS."

"That's you," the woman who sold guns told Jay. "It's going to be a while before they get to you, though. You want something to eat?"

"Yes." He had not realized how hungry he was.

"I don't keep much besides beer in these places. Usually I just phone out. Pizza okay?"

He had not eaten pizza since college. He said it was.

"You've got to get out of here, 'cause I'll have to give the address. Why don't you go in the kitchen?"

A plastic model of a large artery enclosing a very small

artificial heart stood in the middle of the room. He nodded and went into the kitchen.

"Bring me a beer, okay?"

The refrigerator was white, as his mother's had been; he knew vaguely that no one had white refrigerators now, though he did not know why. It held beer in squat plastic bulbs and a deli container of potato salad. He opened a bulb over the small and dirty sink, afraid that the foam might overflow the bulb. When he could no longer hear her voice, he called, "Can I come back in?"

"Sure."

He brought her the beer, and she said, "Pepperoni, hot peppers, and onions, okay? You can have a beer, too."

He shook his head. "Not until the food gets here."

"Don't you think it's coming?"

It had not even occurred to him. He said, "Of course it is," and returned to the kitchen to get a beer for himself.

"I need to make another call. I got to call my baby-sitter and tell her I won't be back tonight. But I'll wait till we see you."

He nodded, careful not to look at her. A towering Christmas tree, shrunken by distance, disappeared into the ceiling. Little firemen in yellow coveralls and Day-Glo red helmets clambered over it like elves.

"I turned off the sound so I could call. All right?"

"Sure," he said.

"Maybe you'd better turn it back on now."

He did, getting it too loud then scaling it back. Reduced to the size of a child's battery-powered CUV, an immense float trundled through the room, appearing at one wall and disappearing into the other while doll-size women feigned to conceal their nakedness with bouquets from which they tossed flowers to the onlookers. Lee-Anne's voice said, ". . . la tourista fiesta queen and her court, Phil. They say the fiesta is worth about three hundred million to the city of Orlando."

Phil's voice replied, "I don't doubt it. And speaking of money, Lee-Anne, here's a lady trying to collect some."

A good-looking woman in a skintight orange jumpsuit

rappelled down a mountain of air, bouncing and swaying. Jay said, "I didn't see that."

"They were shooting from a helicopter, probably," the woman who sold guns told him.

It took about half a second for him to realize that by "shooting" she intended the taking of pictures; in that half second, the swaying woman on the rope became the helmet-less woman he recalled, shaking out her hair in the rear seat of the vanette. "You have a great deal of money belonging to our Federal Government. One hundred thousand, if not more."

The other woman said, "He thinks it belongs to him." Then his own voice, just as he heard it when he spoke: "It was paid me by Globnet."

Their conversation continued, but he paid little attention to what they said. He watched Hayfa Washington's face, discovering that he had forgotten (or had never known) how beautiful she had been.

Too soon it was over, and a woman in a spotless gingham apron coalesced from light to talk about lemon custard. The woman who sold guns said, "You want to turn that off now?" and he did.

"I'm going to call my sitter, okay? You can stay, though. I won't tell her where I am."

"I'll go anyway," he said, and returned to the kitchen. Faintly, through the tiny dining nook and the door he had closed behind him, he heard her tell someone, "It's me, Val. How are the kids?"

The card was in his shirt pocket, under the hunting coat he had been careful not to remove. "Captain H. Washington, Fifth Airborne Brigade." He turned it over, and discovered that her picture was on the reverse, and that her soul was in her huge dark eyes.

"Hey!" the other woman called from the living room. "The pizza's here. Bring out a couple more bulbs."

He did, and opened hers for her while she opened the pizza box on the rickety coffee table, then returned to the kitchen for plastic knives and forks, and paper napkins.

"If we eat in there we'll have to sit facing," she said. "So I figured in here. We can sit side-by-each, like in the car. It'll be easier."

He said that was fine, and asked about her children.

"Oh, they're okay. My girlfriend is sitting them. She's going to take them over to her house till I get back. Ron's eight and Julie's seven. I had them right together, like. Then we broke up, and he didn't want any part of them. You know how that is."

"No," he said. "No, I don't."

"Haven't you ever been married? Or lived with a woman?"

He shook his head.

"Well, why not?"

"I've never been rich, handsome, or exciting, that's all." He paused, thinking. "All right, I'm rich now, or at least have something like riches. But I never did before."

"Neither was he, but he got me."

Jay shrugged.

"He was nice, and he was fun to be with, and he had a pretty good job. Only after the divorce his company sent him overseas and he stopped paying support."

"I've never had a job," Jay said.

"Really?"

"Really. My friends call me a slacker." He found that he was smiling. "Dad called me a woods bum. He's dead now."

"I'm sorry."

"So am I, in a way. We seldom got along, but well . . ." He shrugged and drank beer.

"I know."

"He sent me to college. I thought I was a pretty good baseball player in those days, and a pretty good football player, but I didn't make either team. I tried hard, but I didn't make the cut."

She spoke with her mouth full. "Tha's too bad."

"It was. If I had, it would have been different. I know it would. The way it was, I worked hard up until I was close to graduation." The pizza was half gone. He picked up a square center piece that looked good, bit into it, and chewed and swallowed, tasting only the bitterness of empty years.

"What happened then?" she asked.

"When I was a senior? Nothing, really. It was just that I realized I had been working like a dog to acquire knowledge that nobody wanted. Not even me. That if I did everything right and aced my exams and got my Master's I'd end up teaching in the high school in the little Pennsylvania town where we lived, or someplace like it. I'd teach math and chemistry, and maybe coach the baseball team, and it would be kids who were going to work on farms or get factory jobs when they got out of school. I said to hell with it."

"I don't blame you."

"I went back home and told my folks some story. They didn't believe it, and I don't even know what it was now. I got my camping stuff together and went out into the woods. I had a little tent, an air mattress, and a sleeping bag. The first winter was rough, so I built a cabin about as big as this room in a place where nobody would ever find it." He paused, recalling Hayfa Washington and the helicopter that had let her down on a rope and somehow made their sunroof open. "It's federal land, really. National Forest. I don't think about that much, but it is."

The woman shrugged. "If all the money's theirs, all the land is, too, I guess."

"I suppose you're right." He put his half-eaten piece of pizza back in the box.

"You just live out there? Like that?"

"It was always going to be for a little while."

"But you never came back in?"

"Oh, sometimes I do. For my father's funeral, and then for mom's. She died about a month after he did."

"I'm sorry."

"I was, too. But they left everything to me—I was the only kid. The house and so on. The car and a little money. I sold the house and the car, and I don't spend much. I hunt deer and snare small game, and that's what I eat, mostly. Wild plants in the summer." He smiled. "I use dead leaves for toilet paper."

"Do you want to know about me?"

"If you want to tell me."

"Well, I never got to go to college. I was a clerk in a store and a waitress. Then I got married and had the kids, and you know about that. You want to know how I got started selling guns? A friend wanted to know where she could buy one, so I asked this guy I knew, and he sent me to somebody else. And that guy said he'd sell to me only not to her, because the guy that sent me didn't know her. So I said, okay, sell it to me, and I paid him, and I told him I'd get my money back from her. And he said you ought to charge her about a hundred more, I would. So I charged her fifty over. And after a couple weeks, I guess it was, she sent somebody else to me, another woman in her building that was scared worse than she was. Now here I am."

Softly he said, "I steal from campers, sometimes. From hunters, too. That's how I got this coat. A hunter got hot, and hung it on a tree."

She nodded as though she had expected no less. "You want to get me another beer?"

The telephone buzzed as he rose; a thin-lipped man who wore a business suit as though it were a uniform said, "You still haven't called Captain Washington."

"No," Jay admitted. "No, I haven't."

"We don't like to arrest people over tax matters. You may have heard that."

Jay shook his head.

"We don't. Yet more than half the prison population is made up of tax offenders." The thin-lipped man vanished.

"They know where we are," Jay told the woman.

"Yeah. Get me that beer, will you?"

"Shouldn't we leave?"

She did not speak, and after half a minute or so he brought her another beer from the kitchen.

"Here's how I see it," she said when he (with face averted) held out the beer. "Let me go through it, and you tell me if you think I'm wrong.

"To start with, how do they know we're here? Answer—that FR&SS woman put a bug on our car, I just didn't find it. That means that if we take the car we might as well stay here. And if we don't take the car, we'll have to go on foot.

They'll have people all around this building by now waiting to tail us, and with the streets pretty well empty it would be a cinch."

"Where would we go?" he asked.

"Damned if I know. We might end up walking all night. Next question. Are they about to break down the door and bust us? Answer—no, because they wouldn't have called first if they were. The FR&SS woman made the news, she was good-looking, it was dramatic, and blah blah. It was meant to. Now they'll be watching to see if that phone call makes it. I think what they'll do is get a little rougher every time, because every time they come around the chance that it'll make Globnet's news show gets slimmer. The woman was really pretty nice, on purpose. The guy on the phone wasn't so nice, and next time's going to be worse. Or that's how it looks to me."

"You're probably right. But you're leaving something out. They knew that we were in this apartment, and not in some other apartment in this building."

"Piece of cake. The guys staking it out talked to the pizza man. 'Who paid you?' 'Well, she was a middle-aged woman with red hair.' 'Anybody else in there?' 'Yeah, I could hear somebody moving around in back.' 'Okay, that's them.' They got a look at me when we talked on the phone, and the fed that got into our car probably described us."

Jay said, "You're not middle-aged."

She laughed. "When you've got two kids in school, you're middle-aged. How old are you?"

"Forty-one."

"See, you're middle-aged, too. You're older than I am." To his amazement, her hand had found his.

They kissed, he with his eyes shut; an hour later, turning off the lights in the musty little bedroom hid the stains on the wallpaper and let him look at her face.

Next morning she said, "I want to have breakfast with you. Isn't that funny?"

Not knowing what else to do, he nodded.

"I never used to have breakfast with Chuck. I'd have to

get up early to see about the kids, and he'd sleep till ten or eleven. After he left me I'd have a boyfriend sometimes. Only we'd do it and he'd get up and go. Back to his wife, or where he lived. They weren't ever around for breakfast."

"All right," Jay said, "let's eat breakfast."

"We don't have to take the car. You don't mind walking three or four blocks?"

He smiled. "No."

"Okay. We've got a couple things to settle, and maybe the safest way is while we're walking. I don't know how serious they are, but if they're serious at all they'll have bugged this place while we slept. The café'd be better, but out on the street's probably as good as it gets. Keep your voice down, don't move your lips a lot when you talk, and if it's serious hold your hand in front of your face."

He nodded, and seeing blowing snow through a dirty windowpane, pulled the reversible coat he had bought the day before out of his wheeled duffel and put it on over the hunting coat that still (almost to his dismay) held his money.

Out in the cold and windy street she murmured, "They'll figure we're going back, so first thing is we won't. If they have a man watch it and maybe another guy watch the car, they could get a little shorthanded. We can hope, anyway."

He nodded, although it seemed to him that if there were a homing device in the vanette it would not be necessary to have anyone watch it.

"When we go out of the café we'll split up, see? I'll give you the address—where to go and how to get there. Don't look to see if they're following you. If they're good you won't see them. Just lose them if you can."

"I hope I can," he said.

The little restaurant was small and crowded and noisy. They ate waffles in a tiny booth, he striving to keep his eyes on his plate.

"The way you lose a tail is you do something unexpected where the tail can't follow you," she said. "Say there's a cab, but just the one. You grab it and have him take you someplace fast, all right? Only not to the address I'm going to give you. Someplace else."

He nodded.

"I thought maybe you were going to say there's got to be a thousand cabbies, and they can't talk to them all. Only every cab's got a terminal in it, and it records when fares get picked up, and where they're going. Like if they know you caught the cab at eleven oh two, all they've got to do is check cabs that picked up somebody right about then. It's maybe a dozen cabs, then they can find out where you went."

"I understand," he said.

"Or maybe you go to the john. He's not going to come in the john with you because you'd get too good a look at him. He'll wait outside. Well, if it's got two doors you duck in one and out the other. Or climb out the window, if there's a window. It gets you ten or fifteen minutes to get away."

"Okay," he said.

She had taken a pen and a small notebook from her purse; she scribbled in it, tore out the page, and handed it to him. "Where we're going to meet," she said. "Don't look at it till you're almost there."

He was too stunned to say anything.

"You're finished."

He managed to say, "Yes, but you're not."

"I'm awfully nervous, and when I'm nervous I don't eat a lot. I look at you and see the two dots, and I know they're seeing what you do, your sausages or whatever. Let's go."

Out on the street again, in the cutting wind, she squeezed his hand. "See that subway entrance up ahead? Maybe you can see the escalator through the glass."

"Yes," he said.

"We're going to walk right toward it. When we get there, I'll go in and down. You keep walking."

He did, badly tempted to watch as the moving steps carried her away but staring resolutely ahead.

Soon traffic thinned, and the sidewalks grew dirtier. The vehicles filling every parking space were older and shabbier. He went into a corner store then and asked the middle-aged black man behind the counter for a package of gum. "This a bad neighborhood?"

The counterman did not smile. "It's not good."

"I heard it was really bad," Jay said. "This doesn't look so bad."

The counterman shrugged. "One and a quarter for that."

Jay gave him a hundred. "Where would it be worse?"

"Don't know." The counterman held Jay's hundred up to the light and fingered the paper. "You pushin' queer? I knows what you looks like now."

"Keep the change," Jay said.

The counterman stared.

"Where does it get really bad? Dangerous."

For a second or two, the counterman hesitated. Then he said, "Just keep on north, maybe six blocks?"

Jay nodded.

"Then you turns east. Three blocks. Or fo'. That's 'bout as bad as anythin' gits."

"Thanks." Jay opened the gum and offered a stick to the counterman.

The counterman shook his head. "Gits on my dentures. You goin' up there where I told you?"

He did, and once there he stopped and studied the shabby buildings as though searching for a street number. Two white men—the only other whites in sight—were following him, one behind him with a brown attaché case, the other on the opposite side of the street. Their hats and topcoats looked crisp and new, and they stood out in that neighborhood like two candy bars in a brushpile. He turned down an alley, ran, then halted abruptly where a rusted-out water heater leaned against a dozen rolls of discarded carpet.

Often he had waited immobile for an hour or more until a wary deer ventured within range of his bow. He waited so now, motionless in the wind and the blowing snow, half concealed by the hot-water tank and a roll of carpet, a sleeve breaking the outline of his face; and the men he had seen in the street passed him without a glance, walking purposefully up the alley. Where it met the next street they stopped and talked for a moment or two; then the attaché case was opened, and they appeared to consult an instrument of some kind. They reentered the alley.

He rose and ran—down that alley, across the street and into the next, down another street, a narrow and dirty street on which half or more of the parked cars had been stripped. When he stopped at last, sweating despite the cold, he got out Hayfa Washington's card and tore it in two.

Threadlike wires and their parent microchips bound the halves together still.

He dropped both halves down a sewer grating, pulled off his reversible coat, turned it green-side-out and put it back on, then unbuttoned his hunting coat as well and transferred the hunting knife his father had given him one Christmas to a pocket of the now-green raincoat, sheath and all.

An hour later—long after he had lost count of alleys and wretched streets—he heard running feet behind him, whirled, and met his attacker with the best flying tackle he could muster. He had not fought another human being since boyhood; he fought now as the bobcat had fought him, with the furious strength of desperation, gouging and biting and twice pounding the other's head against the dirty concrete. He heard the bottle that had been the other's weapon break, and felt the heat of the blood streaming from his ear and scalp, and by an immense effort of will stopped the point of the old hunting knife short of the other's right eye.

The other's struggle ended. "Don' do that, man! You don' want to make me blind."

"Give up?"

"Yeah, man. I give up." The jagged weapon the bottle had become clinked on the pavement.

"How much did you think I'd have on me?"

"Man, that don't matter!"

"Yes, it does. How much?"

"Forty. Fifty. Maybe credit cards, man, you know."

"All right." The point of the knife moved a centimeter closer. "I want you to do something for me. I want you to work. If you'll do it, I'll pay you a hundred and send you away. If you won't, you'll never get up. Which is it?"

"I'll do it, man." The other at least sounded sincere. "I'll do whatever you says."

"Good." Jay rose and dropped the knife back into his

pocket. "Maybe you can pull me down. I don't know, but maybe you can. Whenever you want to try . . ." He shrugged.

"You bleedin', man."

"I know. It will stop, or I think it will." Jay got out a hundred. "You see this? It'll be all yours." He tore it in two and gave half to the other. "You get the other half when you've done what I'm hiring you to do."

"Okay if I gets up, man?"

Jay nodded, and the other got slowly to his feet. His Jeens and plastic jacket were old and cracked, his Capribuk athletic shoes nearly new.

"Listen carefully. If you don't do exactly what I tell you, our deal is off. I'm going to give you a piece of paper with an address on it."

The other gave no indication that he had heard.

"I want you to read that address, but I don't want you to tell me what it is. Don't say it, and don't let me see the paper."

"What is this shit, man?"

"Do you watch the news?"

"I got no time for that shit, man. I listens to music."

For two or three seconds Jay stared at the blank screen on the other's forehead, recalling that his own was—or had been—equally blank. "There's no point in explaining. Do you understand what you've got to do?"

"Look at the address. Not tell you. Not let you look, even. You want me to tear it up?"

Jay shook his head. "I want you to keep it, and I want you to take me there. If we have to spend money to get there, I'll pay."

Reluctantly, the other nodded.

"When we get there, you give me the paper so I can see you took me to the right place. When you do, I'll give you the other half of that hundred and you can go."

He had expected the subway, but they took a bus; the ride lasted over an hour. " 'Bout two blocks now," the other said when they left it at last. "You wants to walk?"

Jay nodded.

"You going to turn me in, man?"

"No," Jay said. They were walking side by side. "I'm going to give you the other half of that hundred, and shake hands if you're willing to shake hands, and say good-bye."

"You a pretty fair scrapper, you know? Only you catches me by surprise. I wasn't expectin' you to turn 'round like what you done."

"Wasn't that what you were trying to do to me? Take me by surprise?"

"Sho'!" The other laughed.

"So that's all right. Except that right and wrong really don't count in things like this. I hunt a lot. I hunt animals to eat."

"Do tell?"

"And for hide and bone to make things out of. Generally I try to give the animals a fighting chance."

"Uh-huh."

"But when I'm hungry, really up against it, I don't. I kill any way I can."

"We here." The other waved at one of several squat concrete buildings. "Got a number on it 'n' everythin'. You don' want to look at that?"

"I don't think it matters now," Jay said, and looked.

"Number eighteen." The other fished in his pockets and pulled out the page of notebook paper, now much folded, that the woman who sold guns had given Jay in the café. "All right. It says here Greentree Gardens. An' it says buildin' eighteen. Then it says number eight. Have a look."

Jay did.

"Now this here's Greentree Gardens, all right? You look right over there 'n' there's a sign on top of that buildin'. What do it say?"

"Greentree Gardens."

"Right on, man. Right over there's buildin' number eighteen, like you sees. Number eight will be ground flo', mos' like, or maybe next up. Places like this ain't bad as some other places, you know? Only they ain't real safe neither. You wants me to go in there with you? Be glad to if you wants it."

Jay shook his head, took out the remaining half of the torn

hundred, and handed it to the other. Then he offered his hand, which the other accepted after putting the torn half bill into one of his pockets.

Abruptly his grip tightened. Jay tried to jerk away, but the other's fist caught him under the cheekbone.

He went down, rolling and trying to cover his head with his arms. A kick dizzied him, its shock worse than its pain. Another missed, and another must have struck his forearm, because his arm felt as though it had been clubbed.

Somehow he got to his feet, charged the other and grappled him. *I killed that buck like this*, he thought; the buck had an arrow in its gut, but that had hardly seemed to matter. His knife was in his hand. He stabbed and felt it strike bone.

Then it was gone.

At once the other had it, and there was freezing cold where his shirt pocket should have been, cold followed by burning heat, and he was holding the other's wrist with both hands, and the blade was wet and red. The other's fist pounded his nose and mouth. He did not hear the shot, but he felt the other stiffen and shudder.

He pushed the other's body from him, insanely certain that it was only a trick, only a temporary respite granted so that he might be taken by surprise again in a moment or two. Rising, he kicked something.

It was the knife, and it went clattering over the sidewalk. He pulled it out of some snow, wiped the blade with his handkerchief, returned it to its sheath and the sheath to his pocket.

Then the woman who sold guns was tugging at his sleeve. In her other hand she held a short and slender rifle with a long box magazine. "Come on! We've got to get out of here."

He followed her docilely between the hulking building that was eighteen Greentree Gardens, and a similar building that was probably sixteen or twenty. Two floors down in a dark underground garage, she unlocked a blue CUV. As he climbed in he said, "Borrowed from another friend?"

"This's mine, and if I didn't sell what I do I couldn't afford it."

It reeked of cigar smoke; he said, "In that case, I'd think they'd know about it—the plate number and so forth."

She shook her head. "It's registered under a fake name, and these aren't my plates."

He considered that while she drove eight or ten blocks fast, then up a winding ramp and onto the Interstate.

When they were in the leftmost lane, he said, "Why are we running away?"

She turned her head to look at him. "Are you crazy? Because I killed that guy."

"He was going to kill me." He looked down at his wound, and was mildly surprised to find that it was still bleeding, his blood soaking the two-sided raincoat and, presumably, the hunting coat under it.

"So what? Look, I can't even defend myself, according to the law. Say you were going to rape me and kill me."

"I wouldn't do that."

"Just suppose. I couldn't shoot you or stab you or even hit you, and if I did you could sue me afterward."

"Could I win?"

"Sure. What's more, I'd be defending your suit from a cell. And if I hurt you worse'n you hurt me, you'd be out."

Jay shook his head. "That doesn't make sense."

"Not for us it doesn't." The Interstate sloped sharply down here, but she kept pedal to the floor; for a moment the CUV shook wildly. "For them it does—for the feds. If we got used to the idea of going after somebody who went after us, we'd go after them. *Capisce?*"

"We should."

"Sure. Only for me it's a lot worse. For you, too. I killed that guy. Don't say maybe he's not dead. I saw him when I hit him, and I saw him afterward. He's gone."

"How did you know we were out there?"

"Saw you out the window, that's all. It'd been a while, so I kept looking outside, hoping you were just looking for the right number. I'd stopped off and picked up your gun on the way home, and I was afraid you'd come and gone before I got there. You want to see it? It's on the backseat. Only be careful, it's loaded. I think I put the safety on."

Jay took off his seat belt and picked up the carbine, careful not to touch its trigger.

"Keep it down so the other drivers can't see it."

He did. "This car doesn't talk to us."

"I killed that bastard as soon as I got it. It's pretty easy."

Sensing that she was about to cry, Jay did not speak; he would have tried to hold her hand, perhaps, but both her hands were on the wheel.

"And now I've killed the bastard that was trying to kill you. There's tissues in back somewhere."

He got them, heard her blow her nose.

"I told you how bad that is. It's murder one. He was trying to kill you, but that doesn't make a damned bit of difference. I should have called the cops and showed them your body when they got there. That would have been when? Two or three o'clock. My God, it's lunchtime."

He looked at the clock on the instrument panel. It was nearly one.

"You hungry?"

"No," he said.

"Me neither. Let's skip lunch. We'll stop somewhere for dinner tonight."

He agreed, and asked where they were going.

"Damned if I know."

"Then I'd like you to take Eighty."

"We need to get off the Interstate before too much longer," she said.

He nodded. "We will."

"Listen, I'm sorry I got you into this."

"I feel the same way," he said. "You saved my life."

"Who was he, anyway?"

"The man I'd gotten to read your note. You didn't want Globnet to get it on the air before we'd left, so I had to have somebody who would look at it for me and take me there. I tried to find somebody who wouldn't call the police as soon as we separated. Clearly that was a bad idea." Jay paused. "How did you think I'd handle it?"

"That you'd guess. That you'd go there and look at my note and see that you were right when you got there."

"No more crying?"

"Nope. That's over. You know what made me cry?"

"What?"

"You didn't understand. You can't kill people, not even if they're killing other people, and I did it with a gun. If they get me I'll get life, and you didn't understand that."

"Who'd take care of your kids?" He let his voice tell her what he felt he knew about those kids.

She drove. He glanced over at her, and she was staring straight ahead, both hands on the wheel.

"I'm going back into the woods. Maybe they'll get me in there, but it won't be easy. If the holovid company can't help you, maybe you'd like to come with me."

"You had it all doped out." She sounded bitter.

He shook his head. "I don't think I understand it all even now, and there's a lot of it that I just figured out a minute ago. How much were you supposed to get for this?"

"A couple thousand."

He thought about that. "You're not an employee. Or at least, you don't work for Globnet full-time."

"No." She sniffled. "They did a documentary on the gun trade last year, and I was one of the people they found—the only woman. So I was on holo with this really cool mask over my face, and I thought that was the end of it. Then about a month ago they lined me up to do this."

He nodded.

"They figured you'd want women or drugs, mostly, and they had people set for those. I was kind of an afterthought, okay? Stand by for a couple hundred, or a couple thousand if you called. Another thousand if I sold you a gun. I did, but I'll never collect any of it."

"The bot must have called you after he gave me your number."

"Kaydee Nineteen? Sure. That's how you knew, huh? Because you got it from him."

Jay shook his head. "That was how I should have known, but I didn't. It was mostly the phone call you made last night to somebody who was supposed to be sitting your kids. Real mothers talk about their kids a lot, but you didn't. And just now it hit me that you'd called your friend Val, and James R. Smith's secretary was Valerie. Then I thought about the bot. He took his security work very seriously, or at least it seemed like he did. But he had given me the number of a gun dealer as soon as I asked, and he had been friendly with Valerie."

"So I was lying to you all the time."

He shrugged.

"Don't do that! You're going to get that thing bleeding worse. What happened to your ear?"

He told her, and she pointed. "There's a truck stop. They'll have aid kits for sale." Cutting across five lanes of traffic, they raced down an exit ramp.

That night, in an independent motel very far from Interstate 80, he took off his reversible raincoat and his hunting coat, and his shirt and undershirt as well, and sat with clenched teeth while she did what she could with disinfectant and bandages.

When she had finished, he asked whether she had been able to buy much ammunition.

"Eight boxes. That's four hundred rounds. They come fifty in a box."

He nodded.

"Only we don't have it. It's back in that place in Greentree Gardens."

He swore.

"Listen, you've got money and I've got connections. We can buy more as soon as things quiet down."

"A lot of the money's ruined. It has blood on it."

She shook her head. "It'll wash up. You'll see. Warm water and a little mild detergent, don't treat it rough and let it dry flat. You can always clean up money."

"I thought maybe I could just give it to them," he said. "Show them it wasn't any good anymore."

She kissed him, calling him Skeeter; and he shut his eyes so that Globnet and its audience would not see her kiss.

He had been after deer since before the first gray of dawn; but he had never gotten a shot, perhaps because of the helicopters. Helicopters had been flying over all morning, sweeping up and down this valley and a lot of other valleys. He thought about Arizona or New Mexico, as he sometimes did, but concluded (as he generally had to) that they would be too open, too exposed. Colorado, maybe, or Canada.

The soldiers the helicopters had brought were spread out now, working their way slowly up the valley. Too few, he decided. There weren't enough soldiers and they were spread too thin. They expected him to run, as perhaps he would. He tried to gauge the distance to the nearest.

Two hundred yards. A long two hundred yards that could be as much as two hundred and fifty.

But coming closer, closer all the time, a tall, dark-faced woman in a mottled green, brown, and sand-colored uniform that had been designed for someplace warmer than these snowy Pennsylvania woods. Her height made her an easy target—far easier than even the biggest doe—and she held a dead-black assault rifle slantwise across her chest. That rifle would offer full or semiautomatic operation, with a switch to take it from one to the other.

Less than two hundred yards. Very slowly Jay crouched in the place he had chosen, pulled his cap down to hide the stars of his upgrade, and then raised his head enough to verify that he could keep the woman with the assault rifle in view. His wound felt as hot as his cheeks, and there was blood seeping through the bandage; he was conscious of that, and conscious, too, that it was harder to breathe than it should have been.

A hundred and fifty yards. Surely it was not more than a hundred and fifty, and it might easily be less. He was aware of his breathing, of the pounding of his heart—the old thrill.

Thirty rounds in that black rifle's magazine, possibly. Possibly more, possibly as many as fifty. There would be an ammunition belt, too, if he had time to take it. Another two or three hundred rounds, slender, pointed bullets made to fly flatter than a stretched string and tumble in flesh.

For an instant that was less than a moment, less even than the blink of an eye, a phantom passed between him and the woman with the black assault rifle—a lean man in soiled buckskins who held a slender, graceful gun that must have been almost as long as he was tall.

A hallucination.

Jay smiled to himself. Had they seen that, back at Glob-net? They must have, if they still saw everything he did. Would they put it on the news?

A scant hundred yards now. The little carbine seemed to bring itself to his shoulder.

Seventy yards, if that.

Jay took a deep breath, let it half out, and began to squeeze the trigger.

Anomalies

GREGORY BENFORD

Gregory Benford [www.authorcafe.com/benford] is a plasma physicist and astrophysicist, and one of the leading SF writers of the last twenty-five years. He has been a science columnist for F & SF, and in 1999 published his first popular science book, Deep Time. *One of the chief spokesmen of hard SF of the last three decades, Benford is articulate and contentious, and he has produced some of the best fiction of recent decades about scientists working, and about the riveting and astonishing concepts of cosmology and the nature of the universe. Among his many awards is the 1990 United Nations Medal in Literature. His most famous novel is* Timescape *(1980), his most recent,* Eater *(2000). Many of his (typically hard) SF stories are collected in* In Alien Flesh *(1986) and* Matters End *(1995).*

"Anomalies" is another story from Red Shift; *it is not hard SF, although it is filled with hard SF ideas, but is an entertainment for all SF readers. In it, the Universe misbehaves, making it necessary to found a new science.*

It was not lost upon the Astronomer Royal that the greatest scientific discovery of all time was made by a carpenter and amateur astronomer from the neighboring cathedral town of Ely. Not by a Cambridge man.

Geoffrey Carlisle had a plain directness that apparently came from his profession, a custom cabinet maker. It had enabled him to get past the practiced deflection skills of the receptionist at the Institute for Astronomy, through the assistant director's patented brush-off, and into the Astronomer Royal's corner office.

Running this gauntlet took until early afternoon, as the sun broke through a shroud of soft rain. Geoffrey wasted no time. He dropped a celestial coordinate map on the Astronomer Royal's mahogany desk, hand amended, and said, "The moon's off by better'n a degree."

"You measured carefully, I am sure."

The Astronomer Royal had found that the occasional crank did make it through the institute's screen, and in confronting them it was best to go straight to the data. Treat them like fellow members of the profession and they softened. Indeed, astronomy was the only remaining science that profited from the work of amateurs. They discovered the new comets, found wandering asteroids, noticed new novae, and generally patrolled what the professionals referred to as local astronomy—anything that could be seen in the night sky with a telescope smaller than a building.

That Geoffrey had gotten past the scrutiny of the others

meant this might conceivably be real. "Very well, let us have a look." The Astronomer Royal had lunched at his desk and so could not use a date in his college as a dodge. Besides, this was crazy enough to perhaps generate an amusing story.

An hour later he had abandoned the story-generating idea. A conference with the librarian, who knew the heavens like his own palm, made it clear that Geoffrey had done all the basic work correctly. He had photos and careful, carpenter-sure data, all showing that, indeed, last night after around eleven o'clock the moon was well ahead of its orbital position.

"No possibility of systematic error here?" the librarian politely asked the tall, sinewy Geoffrey.

"Check 'em yerself. I was kinda hopin' you fellows would have an explanation, is all."

The moon was not up, so the Astronomer Royal sent a quick e-mail to Hawaii. They thought he was joking, but then took a quick look and came back, rattled. A team there got right on it and confirmed. Once alerted, other observatories in Japan and Australia chimed in.

"It's out of position by several of its own diameters," the Astronomer Royal mused. "Ahead of its orbit, exactly on track."

The librarian commented precisely, "The tides are off prediction as well, exactly as required by this new position. They shifted suddenly, reports say."

"I don't see how this can happen," Geoffrey said quietly.

"Nor I," the Astronomer Royal said. He was known for his understatement, which could masquerade as modesty, but here he could think of no way to underplay such a result.

"Somebody else's bound to notice, I'd say," Geoffrey said, folding his cap in his hands.

"Indeed," the Astronomer Royal suspected some subtlety had slipped by him.

"Point is, sir, I want to be sure I get the credit for the discovery."

"Oh, of course you shall." All amateurs ever got for their labors was their name attached to a comet or asteroid, but this was quite different. "Best we get on to the IAU, ah, the

International Astronomical Union," the Astronomer Royal said, his mind whirling. "There's a procedure for alerting all interested observers. Establish credit, as well."

Geoffrey waved this away. "Me, I'm just a five-inch 'scope man. Don't care about much beyond the priority, sir. I mean, it's over to you fellows. What I want to know is, what's it mean?"

Soon enough, as the evening news blared and the moon lifted above the European horizons again, that plaintive question sounded all about. One did not have to be a specialist to see that something major was afoot.

"It all checks," the Astronomer Royal said before a forest of cameras and microphones. "The tides being off true has been noted by the naval authorities around the world, as well. Somehow, in the early hours of last evening, Greenwich time, our moon accelerated in its orbit. Now it is proceeding at its normal speed, however."

"Any danger to us?" one of the incisive, investigative types asked.

"None I can see," the Astronomer Royal deflected this mildly. "No panic headlines needed."

"What caused it?" a woman's voice called from the media thicket.

"We can see no object nearby, no apparent agency," the Astronomer Royal admitted.

"Using what?"

"We are scanning the region on all wavelengths, from radio to gamma rays." An extravagant waste, very probably, but the Astronomer Royal knew the price of not appearing properly concerned. Hand-wringing was called for at all stages.

"Has this happened before?" a voice sharply asked. "Maybe we just weren't told?"

"There are no records of any such event," the Astronomer Royal said. "Of course, a thousand years ago, who would have noticed? The supernova that left us the Crab nebula went unreported in Europe, though not in China, though it was plainly visible here."

"What do you think, Mr. Carlisle?" a reporter probed. "As a nonspecialist?"

Geoffrey had hung back at the press conference, which the crowds had forced the Institute to hold on the lush green lawn outside the old Observatory Building. "I was just the first to notice it," he said. "That far off, pretty damned hard not to."

The media mavens liked this and coaxed him further. "Well, I dunno about any new force needed to explain it. Seems to me, might as well say it's supernatural, when you don't know anything."

This the crowd loved. SUPER AMATEUR SAYS MOON IS SUPERNATURAL soon appeared on a tabloid. They made a hero of Geoffrey. "AS OBVIOUS AS YOUR FACE" SAYS GEOFF. The London *Times* ran a full-page reproduction of his log book, from which he and the Astronomer Royal had worked out that the acceleration had to have happened in a narrow window around ten P.M., since no observer to the east had noticed any oddity before that.

Most of Europe had been clouded over that night anyway, so Geoffrey was among the first who could have gotten a clear view after what the newspapers promptly termed the "Anomaly," as in ANOMALY MAN STUNS ASTROS.

Of the several thousand working astronomers in the world, few concerned themselves with "local" events, especially not with anything the eye could make out. But now hundreds threw themselves upon the Anomaly and, coordinated out of Cambridge by the Astronomer Royal, swiftly outlined its aspects. So came the second discovery.

In a circle around where the moon had been, about two degrees wide, the stars were wrong. Their positions had jiggled randomly, as though irregularly refracted by some vast, unseen lens.

Modern astronomy is a hot competition between the quick and the dead—who soon become the untenured.

Five of the particularly quick discovered this Second Anomaly. They had only to search all ongoing observing campaigns and find any that chanced to be looking at that portion of the sky the night before. The media, now in full bay, headlined their comparison photos. Utterly obscure dots of light became famous when blink-comparisons showed them jumping a finger's width in the night sky, within an hour of the ten P.M. Anomaly Moment.

"Does this check with your observations?" a firm-jawed commentator had demanded of Geoffrey at a hastily called meeting one day later, in the auditorium at the Institute for Astronomy. They called upon him first, always—he served as an anchor amid the swift currents of astronomical detail.

Hooting from the traffic jam on Madingley Road nearby nearly drowned out Geoffrey's plaintive, "I dunno. I'm a planetary man, myself."

By this time even the nightly news broadcasts had caught on to the fact that having a patch of sky behave badly implied something of a wrenching mystery. And no astronomer, however bold, stepped forward with an explanation. An old joke with not a little truth in it—that a theorist could explain the outcome of any experiment, as long as he knew it in advance—rang true, and got repeated. The chattering class ran rife with speculation.

But there was still nothing unusual visible there. Days of intense observation in all frequencies yielded nothing.

Meanwhile the moon glided on in its ethereal ellipse, following precisely the equations first written down by Newton, only a mile from where the Astronomer Royal now sat, vexed, with Geoffrey. "A don at Jesus College called, fellow I know," the Astronomer Royal said. "He wants to see us both."

Geoffrey frowned. "Me? I've been out of my depth from the start."

"He seems to have an idea, however. A testable one, he says."

They had to take special measures to escape the media hounds. The institute enjoys broad lawns and ample shrubbery, now being trampled by the crowds. Taking a car would guarantee being followed. The Astronomer Royal had chosen his offices here, rather than in his college, out of a desire to escape the busyness of the central town. Now he found himself trapped. Geoffrey had the solution. The institute kept bicycles for visitors, and upon two of these the men took a narrow, tree-lined path out the back of the institute, toward town. Slipping down the cobbled streets between ancient, elegant college buildings, they went ignored by students and shoppers alike. Jesus College was a famously well-appointed college along the Cam River, approachable across its ample playing fields. The Astronomer Royal felt rather absurd to be pedaling like an undergraduate, but the exercise helped clear his head. When they arrived at the rooms of Professor Wright, holder of the Wittgenstein Chair, he was grateful for tea and small sandwiches with the crusts cut off, one of his favorites.

Wright was a post-postmodern philosopher, reedy and intense. He explained in a compact, energetic way that in some sense, the modern view was that reality could be profitably regarded as a computation.

Geoffrey bridled at this straightaway, scowling with his heavy eyebrows. "It's real, not a bunch of arithmetic."

Wright pointedly ignored him, turning to the Astronomer Royal. "Martin, surely you would agree with the view that when you fellows search for a Theory of Everything, you are pursuing a belief that there is an abbreviated way to express the logic of the universe, one that can be written down by human beings?"

"Of course," the Astronomer Royal admitted uncomfortably, but then said out of loyalty to Geoffrey, "All the same, I do not subscribe to the belief that reality can profitably be seen as some kind of cellular automata, carrying out a program."

Wright smiled without mirth. "One might say you are revolted not by the notion that the universe is a computer, but by the evident fact that someone else is using it."

"You gents have got way beyond me," Geoffrey said.

"The idea is, how do physical laws act themselves out?" Wright asked in his lecturer voice. "Of course, atoms do not know their own differential equations." A polite chuckle. "But to find where the moon should be in in the next instant, in some fashion the universe must calculate where it must go. We can do that, thanks to Newton."

The Astronomer Royal saw that Wright was humoring Geoffrey with this simplification, and suspected that it would not go down well. To hurry Wright along he said, "To make it happen, to move the moon—"

"Right, that we do not know. Not a clue. How to breathe fire into the equations, as that Hawking fellow put it—"

"But look, nature doesn't know maths," Geoffrey said adamantly. "No more than I do."

"But something must, you see," Professor Wright said earnestly, offering them another plate of the little cut sandwiches and deftly opening a bottle of sherry. "Of course, I am using our human way of formulating this, the problem of natural order. The world is usefully described by mathematics, so in our sense the world must have some mathematics embedded in it."

"God's a bloody mathematician?" Geoffrey scowled.

The Astronomer Royal leaned forward over the antique oak table. "Merely an expression."

"Only way the stars could get out of whack," Geoffrey said, glancing back and forth between the experts, "is if whatever caused it came from there, I'd say."

"Quite right." The Astronomer Royal pursed his lips. "Unless the speed of light has gone off, as well, no signal could have rearranged the stars straight after doing the moon."

"So we're at the tail end of something from out there, far away," Geoffrey observed.

"A long, thin disturbance propagating from distant stars. A very tight beam of . . . well, error. But from what?" The Astronomer Royal had gotten little sleep since Geoffrey's appearance, and showed it.

"The circle of distorted stars," Professor Wright said slowly, "remains where it was, correct?"

The Astronomer Royal nodded. "We've not announced it, but anyone with a cheap telescope—sorry, Geoffrey, not you, of course—can see the moon's left the disturbance behind, as it follows its orbit."

Wright said, "Confirming Geoffrey's notion that the disturbance is a long, thin line of—well, I should call it an error."

"Is that what you meant by a checkable idea?" the Astronomer Royal asked irritably.

"Not quite. Though that the two regions of error are now separating, as the moon advances, is consistent with a disturbance traveling from the stars to us. That is a first requirement, in my view."

"Your view of what?" Geoffrey finally gave up handling his small sherry glass and set it down with a decisive rattle.

"Let me put my philosophy clearly," Wright said. "If the universe is an ongoing calculation, then computational theory proves that it cannot be perfect. No such system can be free of a bug or two, as the programmers put it."

Into an uncomfortable silence Geoffrey finally inserted, "Then the moon's being ahead, the stars—it's all a mistake?"

Wright smiled tightly. "Precisely. One of immense scale, moving at the speed of light."

Geoffrey's face scrunched into a mask of perplexity. "And it just—jumped?"

"Our moon hopped forward a bit too far in the universal computation, just as a program advances in little leaps." Wright smiled as though this were an entirely natural idea.

Another silence. The Astronomer Royal said sourly, "That's mere philosophy, not physics."

"Ah!" Wright pounced. "But any universe that is a sort of analog computer must, like any decent digital one, have an error-checking program. Makes no sense otherwise."

"Why?" Geoffrey was visibly confused, a craftsman out of his depth.

"Any good program, whether it is doing accounts in a bank, or carrying forward the laws of the universe, must be able to correct itself." Professor Wright sat back triumphantly and swallowed a Jesus College sandwich, smacking his lips.

The Astronomer Royal said, "So you predict—?"

"That both the moon and the stars shall snap back, get themselves right—and at the same time, as the correction arrives here at the speed of light."

"Nonsense," the Astronomer Royal said.

"A prediction," Professor Wright said sternly. "My philosophy stands upon it."

The Astronomer Royal snorted, letting his fatigue get to him. Geoffrey looked puzzled and asked a question that would later haunt them.

Professor Wright did not have long to wait.

To his credit, he did not enter the media fray with his prediction. However, he did unwisely air his views at High Table, after a particularly fine bottle of claret brought forward by the oldest member of the college. Only a generation or two earlier, such a conversation among the Fellows would have been secure. Not so now. A junior Fellow in political studies proved to be on a retainer from the *Times*, and scarcely a day passed before Wright's conjecture was known in New Delhi and Tokyo.

The furor following from that had barely subsided when the Astronomer Royal received a telephone call from the Max Planck Institute. They excitedly reported that the moon, now under continuous observation, had shifted instantly to the position it should have, had its orbit never been perturbed.

So, too, did the stars in the warped circle return to their rightful places. Once more, all was right with the world. Even so, it was a world that could never again be the same.

Professor Wright was not smug. He received the news from the Astronomer Royal, who had brought along Geoffrey to Jesus College, a refuge now from the institute. "Nothing, really, but common sense." He waved away their congratulations.

Geoffrey sat, visibly uneasily, through some talk about how to handle all this in the voracious media glare. Philosophers are not accustomed to much attention until well after they are dead. But as discussion ebbed Geoffrey repeated his probing question of days before: "What sort of universe has mistakes in it?"

Professor Wright said kindly, "An information-ordered

one. Think of everything that happens—including us talking here, I suppose—as a kind of analog program acting out. Discovering itself in its own development. Manifesting."

Geoffrey persisted, "But who's the programmer of this computer?"

"Questions of first cause are really not germane," Wright said, drawing himself up.

"Which means that he cannot say," the Astronomer Royal allowed himself.

Wright stroked his chin at this and eyed the others before venturing, "In light of the name of this college, and you, Geoffrey, being a humble bearer of the message that began all this . . ."

"Oh, no," the Astronomer Royal said fiercely, "next you'll point out that Geoffrey's a carpenter."

They all laughed, though uneasily.

But as the Astronomer Royal and Geoffrey left the venerable grounds, Geoffrey said moodily, "Y'know, I'm a cabinet maker."

"Uh, yes?"

"We aren't bloody carpenters at all," Geoffrey said angrily. "We're craftsmen."

The distinction was lost upon the Royal Astronomer, but then, much else was, these days.

The Japanese had very fast images of the moon's return to its proper place, taken from their geosynchronous satellite. The transition did indeed proceed at very nearly the speed of light, taking a slight fraction of a second to jerk back to exactly where it should have been. Not the original place where the disturbance occurred, but to its rightful spot along the smooth ellipse. The immense force needed to do this went unexplained, of course, except by Professor Wright's Computational Principle.

To everyone's surprise, it was not a member of the now quite raucous press who made the first telling gibe at Wright, but Geoffrey. "I can't follow, sir, why we can still remember when the moon was in the wrong place."

"What?" Wright looked startled, almost spilling some of

the celebratory tea the three were enjoying. Or rather, that Wright was conspicuously relishing, while the Astronomer Royal gave a convincing impression of a man in a good mood.

"Y'see, if the error's all straightened out, why don't our memories of it get fixed, too?"

The two learned men froze.

"We're part of the physical universe," the Astronomer Royal said wonderingly, "so why not, eh?"

Wright's expression confessed his consternation. "That we haven't been, well, edited . . ."

"Kinda means we're not the same as the moon, right?"

Begrudgingly, Wright nodded. "So perhaps the, ah, 'mind' that is carrying out the universe's computation cannot interfere with our—other—minds."

"And why's that?" the Astronomer Royal a little too obviously enjoyed saying.

"I haven't the slightest."

Light does not always travel at the same blistering speed. Only in a vacuum does it have its maximum velocity.

Light emitted at the center of the sun, for example—which is a million times denser than lead—finds itself absorbed by the close-packed ionized atoms there, held for a tiny sliver of a second, and then released. It travels an infinitesimal distance, then is captured by yet another hot ion of the plasma, and the process repeats. The radiation random-walks its way out to the solar surface. In all, the passage from the core takes many thousands of years. Once free, the photon reaches Earth in a few minutes.

Radiation from zones nearer the sun's fiery surface takes less time because the plasma there is far less dense. That was why a full three months elapsed before anyone paid attention to a detail the astronomers had noticed early on and then neglected.

The "cone of chaos" (as it was now commonly called) that had lanced in from the distant stars and deflected the moon had gone on and intersected the sun at a grazing angle. It had luckily missed Earth, but that was the end of the luck.

On an otherwise unremarkable morning, Geoffrey rose to begin work on a new pine cabinet. He was glad to be out of the media glare, though still troubled by the issues raised by his discovery. Professor Wright had made no progress in answering Geoffrey's persistent questions. The Astronomer Royal was busying himself with a Royal commission appointed to investigate the whole affair, though no one expected a commission to actually produce an idea. Geoffrey's hope—that they could "find out more by measuring," seemed to be at a dead end.

On that fateful morning, out his bedroom window, Geoffrey saw a strange sun. Its lumpy shape he quickly studied by viewing it through his telescope with a dark glass clamped in place. He knew of the arches that occasionally rose from the corona, vast galleries of magnetic field lines bound to the plasma like bunches of wire under tension. Sprouting from the sun at a dozen spots stood twisted parodies of this, snaking in immense weaves of incandescence.

He called his wife to see. Already voices in the cobbled street below were murmuring in alarm. Hanging above the open marsh lands around the ancient cathedral city of Ely was a ruby sun, its grand purple arches swelling like blisters from the troubled rim.

His wife's voice trembled. "What's it mean?"

"I'm afraid to ask."

"I thought everything got put back right."

"Must be more complicated, somehow."

"Or a judgment." In his wife's severe frown he saw an eternal human impulse, to read meaning into the physical world—and a moral message as well.

He thought of the swirl of atoms in the sun, all moving along their hammering trajectories, immensely complicated. The spike of error must have moved them all, and the later spike of correction could not, somehow, undo the damage. Erasing such detail must be impossible. So even the mechanism that drove the universal computation had its limits. Whatever you called it, Geoffrey mused, the agency that made order also made error—and could not cover its tracks completely.

"Wonder what it means?" he whispered.

The line of error had done its work. Plumes rose like angry necklaces from the blazing rim of the star whose fate governed all intelligence within the solar system.

Thus began a time marked not only by vast disaster, but by the founding of a wholly new science. Only later, once studies were restored at Cambridge University, and Jesus College was rebuilt in a period of relative calm, did this new science and philosophy—for now the two were always linked—acquire a name: the field of empirical theology.

Glacial

ALASTAIR REYNOLDS

*Alastair Reynolds [www.members.tripod.com/~voxish/Home.
html] was born in Barry, South Wales (the birthplace of Bob
Hope), raised in Cornwall, educated in Newcastle and St.
Andrews, Scotland (Ph.D. in astronomy), and now lives in
Noordwijk, Holland, and works for the European Space
Agency. He is one of the British space opera writers to
emerge in the mid and late 1990s, and the most "hard SF"
of them. To date his stories have been published almost ex-
clusively in* Interzone *and in* Spectrum SF, *the ambitious
new SF magazine from Scotland. His first novel was* Revela-
tion Space *(2000) and his second,* Chasm City, *was published in 2001.*

"Glacial," from Spectrum SF, *which is now one of the
major small press SF magazines, is a sequel to Reynolds'
2000 novella, "Great Wall of Mars." An almost superhuman
group of the Conjoiners, a group mind composed of individual humans, is exploring systems nearby in the galaxy humans reached centuries before. And they find one, with one
survivor, and a mystery.*

Nevil Clavain picked his way across a mosaic of shattered ice. The field stretched away in all directions, gouged by sleek-sided crevasses. They had mapped the largest cracks before landing, but he was still wary of surprises; his breath caught every time his booted foot cracked through a layer of ice. He was aware of how dangerous it would be to wander from the red path which his implants were painting across the glacier field.

He only had to remind himself what had happened to Martin Setterholm.

They had found his body a month ago, shortly after their arrival on the planet. It had been near the main American base; a stroll from the perimeter of the huge, deserted complex of stilted domes and ice-walled caverns. Clavain's friends had found dozens of dead within the buildings, and most of them had been easily identified against the lists of base personnel which the expedition had pieced together. But Clavain had been troubled by the gaps, and had wondered if any further dead might be found in the surrounding ice fields. He had explored the warrens of the base until he found an air-lock which had never been closed, and though snowfalls had long since obliterated any footprints, there was little doubt in which direction a wanderer would have set off.

Long before the base had vanished over the horizon, Clavain had run into the edge of a deep, wide crevasse. And there at the bottom—just visible if he leaned close to the edge—was a man's outstretched arm and hand. Clavain had gone back to the others and had them return with a winch to lower him into the depths, descending thirty or forty meters into a cathedral of stained and sculpted ice. The body had come into view: a figure in an old-fashioned atmospheric survival suit. The man's legs were bent in a horrible way, like those of a strangely articulated alien. Clavain knew it was a man because the fall had jolted his helmet from its neck-ring; the corpse's well-preserved face was pressed halfway into a pillow of ice. The helmet had ended up a few meters away.

No one died instantly on Diadem. The air was breathable for short periods, and the man had clearly had time to ponder his predicament. Even in his confused state of mind he must have known that he was going to die.

"Martin Setterholm," Clavain had said aloud, picking up the helmet and reading the nameplate on the crown. He felt sorry for him, but could not deny himself the small satisfaction of accounting for another of the dead. Setterholm had been among the missing, and though he had waited the better part of a century for it, he would at least receive a proper funeral now.

There was something else, but Clavain very nearly missed it. Setterholm had lived long enough to scratch out a message in the ice. Sheltered at the base of the glacier, the marks he had gouged were still legible. Three letters, it seemed to Clavain: an I, a V and an F.

IVF.

The message meant nothing to Clavain, and even a deep search of the Conjoiner collective memory threw up only a handful of vaguely plausible candidates. The least ridiculous was *in-vitro fertilization*, but even that seemed to have no immediate connection with Setterholm. But then again, he had been a biologist, according to the base records. Did the message spell out the chilling truth about what had happened to the colony on Diadem: a biology lab experiment which had gone terribly wrong? Something to do with the worms, perhaps?

But after a while, overwhelmed by the sheer number of

dead, Clavain had allowed the exact details of Setterholm's death to slip from his mind. He was hardly unique anyway: just one more example of the way most of them had died; not by suicide or violence but through carelessness, recklessness or just plain stupidity. Basic safety procedures—like not wandering into a crevasse zone without the right equipment—had been forgotten or ignored. Machines had been used improperly. Drugs had been administered incorrectly. Sometimes the victim had taken only themselves to the grave, but in other cases the death-toll had been much higher. And it had all happened swiftly.

Galiana talked about it as if it was some kind of psychosis, while the other Conjoiners speculated about some kind of emergent neural condition, buried in the gene-pool of the entire colony, lurking for years until it was activated by an environmental trigger.

Clavain, while not discounting his friends' theories, could not help but think of the worms. They were everywhere, after all, and the Americans had certainly been interested in them—Setterholm especially. Clavain himself had pressed his faceplate against the ice and seen that the worms reached down to the depth where the man had died. Their fine burrowing trails scratched into the vertical ice walls like the branchings of a river delta; the dark nodes of breeding tangles at the intersections of the larger tunnels. The tiny black worms had infested the glacier completely, and this would only be one distinct colony out of the millions that existed all over Diadem's frozen regions. The worm biomass in this one colony must have been several dozen tons at the very least. Had the Americans' studies of the worms unleashed something which shattered the mind, turning them all into stumbling fools?

He sensed Galiana's quiet presence at the back of his thoughts, where she had not been a moment earlier.

"Nevil," she said. "We're ready to leave again."

"You're done with the ruin already?"

"It isn't very interesting—just a few equipment shacks. There are still some remains to the north we have to look over, and it'd be good to get there before nightfall."

"But I've only been gone half an hour or . . ."

"Two hours, Nevil."

He checked his wrist display unbelievingly, but Galiana was right: he had been out alone on the glacier for all that time. Time away from the others always seemed to fly by, like sleep to an exhausted man. Perhaps the analogy was accurate, at that: sleep was when the mammalian brain took a rest from the business of processing the external universe, allowing the accumulated experience of the day to filter down into long-term memory; collating useful memories and discarding what did not need to be remembered. And for Clavain—who still needed normal sleep—these periods away from the others were when his mind took a rest from the business of engaging in frantic neural communion with the other Conjoiners. He could almost feel his neurones breathing a vast collective groan of relief, now that all they had to do was process the thoughts of a single mind.

Two hours was nowhere near enough.

"I'll be back shortly," Clavain said. "I just want to pick up some more worm samples, then I'll be on my way."

"You've picked up hundreds of the damned things already, Nevil, and they're all the same, give or take a few trivial differences."

"I know. But it can't hurt to indulge an old man's irrational fancies, can it?"

As if to justify himself, he knelt down and began scooping surface ice into a small sample container. The leech-sized worms riddled the ice so thoroughly that he was bound to have picked up a few individuals in this sample, even though he would not know for sure until he got back to the shuttle's lab. If he was lucky, the sample might even hold a breeding tangle; a knot of several dozen worms engaged in a slow, complicated orgy of cannibalism and sex. There, he would complete the same comprehensive scans he had run on all the other worms he had picked up, trying to guess just why the Americans had devoted so much effort to studying them. And doubtless he would get exactly the same results he had found previously. The worms never changed; there was no astonishing mutation buried in every hundredth or even thousandth specimen; no stunning biochemical trickery going on inside them. They secreted a few simple enzymes and they ate pollen grains and ice-bound algae and they wriggled their way through cracks in the ice, and when they met other worms they obeyed the brainless rules of life, death and procreation.

That was all they did.

Galiana, in other words, was right: the worms had simply become an excuse for him to spend time away from the rest of the Conjoiners.

Before any of them had left Earth's solar system, Clavain had been a soldier, fighting on the side of the faction which directly opposed Galiana's experiments in mind-augmentation. He had fought against her Conjoiners on Mars, and she had taken him prisoner at the height of the war. Later—when he was older, and when an uneasy truce looked like it was at the point of collapsing—Clavain had gone back to Mars with the intention of reasoning with Galiana. It was during that peace mission that he realized—for the sake of his conscience— that he had to defect and fight alongside his old enemy, even though that meant accepting Galiana's machines into his head.

Later, along with Galiana, Felka and their allies, Clavain had escaped from the system in a prototype starship, the *Sandra Voi*. Clavain's old side had done their best to stop the ship leaving, but they had failed, and the *Sandra Voi* had safely reached interstellar space. Galiana's intention had been to explore a number of solar systems within a dozen or so light years of Earth, until she found a world that her party could colonize without the risk of persecution.

Diadem had been their first port of call.

At the beginning of the expedition, a month ago, it had been much easier to justify these excursions. Even some of the true Conjoined had been drawn by a primal human urge to walk out into the wilderness, surrounding themselves with kilometers of beautifully tinted, elegantly fractured, unthinking ice. It was good to be somewhere quiet and pristine, after the war-torn solar system that they had left behind.

Diadem was an earthlike planet orbiting the star Ross 248. It had oceans, icecaps, plate tectonics and signs of reasonably advanced multicellular life. Plants had already invaded Diadem's land, and some animals—the equivalents of arthropods, molluscs and worms—had begun to follow in their wake. The largest land-based animals were still small by terrestrial standards, since nothing in the oceans had yet evolved an internal skeleton. There was nothing that showed any signs of intelligence, but that was only a minor disappointment. It would still take a lifetime's study just to explore the fantastic array of body-plans, metabolisms and survival strategies which Diadem life had blindly evolved.

Yet even before Galiana had sent down the first survey shuttles, a shattering truth had become apparent.

Someone had reached Diadem before them.

The signs were unmistakable; glints of refined metal on the surface, picked out by radar. Upon inspection from orbit they turned out to be ruined structures and equipment, obviously of human origin.

"It's not possible," Clavain had said. "We're the first. We have to be the first. No one else has ever built anything like the *Sandra Voi;* nothing capable of traveling this far."

"Somewhere in there," Galiana had answered, "I think there might be a mistaken assumption, don't you?"

Meekly, Clavain had nodded.

Now—later still than he had promised—Clavain made his way back to the waiting shuttle. The red carpet of safety led straight to the access ramp beneath the craft's belly. He climbed up and stepped through the transparent membrane which spanned the entrance door, most of his suit slithering away on contact with the membrane. By the time he was inside the ship he wore only a lightweight breather mask and a few communicational devices. He could have survived outside naked for many minutes—Diadem's atmosphere now had enough oxygen to support humans—but Galiana refused to allow any intermingling of microorganisms.

He returned the equipment to a storage locker, placed the worm sample in a refrigeration rack, and clothed himself in a paper-thin black tunic and trousers, before moving into the aft compartment where Galiana was waiting.

She and Felka were sitting facing each other across the

blank-walled, austerely furnished room. They were staring into the space between them without quite meeting each other's eyes. They looked like a mother and daughter locked in argumentative stalemate, but Clavain knew better.

He issued the mental command, well rehearsed now, which opened his mind to communion with the others. It was like opening a tiny aperture in the side of a dam; he was never adequately prepared for the force with which the flow of data hit him. The room changed; color bleeding out of the walls, lacing itself into abstract structures which permeated the room's volume. Galiana and Felka, dressed dourly a moment earlier, were now veiled in light, and appeared superhumanly beautiful. He could feel their thoughts, as if he were overhearing a heated conversation in the room next door. Most of it was nonverbal; Galiana and Felka playing an intense, abstract game. The thing floating between them was a solid lattice of light, resembling the plumbing diagram of an insanely complex refinery. It was constantly adjusting itself, with colored flows racing this way and that as the geometry changed. About half the volume was green; what remained was lilac, but now the former encroached dramatically on the latter.

Felka laughed; she was winning.

Galiana conceded and crashed back into her seat with a sigh of exhaustion, but she was smiling as well.

"Sorry. I appear to have distracted you," Clavain said.

"No; you just hastened the inevitable. I'm afraid Felka was always going to win."

The girl smiled again, still saying nothing, though Clavain sensed her victory; a hard-edged thing which for a moment outshone all other thoughts from her direction, eclipsing even Galiana's air of weary resignation.

Felka had been a failed Conjoiner experiment in the manipulation of fetal brain development; a child with a mind more machine than human. When he had first met her—in Galiana's nest on Mars—he had encountered a girl absorbed in a profound, endless game; directing the faltering self-repair processes of the terraforming structure known as the Great Wall of Mars, in which the nest sheltered. She had no interest in people—indeed; she could not even discriminate faces. But when the nest was being evacuated, Clavain had risked his life to save hers, even though Galiana had told him that the kindest thing would be to let her die. As Clavain had struggled to adjust to life as part of Galiana's commune, he had set himself the task of helping Felka to develop her latent humanity. She had begun to show signs of recognition in his presence, perhaps sensing on some level that they had a kinship; that they were both strangers stumbling toward a strange new light.

Galiana rose from her chair, carpets of light wrapping around her. "It was time to end the game, anyway. We've got work to do." She looked down at the girl, who was still staring at the lattice. "Sorry, Felka. Later, maybe."

Clavain said: "How's she doing?"

"She's laughing, Nevil. That has to be progress, doesn't it?"

"I'd say that depends what she's laughing about."

"She beat me. She thought it was funny. I'd say that was a fairly human reaction, wouldn't you?"

"I'd still be happier if I could convince myself she recognized my face, and not my smell, or the sound my footfalls make."

"You're the only one of us with a beard, Nevil. It doesn't take vast amounts of neural processing to spot *that*."

Clavain scratched his chin self-consciously as they stepped through into the shuttle's flight deck. He liked his beard, even though it was trimmed to little more than gray stubble so that he could slip a breather mask on without difficulty. It was as much a link to his past as his memories, or the wrinkles Galiana had studiously built into his remodeled body.

"You're right, of course. Sometimes I just have to remind myself how far we've come."

Galiana smiled—she was getting better at that, though there was still something a little forced about it—and pushed her long, gray-veined black hair behind her ears. "I tell myself the same things when I think about you, Nevil."

"Mm. But I have come some way, haven't I?"

"Yes, but that doesn't mean you haven't got a considerable distance ahead of you. I could have put that thought into

your head in a microsecond, if you allowed me to do so—
but you still insist that we communicate by making noises in
our throats, the way monkeys do."

"Well, it's good practice for you," Clavain said, hoping
that his irritation was not too obvious.

They settled into adjacent seats while avionics displays
slithered into take-off configuration. Clavain's implants allowed him to fly the machine without any manual inputs at
all, but—old soldier that he was—he generally preferred
tactile controls. So his implants obliged; hallucinating a joy-
stick inset with buttons and levers, and when he reached out
to grasp it his hands seemed to close around something
solid. He shuddered to think how thoroughly his perceptions
of the real world were being doctored to support this illusion; but once he had been flying for a few minutes he generally forgot about it, lost in the joy of piloting.

He got them airborne, then settled the shuttle into level
flight toward the fifth ruin that they would be visiting today.
Kilometers of ice slid beneath them, only occasionally broken
by a protruding ridge or a patch of dry, boulder-strewn ground.

"Just a few shacks, you said?"

Galiana nodded. "A waste of time, but we had to check it
out."

"Any closer to understanding what happened to them?"

"They died, more or less overnight. Mostly through incidents related to the breakdown of normal thought—although
one or two may have simply died; as if they had some
greater susceptibility to a toxin than the others."

Clavain smiled, feeling that a small victory was his. "Now
you're looking at a toxin, rather than a psychosis?"

"A toxin's difficult to explain, Nevil."

"From Martin Setterholm's worms, perhaps?"

"Not very likely. Their biohazard containment measures
weren't as good as ours—but they were still adequate.
We've analyzed those worms and we know they don't carry
anything obviously hostile to us. And even if there was a
neurotoxin, how would it affect everyone so quickly? Even
if the lab workers had caught something, they'd have fallen
ill before anyone else did, sending a warning to the others—

but nothing like that happened." She paused, anticipating Clavain's next question. "And no; I don't think that what happened to them is necessarily anything we need worry about, though that doesn't mean I'm going to rule anything out. But even our oldest technology's a century ahead of anything they had—and we have the *Sandra Voi* to retreat to if we run into anything the medichines in our heads can't handle."

Clavain always did his best not to think too much about the swarms of sub-cellular machines lacing his brain—supplanting much of it, in fact—but there were times when it was unavoidable. He still had a squeamish reaction to the idea, though it was becoming milder. Now, though, he could not help but view the machines as his allies; as intimately a part of him as his immune system. Galiana was right: they would resist anything which tried to interfere with what now passed as the 'normal' functioning of his mind.

"Still," he said, not yet willing to drop his pet theory. "You've got to admit something: the Americans—Setterholm especially—were interested in the worms. Too interested, if you ask me."

"Look who's talking."

"Ah, but my interest is strictly forensic. And I can't help but put the two things together. They were interested in the worms. And they went mad."

What he said was an oversimplification, of course: it was clear enough that the worms had only preoccupied some of the Americans: those who were most interested in xenobiology. According to the evidence the Conjoiners had so far gathered, the effort had been largely spearheaded by Setterholm, the man he had found dead at the bottom of the crevasse. Setterholm had traveled widely across Diadem's snowy wastes, gathering a handful of allies to assist in his work. He had found worms in dozens of ice-fields, grouped into vast colonies. For the most part the other members of the expedition had let him get on with his activities, even as they struggled with the day-to-day business of staying alive in what was still a hostile, alien environment.

Even before they had all died things had been far from easy. The self-replicating robots which had brought them here in the first place had failed years before, leaving the delicate life-support systems of their shelters to slowly collapse; each malfunction a little harder to rectify than the last. Diadem was getting colder, too—sliding inexorably into a deep ice-age. It had been the Americans' misfortune to arrive at the coming of a great, centuries-long winter. Now, Clavain thought, it was colder still; the polar ice-caps rushing toward each other like long-separated lovers.

"It must have been fast, whatever it was," Clavain mused. "They'd already abandoned most of the outlying bases by then, huddling together back at the main settlement. By then they only had enough spare parts and technical know-how to run a single fusion power-plant."

"Which failed."

"Yes—but that doesn't mean much. It couldn't run itself, not by then—it needed constant tinkering. Eventually the people with the right know-how must have succumbed to the . . . whatever it was—and then the reactor stopped working and they all died of the cold. But they were in trouble long before the reactor failed."

Galiana seemed on the point of saying something. Clavain could always tell when she was about to speak; it was if some leakage from her thoughts reached his brain even as she composed what she would say.

"Well?" he said, when the silence had stretched long enough.

"I was just thinking," she said. "A reactor of that type—it doesn't need any exotic isotopes, does it? No tritium, or deuterium?"

"No. Just plain old hydrogen. You could get all you needed from sea-water."

"Or ice," Galiana said.

They vectored in for the next landing site. Toadstools, Clavain thought: half a dozen black metal towers of varying height surmounted by domed black habitat modules, interlinked by a web of elevated, pressurized walkways. Each of the domes was thirty or forty meters wide, perched a hundred or more meters above the ice, festooned with narrow, armored windows, sensors and communications antennae. A tongue-like extension from one of the tallest domes was clearly a landing pad. In fact, as he came closer, he saw that there was an aircraft parked on it; one of the blunt-winged machines that the Americans had used to get around in. It was dusted with ice, but it would probably still fly with a little persuasion.

He inched the shuttle down, one of its skids only just inside the edge of the pad. Clearly the landing pad had only really been intended for one aircraft at a time.

"Nevil . . ." Galiana said. "I'm not sure I like this."

He felt tension, but could not be sure if it was his own or Galiana's, leaking into his head.

"What don't you like?"

"There shouldn't be an aircraft here," Galiana said.

"Why not?"

She spoke softly, reminding him that the evacuation of the outlying settlements had been orderly, compared to the subsequent crisis. "This base should have been shut down and mothballed with all the others."

"Then someone stayed behind here," Clavain suggested.

Galiana nodded. "Or someone came back."

There was a third presence with them now; another hue of thought bleeding into his mind. Felka had come into the cockpit. He could taste her apprehension.

"You sense it, too," he said, wonderingly, looking into the face of the terribly damaged girl. "Our discomfort. And you don't like it anymore than we do, do you?"

Galiana took the girl's hand. "It's all right,' Felka."

She must have said that just for Clavain's benefit. Before her mouth had even opened Galiana would have planted reassuring thoughts in Felka's mind; attempting to still the disquiet with the subtlest of neural adjustments. Clavain thought of an expert Ikebana artist minutely altering the placement of a single flower in the interests of harmony.

"Everything will be OK," Clavain said. "There's nothing here that can harm you."

Galiana took a moment, blank-eyed, to commune with the other Conjoiners in and around Diadem. Most of them were still in orbit observing things from the ship. She told them about the aircraft and notified them that she and Clavain were going to enter the structure.

He saw Felka's hand tighten around Galiana's wrist.

"She wants to come as well," Galiana said.

"She'll be safer if she stays here."

"She doesn't want to be alone."

Clavain chose his words carefully. "I thought Conjoiners— I mean we—could never be truly alone, Galiana."

"There might be a communicational block inside the structure. It'd be better if she stays physically close to us."

"Is that the only reason?"

"No, of course not." For a moment he felt a sting of her anger prickling his mind like sea-spray. "She's still human, Nevil—no matter what we've done to her mind. We can't erase a million years of evolution. She may not be very good at recognizing faces, but she recognizes the need for companionship."

He raised his hands. "I never doubted it."

"Then why are you arguing?"

Clavain smiled. He'd had this conversation so many times before with so many women. He had been married to some of them. It was oddly comforting to be having it again, light-years from home, wearing a new body, his mind clotted with machines and confronting the matriarch of what should have been a feared and hated hive-mind. It's the epicenter of so much strangeness, a tiff was almost to be welcome.

"I just don't want anything to hurt her."

"Oh. And I do?"

"Never mind," he said, gritting his teeth. "Let's just get in and out, shall we?"

The base, like all the American structures, had been built for posterity. Not by people, however, but by swarms of diligent replicating robots. That was how the Americans had reached Diadem; they had been brought here as frozen fertilized cells in the armor radiation-proofed bellies of star-crossing von Neumann robots. The robots had been launched toward several solar systems about a century be-fore the *Sandra Voi* had left Mars. Upon arrival on Diadem they had set about breeding; making copies of themselves from local ores. When their numbers had reached some threshold they had turned over their energies to the construction of bases; luxurious accommodation for the human children which would then be grown in their wombs.

"The entrance door's intact," Galiana said, when they had crossed from the shuttle to the smooth black side of the dome, stooping against the wind. "And there's still some residual power in its circuits."

That was a Conjoiner trick which always faintly unnerved him. Like sharks, Conjoiners were sensitive to ambient electrical fields. Mapped into her vision, Galiana would see the energized circuits superimposed on the door like a ghostly neon maze. Now she extended her hand toward the lock, palm first.

"I'm accessing the opening mechanism. Interfacing with it now." Behind her mask, he saw her face scrunch in concentration. Galiana only ever frowned when having to think hard. With her hand outstretched she looked like a wizard attempting some particularly demanding enchantment.

"Hmm," she said. "Nice old software protocols. Nothing too difficult."

"Careful," Clavain said. "I wouldn't put it past them to have put some kind of trap here . . ."

"There's no trap," she said. "But there is—ah, yes—a verbal entry code. Well, here goes." She spoke louder, so that her voice could travel through the air to the door even above the howl of the wind. *"Open Sesame."*

Lights flicked from red to green; dislodging a frosting of ice, the door slid ponderously aside to reveal a dimly lit interior chamber. The base must have been running on a trickle of emergency power for decades.

Felka and Clavain lingered while Galiana crossed the threshold. "Well?" she challenged, turning around. "Are you two sissies coming or not?"

Felka offered a hand. He took hers and the two of them—the old soldier and the girl who could barely grasp the difference between two human faces—took a series of tentative steps inside.

"What you just did; that business with your hand and the password . . ." Clavain paused. "That *was* a joke, wasn't it?"

Galiana looked at him blank-faced. "How could it have been? Everyone knows we haven't got anything remotely resembling a sense of humor."

Clavain nodded gravely. "That was my understanding, but I just wanted to be sure."

There was no trace of the wind inside, but it would still have been too cold to remove their suits, even had they not been concerned about contamination. They worked their way along a series of winding corridors, of which some were dark and some were bathed in feeble, pea-green lighting. Now and then they passed the entrance to a room full of equipment, but nothing that looked like a laboratory or living quarters. Then they descended a series of stairs and found themselves crossing one of the sealed walkways between the toadstools. Clavain had seen a few other American settlements built like this one; they were designed to remain useful even as they sank slowly into the ice.

The bridge led to what was obviously the main habitation section. Now there were lounges, bedrooms, laboratories and kitchens—enough for a crew of perhaps fifty or sixty. But there were no signs of any bodies, and the place did not look as if it had been abandoned in a hurry. The equipment was neatly packed away and there were no half-eaten meals on the tables. There was frost everywhere, but that was just the moisture which had frozen out of the air when the base cooled down.

"They were expecting to come back," Galiana said.

Clavain nodded. "They couldn't have had much of an idea of what lay ahead of them."

They moved on, crossing another bridge until they arrived in a toadstool which was almost entirely dedicated to bio-analysis laboratories. Galiana had to use her neural trick to get them inside again, the machines in her head sweet-talking the duller machines entombed in the doors. The low-ceilinged labs were bathed in green light, but Galiana found a wall panel which brought the lighting up a notch and even caused some bench equipment to wake up, pulsing stand-by lights.

Clavain looked around, recognizing centrifuges, gene-sequencers, gas chromatographs and scanning-tunneling microscopes. There were at least a dozen other hunks of gleaming machinery whose function eluded him. A wall-sized cabinet held dozens of pull-out drawers, each of which contained hundreds of culture dishes, test-tubes and gel slides. Clavain glanced at the samples, reading the tiny labels. There were bacteria and single-cell cultures with unpronounceable code names, most of which were marked with Diadem map coordinates and a date. But there were also drawers full of samples with Latin names; comparison samples which must have come from Earth. The robots could easily have carried the tiny parent organisms from which these larger samples had been grown or cloned. Perhaps the Americans had been experimenting with the hardiness of Earth-born organisms, with a view to terraforming Diadem at some point in the future.

He closed the drawer silently and moved to a set of larger sample tubes racked on a desk. He picked one from the rack and raised it to the light, examining the smoky things inside. It was a sample of worms, indistinguishable from those he had collected on the glacier a few hours earlier. A breeding tangle, probably: harvested from the intersection point of two worm tunnels. Some of the worms in the tangle would be exchanging genes; others would be fighting; others would be allowing themselves to be digested by adults or newly hatched young; all behaving according to rigidly deterministic laws of caste and sex. The tangle looked dead, but that meant nothing with the worms. Their metabolism was fantastically slow; each individual easily capable of living for thousands of years. It would take them months just to crawl along some of the longer cracks in the ice, let alone move between some of the larger tangles.

But the worms were really not all that alien. They had a close terrestrial analog; the sun-avoiding ice-worms which had first been discovered in the Malaspina Glacier in Alaska toward the end of the nineteenth century. The Alaskan ice-worms were a lot smaller than their Diadem counterparts, but they also nourished themselves on the slim pickings that drifted onto the ice, or had been frozen into it years earlier. Like the Diadem worms, their most notable anatomical feature was a pore at the head end, just above the mouth. In the case of the terrestrial worms the pore served a single function: secreting a salty solution which helped the worms melt their way into ice when there was no tunnel already present— an escape strategy that helped them get beneath the ice before the sun dried them up. The Diadem worms had a similar structure, but according to Setterholm's notes they have evolved a second use for it; secreting a chemically rich "scent trail" which helped other worms navigate through the tunnel system. The chemistry of that scent-trail turned out to be very complex, with each worm capable of secreting not merely a unique signature but a variety of flavors. Conceivably, more complex message schemes were embedded in some of the other flavors: not just "follow me" but "follow me only if you are female—" the Diadem worms had at least three sexes "—and this is breeding season." There were many other possibilities, which Setterholm seemed to have been attempting to decode and catalog when the end had come.

It was interesting . . . up to a point. But even if the worms followed a complex set of rules dependent on the scent-trails they were picking up, and perhaps other environmental cues, it would still only be rigidly mechanistic behavior.

"Nevil, come here."

That was Galiana's voice, but it was in a tone he had barely heard before. It was one that made him run, to where Felka and Galiana were waiting on the other side of the lab.

They were facing an array of lockers which occupied an entire wall. A small status panel was set into each locker, but only one locker—placed at chest height—showed any activity. Clavain looked back to the door they had come in through, but from here it was hidden by intervening lab equipment. They would not have seen this locker even if it had been illuminated before Galiana brought the room's power back on.

"It might have been on all along," he said.

"I know," Galiana agreed.

She reached a hand up to the panel, tapping the control

keys with unnerving fluency. Machines to Galiana were like musical instruments to a prodigy. She could pick one up cold and play it like an old friend.

The array of status lights changed configuration abruptly, then there was a bustle of activity somewhere behind the locker's metal face—latches and servo-motors clicking after decades of stasis.

"Stand back," Galiana said.

A rime of frost shattered into a billion sugary pieces. The locker began to slide out of the wall, the unhurried motion giving them adequate time to digest what lay inside. He felt Felka grip his hand, and then noticed that her other hand was curled tightly around Galiana's wrist. For the first time, he began to wonder if it had really been such a good idea to allow the girl to join them.

The locker was two meters in length and half that in width and height; just sufficient to contain a human body. It had probably been designed to hold animal specimens culled from Diadem's oceans, but it was equally capable of functioning as a mortuary tray. That the man inside the locker was dead was beyond question, but there was no sign of injury. His composure—flat on his back, his blue-gray face serenely blank, his eyes closed and his hands clasped neatly just below his ribcage—suggested to Clavain a saint lying in grace. His beard was neatly pointed and his hair long, frozen into a solid sculptural mass. He was still wearing several heavy layers of thermal clothing.

Clavain knelt closer and read the name-tag above the man's heart.

"Andrew Iverson. Ring a bell?"

A moment while Galiana established a link to the rest of the Conjoiners, ferreting the name out of some database. "Yes. One of the missing. Seems he was a climatologist with an interest in terraforming techniques."

Clavain nodded shrewdly. "That figures, with all the microorganisms I've seen in this place. Well: the trillion dollar question. How do you think he got in there?"

"I think he climbed in," Galiana said. And nodded at something which Clavain had missed, almost tucked away beneath the man's shoulder. Clavain reached into the gap, his finger brushing against the rock-hard fabric of Iverson's outfit. A catheter vanished into the man's forearm, where he had cut away a square of fabric. The catheter's black feed-line reached back into the cabinet, vanishing into a socket at the rear.

"You're saying he killed himself?"

"He must have put something in that which would stop his heart. Then he probably flushed out his blood and replaced it with glycerol, or something similar, to prevent ice-crystals forming in his cells. It would have taken some automation to make it work, but I'm sure everything he needed was here."

Clavain thought back to what he knew about the cryonic immersion techniques that had been around a century or so earlier. They left something to be desired now, but back then they had not been much of an advance over mummification.

"When he sank that catheter into himself, he can't have been certain we'd ever find him," Clavain remarked.

"Which would still have been preferable to suicide."

"Yes, but . . . the thoughts which must have gone through his head. Knowing he had to kill himself first, to stand a chance of living again—and then hope someone else stumbled on Diadem."

"You made a harder choice than that, once."

"Yes. But at least I wasn't alone when I made it."

Iverson's body was astonishingly well-preserved, Clavain thought. The skin tissue looked almost intact, even if it had a deathly, granitelike color. The bones of his face had not ruptured under the strain of the temperature drop. Bacterial processes had stopped dead. All in all, things could have been a lot worse.

"We shouldn't leave him like this," Galiana said, pushing the locker so that it began to slide back into the wall.

"I don't think he cares much about that now," Clavain said.

"No. You don't understand. He mustn't warm—not even to the ambient temperature of the room. Otherwise we won't be able to wake him up."

* * *

It took five days to bring him back to consciousness.

The decision to reanimate had not been taken lightly; it had only been arrived at after intense discussion among the Conjoined, debates in which Clavain participated to the best of his ability. Iverson, they all agreed, could probably be resurrected with current Conjoiner methods. In-situ scans of his mind had revealed preserved synaptic structures which a scaffold of machines could coax back toward consciousness. However, since they had not yet identified the cause of the madness which had killed Iverson's colleagues—and the evidence was pointing toward some kind of infectious agent—Iverson would be kept on the surface, reborn on the same world where he had died.

They had, however, moved him: shuttling him halfway across the world back to the main base. Clavain had traveled with the corpse, marveling at the idea that this solid chunk of man-shaped ice—tainted, admittedly, with a few vital impurities—would soon be a breathing, thinking, human being with memories and feelings. To him it seemed astonishing that this was possible; that so much latent structure had been preserved across the decades. Even more astonishing that the infusions of tiny machines which the Conjoiners were brewing would be able to stitch together damaged cells and kick-start them back to life. And out of that inert loom of frozen brain structure—a thing that was at this moment nothing more than a fixed geometric entity, like a finely eroded piece of rock—something as malleable as consciousness would emerge.

But the Conjoiners were blasé at the prospect, viewing Iverson the way expert picture restorers might view a damaged old master. Yes, there would be difficulties ahead—work that would require great skill—but nothing to lose sleep over.

Except, Clavain reminded himself, none of them slept anyway.

While the others were working to bring Iverson back to life, Clavain wandered the outskirts of the base, trying to get a better feel for what it must have been like in the last days. The debilitating mental illness must have been terrifying, as it struck even those who might have stood some chance of developing some kind of counteragent to it. Perhaps in the old days, when the base had been under the stewardship of the von Neumann machines, something might have been done . . . but in the end it must have been like trying to crack a particularly tricky algebra problem while growing steadily more drunk; losing first the ability to focus sharply, then to focus on the problem at all, and then to remember what was so important about it anyway. The labs in the main complex had an abandoned look to them: experiments half-finished; notes on the wall scrawled in ever more incoherent handwriting.

Down in the lower levels—the transport bays and storage areas—it was almost as if nothing had happened. Equipment was still neatly racked; surface vehicles neatly parked, and—with the base subsystems back on—the place was bathed in light and not so cold as to require extra clothing. It was quite therapeutic, too: the Conjoiners had not extended their communicational fields into these regions, so Clavain's mind was mercifully isolated again; freed of the clamor of other voices. Despite that, he was still tempted by the idea of spending some time outdoors.

With that in mind he found an airlock; one that must have been added late in the base's history, as it was absent from the blueprints. There was no membrane stretched across this one; if he stepped through it he would be outside as soon as the doors cycled, with no more protection than the clothes he was wearing now. He considered going back into the base proper to find a membrane suit, but by the time he did that, the mood—the urge to go outside—would be gone.

Clavain noticed a locker. Inside, to his delight, was a rack of old-style suits such as Setterholm had been wearing. They looked brand new, alloy neck-rings gleaming. Racked above each was a bulbous helmet. He experimented until he found a suit that fitted him, then struggled with the various latches and seals which coupled the suit parts together. Even when he thought he had donned the suit properly, the airlock detected that one of his gloves wasn't latched correctly. It refused to let him outside until he reversed the cycle and fixed the problem.

But then he was outside, and it was glorious.

He walked around the base until he found his bearings, and then—always ensuring that the base was in view and that his air-supply was adequate—he set off across the ice. Above, Diadem's sky was a deep enameled blue, and the ice—though fundamentally white—seemed to contain in itself a billion nuances of pale turquoise, pale aquamarine; even hints of the palest of pinks. Beneath his feet he imagined the cracklike networks of the worms, threading down for hundreds of meters; and he imagined the worms themselves, wriggling through that network, responding to and secreting chemical scent trails. The worms themselves were biologically simple—almost dismayingly so—but that network was a vast, intricate thing. It hardly mattered that the traffic along it—the to-and-fro motions of the worms as they went about their lives—was so agonizingly slow. The worms, after all, had endured longer than human comprehension. They had seen people come and go in an eyeblink.

He walked on until he arrived at the crevasse where he had found Setterholm. They had long since removed Setterholm's body, of course, but the experience had imprinted itself deeply on Clavain's mind. He found it easy to relive the moment at the lip of the crevasse, when he had first seen the end of Setterholm's arm. At the time he had told himself that there must be worse places to die; surrounded by beauty that was so pristine; so utterly untouched by human influence. Now, the more that he thought about it, the more that Setterholm's death played on his mind—he wondered if there could be any worse place. It was undeniably beautiful, but it was also crushingly dead; crushingly oblivious to life. Setterholm must have felt himself draining away, soon to become as inanimate as the palace of ice that was to become his tomb.

Clavain thought about it for many more minutes, enjoying the silence and the solitude and the odd awkwardness of the suit. He thought back to the way Setterholm had been found, and his mind niggled at something not quite right; a detail that had not seemed wrong at the time but which now troubled him.

It was Setterholm's helmet.

He remembered the way it had been lying away from the man's corpse, as if the impact had knocked it off. But now that Clavain had locked an identical helmet onto his own suit, that was harder to believe. The latches were sturdy, and he doubted that the drop into the crevasse would have been sufficient to break the mechanism. He considered the possibility that Setterholm had put his suit on hastily, but even that seemed unlikely now. The airlock had detected that Clavain's glove was badly attached; it—or any of the other locks—would have surely refused to allow Setterholm outside if his helmet had not been correctly latched.

Clavain wondered if Setterholm's death had been something other than an accident.

He thought about it, trying the idea on for size, then slowly shook his head. There were a myriad possibilities he had yet to rule out. Setterholm could have left the base with his suit intact and then—confused and disoriented—he could have fiddled with the latch, depriving himself of oxygen until he stumbled into the crevasse. Or perhaps the airlocks were not as foolproof as they seemed; the safety mechanism capable of being disabled by people in a hurry to get outside.

No. A man had died, but there was no need to assume it had been anything other than an accident. Clavain turned, and began to walk back to the base.

"He's awake," Galiana said, a day or so after the final wave of machines had swum into Iverson's mind. "I think it might be better if he spoke to you first, Nevil, don't you? Rather than one of us?" She bit her tongue. "I mean, rather than someone who's been Conjoined for as long as the rest of us?"

Clavain shrugged. "Then again, an attractive face might be preferable to a grizzled old relic like myself. But I take your point. Is it safe to go in now?"

"Perfectly. If Iverson was carrying anything infectious, the machines would have flagged it."

"I hope you're right."

"Well, look at the evidence. He was acting rationally up to the end. He did everything to ensure we'd have an excellent chance of reviving him. His suicide was just a coldly calculated attempt to escape his then situation."

"Coldly calculated," Clavain echoed. "Yes, I suppose it would have been. Cold, I mean."

Galiana said nothing, but gestured toward the door into Iverson's room.

Clavain stepped through the opening. And it was as he crossed the threshold that a thought occurred to him. He could once again see, in his mind's eye, Martin Setterholm's body lying at the bottom of the crevasse, his fingers pointing to the letters IVF.

In-vitro fertilization.

But suppose Setterholm had been trying to write IVER-SON, but had died before finishing the word? If Setterholm had been murdered—pushed into the crevasse—he might have been trying to pass on a message about his murderer. Clavain imagined his pain, legs smashed; knowing with absolute certainty he was going to die alone and cold, but willing himself to write Iverson's name . . .

But why would the climatologist have wanted to kill Setterholm? Setterholm's fascination with the worms was perplexing but harmless. The information Clavain had collected pointed to Setterholm being a single-minded loner; the kind of man who would inspire pity or indifference in his colleagues, rather than hatred. And everyone was dying anyway—against such a background, a murder seemed almost irrelevant.

Maybe he was attributing too much to the six faint marks a dying man had scratched on the ice.

Forcing suspicion from his mind—for now—Clavain stepped into Iverson's room. The room was spartan but serene, with a small blue holographic window set high in one white wall. Clavain was responsible for that. Left to the Conjoiners—who had taken over an area of the main American base and filled it with their own pressurized spaces—Iverson's room would have been a grim, gray cube. That was fine for the Conjoiners—they moved through informational fields draped like an extra layer over reality. But though Iverson's head was now drenched with their machines, they were only there to assist his normal patterns of thought, reinforcing weak synaptic signals and compensating for a far-from-equilibrium mix of neurotransmitters.

So Clavain had insisted on cheering the place up a bit; Iverson's bedsheets and pillow were now the same pure white as the walls, so that his head bobbed in a sea of whiteness. His hair had been trimmed, but Clavain had made sure that no one had done more than neaten Iverson's beard.

"Andrew?" he said. "I'm told you're awake now. I'm Nevil Clavain. How are you feeling?"

Iverson wet his lips before answering. "Better, I suspect, than I have any reason to feel."

"Ah." Clavain beamed, feeling that a large burden had just been lifted from his shoulders. "Then you've some recollection of what happened to you."

"I died, didn't I? Pumped myself full of anti-freeze and hoped for the best. Did it work, or is this just some weird-ass dream as I'm sliding toward brain-death?"

"No, it sure as hell worked. That was one weird-heck-ass of a risk . . ." Clavain halted, not entirely certain that he could emulate Iverson's century-old speech patterns. "That was quite some risk you took. But it did work, you'll be glad to hear."

Iverson lifted a hand from beneath the bedsheets, examining his palm and the pattern of veins and tendons on the rear. "This is the same body I went under with? You haven't stuck me in a robot, or cloned me, or hooked up my disembodied brain to a virtual-reality generator?"

"None of those things, no. Just mopped up some cell damage, fixed a few things here and there and—um—kick-started you back to the land of the living."

Iverson nodded, but Clavain could tell he was far from convinced. Which was unsurprising: Clavain, after all, had already told a small lie. "So how long was I under?"

"About a century, Andrew. We're an expedition from back home. We came by starship."

Iverson nodded again, as if this was mere, incidental detail. "We're aboard it now, right?"

"No . . . no. We're still on the planet. The ship's parked in orbit."

"And everyone else?"

No point sugaring the pill. "Dead, as far as we can make out. But you must have known that would happen."

"Yeah. But I didn't know for sure, even at the end."

"So what happened? How did you escape the infection, or whatever it was?"

"Sheer luck." Iverson asked for a drink. Clavain fetched him one, and at the same time had the room extrude a chair next to the bed.

"I didn't see much sign of luck," Clavain said.

"No; it was terrible. But I was the lucky one; that's all I meant. I don't know how much you know. We had to evacuate the outlying bases toward the end, when we couldn't keep more than one fusion reactor running." Iverson took a sip from the glass of water Clavain had brought him. "If we'd still had the machines to look after us . . ."

"Yes. That's something we never really understood." Clavain leaned closer to the bed. "Those von Neumann machines were built to self-repair themselves, weren't they? We still don't see how they broke down."

Iverson eyed him. "They didn't. Break down, I mean."

"No? Then what happened?"

"We smashed them up. Like rebellious teenagers overthrowing parental control. The machines were nannying us, and we were sick of it. In hindsight, it wasn't such a good idea."

"Didn't the machines put up a fight?"

"Not exactly. I don't think the people who designed them ever thought they'd get trashed by the kids they'd lovingly cared for."

So, Clavain thought—whatever had happened here; whatever he went onto learn, it was clear that the Americans had been at least partially the authors of their own misfortunes. He still felt sympathy for them, but now it was cooler; tempered with something close to disgust. He wondered if that feeling of disappointed appraisal would have come so easily without Galiana's machines in his head. *It would be just a tiny step to go from feeling that way toward Iverson's people to feeling that way about the rest of humanity . . . and then I'd know that I'd truly attained Transenlightenment . . .*

Clavain snapped out of his morbid line of thinking. It was not Transenlightenment that engendered those feelings; just ancient, bone-deep cynicism.

"Well, there's no point dwelling on what was done years ago. But how did you survive?"

"After the evacuation, we realized that we'd left something behind—a spare component for the fusion reactor. So I went back for it, taking one of the planes. I landed just as a bad weather front was coming in, which kept me grounded there for two days. That was when the others began to get sick. It happened pretty quickly, and all I knew about it was what I could figure out from the comm links back to the main base."

"Tell me what you did figure out."

"Not much," Iverson said. "It was fast, and it seemed to attack the central nervous system. No one survived it. Those who didn't die of it directly seemed to get themselves killed through accidents or sloppy procedure."

"We noticed. Eventually someone died who was responsible for keeping the fusion reactor running properly. It didn't blow up, did it?"

"No. Just spewed out a lot more neutrons than normal; too much for the shielding to contain. Then it went into emergency shutdown mode. Some people were killed by the radiation, but most died of the cold that came afterward."

"Hm. Except you."

Iverson nodded. "If I hadn't had to go back for that component, I'd have been one of them. Obviously, I couldn't risk returning. Even if I could have got the reactor working again, there was still the problem of the contaminant." He breathed in deeply, as if steeling himself to recollect what had happened next. "So I weighed my options, and decided dying—freezing myself—was my only hope. No one was going to come from Earth to help me, even if I could have kept myself alive. Not for decades, anyway. So I took a chance."

"One that paid off."

"Like I said, I was the lucky one." Iverson took another sip from the glass Clavain had brought him. "Man, that tastes better than anything I've ever drunk in my life. What's in this, by the way?"

"Just water. Glacial water. Purified, of course."

Iverson nodded, slowly, and put the glass down next to his bed.

"Not thirsty now?"

"Quenched my thirst nicely, thank you."

"Good." Clavain stood up. "I'll let you get some rest, Andrew. If there's anything you need; anything we can do—just call out."

"I'll be sure to."

Clavain smiled and walked to the door, observing Iverson's obvious relief that the questioning session was over for now. But Iverson had said nothing incriminating, Clavain reminded himself, and his responses were entirely consistent with the fatigue and confusion anyone would feel after so long asleep—or dead, depending on how you defined Iverson's period on ice. It was unfair to associate him with Setterholm's death just because of a few indistinct marks gouged in ice, and the faint possibility that Setterholm had been murdered.

Still, Clavain paused before leaving the room. "One other thing, Andrew—just something that's been bothering me, and I wondered if you could help."

"Go ahead."

"Would the initials I, V and F mean anything to you?"

Iverson thought about it for a moment, then shook his head. "Sorry, Nevil. You've got me there."

"Well, it was just a shot in the dark," Clavain said.

Iverson was strong enough to walk around the next day. He insisted on exploring the rest of the base, not simply the parts of it which the Conjoiners had taken over. He wanted to see for himself the damage that he had heard about, and see the lists of the dead—and the manner in which they had died—which Clavain and his friends had assiduously compiled. Clavain kept a watchful eye on the man, aware of how emotionally traumatic the whole experience must be. He was bearing it well, but that could easily have been a front. Galiana's machines could tell a lot about how his brain was functioning, but they were unable to probe Iverson's state of mind at the resolution needed to map emotional well-being.

Clavain, meanwhile, strove as best he could to keep Iverson in the dark about the Conjoiners. He did not want to overwhelm Iverson with strangeness at this delicate time; did not want to shatter the man's illusion that he had been rescued by a group of "normal" human beings. But it turned out to be easier than he had expected, as Iverson showed surprisingly little interest in the history he had missed. Clavain had gone as far as telling him that the *Sandra Voi* was technically a ship full of refugees, fleeing the aftermath of a war between various factions of solar-system humanity—but Iverson had done little more than nod, never probing Clavain for more details about the war. Once or twice Clavain had even alluded accidentally to the Transenlightenment—that shared consciousness state which the Conjoiners had reached—but Iverson had shown the same lack of interest. He was not even curious about the *Sandra Voi* herself; never once asking Clavain what the ship was like. It was not quite what Clavain had been expecting.

But there were rewards, too.

Iverson, it turned out, was fascinated by Felka, and Felka herself seemed pleasantly amused by the newcomer. It was, perhaps, not all that surprising: Galiana and the others had been busy helping Felka grow the neural circuitry necessary for normal human interactions, adding new layers to supplant the functional regions which had never worked properly— but in all that time, they had never introduced her to another human being whom she had not already met. And here was Iverson: not just a new voice but a new smell; a new face; a new way of walking—a deluge of new input for her starved mental routines. Clavain watched the way Felka latched onto Iverson when he entered a room; her attention snapping to him, her delight evident. And Iverson seemed perfectly happy to play the games that so wearied the others; the kinds of intricate challenge which Felka adored. For hours on end he watched the two of them lost in concentration; Iverson pulling mock faces of sorrow or—on the rare occasions when he beat her—extravagant joy. Felka responded in kind, her face more animated—more plausibly human—than Clavain had ever believed possible. She spoke more often in Iverson's presence than she had ever done in his, and the utterances she made more closely approximated well-formed, grammatically sound sentences than the disjointed shards of language Clavain had grown to recognize. It was like watching a difficult, backward child suddenly come alight in the presence of a skilled teacher. Clavain thought back to the time when he had rescued Felka from Mars, and how unlikely it had seemed then that she would ever grow into something resembling a normal adult human, as sensitized to others' feelings as she was to her own. Now, he could almost believe it would happen—yet half the distance she had come had been due to Iverson's influence, rather than his own.

Afterward, when even Iverson had wearied of Felka's ceaseless demands for games, Clavain spoke to him quietly, away from the others.

"You're good with her, aren't you."

Iverson shrugged, as if the matter was of no great consequence to him. "Yeah. I like her. We both enjoy the same kinds of game. If there's a problem—"

He must have detected Clavain's irritation. "No—no problem at all." Clavain put a hand on his shoulder. "There's more to it than just games, though, you have to admit . . ."

"She's a pretty fascinating case, Nevil."

"I don't disagree. We value her highly." He flinched, aware of how much the remark sounded like one of Galiana's typically flat statements. "But I'm puzzled. You've been revived after nearly a century asleep. We've come here by a ship that couldn't even have been considered a distant possibility in your own era. We've undergone massive social and technical upheavals in the last hundred years. There are things about us—things about me—I haven't told you yet. Things about *you* I haven't even told you yet."

"I'm just taking things one step at a time, that's all." Iverson shrugged and looked distantly past Clavain, through the window behind him. His gaze must have been skating across kilometers of ice toward Diadem's white horizon, unable to find a purchase. "I admit, I'm not really interested in technological innovations. I'm sure your ship's really nice, but . . . it's just applied physics. Just engineering. There may be some new quantum principles underlying your propulsion system, but if that's the case, it's probably just an elaborate curlicue on something that was already pretty baroque to begin with. You haven't smashed the light barrier, have you?" He read Clavain's expression accurately. "No—didn't think so. Maybe if you had . . ."

"So what exactly does interest you?"

Iverson seemed to hesitate before answering, but when he did speak Clavain had no doubt that he was telling the truth. There was a sudden, missionary fervor in his voice. "Emergence. Specifically, the emergence of complex, almost unpredictable, patterns from systems governed by a few, simple laws. Consciousness is an excellent example. A human mind's really just a web of simple neuronal cells wired together in a particular way. The laws governing the functioning of those individual cells aren't all that difficult to grasp—a cascade of well-studied electrical, chemical and enzymic processes. The tricky part is the wiring diagram. It certainly isn't encoded in DNA in any but the crudest sense. Otherwise why would a baby bother growing neural connections that are pruned down before birth? That'd be a real waste—if you had a perfect blueprint for the conscious mind, you'd only bother forming the connections you needed. No; the mind organizes itself during growth, and that's why it needs so many more neurones than it'll eventually incorporate into functioning networks. It needs the raw material to work with, as it gropes its way toward a functioning consciousness. The pattern emerges, bootstrapping itself into existence, and the pathways that aren't used—or aren't as efficient as others—are discarded." Iverson paused. "But how this organization happens really isn't understood in any depth. Do you know how many neurones it takes to control the first part of a lobster's gut, Nevil? Have a guess, to the nearest hundred."

Clavain shrugged. "I don't know. Five hundred? A thousand?"

"No. Six. Not six hundred, just six. Six damned neurones. You can't get much simpler than that. But it took decades to understand how those six worked together, let alone how that particular network evolved. The problems aren't inseparable, either. You can't really hope to understand how ten billion neurones organize themselves into a functioning whole unless you understand how the whole actually functions. Oh, we've made some progress—we can tell you exactly which spinal neurones fire to make a lamprey swim, and how that firing pattern maps into muscle motion—but we're a long way from understanding how something as elusive as the concept of 'I' emerges in the developing human mind. Well, at least we were before I went under. You may be about to tell me you've achieved stunning progress in the last century, but something tells me you were too busy with social upheaval for that."

Clavain felt an urge to argue—angered by the man's tone—but suppressed it, willing himself into a state of serene acceptance. "You're probably right. We've made progress in the other direction—augmenting the mind as it is—but if we genuinely understood brain development, we wouldn't have ended up with a failure like Felka."

"Oh, I wouldn't call her a failure, Nevil."

"I didn't mean it like that."

"Of course not." Now it was Iverson's turn to place a hand on Clavain's shoulder. "But you must see now why I find Felka so fascinating. Her mind is damaged—you told me that yourself, and there's no need to go into the details—but despite that damage, despite the vast abysses in her head, she's beginning to self-assemble the kinds of higher-level neural routines we all take for granted. It's as if the patterns were always there as latent potentials, and it's only now that they're beginning to emerge. Isn't that fascinating? Isn't it something worthy of study?"

Delicately, Clavain removed the man's hand from his

shoulder. "I suppose so. I had hoped, however, that there might be something more to it than study."

"I've offended you, and I apologize. My choice of phrase was poor. Of course I care for her."

Clavain felt suddenly awkward, as if he had misjudged a fundamentally decent man. "I understand. Look, ignore what I said."

"Yeah, of course. It—um—will be all right for me to see her again, won't it?"

Clavain nodded. "I'm sure she'd miss you if you weren't around."

Over the next few days Clavain left the two of them to their games, only rarely eavesdropping to see how things were going on. Iverson had asked permission to show Felka around some of the other areas of the base, and after some initial misgivings Clavain and Galiana had both agreed to his request. After that, long hours went by when the two of them were not to be found. Clavain had tracked them once, watching as Iverson led the girl into a disused lab and showed her intricate molecular models. They clearly delighted her; vast fuzzy holographic assemblages of atoms and chemical bonds which floated in the air like Chinese dragons. Wearing cumbersome gloves and goggles, Iverson and Felka were able to manipulate the mega-molecules; forcing them to fold into minimum-energy configurations which brute-force computation would have struggled to predict. As they gestured into the air and made the dragons contort and twist, Clavain watched for the inevitable moment when Felka would grow bored and demand something harder. But it never came. Afterward—when she had returned to the fold, her face shining with wonder—it was as if Felka had undergone a spiritual experience. Iverson had shown her something which her mind could not instantly encompass; a problem too large and subtle to be stormed in a flash of intuitive insight.

Seeing that, Clavain again felt guilty about the way he had spoken to Iverson, and knew that he had not completely put aside his doubts about the message Setterholm had left in the ice. But—the riddle of the helmet aside—there was no reason to think that Iverson might be a murderer beyond those haphazard marks. Clavain had looked into Iverson's personnel records from the time before he was frozen, and the man's history was flawless. He had been a solid, professional member of the expedition, well-liked and trusted by the others. Granted, the records were patchy, and since they were stored digitally they could have been doctored to almost any extent. But then much the same story was told by the handwritten diary and verbal log entries of some of the other victims. Andrew Iverson's name came up again and again as a man regarded with affection by his fellows; most certainly not someone capable of murder. Best, then, to discard the evidence of the marks and give him the benefit of the doubt.

Clavain spoke of his fears to Galiana, and while she listened to him, she only came back with exactly the same rational counter-arguments that he had already provided for himself.

"The problem is," Galiana said, "that the man you found in the crevasse could have been severely confused; perhaps even hallucinatory. That message he left—if it was a message, and not a set of random gouge marks he left while convulsing—could mean anything at all."

"We don't know that Setterholm was confused," Clavain protested.

"We don't? Then why didn't he make sure his helmet was on properly? It can't have been latched fully, or it wouldn't have rolled off him when he hit the bottom of the crevasse."

"Yes," Clavain said. "But I'm reasonably sure he wouldn't have been able to leave the base if his helmet hadn't been latched."

"In which case he must have undone it afterward."

"Yes, but there's no reason for him to have done that, unless . . ."

Galiana gave him a thin-lipped smile. "Unless he was confused. Back to square one, Nevil."

"No," he said, conscious that he could almost see the

shape of something; something that was close to the truth if not the truth itself. "There's another possibility, one I hadn't thought of until now."

Galiana squinted at him, that rare frown appearing. "Which is?"

"That someone else removed his helmet for him."

They went down into the bowels of the base. In the dead space of the equipment bays Galiana became ill at ease. She was not used to being out of communicational range of her colleagues. Normally systems buried in the environment picked up neural signals from individuals, amplifying and rebroadcasting them to other people, but there were no such systems here. Clavain could hear Galiana's thoughts, but they came in weakly, like a voice from the sea almost drowned by the roar of surf.

"This had better be worth it," Galiana said.

"I want to show you the airlock," Clavain answered. "I'm sure Setterholm must have left here with his helmet properly attached."

"You still think he was murdered?"

"I think it's a remote possibility that we should be very careful not to discount."

"But why would anyone kill a man whose only interest was a lot of harmless ice worms?"

"That's been bothering me as well."

"And?"

"I think I have an answer. Half of one, anyway. What if his interest in the worms brought him into conflict with the others? I'm thinking about the reactor."

Galiana nodded. "They'd have needed to harvest ice for it."

"Which Setterholm might have seen as interfering with the worms' ecology. Maybe he made a nuisance of himself and someone decided to get rid of him."

"That would be a pretty extreme way of dealing with him."

"I know," Clavain said, stepping through a connecting door into the transport bay. "I said I had half an answer, not all of one."

As soon as he was through he knew something was amiss. The bay was not as it had been before, when he had come down here scouting for clues. He dropped his train of thought immediately, focusing only on the now.

The room was much, much colder than it should have been. And lighter. There was an oblong of chill blue daylight spilling across the floor, from the huge open door of one of the vehicle exit ramps. Clavain looked at it in mute disbelief, wanting it to be a temporary glitch in his vision. But Galiana was with him, and she had seen it too.

"Someone's left the base," she said.

Clavain looked out across the ice. He could see the wake which the vehicle had left in the snow, arcing out toward the horizon. For a long moment they stood at the top of the ramp, frozen into inaction. Clavain's mind screamed with the implications. He had never really liked the idea of Iverson taking Felka away with him elsewhere in the base, but he had never considered the possibility that he might take her into one of the blind zones. From here, Iverson must have known enough little tricks to open a surface door, start a rover and leave, without any of the Conjoiners realizing.

"Nevil, listen to me," Galiana said. "He doesn't necessarily mean her any harm. He might just want to show her something."

He turned to her. "There isn't time to arrange a shuttle. That trick you did a few days ago—talking to the door? Do you think you can manage it again?"

"I don't need to. The door's already open."

Clavain nodded at one of the other rovers, hulking behind them. "It's not the door I'm thinking about."

Galiana was disappointed; it took her three minutes to convince the machine to start, rather than the few dozen seconds she said it should have taken. She was, she told Clavain, in serious danger of getting rusty at this sort of thing. Clavain just thanked the gods that there had been no mechanical sabotage to the rover; no amount of neural intervention could have fixed that.

"That's another thing that makes it look like this is just an innocent trip outside," Galiana said. "If he'd really wanted to abduct her, it wouldn't have taken much additional effort to stop us following him. If he'd closed the door, as well, we might not even have noticed he was gone."

"Haven't you ever heard of reverse psychology?" Clavain said.

"I still can't see Iverson as a murderer, Nevil." She checked his expression, her own face calm despite her driving the machine. Her hands were folded in her lap. She was less isolated now, having used the rover's comm systems to establish a link back to the other Conjoiners. "Setterholm, maybe. The obsessive loner and all that. Just a shame he's the dead one."

"Yes," Clavain said, uneasily.

The rover itself ran on six wheels; a squat, pressurized hull perched low between absurd-looking balloon tires. Galiana gunned them hard down the ramp and across the ice, trusting the machine to glide harmlessly over the smaller crevasses. It seemed reckless, but if they followed the trail that Iverson had left, they were almost guaranteed not to hit any fatal obstacles.

"Did you get anywhere with the source of the sickness?" Clavain asked.

"No breakthroughs yet . . ."

"Then here's a suggestion. Can you read my visual memory accurately?" Clavain did not need an answer. "While you were finding Iverson's body, I was looking over the lab samples. There were a lot of terrestrial organisms there. Could one of those have been responsible?"

"You'd better replay the memory."

Clavain did; picturing himself looking over the rows of culture dishes, test-tubes and gel-slides; concentrating especially on those that had come from Earth rather than the locally obtained samples. In his mind's eye the sample names refused to snap into clarity, but the machines which Galiana had seeded through his mind would already be locating the eidetically stored short-term memories and retrieving them with a clarity beyond the capabilities of Clavain's own brain.

"Now see if there's anything there which might do the job."

"A terrestrial organism?" Galiana sounded surprised. "Well, there might be something there, but I can't see how it could have spread beyond the laboratory unless someone wanted it to."

"I think that's exactly what happened."

"Sabotage?"

"Yes."

"Well, we'll know sooner or later. I've passed the information to the others. They'll get back to me if they find a candidate. But I still don't see why anyone would sabotage the entire base, even if it was possible. Overthrowing the von Neumann machines is one thing . . . mass suicide is another."

"I don't think it was mass suicide. Mass murder, maybe."

"And Iverson's your main suspect?"

"He survived, didn't he? And Setterholm scrawled a message in the ice just before he died. It must have been a warning about him." But even as he spoke, he knew there was a second possibility; one that he could not quite focus on.

Galiana swerved the rover to avoid a particularly deep and yawning chasm, shaded with vivid veins of turquoise blue.

"There's a small matter of missing motive."

Clavain looked ahead, wondering if the thing he saw glinting in the distance was a trick of the eye. "I'm working on that," he said.

Galiana halted them next to the other rover. The two machines were parked at the lip of a slope-sided depression in the ice. It was not really steep enough to call a crevasse, although it was at least thirty or forty meters deep. From the rover's cab it was not possible to see all the way into the powdery-blue depths, although Clavain could certainly see the fresh footprints which descended into them. Up on the surface marks like that would have been scoured away by the wind in days or hours, so these prints were very fresh. There were, he observed, two sets—someone heavy and confident and someone lighter, less sure of her footing.

Before they had taken the rover they had made sure there were two suits aboard it. They struggled into them, fiddling with the latches.

"If I'm right," Clavain said, "this kind of precaution isn't really necessary. Not for avoiding the sickness, anyway. But better safe than sorry."

"Excellent timing," Galiana said, snapping down her helmet and giving it a quarter twist to lock into place. "They've just pulled something from your memory, Nevil. There's a family of single-celled organisms called dinoflagellates, one of which was present in the lab where we found Iverson. Something called *pfiesteria piscicida*. Normally it's an ambush predator that attacks fish."

"Could it have been responsible for the madness?"

"It's at least a strong contender. It has a taste for mammalian tissue as well. If it gets into the human nervous system it produces memory loss, disorientation—as well as a host of physical effects. It could have been dispersed as a toxic aerosol; released into the base's air-system. Someone with access to the lab's facilities could have turned it from something merely nasty to something deadly, I think."

"We should have pinpointed it, Galiana. Didn't we swab the air ducts?"

"Yes, but we weren't looking for something terrestrial. In fact we were excluding terrestrial organisms; only filtering for the basic biochemical building blocks of Diadem life. We just weren't thinking in criminal terms."

"More fool us," Clavain said.

Suited now, they stepped outside. Clavain began to regret his haste in leaving the base so quickly; at having to make do with these old suits and lacking any means of defense. Wanting something in his hand for moral support, he examined the equipment stowed around the outside of the rover until he found an ice-pick. It would not be much of a weapon, but he felt better for it.

"You won't need that," Galiana said.

"What if Iverson turns nasty?"

"You still won't need it."

But he kept it anyway—an ice-pick was an ice-pick, after

all—and the two of them walked to the point where the icy ground began to curve over. Clavain examined the wrist of his suit, studying the cryptic and old-fashioned matrix of keypads which controlled the suit's functions. On a whim he pressed something promising and was gratified when he felt crampons spike from the soles of his boots, anchoring him to the ice.

"Iverson!" he shouted. "Felka!"

But sound carried poorly beyond his helmet, and the ceaseless, whipping wind would have snatched his words away from the crevasse. There was nothing for it but to make the difficult trek into the blue depths. He led the way, his heart pounding in his chest, the old suit awkward and top-heavy. He almost lost his footing once or twice, and had to stop to catch his breath once he reached the level bottom of the depression, sweat running into his eyes.

He looked around. The footprints led horizontally for ten or fifteen meters, weaving between fragile, curtainlike formations of opal ice. On some clinical level he acknowledged that the place had a sinister charm—he imagined the wind breathing through those curtains of ice, making ethereal music—but the need to find Felka eclipsed such considerations. He focused only on the low, dark blue hole of a tunnel in the ice ahead of them. The footprints vanished into the tunnel.

"If the bastard's taken her . . ." Clavain said, tightening his grip on the pick. He switched on his helmet light and stooped into the tunnel, Galiana behind him. It was hard going; the tunnel wriggled, rose and descended for many tens of meters, and Clavain was unable to decide whether it was some weird natural feature—carved, perhaps, by a hot subglacial river—or whether it had been dug by hand, much more recently. The walls were veined by worm tracks; a marbling like an immense magnification of the human retina. Here and there Clavain saw the dark smudges of worms moving through cracks that were very close to the surface, though he knew it was necessary to stare at them for long seconds before any movement was discernible. He groaned, the stooping becoming painful, and then the tunnel widened out dramatically. He realized that he had emerged in a much larger space.

It was still underground, although the ceiling glowed with the blue translucence of filtered daylight. The covering of ice could not have been more than a meter or two thick; a thin shell stretched like a dome over tens of meters of yawing nothing. Nearly sheer walls of delicately patterned ice rose up from a level, footprint-dappled floor.

"Ah," said Iverson, who was standing near one wall of the chamber. "You decided to join us."

Clavain felt a stab of relief, seeing that Felka was standing not far from him, next to a piece of equipment Clavain failed to recognize. Felka seemed unharmed. She turned toward him, the peculiar play of light and shade on her helmeted face making her seem older than she was.

"Nevil," he heard Felka say. "Hello."

He crossed the ice, fearful that the whole marvelous edifice was about to come crashing down on them all.

"Why did you bring her here, Iverson?"

"There's something I wanted to show her. Something I knew she'd like, even more than the other things." He turned to the smaller figure near him. "Isn't that right, Felka?"

"Yes."

"And do you like it?"

Her answer was matter of fact, but it was closer to conversation than anything Clavain had ever heard from her lips.

"Yes. I do like it."

Galiana stepped ahead of him and extended a hand to the girl. "Felka? I'm glad you like this place. I like it too. But now it's time to come back home."

Clavain steeled himself for an argument; some kind of showdown between the two women, but to his immense relief Felka walked casually toward Galiana.

"I'll take her back to the rover," Galiana said. "I want to make sure she hasn't had any problems breathing with that old suit on."

A transparent lie, but it would suffice.

Then she spoke to Clavain. It was a tiny thing, almost inconsequential, but she placed it directly in his head.

And he understood what he would have to do.

* * *

When they were alone, Clavain said: "You killed him."

"Setterholm?"

"No. You couldn't have killed Setterholm because you *are* Setterholm." Clavain looked up, the arc of his helmet light tracing the filamentary patterning until it became too tiny to resolve; blurring into an indistinct haze of detail that curved over into the ceiling itself. It was like admiring a staggeringly ornate fresco.

"Nevil—do me a favor? Check the settings on your suit, in case you're not getting enough oxygen?"

"There's nothing wrong with my suit." Clavain smiled, the irony of it all delicious. "In fact, it was the suit which really tipped me off. When you pushed Iverson into the crevasse, his helmet came off. That couldn't have happened unless it wasn't fixed on properly in the first place—and *that* couldn't have happened unless someone had removed it after the two of you left the base."

Setterholm—he was sure the man was Setterholm— snorted derisively, but Clavain continued speaking.

"Here's my stab at what happened, for what it's worth. You needed to swap identities with Iverson because Iverson had no obvious motive for murdering the others, whereas Setterholm certainly did."

"And I don't suppose you have any idea what that motive might have been?"

"Give me time; I'll get there eventually. Let's just deal with the lone murder first. Changing the electronic records was easy enough—you could even swap Iverson's picture and medical data for your own—but that was only part of it. You also needed to get Iverson into your clothes and suit, so that we'd assume the body in the crevasse belonged to you, Setterholm. I don't know exactly how you did it."

"Then perhaps . . ."

Clavain carried on. "But my guess is you let him catch a dose of the bug you let loose in the main base—*pfiesteria*, wasn't it?—then followed him while he went walking outside. You jumped him, knocked him down on the ice and got him out of the suit and into yours. He was probably unconscious by then, I suppose. But then he must have started coming round, or you panicked for another reason. You jammed the helmet on and pushed him into the crevasse. Maybe if all that had happened was his helmet coming off, I wouldn't have dwelled on it. But he wasn't dead, and he lived long enough to scratch a message in the ice. I thought it concerned his murderer, but I was wrong. He was trying to tell me who he was. Not Setterholm, but Iverson."

"Nice theory." Setterholm glanced down at a display screen in the back of the machine which squatted next to him. Mounted on a tripod, it resembled a huge pair of binoculars, pointed with a slight elevation toward one wall of the chamber.

"Sometimes, a theory's all you need. That's quite a toy you've got there, by the way. What is it, some kind of ground-penetrating radar?"

Setterholm brushed aside the question. "If I was him—why would I have done it? Just because I was interested in the ice-worms?"

"It's simple," Clavain said, hoping the uncertainty he felt was not apparent in his voice. "The others weren't as convinced as you were of the worms' significance. Only you saw them for what they were." He was treading carefully here; masking his ignorance of Setterholm's deeper motives by playing on the man's vanity.

"Clever of me if I did."

"Oh, yes. I wouldn't doubt that at all. And it must have driven you to distraction, that you could see what the others couldn't. Naturally, you wanted to protect the worms, when you saw them under threat."

"Sorry, Nevil, but you're going to have to try a lot harder than that." He paused and patted the machine's matt-silver casing, clearly unable to pretend that he did not know what it was. "It's radar, yes. It can probe the interior of the glacier with sub-centimeter resolution, to a depth of several tens of meters."

"Which would be rather useful if you wanted to study the worms."

Setterholm shrugged. "I suppose so. A climatologist interested in glacial flow might also have use for the information."

"Like Iverson?" Clavain took a step closer to Setterholm and the radar equipment. He could see the display more clearly now: a fibrous tangle of mainly green lines slowly spinning in space, with a denser structure traced out in red near its heart. "Like the man you killed?"

"I told you, I'm Iverson."

Clavain stepped toward him with the ice-pick held double-handed, but when he was a few meters from the man he veered past and made his way to the wall. Setterholm had flinched, but he had not seemed unduly worried that Clavain was about to try and hurt him.

"I'll be frank with you," Clavain said, raising the pick. "I don't really understand what it is about the worms."

"What are you going to do?"

"This."

Clavain smashed the pick against the wall as hard as he was able. It was enough: a layer of ice fractured noisily away, sliding down like a miniature avalanche to land in pieces at his feet; each fist-sized shard veined with worm trails.

"Stop," Setterholm said.

"Why? What do you care, if you're not interested in the worms?"

Clavain smashed the ice again, dislodging another layer.

"You . . ." Setterholm paused. "You could bring the whole place down on us if you're not careful."

Clavain raised the pick again, letting out a groan of effort as he swung. This time he put all his weight behind the swing; all his fury, and a chunk the size of his upper body calved noisily from the wall.

"I'll take that risk," Clavain said.

"No. You've got to stop."

"Why? It's only ice."

"No!"

Setterholm rushed him, knocking him to his feet. The ice-pick spun from his hand and the two of them crashed into the ground, Setterholm landing on his chest. He pressed his faceplate close to Clavain's, every bead of sweat on his forehead gleaming like a precise little jewel.

"I told you to stop."

Clavain found it hard to speak with the pressure on his chest, but forced out the words with effort. "I think we can dispense with the charade that you're Iverson now, can't we?"

"You shouldn't have harmed it."

"No . . . and neither should the others, eh? But they needed that ice very badly."

Now Setterholm's voice held a tone of dull resignation. "The reactor, you mean?"

"Yes. The fusion plant." Clavain allowed himself to feel some small satisfaction, before adding: "Actually, it was Galiana who made the connection, not me. That the reactor ran on ice, I mean. And after all the outlying bases had been evacuated, they had to keep everyone alive back at the main one. And that meant more load on the reactor. Which meant it needed more ice, of which there was hardly a shortage in the immediate vicinity."

"But they couldn't be allowed to harvest the ice. Not after what I'd discovered."

Clavain nodded, observing that the reversion from Iverson to Setterholm was now complete.

"No. The ice was precious, wasn't it. Infinitely more so than anyone else realized. Without that ice the worms would have died . . ."

"You don't understand either, do you?"

Clavain swallowed. "I think I understand more than the others, Setterholm. You realized that the worms—"

"It wasn't the damned worms!" He had shouted—Setterholm had turned on a loudspeaker function in his suit which Clavain had not located yet—and for a moment the words crashed around the great ice chamber, threatening to start the tiny chain reaction of fractures which would collapse the whole. But when silence had returned—disturbed only by the rasp of Clavain's breathing—nothing had changed.

"It wasn't the worms?"

"No." Setterholm was calmer now, as if the point had been made. "No—not really. They were important, yes—but as low-level elements in a much more complex system. Don't you understand?"

Clavain strove for honesty. "I never really understood what it was that fascinated you about them. They seemed quite simple to me."

Setterholm removed his weight from Clavain and rose up onto his feet again. "That's because they are. A child could grasp the biology of a single ice worm in an afternoon. Felka did, in fact. Oh, she's wonderful, Nevil." Setterholm's teeth flashed a smile that chilled Clavain. "The things she could unravel . . . she isn't a failure; not at all. I think she's something miraculous we barely comprehend."

"Unlike the worms."

"Yes. They're like clockwork toys; programmed with a few simple rules." Setterholm stooped down and grabbed the ice-pick for himself. "They always respond in exactly the same way to the same input stimulus. And the kinds of stimuli they respond to are simple in the extreme: a few gradations of temperature; a few biochemical cues picked up from the ice itself. But the emergent properties . . ."

Clavain forced himself to a sitting position. "There's that word again."

"It's the network, Nevil. The system of tunnels the worms dig through the ice. Don't you understand? That's where the real complexity lies. That's what I was always more interested in. Of course, it took me years to see it for what it was . . ."

"Which was?"

"A self-evolving network. One that has the capacity to adapt; to learn."

"It's just a series of channels bored through ice, Setterholm."

"No. It's infinitely more than that." The man craned his neck as far as the architecture of his suit would allow, reveling in the palatial beauty of the chamber. "There are two essential elements in any neural network, Nevil. Connections and nodes are necessary, but not enough. The connections must be capable of being weighted; adjusted in strength according to usefulness. And the nodes must be capable of processing the inputs from the connections in a deterministic manner, like logic gates." He gestured around the chamber. "Here, there is no absolutely sharp distinction between the connections and the nodes, but the essences remain. The worms lay down secretions when they travel, and those secretions determine how other worms make use of the same channels; whether they utilize one route or another. There are many determining factors—the sexes of the worms, the seasons; others I won't bore you with. But the point is simple. The secretions—and the effect they have on the worms—mean that the topology of the network is governed by subtle emergent principles. And the breeding tangles function as logic gates; processing the inputs from their connecting nodes according to the rules of worm sex, caste and hierarchy. It's messy, slow and biological—but the end result is that the worm colony as a whole functions as a neural network. It's a program that the worms themselves are running, even though any given worm hasn't a clue that it's a part of a larger whole."

Clavain absorbed all that and thought carefully before asking the question that occurred to him. "How does it change?"

"Slowly," Setterholm said. "Sometimes routes fall into disuse because the secretions inhibit other worms from using them. Gradually, the glacier seals them shut. At the same time other cracks open by chance—the glacier's own fracturing imposes a constant chaotic background on the network— or the worms bore new holes. Seen in slow-motion—our time frame—almost nothing ever seems to happen, let alone change. But imagine speeding things up, Nevil. Imagine if we could see the way the network has changed over the last century, or the last thousand years . . . imagine what we might find. A constantly evolving loom of connections; shifting and changing eternally. Now. Does that remind you of anything?"

Clavain answered in the only way that he knew would satisfy Setterholm. "A mind, I suppose. A newborn one, still forging neural connections."

"Yes. Oh, you'd doubtless like to point out that the network is isolated, so it can't be responding to stimuli beyond itself—but we can't know that for certain. A season is like a heartbeat here, Nevil! What we think of as geologically slow processes—a glacier cracking; two glaciers colliding—those events could be as forceful as caresses and sounds to a blind child." He paused and glanced at the screen in the back of the imaging radar. "That's what I wanted to find out. A century ago, I was able to study the network for a handful of decades. And I found something that astonished me. The colony moves; reshapes itself constantly, as the glacier shifts and breaks up. But no matter how radically the network changes its periphery; no matter how thoroughly the loom evolves, there are deep structures inside the network that are always preserved." Setterholm's finger traced the red mass at the heart of the green tunnel map. "In the language of network topology, the tunnel system is scale-free rather than exponential. It's the hallmark of a highly organized network with a few rather specialized processing centers—hubs, if you like. This is one. I believe its function is to cause the whole network to move away from a widening fracture in the glacier. It would take me much more than a century to know for sure, although everything I've seen here confirms what I thought originally. I mapped other structures in other colonies, too. They can be huge; spread across cubic kilometers of ice. But they always persist. Don't you see what that means? The network has begun to develop specialized areas of function. It's begun to process information, Nevil. It's begun to creep its way toward thought."

Clavain looked around him once more, trying to see the chamber in the new light that Setterholm had revealed. Think not of the worms as entities in their own right, he thought, but as electrical signals, ghosting along synaptic pathways in a neural network made of solid ice . . .

He shivered. It was the only appropriate response.

"Even if the network processes information . . . there's no reason to think it could ever become conscious."

"Why, Nevil? What's the fundamental difference between perceiving the universe via electrical signals transmitted along nerve tissue, and via fracture patterns moving through a vast block of ice?"

"I suppose you have a point."

"I had to save them, Nevil. Not just the worms, but the network they were a part of. We couldn't come all this way and just wipe out the first thinking thing we'd ever encountered in the universe, just because it didn't fit into our neat little preconceived notions of what alien thought would actually be like."

"But saving the worms meant killing everyone else."

"You think I didn't realize that? You think it didn't agonize me to do what I had to do? I'm a human being, Nevil—not a monster. I knew exactly what I was doing and I knew exactly what it would make me look like to anyone who came here afterward."

"But you still did it."

"Put yourself in my shoes. How would you have acted?"

Clavain opened his mouth, expecting an answer to spring to mind. But nothing came; not for several seconds. He was thinking about Setterholm's question, more thoroughly than he had done so far. Until then he had satisfied himself with the quiet, unquestioned assumption that he would not have acted the way Setterholm had done. But could he really be so sure? Setterholm, after all, had truly believed that the network formed a sentient whole; a thinking being. Possessing that knowledge must have made him feel divinely chosen; sanctioned to commit any act to preserve the fabulously rare thing he had found. And he had, after all, been right.

"You haven't answered me."

"That's because I thought the question warranted something more than a flippant answer, Setterholm. I like to think I wouldn't have acted the way you did, but I don't suppose I can ever be sure of that."

Clavain stood up, inspecting his suit for damage; relieved that the scuffle had not injured him.

"You'll never know."

"No. I never will. But one thing's clear enough. I've heard you talk; heard the fire in your words. You believe in your network, and yet you still couldn't make the others see it. I doubt I'd have been able to do much better, and I doubt that I'd have thought of a better way to preserve what you'd found."

"Then you'd have killed everyone, just like I did?"

The realization of it was like a hard burden someone had just placed on his shoulders. It was so much easier to feel incapable of such acts. But Clavain had been a soldier. He had killed more people than he could remember, even though those days had been a long time ago. It was really a lot less difficult to do, when you had a cause to believe in.

And Setterholm had definitely had a cause.

"Perhaps," Clavain said. "Perhaps I might have, yes."

He heard Setterholm sigh. "I'm glad. For a moment there . . ."

"For a moment what?"

"When you showed up with that pick, I thought you were planning to kill me." Setterholm hefted the pick, much as Clavain had done earlier. "You wouldn't have done that, would you? I don't deny that what I did was regrettable, but I had to do it."

"I understand."

"But what happens to me now? I can stay with you all, can't I?"

"We probably won't be staying on Diadem, I'm afraid. And I don't think you'd really want to come with us; not if you knew what we're really like."

"You can't leave me alone here, not again."

"Why not? You'll have your worms. And you can always kill yourself again and see who shows up next." Clavain turned to leave.

"No. You can't go now."

"I'll leave your rover on the surface. Maybe there are

some supplies in it. Just don't come anywhere near the base again. You won't find a welcome there."

"I'll die out here," Setterholm said.

"Start getting used to it."

He heard Setterholm's feet scuffing across the ice; a walk breaking into a run. Clavain turned around calmly, unsurprised to see Setterholm coming toward him with the pick raised high, as a weapon.

Clavain sighed.

He reached into Setterholm's skull; addressing the webs of machines which still floated in the man's head, and instructed them to execute their host in a sudden, painless orgy of neural deconstruction. It was not a trick he could have done an hour ago, but after Galiana had planted the method in his mind, it was easy as sneezing. For a moment he understood what it must feel like to be a god.

And in that same moment Setterholm dropped the ice-pick, and stumbled, falling forward onto one end of the pick's blade. It pierced his faceplate, but by then he was dead anyway.

"What I said was the truth," Clavain said. "I might have killed them as well, just like I said. I don't like to think so, but I can't say it isn't in me. No; I don't blame you for that; not at all."

With his boot he began to kick a dusting of frost over the dead man's body. It would be too much bother to remove Setterholm from this place, and the machines inside him would sterilize his body, ensuring that none of his cells ever contaminated the glacier. And, as Clavain had told himself only a few days earlier, there were worse places to die than here. Or worse places to be left for dead, anyway.

When he was done; when what remained of Setterholm was just an ice-covered mound in the middle of a cavern, Clavain addressed him for one final time.

"But that doesn't make it right, either. It was still murder, Setterholm." He kicked a final divot of ice over the corpse. "Someone had to pay for it."

Undone

JAMES PATRICK KELLY

James Patrick Kelly [www.jimkelly.net] wrote "Think Like a Dinosaur," a critique of the hard SF classic, Tom Godwin's "The Cold Equations." It was the lead story in Year's Best SF 1, *and won the Hugo Award in 1996. If there was a new synthesis in 1990s hard SF, it is at the point where Gregory Benford, Kelly, and Bruce Sterling meet. Though identified with the Sycamore Hill workshop in the 1980s, the hotbed of Humanist opposition to the cyberpunks, he was also chosen as one of the original cyberpunks by Bruce Sterling for inclusion in* Mirrorshades, the Cyberpunk Anthology. *Much of Kelly's fiction has a serious hard SF side that appeals broadly to all readers in the field. His novel,* Wildlife, *which includes his novella "Mr. Boy," appeared in 1994, and since then he has been publishing more frequent short stories. His stories are collected in* Think Like a Dinosaur and Other Stories *(1997), and the forthcoming* Strange but Not a Stranger *(2002).*

"Undone" appeared in Asimov's, *with a blurb that said Kelly claims Alfred Bester and Cordwainer Smith as influences on this piece. It's an excellent story, with a vast scale, set in the distant future, with an engaging central character, big ideas, political satire, even typographical tricks in the Bester, Ellison, and Delany tradition. SF doesn't get more fun than this story, the capstone of this* Year's Best.

The ship screamed. Its screens showed Mada that she was surrounded in threespace. A swarm of Utopian asteroids was closing on her, brain clans and mining DIs living in hollowed-out chunks of carbonaceous chondrite, any one of which could have mustered enough votes to abolish Mada in all ten dimensions.

"I'm going to die," the ship cried, "I'm going to die, I'm going to . . ."

"I'm not." Mada waved the speaker off impatiently and scanned downwhen. She saw that the Utopians had planted an identity mine five minutes into the past that would boil her memory to vapor if she tried to go back in time to undo this trap. Upwhen, then. The future was clear, at least as far as she could see, which wasn't much beyond next week. Of course, that was the direction they wanted her to skip. They'd be happiest making her their great-great-great-grandchildren's problem.

The Utopians fired another spread of panic bolts. The ship tried to absorb them, but its buffers were already overflowing. Mada felt her throat tighten. Suddenly she couldn't remember how to spell *luck*, and she believed that she could feel her sanity oozing out of her ears.

"So let's skip upwhen," she said.

"You s-sure?" said the ship. "I don't know if . . . how far?"

"Far enough so that all of these drones will be fossils."

"I can't just . . . I need a number, Mada."

A needle of fear pricked Mada hard enough to make her

reflexes kick. "Skip!" Her panic did not allow for the luxury of numbers. "Skip now!" Her voice was tight as a fist. "Do it!"

Time shivered as the ship surged into the empty dimensions. In three-space, Mada went all wavy. Eons passed in a nanosecond, then she washed back into the strong dimensions and solidified.

She merged briefly with the ship to assess damage. "What have you done?" The gain in entropy was an ache in her bones.

"I-I'm sorry, you said to skip so . . ." The ship was still jittery.

Even though she wanted to kick its sensorium in, she bit down hard on her anger. They had both made enough mistakes that day. "That's all right," she said, "we can always go back. We just have to figure out when we are. Run the star charts."

two-tenths of a spin

The ship took almost three minutes to get its charts to agree with its navigation screens—a bad sign. Reconciling the data showed that it had skipped forward in time about two-tenths of a galactic spin. Almost twenty million years had passed on Mada's home world of Trueborn, time enough for its crust to fold and buckle into new mountain ranges, for the Green Sea to bloom, for the glaciers to march and melt. More than enough time for everything and everyone Mada had ever loved—or hated—to die, turn to dust and blow away.

Whiskers trembling, she checked downwhen. What she saw made her lose her perch and float aimlessly away from the command mod's screens. There had to be something wrong with the ship's air. It settled like dead, wet leaves in her lungs. She ordered the ship to check the mix.

The ship's deck flowed into an enormous plastic hand, warm as blood. It cupped Mada gently in its palm and raised her up so that she could see its screens straight on.

"Nominal, Mada. Everything is as it should be."

That couldn't be right. She could breathe ship-nominal atmosphere. "Check it again," she said.

"Mada, I'm sorry," said the ship.

The identity mine had skipped with them and was still dogging her, five infuriating minutes into the past. There was no getting around it, no way to undo their leap into the future. She was trapped two-tenths of a spin upwhen. The knowledge was like a sucking hole in her chest, much worse than any wound the Utopian psychological war machine could have inflicted on her.

"What do we do now?" asked the ship.

Mada wondered what she should say to it. Scan for hostiles? Open a pleasure sim? Cook a nice, hot stew? Orders twisted in her mind, bit their tails and swallowed themselves.

She considered—briefly—telling it to open all the air locks to the vacuum. Would it obey this order? She thought it probably would, although she would as soon chew her own tongue off as utter such cowardly words. Had not she and her sibling batch voted to carry the revolution into all ten dimensions? Pledged themselves to fight for the Three Universal Rights, no matter what the cost the Utopian brain clans extracted from them in blood and anguish?

But that had been two-tenths of a spin ago.

bean thoughts

"Where are you going?" said the ship.

Mada floated through the door bubble of the command mod. She wrapped her toes around the perch outside to steady herself.

"Mada, wait! I need a mission, a course, some line of inquiry."

She launched down the companionway.

"I'm a Dependent Intelligence, Mada." Its speaker buzzed with self-righteousness. "I have the right to proper and timely guidance."

The ship flowed a veil across her trajectory; as she approached, it went taut. That was DI thinking: the ship was sure that it could just bounce her back into its world. Mada flicked her claws and slashed at it, shredding holes half a meter long.

"And I have the right to be an individual," she said. "Leave me alone."

She caught another perch and pivoted off it toward the greenhouse blister. She grabbed the perch by the door bubble and paused to flow new alveoli into her lungs to make up for the oxygen-depleted, carbon-dioxide-enriched air mix in the greenhouse. The bubble shivered as she popped through it and she breathed deeply. The smells of life helped ground her whenever operation of the ship overwhelmed her. It was always so needy and there was only one of her.

It would have been different if they had been designed to go out in teams. She would have had her sibling Thiras at her side; together they might have been strong enough to withstand the Utopian's panic . . . *no!* Mada shook him out of her head. Thiras was gone; they were all gone. There was no sense in looking for comfort, downwhen or up. All she had was the moment, the tick of the relentless present, filled now with the moist, bittersweet breath of the dirt, the sticky savor of running sap, the bloom of perfume on the flowers. As she drifted through the greenhouse, leaves brushed her skin like caresses. She settled at the potting bench, opened a bin and picked out a single bean seed.

Mada cupped it between her two hands and blew on it, letting her body's warmth coax the seed out of dormancy. She tried to merge her mind with its blissful unconsciousness. Cotyledons stirred and began to absorb nutrients from the endosperm. A bean cared nothing about proclaiming the Three Universal Rights: the right of all independent sentients to remain individual, the right to manipulate their physical structures and the right to access the timelines. Mada slowed her metabolism to the steady and deliberate rhythm of the bean—what Utopian could do that? They held that individuality bred chaos, that function alone must determine form and that undoing the past was sacrilege. Being

Utopians, they could hardly destroy Trueborn and its handful of colonies. Instead they had tried to put the Rights under quarantine.

Mada stimulated the sweat glands in the palms of her hands. The moisture wicking across her skin called to the embryonic root in the bean seed. The tip pushed against the seed coat. Mada's sibling batch on Trueborn had pushed hard against the Utopian blockade, to bring the Rights to the rest of the galaxy.

Only a handful had made it to open space. The brain clans had hunted them down and brought most of them back in disgrace to Trueborn. But not Mada. No, not wily Mada, Mada the fearless, Mada whose heart now beat but once a minute.

The bean embryo swelled and its root cracked the seed coat. It curled into her hand, branching and rebranching like the timelines. The roots tickled her.

Mada manipulated the chemistry of her sweat by forcing her sweat ducts to reabsorb most of the sodium and chlorine. She parted her hands slightly and raised them up to the grow lights. The cotyledons emerged and chloroplasts oriented themselves to the light. Mada was thinking only bean thoughts as her cupped hands filled with roots and the first true leaves unfolded. More leaves budded from the nodes of her stem, her petioles arched and twisted to the light, *the light*. It was only the light—violet-blue and orange-red—that mattered, the incredible shower of photons that excited her chlorophyll, passing electrons down carrier molecules to form adenosine diphosphate and nicotinamide adenine dinucleo. . . .

"Mada," said the ship. "The order to leave you alone is now superseded by primary programming."

"What?" The word caught in her throat like a bone.

"You entered the greenhouse forty days ago."

Without quite realizing what she was doing, Mada clenched her hands, crushing the young plant.

"I am directed to keep you from harm, Mada," said the ship. "It's time to eat."

She glanced down at the dead thing in her hands. "Yes, all right." She dropped it onto the potting bench. "I've got something to clean up first but I'll be there in a minute." She wiped the corner of her eye. "Meanwhile, calculate a course for home."

natural background

Not until the ship scanned the quarantine zone at the edge of the Trueborn system did Mada begin to worry. In her time the zone had swarmed with the battle asteroids of the brain clans. Now the Utopians were gone. Of course, that was to be expected after all this time. But as the ship reentered the home system, dumping excess velocity into the empty dimensions, Mada felt a chill that had nothing to do with the temperature in the command mod.

Trueborn orbited a spectral type G3V star, which had been known to the discoverers as HR3538. Scans showed that the Green Sea had become a climax forest of deciduous hardwood. There were indeed new mountains—knife edges slicing through evergreen sheets—that had upthrust some eighty kilometers off the Fire Coast, leaving Port Henoch landlocked. A rain forest choked the plain where the city of Blair's Landing had once sprawled.

The ship scanned life in abundance. The seas teemed and flocks of Trueborn's flyers darkened the skies like storm clouds: kippies and bluewings and warblers and migrating stilts. Animals had retaken all three continents, lowland and upland, marsh and tundra. Mada could see the dust kicked up by the herds of herbivorous aram from low orbit. The forest echoed with the clatter of shindies and the shriek of blowhards. Big hunters like kar and divil padded across the plains. There were new species as well, mostly invertebrates but also a number of lizards and something like a great, mossy rat that built mounds five meters tall.

None of the introduced species had survived: dogs or turkeys or llamas. The ship could find no cities, towns, buildings—not even ruins. There were neither tubeways nor roads, only the occasional animal track. The ship looked across the entire electromagnetic spectrum and saw nothing but the natural background.

There was nobody home on Trueborn. And as far as they could tell, there never had been.

"Speculate," said Mada.

"I can't," said the ship. "There isn't enough data."

"There's your data." Mada could hear the anger in her voice. "Trueborn, as it would have been had we never even existed."

"Two-tenths of a spin is a long time, Mada."

She shook her head. "They ripped out the foundations, even picked up the dumps. There's nothing, *nothing* of us left." Mada was gripping the command perch so hard that the knuckles of her toes were white. "Hypothesis," she said, "the Utopians got tired of our troublemaking and wiped us out. Speculate."

"Possible, but that's contrary to their core beliefs." Most DIs had terrible imaginations. They couldn't tell jokes, but then they couldn't commit crimes, either.

"Hypothesis: they deported the entire population, scattered us to prison colonies. Speculate."

"Possible, but a logistical nightmare. The Utopians prize the elegant solution."

She swiped the image of her home planet off the screen, as if to erase its unnerving impossibility. "Hypothesis: there are no Utopians anymore because the revolution succeeded. Speculate."

"Possible, but then where did everyone go? And why did they return the planet to its pristine state?"

She snorted in disgust. "What if," she tapped a finger to her forehead, "maybe we *don't* exist. What if we've skipped to another timeline? One in which the discovery of Trueborn never happened? Maybe there has been no Utopian Empire in this timeline, no Great Expansion, no Space Age, maybe no human civilization at all."

"One does not just skip to another timeline at random." The ship sounded huffy at the suggestion. "I've monitored all our dimensional reinsertions quite carefully, and I can assure you that all these events occurred in the timeline we currently occupy."

"You're saying there's no chance?"

"If you want to write a story, why bother asking my opinion?"

Mada's laugh was brittle. "All right then. We need more data." For the first time since she had been stranded upwhen, she felt a tickle stir the dead weight she was carrying inside her. "Let's start with the nearest Utopian system."

chasing shadows

The HR683 system was abandoned and all signs of human habitation had been obliterated. Mada could not be certain that everything had been restored to its pre-Expansion state because the ship's database on Utopian resources was spotty. HR4523 was similarly deserted. HR509, also known as Tau Ceti, was only 11.9 light years from earth and had been the first outpost of the Great Expansion.

Its planetary system was also devoid of intelligent life and human artifacts—with one striking exception.

Nuevo LA was spread along the shores of the Sterling Sea like a half-eaten picnic lunch. Something had bitten the roofs off its buildings and chewed its walls. Metal skeletons rotted on its docks, transports were melting into brown and gold stains. Once-proud boulevards crumbled in the orange light; the only traffic was windblown litter chasing shadows.

Mada was happy to survey the ruin from low orbit. A closer inspection would have spooked her. "Was it war?"

"There may have been a war," said the ship, "but that's not what caused this. I think it's deliberate deconstruction." In extreme magnification, the screen showed a concrete wall pockmarked with tiny holes, from which dust puffed intermittently. "The composition of that dust is limestone, sand, and aluminum silicate. The buildings are crawling with nanobots and they're eating the concrete."

"How long has this been going on?"

"At a guess, a hundred years, but that could be off by an order of magnitude."

"Who did this?" said Mada. "Why? Speculate."

"If this is the outcome of a war, then it would seem that

the victors wanted to obliterate all traces of the vanquished. But it doesn't seem to have been fought over resources. I suppose we could imagine some deep ideological antagonism between the two sides that led to this, but such an extreme of cultural psychopathology seems unlikely."

"I hope you're right." She shivered. "So they did it themselves, then? Maybe they were done with this place and wanted to leave it as they found it?"

"Possible," said the ship.

Mada decided that she was done with Nuevo LA, too. She would have been perversely comforted to have found her enemies in power somewhere. It would have given her an easy way to calculate her duty. However, Mada was quite certain that what this mystery meant was that twenty thousand millennia had conquered both the revolution *and* the Utopians and that she and her sibling batch had been designed in vain.

Still, she had nothing better to do with eternity than to try to find out what had become of her species.

a never-ending vacation

The Atlantic Ocean was now larger than the Pacific. The Mediterranean Sea had been squeezed out of existence by the collision of Africa, Europe and Asia. North America floated free of South America and was nudging Siberia. Australia was drifting toward the equator.

The population of earth was about what it had been in the fifteenth century CE, according to the ship. Half a billion people lived on the home world and, as far as Mada could see, none of them had anything important to do. The means of production and distribution, of energy-generation and waste disposal were in the control of Dependent Intelligences like the ship. Despite repeated scans, the ship could detect no sign that any independent sentience was overseeing the system.

There were but a handful of cities, none larger than a quarter of a million inhabitants. All were scrubbed clean and kept scrupulously ordered by the DIs; they reminded Mada of databases populated with people instead of information. The majority of the population spent their bucolic lives in pretty hamlets and quaint towns overlooking lakes or oceans or mountains.

Humanity had booked a never-ending vacation.

"The brain clans could be controlling the DIs," said Mada. "That would make sense."

"Doubtful," said the ship. "Independent sentients create a signature disturbance in the sixth dimension."

"Could there be some secret dictator among the humans, a hidden oligarchy?"

"I see no evidence that anyone is in charge. Do you?"

She shook her head. "Did they choose to live in a museum," she said, "or were they condemned to it? It's obvious there's no First Right here; these people have only the *illusion* of individuality. And no Second Right either. Those bodies are as plain as uniforms—they're still slaves to their biology."

"There's no disease," said the ship. "They seem to be functionally immortal."

"That's not saying very much, is it?" Mada sniffed. "Maybe this is some scheme to start human civilization over again. Or maybe they're like seeds, stored here until someone comes along to plant them." She waved all the screens off. "I want to go down for a closer look. What do I need to pass?"

"Clothes, for one thing." The ship displayed a selection of current styles on its screen. They were extravagantly varied, from ballooning pastel tents to skin-tight sheaths of luminescent metal, to feathered camouflage to jumpsuits made of what looked like dried mud. "Fashion design is one of their principal pastimes," said the ship. "In addition, you'll probably want genitalia and the usual secondary sexual characteristics."

It took her the better part of a day to flow ovaries, fallopian tubes, a uterus, cervix, and vulva and to rearrange her vagina. All these unnecessary organs made her feel bloated. She saw breasts as a waste of tissue; she made hers as small as the ship thought acceptable. She argued with it about the several substantial patches of hair it claimed she needed. Clearly, grooming them would require constant attention. She didn't mind taming her claws into fingernails but she hated giving up her whiskers. Without them, the air was practically invisible. At first her new vulva tickled when she walked, but she got used to it.

The ship entered earth's atmosphere at night and landed in what had once been Saskatchewan, Canada. It dumped most of its mass into the empty dimensions and flowed itself into baggy black pants, a moss-colored boat neck top and a pair of brown, gripall loafers. It was able to conceal its complete sensorium in a canvas belt.

It was 9:14 in the morning on June 23, 19,834,004 CE when Mada strolled into the village of Harmonious Struggle.

the devil's apple

Harmonious Struggle consisted of five clothing shops, six restaurants, three jewelers, eight art galleries, a musical instrument maker, a crafts workshop, a weaver, a potter, a woodworking shop, two candle stores, four theaters with capacities ranging from twenty to three hundred and an enormous sporting goods store attached to a miniature domed stadium. There looked to be apartments over most of these establishments; many had views of nearby Rabbit Lake.

Three of the restaurants—Hassam's Palace of Plenty, The Devil's Apple, and Laurel's—were practically jostling each other for position on Sonnet Street, which ran down to the lake. Lounging just outside of each were waiters eyeing handheld screens. They sprang up as one when Mada happened around the corner.

"Good day, Madame. Have you eaten?"

"Well met, fair stranger. Come break bread with us."

"All natural foods, friend! Lightly cooked, humbly served."

Mada veered into the middle of the street to study the situation as the waiters called to her. *~So I can choose whichever I want?~* she subvocalized to the ship.

~In an attention-based economy,~ subbed the ship in reply, *~all they expect from you is an audience.~*

Just beyond Hassam's, the skinny waiter from The Devil's Apple had a wry, crooked smile. Black hair fell to the padded shoulders of his shirt. He was wearing boots to the knee and loose rust-colored shorts, but it was the little red cape that decided her.

As she walked past her, the waitress from Hassam's was practically shouting. "Madame, *please*, their batter is dull!" She waved her handheld at Mada. "Read the *reviews*. Who puts shrimp in *muffins*?"

The waiter at The Devil's Apple was named Owen. He showed her to one of three tables in the tiny restaurant. At his suggestion, Mada ordered the poached peaches with white cheese mousse, an asparagus breakfast torte, baked orange walnut French toast and coddled eggs. Owen served the peaches, but it was the chef and owner, Edris, who emerged from the kitchen to clear the plate.

"The mousse, Madame, you liked it?" she asked, beaming.

"It was good," said Mada.

Her smile shrank a size and a half. "Enough lemon rind, would you say that?"

"Yes. It was very nice."

Mada's reply seemed to dismay Edris even more. When she came out to clear the next course, she blanched at the corner of breakfast torte that Mada had left uneaten.

"I knew this." She snatched the plate away. "The pastry wasn't fluffy enough." She rolled the offending scrap between thumb and forefinger.

Mada raised her hands in protest. "No, no, it was delicious." She could see Owen shrinking into the far corner of the room.

"Maybe too much colby, not enough gruyere?" Edris snarled. "But you have no comment?"

"I wouldn't change a thing. It was perfect."

"Madame is kind," she said, her lips barely moving, and retreated.

A moment later Owen set the steaming plate of French toast before Mada.

"Excuse me." She tugged at his sleeve.

"Something's wrong?" He edged away from her. "You must speak to Edris."

"Everything is fine. I was just wondering if you could tell me how to get to the local library."

Edris burst out of the kitchen. "What are you doing, bean-headed boy? You are distracting my patron with absurd chitterchat. Get out, get out of my restaurant now."

"No, really, he . . ."

But Owen was already out the door and up the street, taking Mada's appetite with him.

~*You're doing something wrong*,~ the ship subbed.

Mada lowered her head. ~*I know that!*~

Mada pushed the sliver of French toast around the pool of maple syrup for several minutes but could not eat it. "Excuse me," she called, standing up abruptly. "Edris?"

Edris shouldered through the kitchen door, carrying a tray with a silver egg cup. She froze when she saw how it was with the French toast and her only patron.

"This was one of the most delicious meals I have ever eaten." Mada backed toward the door. She wanted nothing to do with eggs, coddled or otherwise.

Edris set the tray in front of Mada's empty chair. "Madame, the art of the kitchen requires the tongue of the patron," she said icily.

She fumbled for the latch. "Everything was very, very wonderful."

no comment

Mada slunk down Lyric Alley, which ran behind the stadium, trying to understand how exactly she had offended. In this attention-based economy, paying attention was obviously not enough. There had to be some other cultural protocol she and the ship were missing. What she probably ought to do was go back and explore the clothes shops, maybe pick up a pot or some candles and see what additional information she could blunder into. But making a fool of herself had never much appealed to Mada as a learning strategy. She wanted the map, a native guide—some edge, preferably secret.

~Scanning, ~ subbed the ship. ~Somebody is following you. He just ducked behind the privet hedge twelve-point-three meters to the right. It's the waiter, Owen.~

"Owen," called Mada, "is that you? I'm sorry I got you in trouble. You're an excellent waiter."

"I'm not really a waiter." Owen peeked over the top of the hedge. "I'm a poet."

She gave him her best smile. "You said you'd take me to the library." For some reason, the smile stayed on her face "Can we do that now?"

"First listen to some of my poetry."

"No," she said firmly. "Owen, I don't think you've been paying attention. I said I would like to go to the library."

"All right then, but I'm not going to have sex with you."

Mada was taken aback. "Really? Why is that?"

"I'm not attracted to women with small breasts."

For the first time in her life, Mada felt the stab of outraged hormones. "Come out here and talk to me."

There was no immediate break in the hedge, so Owen had to squiggle through. "There's something about me that you don't like," he said as he struggled with the branches.

"Is there?" She considered. "I like your cape."

"That you don't like." He escaped the hedge's grasp and brushed leaves from his shorts.

"I guess I don't like your narrow-mindedness. It's not an attractive quality in a poet."

There was a gleam in Owen's eye as he went up on his tiptoes and began to declaim:

> That spring you left I thought I might expire
> And lose the love you left for me to keep.
> To hold you once again is my desire
> Before I give myself to death's long sleep.

He illustrated his poetry with large, flailing gestures. At "death's long sleep" he brought his hands together as if to pray, laid the side of his head against them and closed his eyes. He held that pose in silence for an agonizingly long time.

"It's nice," Mada said at last. "I like the way it rhymes."

He sighed and went flat-footed. His arms drooped and he fixed her with an accusing stare. "You're not from here."

"No," she said. ~Where am I from?~ she subbed. ~Some-place he'll have to look up.~

~Marble Bar. It's in Australia~

"I'm from Marble Bar."

"No, I mean you're not one of us. You don't comment."

At that moment, Mada understood. ~I want to skip down-when four minutes. I need to undo this.~

~this undo to need I minutes four downwhen skip to want I~ understood Mada, moment that At ".comment don't You .us of one not you're mean I ,No" ".Bar Marble from I'm" ~Australia in It's .Bar Marble~ ~up look to have he'll Some-place~ .subbed she ~?from I am Where~ .said she ",No" ".here from not You're" .stare accusing an with her fixed he and drooped arms His .flatfooted went and sighed He ".rhymes it way the like I." .last at said Mada ",nice It's" .time long agonizingly an for silence in pose that held He .eyes his closed and them against head his of side the laid ,pray to if as together hands his brought he "sleep long death's" At .gestures flailing ,large with poetry his illustrated He ".sleep long death's to myself give I Before desire my is again once you hold To keep to me for left you love the lose And expire might I thought I left you spring That" :declaim to began and tiptoes his on up went he as eye Owen's in gleam a was There ".poet a in quality attractive an not It's .narrow-mindedness your like don't I guess I" .shorts his from leaves brushed and grasp hedge's the escaped He ".like don't you That" ".cape your like I'"

As the ship surged through the empty dimensions, threespace became as liquid as a dream. Leaves smeared and buildings ran together. Owen's face swirled.

"They want criticism," said Mada. "They like to think of themselves as artists but they're insecure about what they've accomplished. They want their audience to engage with what they're doing, help them make it better—the comments they both seem to expect."

"I see it now," said the ship. "But is one person in a backwater worth an undo? Let's just start over somewhere else."

.considered She "?there Is" .branches the
with struggled he as said he ",like don't you
that me about something There's" .through
squiggle to had Owen so ,hedge the in
break immediate no was There ".me to talk
and here out Come" .hormones wronged of
stab the felt Mada ,life her in time first the
For ".breasts small with women to attracted
not I'm" "?that is Why ?Really" .aback
taken was Mada ".you with sex have to going not I'm but ,then right All" ".library the
to go to like would I said I .attention paying been you've think don't I ,Owen" .firmly
said she ",No" ".poetry my of some to listen First"

"No, I have an idea." She began flowing more fat cells to her breasts. For the first time since she had skipped upwhen, Mada had a glimpse of what her duty might now be. "I'm going to need a big special effect on short notice. Be ready to reclaim mass so you can re-substantiate the hull at my command."

"First listen to some of my poetry."

"Go ahead." Mada folded her arms across her chest. "Say it then."

Owen stood on tiptoes to declaim:

"That spring you left I thought I might expire
And lose the love you left for me to keep.
To hold you once again is my desire
Before I give myself to death's long sleep."

He illustrated his poetry with large, flailing gestures. At "death's long sleep" he brought his hands together as if to pray, moved them to the side of his head, rested against them and closed his eyes. He had held the pose for just a beat before Mada interrupted him.

"Owen," she said. "You look ridiculous."

He jerked as if he had been hit in the head by a shovel.

She pointed at the ground before her: "You'll want to take these comments sitting down."

He hesitated, then settled at her feet.

"You hold your meter well, but that's purely a mechanical skill." She circled behind him. "A smart oven could do as much. Stop fidgeting!"

She hadn't noticed the ant hills near the spot she had chosen for Owen. The first scouts were beginning to explore him. That suited her plan exactly.

"Your real problem," she continued, "is that you know nothing about death and probably very little about desire."

"I know about death." Owen drew his feet close to his body and grasped his knees. "Everyone does. Flowers die, squirrels die."

"Has anyone you've ever known died?"

He frowned. "I didn't know her personally, but there was the woman who fell off that cliff in Merrymeeting."

"Owen, did you have a mother?"

"Don't make fun of me. Everyone has a mother."

Mada didn't think it was time to tell him that she didn't; that she and her sibling batch of a thousand revolutionaries had been autoflowed. "Hold out your hand." Mada scooped up an ant. "That's your mother." She crunched it and dropped it onto Owen's palm.

Owen looked down at the dead ant and up again at Mada. His eyes filled.

"I think I love you," he said. "What's your name?"

"Mada." She leaned over to straighten his cape. "But loving me would be a very bad idea."

all that's left

Mada was surprised to find a few actual books in the library, printed on real plastic. A primitive DI had catalogued the rest of the collection, billions of gigabytes of print, graphics, audio, video, and VR files. None of it told Mada what she wanted to know. The library had sims of Egypt's New Kingdom, Islam's Abbasid dynasty, and the International Moonbase—but then came an astonishing void. Mada's searches on Trueborn, the Utopians, Tau Ceti, intelligence engineering and dimensional extensibility theory turned up no results. It was only in the very recent past that history resumed. The DI could reproduce the plans that the workbots had left when they built the library twenty-two years ago, and the menu The Devil's Apple had offered the previous summer, and the complete won-lost record of the Black

Minks, the local scatterball club, which had gone 533-905 over the last century. It knew that the name of the woman who died in Merrymeeting was Agnes and that two years after her death, a replacement baby had been born to Chandra and Yuri. They named him Herrick.

Mada waved the screen blank and stretched. She could see Owen draped artfully over a nearby divan, as if posing for a portrait. He was engrossed by his handheld. She noticed that his lips moved as he read. She crossed the reading room and squeezed onto it next to him, nestling into the crook in his legs. "What's that?" she asked.

He turned the handheld toward her. "Nadeem Jerad's *Burning the Snow*. Would you like to hear one of his poems?"

"Maybe later." She leaned into him. "I was just reading about Moonbase."

"Yes, ancient history. It's sort of interesting, don't you think? The Greeks and the Renaissance and all that."

"But then I can't find any record of what came after."

"Because of the nightmares." He nodded. "Terrible things happened, so we forgot them."

"What terrible things?"

He tapped the side of his head and grinned.

"Of course," she said, "nothing terrible happens anymore."

"No. Everyone's happy now." Owen reached out and pushed a strand of her hair off her forehead. "You have beautiful hair."

Mada couldn't even remember what color it was. "But if something terrible did happen, then you'd want to forget it."

"Obviously."

"The woman who died, Agnes. No doubt her friends were very sad."

"No doubt." Now he was playing with her hair.

~Good question,~ subbed the ship. *~They must have some mechanism to wipe their memories.~*

"Is something wrong?" Owen's face was the size of the moon; Mada was afraid of what he might tell her next.

"Agnes probably had a mother," she said.

"A mom and a dad."

"It must have been terrible for them."

He shrugged. "Yes, I'm sure they forgot her."

Mada wanted to slap his hand away from her head. "But how could they?"

He gave her a puzzled look. "Where are you from, anyway?"

"Trueborn," she said without hesitation. "It's a long, long way from here."

"Don't you have libraries there?" He gestured at the screens that surrounded them. "This is where we keep what we don't want to remember."

~*Skip!*~ Mada could barely sub; if what she suspected were true . . . ~ *Skip downwhen two minutes.*~

~.minutes two downwhen skip~ . . . true were suspected she what if ;sub barely could Mada ~!Skip!~ ".remember to want don't we what keep we where is This" .them surrounded that screen the at gestured He "?there libraries have you Don't" ".here from way long ,long a It's" .hesitation without said she ",Trueborn" "?anyway, from you are Where" .look puzzled a her gave He "?they could how But" .head her from away hand his slap to wanted Mada ".her forgot I'm, Yes" .shrugged He ".them for terrible been have must It" ".dad a and mom A" ".mother a had probably Agnes" .next her tell might he what of afraid was Mada .moon the of size of the was face Owen's "?wrong something Is" ~.*memories their wipe to mechanism some have must They*".ship the subbed ~.*question Good*~ .hair her with playing was he Now ".doubt No" ".sad very were friends her doubt no ,Agnes ,died who woman The" ".Obviously" ".it forget to want you'd then ,happen did terrible something if But" .was it color what remember even couldn't even Mada

She wrapped her arms around herself to keep the empty dimensions from reaching for the emptiness inside her. Was something wrong?

Of course there was, but she didn't expect to say it out loud. "I've lost everything and all that's left is *this*."

Owen shimmered next to her like the surface of Rabbit Lake.

"Mada, what?" said the ship.

"Forget it," she said. She thought she could hear something cracking when she laughed.

Mada couldn't even remember what color her hair was. "But if something terrible did happen, then you'd want to forget it."

"Obviously."

"Something terrible happened to me."

"I'm sorry." Owen squeezed her shoulder. "Do you want me to show you how to use the headbands?" He pointed at a rack of metal-mesh strips.

~Scanning,~ subbed the ship. *"Microcurrent taps capable of modulating post-synaptic outputs. I thought they were some kind of virtual reality 1/0."*

"No." Mada twisted away from him and shot off the divan. She was outraged that these people would deliberately burn memories. How many stubbed toes and unhappy love affairs had Owen forgotten? If she could have, she would have skipped the entire village of Harmonious Struggle downwhen into the identity mine. When he rose up after her, she grabbed his hand. "I have to get out of here *right now.*"

She dragged him out of the library into the innocent light of the sun.

"Wait a minute," he said. She continued to tow him up Ode Street and out of town. "Wait!" He planted his feet, tugged at her and she spun back to him. "Why are you so upset?"

"I'm not upset." Mada's blood was hammering in her temples and she could feel the prickle of sweat under her arms. *~Now I need you,~* she subbed. "All right then. It's time you knew." She took a deep breath. "We were just talking about ancient history, Owen. Do you remember back then that the gods used to intervene in the affairs of humanity?"

Owen goggled at her as if she were growing beans out of her ears.

"I am a goddess, Owen, and I have come for you. I am calling you to your destiny. I intend to inspire you to great poetry."

His mouth opened and then closed again.

"My worshippers call me by many names." She raised a hand to the sky. *~Help?~*

~Try Athene? Here's a databurst.~

"To the Greeks, I was Athene," Mada continued, "the goddess of cities, of technology and the arts, of wisdom and of war." She stretched a hand toward Owen's astonished face, forefinger aimed between his eyes. "Unlike you, I had no mother. I sprang full-grown from the forehead of my maker. I am Athene, the virgin goddess."

"How stupid do you think I am?" He shivered and glanced away from her fierce gaze. "I used to live in Maple City, Mada. I'm not some simple-minded country lump. You don't seriously expect me to believe this goddess nonsense?"

She slumped, confused. Of course she had expected him to believe her. "I meant no disrespect, Owen. It's just that the truth is . . ." This wasn't as easy as she had thought. "What I expect is that you believe in your own potential, Owen. What I expect is that you are brave enough to leave this place and come with me. To the stars, Owen, to the stars to start a new world." She crossed her arms in front of her chest, grasped the hem of her moss-colored top, pulled it over her head and tossed it behind her. Before it hit the ground the ship augmented it with enough reclaimed mass from the empty dimensions to resubstantiate the command and living mods.

Mada was quite pleased with the way Owen tried—and failed—not to stare at her breasts. She kicked the gripall loafers off and the deck rose up beneath them. She stepped out of the baggy, black pants; when she tossed them at Owen, he flinched. Seconds later, they were eyeing each other in the metallic light of the ship's main companionway.

"Well?" said Mada.

duty

Mada had difficulty accepting Trueborn as it now was. She could see the ghosts of great cities, hear the murmur of dead friends. She decided to live in the forest that had once been the Green Sea, where there were no landmarks to remind her of what she had lost. She ordered the ship to begin constructing an infrastructure similar to that they had found on earth, only capable of supporting a technologically advanced population. Borrowing orphan mass from the empty dimensions, it was soon consumed with this monumental task. She missed its company; only rarely did she use the link it had left her—a silver ring with a direct connection to its sensorium.

The ship's first effort was the farm that Owen called Athens. It consisted of their house, a flow works, a gravel pit and a barn. Dirt roads led to various mines and domed fields that the ship's bots tended. Mada had it build a separate library, a little way into the woods, where, she declared, information was to be acquired only, never destroyed. Owen spent many evenings there. He said he was trying to make himself worthy of her.

He had been deeply flattered when she told him that, as part of his training as a poet, he was to name the birds and beasts and flowers and trees of Trueborn.

"But they must already have names," he said, as they walked back to the house from the newly tilled soya field.

"The people who named them are gone," she said. "The names went with them."

"Your people." He waited for her to speak. The wind sighed through the forest. "What happened to them?"

"I don't know." At that moment, she regretted ever bringing him to Trueborn.

He sighed. "It must be hard."

"You left *your* people," she said. She spoke to wound him, since he was wounding her with these rude questions.

"For you, Mada." He let go of her. "I know you didn't leave them for *me*." He picked up a pebble and held it in front of his face. "You are now Mada-stone," he told it, "and whatever you hit . . ." He threw it into the woods and it *thwocked* off a tree. ". . . is Mada-tree. We will plant fields of Mada-seed and press Mada-juice from the sweet Mada-fruit and dance for the rest of our days down Mada Street." He laughed and put his arm around her waist and swung her around in circles, kicking up dust from the road. She was so surprised that she laughed too.

Mada and Owen slept in separate bedrooms, so she was not exactly sure how she knew that he wanted to have sex with her. He had never spoken of it, other than on that first day when he had specifically said that he did not want her. Maybe it was the way he continually brushed up against her for no apparent reason. This could hardly be chance, considering that they were the only two people on True-born. For herself, Mada welcomed his hesitancy. Although she had been emotionally intimate with her batch siblings, none of them had ever inserted themselves into her body cavities.

But, for better or worse, she had chosen this man for this course of action. Even if the galaxy had forgotten Trueborn two-tenths of a spin ago, the revolution still called Mada to her duty.

"What's it like to kiss?" she asked that night, as they were finishing supper.

Owen laid his fork across a plate of cauliflower curry. "You've never kissed anyone before?"

"That's why I ask."

Owen leaned across the table and brushed his lips across hers. The brief contact made her cheeks flush, as if she had just jogged in from the gravel pit. "Like that," he said. "Only better."

"Do you still think my breasts are too small?"

"I never said that." Owen's face turned red.

"It was a comment you made—or at least thought about making."

"A comment?" The word *comment* seemed to stick in his throat; it made him cough. "Just because you make a comment on some aspect doesn't mean you reject the work as a whole."

Mada glanced down the neck of her shift. She hadn't re-ally increased her breast mass all that much, maybe ten or twelve grams, but now vasocongestion had begun to swell them even more. She could also feel blood flowing to her re-productive organs. It was a pleasurable weight that made her feel light as pollen. "Yes, but do you think they're too small?"

Owen got up from the table and came around behind her chair. He put his hands on her shoulders and she leaned her head back against him. There was something between her cheek and his stomach. She heard him say, "Yours are the most perfect breasts on this entire planet," as if from a great distance and then realized that the *something* must be his penis.

After that, neither of them made much comment.

nine hours

Mada stared at the ceiling, her eyes wide but unseeing. Her concentration had turned inward. After she had rolled off him, Owen had flung his left arm across her belly and drawn her hip toward his and given her the night's last kiss. Now the muscles of his arm were slack, and she could hear his seashore breath as she released her ovum into the cloud of his sperm squiggling up her fallopian tubes. The most vigorous of the swimmers butted its head through the ovum's membrane and dissolved, releasing its genetic material. Mada immediately started raveling the strands of DNA before the fertilized egg could divide for the first time. Without the necessary diversity, they would never revive the revolution. Satisfied with her intervention, she flowed the blastocyst down her fallopian tubes where it locked onto the wall of her uterus. She prodded it and the ball of cells became a comma with a big head and a thin tail. An array of cells specialized and folded into a tube that ran the length of the embryo, weaving into nerve fibers. Dark pigment swept across two cups in the blocky head and then bulged into eyes. A mouth slowly opened; in it was a one-chambered, beating heart. The front end of the neural tube blossomed into the vesicles that would become the brain. Four buds swelled, two near the head, two at the tail. The uppermost pair sprouted into paddles, pierced by rays of cells that Mada immediately began to ossify into fingerbone. The lower buds stretched into delicate legs. At midnight, the embryo was as big as her fingernail; it began to move and so became a fetus. The eyes opened for a few minutes, but then the eyelids fused. Mada and Owen were going to have a son; his penis was now a nub of flesh. Bubbles of tissue blew inward from the head and became his ears. Mada listened to him listen to her heartbeat. He lost his tail and his intestines slithered down the umbilical cord into his abdomen. As his fingerprints looped and whorled, he stuck his thumb into his mouth. Mada was having trouble breathing because the fetus was floating so high in her uterus. She eased herself into a sitting position and Owen grumbled in his sleep. Suddenly the curry in the cauliflower was giving her heartburn. Then the muscles of her uterus tightened and pain sheeted across her swollen belly.

~*Drink this.*~ The ship flowed a tumbler of nutrient nano onto the bedside table. ~*The fetus gains mass rapidly from now on.*~ The stuff tasted like rusty nails. ~*You're doing fine.*~

When the fetus turned upside down, it felt like he was trying out a gymnastic routine. But then he snuggled headfirst into her pelvis, and calmed down, probably because there wasn't enough room left inside her for him to make large, flailing gestures like his father. Now she could feel electrical buzzes down her legs and inside her vagina as the baby bumped her nerves. He was big now, and growing by almost a kilogram an hour, laying down new muscle and brown fat. Mada was tired of it all. She dozed. At six-thirty-seven her water broke, drenching the bed.

"Hmm." Owen rolled away from the warm, fragrant spill of amniotic fluid. "What did you say?"

The contractions started; she put her hand on his chest and pressed down. "Help," she whimpered.

"Wha . . . ?" Owen propped himself up on his elbows. "Hey, I'm wet. How did I get . . . ?"

"O-Owen!" She could feel the baby's head stretching her vagina in a way mere flesh could not possibly stretch.

"Mada! What's wrong?" Suddenly his face was very close to hers. "Mada, what's happening?"

But then the baby was slipping out of her, and it was *sooo* much better than the only sex she had ever had. She caught her breath and said, "I have begotten a son."

She reached between her legs and pulled the baby to her breasts. They were huge now, and very sore.

"We will call him Owen," she said.

begot

And Mada begot Enos and Felicia and Malaleel and Ralph and Jared and Elisa and Tharsis and Masahiko and Thema and Seema and Casper and Hevila and Djanka and Jennifer and Jojo and Regma and Elvis and Irina and Dean and Marget and Karoly and Sabatha and Ashley and Siobhan and Mei-Fung and Neil and Gupta and Hans and Sade and Moon and Randy and Genevieve and Bob and Nazia and Eiichi and Justine and Ozma and Khaled and Candy and Pavel and Isaac and Sandor and Veronica and Gao and Pat and Marcus and Zsa Zsa and Li and Rebecca.

Seven years after her return to Trueborn, Mada rested.

ever after

Mada was convinced that she was not a particularly good mother, but then she had been designed for courage and quick-thinking, not nurturing and patience. It wasn't the crying or the dirty diapers or the spitting-up, it was the utter uselessness of the babies that the revolutionary in her could not abide. And her maternal instincts were often skewed. She would offer her children the wrong toy or cook the wrong dish, fall silent when they wanted her to play, prod them to talk when they needed to withdraw. Mada and the ship had calculated that fifty of her genetically manipulated offspring would provide the necessary diversity to repopulate Trueborn. After Rebecca was born, Mada was more than happy to stop having children.

Although the children seemed to love her despite her awkwardness, Mada wasn't sure she loved them back. She constantly teased at her feelings, peeling away what she considered pretense and sentimentality. She worried that the capacity to love might not have been part of her emotional design. Or perhaps begetting fifty children in seven years had left her numb.

Owen seemed to enjoy being a parent. He was the one whom the children called for when they wanted to play.

They came to Mada for answers and decisions. Mada liked to watch them snuggle next to him when he spun his fantastic stories. Their father picked them up when they stumbled, and let them climb on his shoulders so they could see just what he saw. They told him secrets they would never tell her.

The children adored the ship, which substantiated a bot companion for each of them, in part for their protection. All had inherited their father's all-but-invulnerable immune system; their chromosomes replicated well beyond the Hayflick limit with integrity and fidelity. But they lacked their mother's ability to flow tissue and were therefore at peril of drowning or breaking their necks. The bots also provided the intense individualized attention that their busy parents could not. Each child was convinced that his or her bot companion had a unique personality. Even the seven-year-olds were too young to realize that the bots were reflecting their ideal personality back at them. The bots were in general as intelligent as the ship, although it had programmed into their DIs a touch of naïveté and a tendency to literalness that allowed the children to play tricks on them. Pranking a brother or sister's bot was a particularly delicious sport.

Athens had begun to sprawl after seven years. The library had tripled in size and grown a wing of classrooms and workshops. A new gym overlooked three playing fields. Owen had asked the ship to build a little theater where the children could put on shows for each other. The original house became a ring of houses, connected by corridors and facing a central courtyard. Each night Mada and Owen moved to their bedroom in a different house. Owen thought it important that the children see them sleeping in the same bed; Mada went along.

After she had begotten Rebecca, Mada needed something to do that didn't involve the children. She had the ship's farmbots plow up a field and for an hour each day she tended it. She resisted Owen's attempts to name this "Mom's Hobby." Mada grew vegetables; she had little use for flowers. Although she made a specialty of root crops, she was not a particularly accomplished gardener. She did, however, enjoy weeding.

It was at these quiet times, her hands flicking across the dark soil, that she considered her commitment to the Three Universal Rights. After two-tenths of a spin, she had clearly lost her zeal. Not for the first, that independent sentients had the right to remain individual. Mada was proud that her children were as individual as any intelligence, flesh or machine, could have made them. Of course, they had no pressing need to exercise the second right of manipulating their physical structures—she had taken care of that for them. When they were of age, if the ship wanted to introduce them to molecular engineering, that could certainly be done. No, the real problem was that down-when was forever closed to them by the identity mine. How could she justify her new Trueborn society if it didn't enjoy the third right: free access to the timelines?

undone

"Mada!" Owen waved at the edge of her garden. She blinked; he was wearing the same clothes he'd been wearing when she had first seen him on Sonnet Street in front of The Devil's Apple—down to the little red cape. He showed her a picnic basket. "The ship is watching the kids tonight," he called. "Come on, it's our anniversary. I did the calculations myself. We met eight earth years ago today."

He led her to a spot deep in the woods, where he spread a blanket. They stretched out next to each other and sorted through the basket. There was a curley salad with alperts and thumbnuts, brainboy and chive sandwiches on cheese bread. He toasted her with mada-fruit wine and told her that Siobhan had let go of the couch and taken her first step and that Irina wanted everyone to learn to play an instrument so that she could conduct the family orchestra and that Malaleel had asked him just today if ship was a person.

"It's not a person," said Mada. "It's a DI."

"That's what I said." Owen peeled the crust off his cheese bread. "And he said if it's not a person, how come it's telling jokes?"

"It told a joke?"

"It asked him, 'How come you can't have everything?' and then it said, 'Where would you put it?'"

She nudged him in the ribs. "That sounds more like you than the ship."

"I have a present for you," he said after they were stuffed. "I wrote you a poem." He did not stand; there were no large, flailing gestures. Instead he slid the picnic basket out of the way, leaned close and whispered into her ear.

> *Loving you is like catching rain on my tongue.*
> *You bathe the leaves, soak indifferent ground;*
> *Why then should I get so little of you?*
> *Yet still, like a flower with a fool's face,*
> *I open myself to the sky.*

Mada was not quite sure what was happening to her; she had never really cried before. "I like that it doesn't rhyme." She had understood that tears flowed from a sadness. "I like that a lot." She sniffed and smiled and daubed at edges of her eyes with a napkin. "Never rhyme anything again."

"Done," he said.

Mada watched her hand reach for him, caress the side of his neck, and then pull him down on top of her. Then she stopped watching herself.

"No more children." His whisper seemed to fill her head.

"No," she said, "no more."

"I'm sharing you with too many already." He slid his hand between her legs. She arched her back and guided him to her pleasure.

When they had both finished, she ran her finger through the sweat cooling at the small of his back and then licked it. "Owen," she said, her voice a silken purr. "That was the one."

"Is that your comment?"

"No." She craned to see his eyes. "This is my comment," she said. "You're writing love poems to the wrong person."

"There is no one else," he said.

She squawked and pushed him off her. "That may be true," she said, laughing, "but it's not something you're supposed to say."

"No, what I meant was . . ."

"I know." She put a finger to his lips and giggled like one

of her babies. Mada realized then how dangerously happy she was. She rolled away from Owen; all the lightness crushed out of her by the weight of guilt and shame. It wasn't her duty to be happy. She had been ready to betray the cause of those who had made her for what? For this man? "There's something I have to do." She fumbled for her shift. "I can't help myself, I'm sorry."

Owen watched her warily. "Why are you sorry?"

"Because after I do it, I'll be different."

"Different how?"

"The ship will explain." She tugged the shift on. "Take care of the children."

"What do you mean, take care of the children? What are you doing?" He lunged at her and she scrabbled away from him on all fours. "Tell me."

"The ship says my body should survive." She staggered to her feet. "That's all I can offer you, Owen." Mada ran.

She didn't expect Owen to come after her—or to run so fast.

~I need you.~ she subbed to the ship. "Substantiate the command mod.~

He was right behind her. Saying something. Was it to her? "No," he panted, "no, no, no."

~Substantiate the com. . . . ~

Suddenly Owen was gone; Mada bit her lip as she crashed into the main screen, caromed off it and dropped like a dead woman. She lay there for a moment, the cold of the deck seeping into her cheek. "Goodbye," she whispered. She struggled to pull herself up and spat blood.

"Skip downwhen," she said, "six minutes."

".minutes six" ,said she ",downwhen Skip" .blood spat and up herself pull to struggled She .whispered she ",Goodbye" .cheek her into seeping deck the of cold the ,moment a for there lay She .woman dead a like dropped and it off caromed ,screen main the into crashed she as lip her bit Mada ;gone was Owen Suddenly~. . . . com the Substantiate~ ".no ,no ,no" ,panted he ",No" ?her to it Was .something Saying .her behind right was He ~.mod command the

When threespace went blurry, it seemed that her duty did too. She waved her hand and watched it smear.

"You know what you're doing," said the ship.

"What I was designed to

Substantiate~ .ship the to subbed she ~ .you need I~ .fast so run to or—her after come to Owen expect didn't She .ran Mada ".Owen ,you offer can I all That's" feet her to staggered She ".survive should body my says ship The" ".me Tell" .fours all on him from away scrabbled she and her at lunged He "?doing you are What ?children the of care take ,mean you do What." ".children the of care Take" .on shift the tugged She ".explain will ship The" "?how Different" ".different be I'll ,it do I after Because" "?sorry you are Why" .warily her watched Owen ".sorry I'm ,myself help can't I" .shift her for fumbled She .her made had who those of cause the betrayed have would she easily How ".do to have I something There's" .happy be to duty her wasn't It .shame and guilt of weight the by her of out crushed lightness the all ,Owen from away rolled She .was she happy dangerously how then realized Mada .babies her of one like giggled and lips his to finger a put She ".know I" "....was meant I what ,No" ".say to supposed you're something not it's but" ,laughing ,said she ",true be may That" .her off him pushed and squawked She .said he ",else one no is There" ".person wrong the to poems love writing You're" .said she ",comment my is This" .eyes his see to craned She ".No" "?comment your that Is" ".one the was That" .purr silken a voice her ,said she ",Owen"

do. What all my batch siblings pledged to do." She waved her hand again; she could actually see through herself. "The only thing I can do."

"The mine will wipe your identity. There will be nothing of you left."

"And then it will be gone and the timelines will open. I believe that I've known this was what I had to do since we first skipped up-when."

"The probability was always high," said the ship. "But not certain."

"Bring me to him, afterward. But don't tell him about the timelines. He might want to change them. The timelines are for the children, so that they can finish the revol . . . .
. . . .
. . . .

. . . .

"Owen," she said, her voice a silken purr. Then she paused.

The woman shook her head, trying to clear it. Lying on top of her was the handsomest man she had ever met. She felt warm and sexy and wonderful. What was this? "I . . . I'm . . . ," she said. She reached up and touched the little red cloth hanging from his shoulders. "I like your cape."

done

".minutes six" ,said she ",downwhen Skip"
.blood spat and up herself pull to struggled
She .whispered she ",Goodbye" .cheek her
into seeping deck the of cold the ,moment
a for there lay She .woman dead a like
dropped and it off caromed ,screen main
the into crashed she as lip her bit Mada
;gone was Owen Suddenly~. . . .*com the
Substantiate~* ".*no* ,*no* ,*no*" ,panted he
",No" ?her to it Was something Saying .her
behind right was He ~.*mod command the
Substantiate~* .ship the to subbed she ~*you
need I~* .fast so run to or—her after come
to Owen expect didn't She .ran Mada
".Owen ,you offer can I all That's" feet her
to staggered She ".survive should body my
says ship The" ".me Tell" .fours all on him
from away scrabbled she and her at lunged
He "?doing you are What ?children the of
care take ,mean you do What." ".children
the of care Take".on shift the tugged She
".explain will ship The" "?how Different"
".different be I'll ,it do I after Because"
"?sorry you are Why" .warily her watched
Owen. ".sorry I'm ,myself help can't I"
.shift her for fumbled She .her made had
who those of cause the betrayed have
would she easily How ".do to have I something There's" .happy be to duty her wasn't
It .shame and guilt of weight the by her of
out crushed lightness the all ,Owen from
away rolled She .was happy dangerously
how then realized Mada .babies her of one
like giggled and lips his to finger a put She
".know I" " . . . .was meant I what ,No"
".say to supposed you're something not it's
but" ,laughing, said she ",true be may
That" .her off him pushed and squawked
She .said he ",else one no is There" ".per-
son wrong the to poems love writing
You're" .said she ",comment my is This"
.eyes his see to craned She ".No" "?com-
ment your that Is" ".one the was That"
.purr silken a voice her ,said she ",Owen"

Mada waved her hand and saw it smear in three-space. "What are you doing?" said the ship.

"What I was designed to do." She waved; she could actually see through herself. "The only thing I can do."

"The mine will wipe your identity. None of your memories will survive."

"I believe that I've known that's what would happen since we first skipped up-when."

"It was probable," said the ship "But not certain."

Trueborn scholars pin-point what the ship did next as its first step toward independent sentience. In its memoirs, the ship credits the children with teaching it to misbehave.

It played a prank.

"Loving you," said the ship, "is like catching rain on my tongue. You bathe . . ."

"Stop," Mada shouted. "Stop right now!"

"Got you!" The ship gloated. "Four minutes, fifty-one seconds."

"Owen," she said, her voice a silken purr. "That was the one."
"Is that your comment?"

"No." Mada was astonished—and pleased—that she still existed. She knew that in most timelines her identity must have been obliterated by the mine. Thinking about those brave, lost selves made her more sad than proud. "This is my comment," she said. "I'm ready now."

Owen coughed uncertainly. "Umm, already?"

She squawked and pushed him off her. "Not for *that*." She sifted his hair through her hands. "To be with you forever."

Story Copyrights

Astonishing tales of new worlds
and remarkable visions
edited by
David G. Hartwell

YEAR'S BEST SF 7
0-06-106143-3/$7.99 US/$10.99 Can
New tales from Brian Aldiss, Poul Anderson,
Stephen Baxter, Gregory Benford, Terry Bisson,
Ursula K. Le Guin, David Morrell, Michael Swanwick,
Gene Wolfe and many more.

YEAR'S BEST SF 6
0-06-102055-9/$7.50 US/$9.99 Can

YEAR'S BEST SF 5
0-06-102054-0/$6.99 US/$9.99 Can

YEAR'S BEST SF 4
0-06-105902-1/$6.50 US/$8.99 Can

YEAR'S BEST SF 3
0-06-105901-3/$6.50 US/$8.50 Can

YEAR'S BEST SF 2
0-06-105746-0/$6.50 US/$8.99 Can

YEAR'S BEST SF
0-06-105641-3/$6.99 US/$9.99 Can

Discover adventure, magic, and intrigue in
Robert Silverberg's

MAJIPOOR

LORD VALENTINE'S CASTLE
0-06-105487-9/$6.99 U.S./$9.99 Canada

VALENTINE PONTIFEX
0-06-105486-0/$6.99 U.S./$9.99 Canada

MAJIPOOR CHRONICLES
0-06-105485-2/$6.99 U.S./$6.99 Canada

SORCERERS OF MAJIPOOR
0-06-105780-0/$6.99 U.S./$8.99 Canada

LORD PRESTIMION
0-06-105810-6/$6.99 U.S./$9.99 Canada

THE KING OF DREAMS
0-06-102052-4/$7.50 U.S./$9.99 Canada